W9-CMH-649

SUPERSONIC THUNDER

FORGE BOOKS BY WALTER J. BOYNE

Dawn Over Kitty Hawk

Operation Iraqi Freedom

Roaring Thunder

Supersonic Thunder

Today's Best Military Writing (editor)

SUPERSONIC THUNDER

A Novel of the Jet Age

WALTER J. BOYNE

A Tom Doherty Associates Book
New York

This is a work of fiction. All the characters and events portrayed in this novel are either fictitious or are used fictitiously.

SUPERSONIC THUNDER: A NOVEL OF THE JET AGE

This book is printed on acid-free paper.

A Forge Book
Published by Tom Doherty Associates, LLC
175 Fifth Avenue
New York, NY 10010

www.tor.com

Forge® is a registered trademark of Tom Doherty Associates, LLC.

Library of Congress Cataloging-in-Publication Data

Boyne, Walter J. 1929–
Supersonic thunder : a novel of the jet age / Walter J. Boyne.—1st hardcover ed.
p. cm.
"A Tom Doherty Associates Book."
ISBN-13: 978-0-765-30844-3
ISBN-10: 0-765-30844-4
1. Johnson, Clarence L.—Fiction. 2. LeVier, Tony, 1913–1998—Fiction. 3. Aeronautical engineers—Fiction. 4. Test pilots—Fiction. 5. Jet planes—Fiction. 6. Aircraft Industry—Fiction. 7. Inventors—Fiction. I. Title.
PS3552.0937S87 2006
813'.54—dc22

2006030409

First Edition: January 2007

Printed in the United States of America

0 9 8 7 6 5 4 3 2 1

THIS BOOK IS DEDICATED TO ALL THE
AMERICAN AIRMEN WHO SERVED IN THE VIETNAM WAR
AND ESPECIALLY TO THOSE WHO GAVE THEIR LIVES.

AUTHOR'S NOTE

THIS IS THE story of the fantastically swift rise of jet aviation from a military curiosity to a system of civil and military aircraft that has revolutionized the world.

All of the events pertaining to the advance of jet aviation in this trilogy of novels are real—production decisions, rollouts, cancellations, first flights, records set, crashes, everything. These incredible accomplishments are properly credited to the people who made them possible, for example, Sir Frank Whittle and Hans von Ohain for the invention of the jet engine, Kelly Johnson for the creation of the U-2, Bill Allen and Juan Trippe for initiating the Boeing 747, Andrei and Alexei Tupolev for creating the Tu-144 supersonic transport, and so on through the years.

But these giants would be the first to recognize that the projects attributed to them are the work of a vast system of people—engineers, pilots, mechanics, sales personnel, accountants, and so on. It is, of course, impossible to recognize all of the participants in real time in a novel. Instead, a fictional family, the Shannons, and their associates have been created to provide continuity and insight and to substitute for all of the thousands of important people who cannot be recognized individually.

Thus Vance Shannon, the patriarch of the Shannon family, finds his way around the world of jet aviation, acting as a facilitator, a lubricant, a pressure pump, for telling the story of the momentous rise of jet aviation from the first successful jet airplanes in 1939 to the hypersonic scramjets of the future. The Shannons are on-scene for most of the major events or create relationships with those who are.

In some instances, real events have been compressed in time and space so that they can be related as fiction in the form of the actions of the Shannon family. In all cases, however, there has been no alteration to the effect of the events on the development of jet aviation.

WALTER J. BOYNE
Ashburn, Virginia,
November 28, 2004

SUPERSONIC THUNDER

CHAPTER ONE

August 1, 1955
Groom Lake, one hundred miles
northwest of Las Vegas, Nevada

Vance Shannon had made many first flights in experimental aircraft, but standing in the shadow of Kelly Johnson's latest triumph, he was glad he wasn't making this one. Called either the Angel, for its high-altitude capability, or the Article, as an informal code name, the beautifully strange aircraft was so secret that it had not yet been given an official designation.

Working with Kelly as a consulting engineer was difficult enough, for Johnson was a genius with a low tolerance for opposition or even suggestions unless they were overburdened with merit. But to be a test pilot for him was a nightmare, as the equally testy and opinionated Tony LeVier had long since discovered.

As he stood listening to their argument while trying not to appear to be eavesdropping, Shannon motioned Bob Rodriquez to his side. Bob had just been made a partner in Shannon's firm, Aviation Consultants, something Vance had not yet disclosed to his twin sons, Tom and Harry, knowing that they would not approve.

"Listen to this, Bob; it's a once-in-a-lifetime chance to hear a genius engineer and a genius test pilot going toe-to-toe!"

The short, dark, and handsome Rodriquez rather resembled a miniature Cesar Romero. He conscientiously cast his eyes up to the empty skies, appearing to be searching for a break in the clouds, as he listened to the increasingly loud argument.

Kelly Johnson was big, five feet, eleven inches, tall and weighing well over two hundred pounds. He had developed his stevedore build—huge chest, massive arms and thighs—as a youth working in construction, making and putting up laths for plaster work in the days before drywall. All the muscle supported a giant intellect, for Kelly had earned stellar marks working his way through the University of Michigan, doing everything from washing dishes to subcontracting out the university's wind tunnel for the design of Studebaker racing cars. Then he had talked his way into a job at Lockheed, where his first contribution was to criticize his boss's design for a new transport—and be right.

From then on there was no stopping Kelly and all his personality quirks were overlooked in appreciation of his raw genius. As a boss, he could be a genial collaborator, given to spine-collapsing congratulatory slaps on the back. He could also be a monster, reacting chemically when he discovered an error and seldom hesitating to administer a good kick to the rear of the erring engineer. It could not be said that Kelly was loved by his subordinates, but he was admired enormously—almost religiously by some—for his brilliant insights, his ability to not only "see the air" around a new design but also sense intuitively the points where heat or stress or fatigue or production costs might be a problem.

Today the problem was that Tony LeVier dared to have a different opinion. At forty-two, LeVier was only three years younger than Kelly, and as the dean of Lockheed test pilots was confident enough to stand up to Johnson in a way few men dared. Before the war, LeVier had set the pylons blazing at the Cleveland Air Races, flying cobbled-up aircraft with tiny wings and big engines. Lockheed hired him as a test pilot, and he became an expert in the P-38 Lightning, sent around the world to show pilots how to fly it with one engine dead, the propeller feathered. After the war he was the first to fly the F-94, the T-33, and Kelly's latest product from the Skunk Works, the "missile with a man in it," the XF-104 Starfighter. LeVier had crashed at least eight times in his test work and was not a whit intimidated by Kelly. With the build of a rangy middleweight boxer, LeVier stood up straight in front of Kelly so that they went at it nose-to-nose.

Shannon dropped down and pretended to draw a sketch on the ground. Rodriquez pretended to be absorbed in it as LeVier's voice rose another octave.

"Goddammit, Kelly, you may be a great engineer, but you are no pilot. This bucket has a tail wheel, just like a Mustang or a P-47. I'm going to have to land it in a three-point attitude."

"You dumb son of a bitch, look at this airplane. Do you see three landing gears?"

Rodriquez's face flinched; in his youth, insults like this would have meant a fistfight. He raised an eyebrow at Shannon, who looked down steadfastly at the meaningless drawing he'd made in the sand.

Kelly went on, "No, you see one undercarriage strut with two wheels in the middle, and one tiny wheel at the tail. I want you to land on the main gear! But that's not the problem. Look at that wing, for God's sake."

It was an extraordinary wing to be sure, eighty feet long, narrow as a sailplane's, and seemingly too fragile to bear the weight of the fuselage. Each tip was bent down, supported by an outrigger wheel that was jettisoned after takeoff.

"I don't want you stalling this airplane! If you are just a little off in your judgment of height, or if you pick up a little lift from ground effect and stall it, you'll drop it in and it will shed its wings like a snake sheds its skin."

LeVier was getting ready to counter when Kelly said, "Look, LeVier, case closed, land on the main gear like I'm telling you to, or I'll get another boy."

LeVier said something too low for Shannon and Rodriquez to hear, but not for Kelly, who replied, "The same to you, LeVier. Now get your ass in that airplane and land it like I've told you to land it."

As the Lockheed ground crew busied itself, Shannon took Rodriquez aside.

"Don't get the wrong impression. These guys are professionals, the best in the field, and they've worked together a long time. Kelly has a lot at stake in this airplane, and he absolutely cannot afford to have something go wrong. I'm surprised at his advice—I think Tony is right; he'll need to land it like a conventional aircraft. But Kelly is a design genius, and maybe he knows something we pilots don't know."

Rodriquez nodded toward the airplane, saying, "That thing looks like they took an F-104 fuselage and bolted glider wings to it."

"Looks like it. But let me tell you the real story—it's a knockout."

The clouds were still drifting over the field, freighted with rain and threatening to postpone the first flight for another day. Moving over to his maroon Cadillac Coupe de Ville, Shannon began his story, "By all conventional standards, that airplane should not be there. Kelly had been trying to sell the Air Force on the idea of a long-range reconnaissance plane for a couple of years, but the real impetus came from the Central Intelligence Agency. Now that Russia has the hydrogen bomb, and is building big bombers and maybe even intercontinental missiles, they have to get some hard information. It isn't coming from anywhere else—Soviet security is virtually airtight."

Shannon pulled out a briefcase that contained two thermos bottles. "Water or coffee, or both?"

Rodriquez opted for coffee and said quietly, "Don't stop now."

Shannon resumed, "The Air Force gave a contract to Bell Aircraft for twenty-eight planes, X-16s, they called them. Two engines, long, thin wing, somewhat the same formula as the Angel here, but bigger and heavier."

"Didn't that freeze Lockheed out?"

"It should have, and would have anybody else but Kelly. It didn't faze him a bit. He went to the Pentagon, sold his idea to some big wheels including Trevor Gardner and General Don Putt, and they went right to the secretary of the Air Force, a nice guy named Harold Talbott. Kelly Johnson promised to furnish twenty planes for twenty-two million, and to fly the first plane in eight months."

"Jesus, nobody could buy that."

"Well, that's what Secretary Talbott thought. He said, 'How do we know you can deliver?' And General Putt says, 'He's already proved it three times on previous projects'—meaning the XP-80, the P-80A, and the F-104. That did it! Talbott agreed to give Lockheed the contract."

"What about the Bell contract?" Rodriquez, almost compulsively straightforward, didn't like what he was hearing.

"They canceled it, and it is sinking Bell; it may put them out of the fixed-wing business. That's why Kelly is so fired up. His name, his reputation, maybe even his ass is on the line with this airplane. If this doesn't work, he won't be able to peddle apples in the Pentagon courtyard."

There was activity over by the Angel. Tony LeVier, wearing his customary immaculate flight suit, was in the cockpit, with Kelly uneasily leaning from a maintenance stand, still talking a mile a minute.

Three days before, LeVier was making some taxi tests when a wind gust forced the Angel into an inadvertent takeoff. It flew for half a mile with the throttle at idle, then bounced heavily into the ground and spun around, blowing both main tires and setting the brakes on fire. For a breathless moment it seemed that the Angel might go up in flames, but the fire trucks, Johnny-on-the-spot, quickly suppressed the fire.

Remarkably enough, the damage was slight and easily repaired, but the incident made Johnson nervous and put LeVier under the gun. Both men had to prove themselves today.

Despite the lowering clouds and the prospects of a thunderstorm, LeVier applied power at five minutes to four and the Angel shot down the runway into a threatening sky. Climbing out steeply, to keep the airspeed below the gear retraction limits, LeVier called, "It flies like a baby buggy," to Bob Mayte, the pilot of the T-33 chase plane. Johnson was airborne right behind him, flying chase in a C-47.

LeVier climbed to 12,500 feet and went through a series of gentle basic maneuvers, easing the Angel around the sky with kid gloves. The aircraft handled conventionally enough and LeVier cycled the landing gear and the flaps, then made a few entries to the stall. After about forty minutes he set up an approach for landing, determined, despite his gut feel, to land the aircraft on its main gear, just as Kelly had demanded.

Lining up on final approach, LeVier closed the throttle and checked with the chase plane to confirm that his gear was down. He slipped in twenty degrees of flaps, but the airplane was so low-drag that it kept on flying as if nothing had happened. Shrugging his shoulders, LeVier extended the fuselage speed brakes, and the nose dropped slightly enough to force him to apply a little back pressure to maintain the correct airspeed.

LeVier brought it in over the end of the runway and greased it in at about seventy knots, touching down on the main wheels, just as Kelly ordered. The aircraft immediately began to bounce down the runway in great leaps that both LeVier and Kelly knew would be fatal if sustained. LeVier advanced power, and the Angel leaped skyward, its high power-to-weight ratio sending it up so fast that it seemed sure to stall. LeVier brought it around for another approach, listening to a constant stream of advice from an agitated Kelly Johnson.

Rodriquez nudged Shannon in the ribs with his elbow, saying, "Look, he's trying the main gear again."

Once again LeVier put the Angel down perfectly on the main gear, and once again the Angel bounded back in the air, forcing LeVier to make another circuit.

Inside the cramped cockpit, LeVier checked the setting sun and the thunderstorm-ringed horizon and knew he had to get the airplane on the ground on this attempt. He contemplated making a wheels-up landing but decided against it. The absolute requirement for saving weight had left the Angel with a frail structure, and a wheels-up landing would probably destroy it.

Murmuring to himself, "OK Kelly, this time we'll do it my way," he set up the third approach. He came down finally at ninety knots, then bled the speed off, raising the Angel's nose just above the horizon and looking at some buildings far down the runway to keep his depth perception accurate.

Crossing the runway threshold at seventy-five knots, he kept flying the airplane until he touched down, main gear and tail wheel simultaneously, at about sixty-five knots. On each side, cars bearing men with steady hands raced out to meet him, one man on each side ready to insert the outrigger gears into the wingtip. LeVier shut the engine down, popped his canopy, and began formulating the "I told you sos" for Johnson.

Shannon and Rodriquez watched with amusement as LeVier began jawing at Kelly as soon as he arrived. They were too far away to hear, but they knew the subject was how to land the Angel.

As they watched the two men, alternately shaking hands and shaking fists at each other, laughing and walking around, their arms around each other's shoulders, obviously delighted with themselves, with the Angel, with everything, Rodriquez asked, "Do you think it can do what it's supposed to do?"

"You mean fly unescorted over Russia and take photographs?"

"Yes—and, more important, bring them back."

"Sure, at least for a couple of years. It will take the Russians time to get an interceptor that can climb to where this baby will fly—it has to be designed for over sixty thousand feet, don't you think?" Shannon had been heavily involved in the tricky cockpit layout of the Angel, but secrecy was so tight that he was still unaware of the aircraft's potential performance. Kelly ruled with an iron hand, and if there was something you didn't need to know, he made sure that you didn't know it.

"Yes, and it may be that they won't be able to track it on their radar at that height. The cameras they are planning to use are fantastic—maybe they will let us see just how far ahead of us those blasted Commies are."

The thunderstorms had finally reached Groom Lake, and they bolted into Shannon's car just as the deluge hit. Rodriquez, a car guy, paused to run his hand over the subdued fins of the Cadillac. As he slid behind the wheel, Shannon asked, "Bob, what do you think we just witnessed?"

"Vance, it's a new era in reconnaissance, that's for sure, if the blasted thing holds together in turbulent weather. It's built very lightly and it is going to be very demanding on the pilots. But more than anything else it's just a first step in the right direction."

"Meaning?"

"Well, if this works, there'll have to be a follow-on airplane in a few years, depending upon how the Soviets react. Lockheed won't be able to refine this design much—it seems to be at the absolute limits in terms of structure. And it's not going to be nearly fast enough. So I suspect Kelly and the boys already have some drawings of something a lot bigger, stronger, faster, and maybe harder to see."

Vance listened approvingly. "You mean like camouflage?"

"In a way, but far more refined than just using paint schemes. They tried a lighting system during the war that would make a plane invisible, and it worked, too, under precise conditions. But it didn't work for radar, of course. That's the big thing. The Germans were way ahead on that. They were using radar-absorbent material on their periscopes and snorkels, and they had one airplane that flew, the Gotha Go 229, that would have been virtually invisible to radar."

Shannon knew all about the Go 229, had even supervised the packing of its prototype, a Horten design, for its return to the United States. He commented, "The Mosquito was almost invisible to the Germans."

"Yes, for a while, but it still had the propellers and the big Merlin engines up front. Why couldn't Lockheed make an airplane that was covered with radar-absorbent material? For that matter, why couldn't you use radar-absorbent material for some of the structure, say the skin?"

Rodriquez was getting wound up; he dove into his briefcase and brought out a drawing pad and began making sketches. "They could shape it to deflect signals, just like they shape armor on ships or tanks to deflect shells. They could—"

Vance tapped him on the shoulder. "Slow down, Bob, one airplane at a time. We've had ours for today, the Angel. Say, are you a drinker? And can you arm wrestle?"

Rodriquez looked blankly at him. "I don't drink much, a beer once in a while. And I guess I can arm wrestle, depends upon who it is."

"Well, tonight plan on doing a lot of both. Kelly always throws a big shindig after a successful flight like this, and he'll take it amiss if you don't keep up with him—or try to. And don't feel bad if he beats you arm wrestling—he will; he wins every time; nobody ever beats him."

CHAPTER TWO

December 18, 1955
Palos Verdes, California

The sons almost never disagreed with their father, not so much out of filial respect but rather because Vance Shannon was usually correct in his arguments. This was different, however. Six months before, the elder Shannon had promoted a relatively new man, Bob Rodriquez, to be a partner in the firm. Six days before, Vance Shannon had finally told his sons about it. Tom and Harry were furious, as much at the delay in learning about something so important as the fact that Vance had not consulted them about it in the first place. Too angry to discuss it at the time, they knew instinctively that they needed time to cool off and arranged today's meeting to discuss it. Not that they were any cooler today.

Tom, the more volatile of the twins, waved his arms around as he paced the polished Mexican tile floor of their dad's library/home office.

"It just doesn't make sense, Harry! Bob's a good guy, but what does he bring to the party?" The question was rhetorical. In these sessions, Tom did most of the talking, while the more reflective Harry listened and thought before responding.

The twins were thirty-seven years old and had oddly varied but equally successful flying careers. Tom had graduated from Annapolis, become an ace flying Wildcats early in World War II, then volunteered for test work, flying captured enemy fighters at Eglin Army Air Field. Harry was a West Pointer whose Air Corps career had taken him immediately into flight test work—having Vance Shannon for a father was a big help—and then into heavy bombers. Both men saw service in the Korean War, with Tom, having transferred to the Air Force, adding to his score while flying F-86 Sabres in MiG Alley. For family reasons, both men had resigned from promising careers in the Air Force. They regretted it and they missed flying high-performance aircraft, but it was a sad necessity for both of them. Both stayed in the Air Force Reserve, but it was not the same.

"It beats me, Tom. He's never done anything like this before."

"Bullshit! What about Madeline and all the problems she caused? It was the same goddamn thing; he rammed her down our throats just like he's ramming Gonzalez, Rodriguez, whatever his wetback name is."

Harry shook his head. It was true that their marital careers were not as successful as their martial careers, but it wasn't entirely Madeline's fault. In 1947, Madeline Behar, their father's mistress, had arranged a party for them. As a friendly joke she had fixed them up with another set of twins, the Capestro sisters, Marie and Anna, as blind dates. Madeline's joke backfired when Tom and Marie fell immediately in love, as did Harry and Anna. Madeline masterminded a wonderful wedding for the two sets of twins, and that was the beginning of the end of the happy part of the story. Within a few months, both marriages began to unravel. Marie had serious mental problems manifested in her increasingly fanatical devotion to her Catholic religion, and her marriage to Tom, never consummated, was annulled. Anna tended in the opposite direction, drinking heavily and giving ample reason for Harry to suspect that she might not be faithful. Both men felt they had contributed to the problem by being away on duty so much. There was no help for Marie, but Anna was gradually brought around to a functioning state through Alcoholics Anonymous—and Harry's persistent, dutiful care.

Tom had rebounded, marrying Nancy Strother, and they were the proud parents of two-year-old Vance Robert Shannon. Nancy had given Tom an ultimatum: the Air Force or her, and after one last tour in Korea, he chose her. Harry left the Air Force to care for Anna. Fortunately, both men liked working with their father—until now.

Harry spoke jokingly at last. "The only thing positive about Bob's being a partner is at least Madeline didn't bring him in."

There was sad truth to what he said. Madeline had completely captivated their father. She was French, working in the American embassy in London in 1941, and they became lovers almost immediately. Although apparently completely devoted, she had always refused to marry him. Vance had total confidence in her, and after the war, until 1949, she administered his business and his family life with competence and authority. Vance was totally absorbed in aviation and made an excellent income in the process. Madeline shrewdly invested his funds in real estate and, to a far lesser degree, the stock market. She kept a good account of all the transactions and turned a considerable fortune over to him in its entirety when on August 6, 1949—he'd never forget the date, his own personal Hiroshima—she left him abruptly and without explanation. Vance had been devastated, unable to understand what had happened. He had always considered himself too lucky and even anticipated that she might leave him someday for a younger or more interesting man. Yet she had given him no warning; the day before she left she was as loving as she had always been.

It was not until a few years later that the reasons for her refusal to marry and her abrupt departure were suddenly made clear to him. His old friend and confidant at Boeing, the masterful engineer George Schairer, had presented him with hard evidence that she had been a spy for the French government all along.

Vance was shattered by her departure and utterly demolished by the revelation that she was a spy. It became apparent that over the years she had removed papers from his safe, photographed them, and passed them to the French. Fortunately for Vance, all the material was Boeing-proprietary rather than U.S. government classified. There was no official action, but Boeing fired him and the word spread throughout the aviation community. He was virtually without work until circumstances forced Boeing to bring him back on. Since then his business had built beyond its former limits.

As well as Madeline had managed his financial affairs, she did even better in the emotional department, using great skill and discretion when hiring people to help her in the business. No one noticed, but her hiring practices had two goals. One was to substitute for her in administering the business. The other was to substitute for her with Vance when she left. Her choice was impeccable: Jill Abernathy as her main assistant, selected for her looks, her personality, her ability—and her suitability for Vance. Madeline had chosen well, and within six months of her leaving, Jill moved in with Vance. They subsequently married and were able to joke together about Madeline's cleverness.

Madeline had equal, if unintended, success with her other hire, Nancy Strother, who became Tom's lover first, than his wife and the mother of his son.

Tom nodded in agreement. "I still don't know whether to love or hate Madeline. She was a spy, which is rotten enough by itself, and she deceived Dad totally about that, but she took wonderful care of him otherwise. Who else would ever have hired a substitute wife for him?"

"But as I say, at least she didn't hire Rodriquez. What do you know about him? You're really the one to blame; you introduced him to Dad, told him we ought to hire him." Harry's tone of reproach verged on anger.

"I'd met him a couple of times in Korea, of course, and I followed his progress, but I didn't really know him until he came back to the States and got out of the Air Force. I couldn't believed it—he had twelve MiGs to his credit, and you'd think he would have been planning to be a general. But he was furious with the Air Force, and wanted out."

"The race business?"

Tom snorted. "Yeah, he was convinced that headquarters made him go home early to be sure that Jabara or McConnell wound up as the top ace. He claims that they were prejudiced against him because he was of Mexican descent."

"You were there—were they?"

"No, of course not, not on base. Everybody looked up to the MiG killers; they even looked up to me. But there might have been somebody in Washington, somebody in public affairs, who decided that they didn't want a man of Mexican descent to be the top ace of the Korean War. Stranger things have happened."

"Seems far-fetched to me. The Air Force has gone further and faster with integration than anybody—Army, Navy, Marines, General Motors, UCLA—anybody. As long as he was an American, not a foreign citizen, why wouldn't they want someone with Mexican blood to be the top ace?"

"I've tried to tell him that, but there's no convincing him. He's sure it happened, and that's that. And I didn't convince Dad to hire him. I introduced him, and when Dad looked over his record and talked to him, they hit it off like Mutt and Jeff. Rodriquez specialized in electronics, and had some interesting experience working with high-performance cameras over in Korea."

They both grew silent when they heard the door upstairs open and their father's footsteps pounded down the hallway to the door to the offices in the basement.

It was an affectionate family, no matter what the circumstances, and Vance came in and hugged both of his boys, just as he had been doing for the past thirty-seven years.

"Is the jury still out, or have you pronounced sentence on me?"

Unusually for him, Harry spoke first and with real vehemence.

"Not yet, Dad, but this is serious business. Tom and I are both angry, hurt, pissed off, and otherwise furious about this deal. I don't know if we are madder about your doing it without talking to us or because you kept it from us."

Tom shook his head in agreement. "It's not like you, Dad; you've never done anything like this before."

Vance felt he might as well get all the arguments on the table right away.

"Well, how about Madeline? I made the same sort of decision with her, didn't I?"

Quick responses came to the lips of both his sons, but both kept quiet. Madeline had been gone for six years now, Vance had married Jill—but the twins knew he still had a soft spot in his heart for the young French refugee girl he had met during the war.

Tom finally said, "That was altogether different. This is a simple business deal; there's no romance in it. We had a partnership, the three of us, and then suddenly we find there are four partners. What the hell are we supposed to think?"

"Well, what was the arrangement when there were three of us? How did we split the profits?"

"You had fifty-two percent, and we each had twenty-four percent. That was more than fair. What is the new arrangement?"

"You both still have twenty-four percent. I have forty-two percent and Bob Rodriquez has ten percent. This hasn't cost you a dime."

"It's not the money—it's the principal of the thing. What does Rodriquez bring to the table? Why should he start out with ten percent after we've put in our time building up the business?"

Harry stood up and put his arm around his father's shoulder.

"Dad, you usually turn out to be right. But not this time. You really should have asked us about making Bob a partner, and worse, you should have told us right away when you did."

Tom elected to be quiet. If someone was going to catch hell for this, he preferred it to be Harry.

"You are absolutely right, Harry; I should have talked to you and I should have told you sooner. I didn't, for what I thought—and still think—were good reasons. You'll probably disagree with me, but hear me out."

Tom volunteered a safe, "Shoot."

"Tom, it was you that introduced me to Bob, and I'm glad you did. I looked into his background, and saw that besides being a war hero—like you two are—he had a brilliant academic record in aeronautical engineering. Straight As. But what was more significant to me, he's been attending classes in electronic engineering whenever he was in the States, and even when he was overseas, shooting down MiGs, he was taking all kinds of correspondence courses, building his own television sets, and so on. The thing that really impressed me was that every minute he wasn't flying he was down on the flight line, working with the cameras and the communication gear."

Tom shrugged. "We grant that he's a good guy, and well qualified, Dad, but this business of being a partner and not telling us—"

"Give me a minute. I'd made my mind up to hire him, because the future is going to be as much electronics as airframes or engines, maybe more, and none of us are strong in that area. You know how long I've worked with Kelly on this high-altitude reconnaissance plane—by the way, they are calling it the U-2 now as a disguise, trying to make people think it's a little utility aircraft; it's still hush-hush. Where was I?"

Tom chipped in, "You were at 'none of us are strong in that area.' "

"Right. I saw we needed someone with talent if we are going to continue to be viable as consultants. It's not going to be so much like the old days, when you had a new model every year. I think airplanes are going to be used over much longer periods of time, and be updated with electronic equipment as time goes on. Look how many types of radar sets they've had already since about 1944."

"Why? What's different now?"

"Well, expense for one thing; airplanes are already ten times as expensive as they were in World War II, and the ratio is going up. Development time is another; before the war, you could go from an idea to production in four years for sure and, if you pushed it, in three. Nowadays, it looks like it's going to take ten to twelve years to get a model into production and, once you get it operational, you have to keep it going for years to amortize its costs."

"So?"

"Well, we are going to have to be working on updating aircraft, rather than just consulting and testing new ones. And the updating is going to come in the electronics. I saw that Bob had the skills I wanted, he has a good personality—a little standoffish at times, I'll admit—so I offered him a job, and he didn't take it."

"Didn't take it? Why not?"

"He already had a job offer, from Lockheed, paying about twice what I was going to offer him. He has talents they want for the U-2 and for some other aircraft they have coming down the line in the Skunk Works. I don't blame them; Bob's a shrewd, hardworking guy."

"Well, what happened? Give it to us; we already know we're beat."

"I knew we couldn't match Lockheed's salary offer—he'd be making more than the three of us combined. So I upped my salary offer a little—it's still a little less than you or I take home—and offered to make him a partner. He thought it over, realized he'd have a lot more opportunity to do things with a small company like ours and could make a lot of money if we succeed. He agreed. I'm glad he did, and I want you to make him feel absolutely welcome. Also I wanted to give him a chance to prove himself before I told you what I had done."

Tom said, "I don't know if I can make him feel welcome as a partner. As an employee, sure, but not as a partner. I still think you made the wrong decision."

Harry caught a vein throbbing in Vance's temple and knew that he was angry. Harry waved at Tom to shut up, but Tom pressed on, "He is a damn good pilot, we all know that, but we're not shooting down MiGs; we're trying for contracts in a tight market. Where are his connections?"

Vance walked over to the carved mahogany table where his latest pride and joy sat. It was a Telefunken Operette six-tube shortwave radio, and he played with it almost every evening, enjoying getting news and music from around the world.

Without a word, he raised it full-length over his head and smashed it down on the tile floor, parts flying and tubes popping. Both of his sons dropped their jaws—they had never seen a similar display of temper from their father.

"Which one of you geniuses can fix this radio?"

Neither son spoke.

"I'll tell you. Neither one of you. You are great stick and rudder men, and you are great salesmen with the airframe and engine manufacturers. But the future is going to be in electronics. If I swept up this mess and handed it to Bob Rodriquez, he'd have it fixed in an hour. He's an electronic genius. I hired him away from Lockheed. They are starting up a new missile division, under Willis Hawkins, and Willis says he'll never forgive me!"

Hawkins was second only to Kelly Johnson at Lockheed; at any other company he would have been chief engineer.

"Like I said, I couldn't match Hawkins's offer to him, I wanted him on staff, so I offered him half as much salary and a ten percent equity. You'll see—it was one of the smartest things I've ever done, even if it pissed Hawkins off; he knows how good Rodriquez is. You know what he told me?"

Tom, still shaken by the smashing of the radio, a gesture so uncharacteristic of his father, muttered in a low voice, "Who told you?"

"Dammit, aren't you listening to me? Willis Hawkins, that's who. He told me that if Rodriquez had gone anywhere else, he would have outbid anybody to get him, but he figured that if Rodriquez worked for us, he'd always have him on call. Now do you think I did the right thing?"

Tom shook his head. "I don't know, Dad. I'm still not sure you did."

"Tom, would it sweeten the pot to tell you that Bob has already secured a four-million-dollar contract for us with the company making the cameras for the U-2?"

Tom looked at Harry and said, "We give in, Dad. Bring Bob around, and we'll welcome him aboard."

"I will. He's out waiting in my car. I'll go get him."

Harry stood up and ran for the door. "Fat chance. I'm going to get him, and I'm taking him out to dinner."

Tom chimed in, "Correction. *We* are taking him out to dinner."

"You're both wrong. All three of us are taking him out to dinner. And after dinner, you two are going out and buy me another radio. It's getting to be expensive educating you in the business facts of life."

CHAPTER THREE

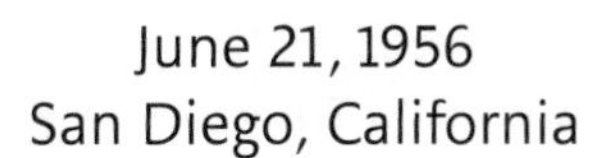

June 21, 1956
San Diego, California

The sunny conference room on the top floor of Convair's main building brought back a lot of bad memories to Vance. He'd arranged for Madeline to have a job at Consolidated in 1941, long before it became Convair, and she had promptly worked her way up in the hierarchy on the basis of her personality and her language capability—she spoke several languages, including Russian. The Soviet Union had arranged a license agreement to build the Consolidated PBY Catalina, and Madeline had been invaluable in dealing with the tough Soviet negotiators.

Things didn't get any better when Lou Capestro walked in, shook Vance's hand warmly, and sat down beside him. They saw each other fairly often and could talk comfortably about their children's sad marriages. Lou's twins had married Vance's twins, and nothing had worked out well. And Lou was the only person with whom Vance ever discussed Madeline. She had worked for Lou, he had been more than fond of her, and he felt her loss almost as much as Vance did. Fortunately, Lou was tactful and for the most part tried to talk about the early days, when he had hired Vance to work with him on the retractable wingtip floats that became a trademark of the Catalina.

"Those were the days, Vance. In 1937 we were glad if we could get one hundred and sixty mph top speed out of a Catalina, and now, nineteen years later, we're talking six hundred miles per hour for our new jets."

Vance knew Capestro too well; there was something wrong here. He was doing his "boisterous Italian" routine, laughing and clowning with others in the room, and that usually meant he was nervous and unhappy.

The meeting was to announce the new airplane, the Convair 600, so-called because of its top speed, to the media. Vance had been integral to the design, working with Gerhard Neumann at General Electric to "civilianize" the J79 engine the new jet employed. The J79 was the engine intended for supersonic fighters and bombers, and Neumann—Herman the German, they called him—was an engineering and managerial genius. Vance enjoyed working with him, learning something new every time they met.

"Seriously, Lou, is everybody still happy with this idea? Boeing and Douglas are really tooling up, and *Aviation Week* says Boeing is bringing out a new model, the 720, specifically to compete. Is the market big enough?"

Capestro's face went sour. "The only guy happy with this airplane is Howard Hughes. He wants to have the fastest airliner in the business, and he has ordered thirty of them for TWA, so we cannot complain. Delta is picking up another ten."

"Well, I'm probably just sore because I lost most of the arguments on this airplane, but I think going for five-abreast seating instead of six-abreast is crazy. The jets make money on cost-per-seat-mile, and it's a hell of a lot easier to cram in a row of seats than to add twenty knots to the airspeed."

There was a fanfare, and a movie screen dropped down at the end of the hall. Capestro whispered, "Watch this and keep your fingers crossed."

The film was the usual corporate pabulum, starting off with historical footage of great Consolidated aircraft of the past—the Catalina, the B-24, the B-36, even some shots of the jet-powered B-46—then cutting to scenes of stewardesses serving blissful customers in cabin mock-ups of the new jet. It ended with a powerful sales pitch on the attraction that "the fastest jet in the sky" would have to customers.

The usual bags of goodies were passed out, filled with brochures, pins, and even a neat little model of the Convair 660 in TWA livery.

"It's a great-looking airplane, Lou. When are you going to roll the first one out?"

"Mr. Hughes says January 1959, and what Mr. Hughes says is usually what happens."

Vance started to get up to leave, but Lou tugged at his sleeve. "Have lunch with me, Vance. I'm meeting a guy at Anthony's; he's making a pitch to me that I'd like you to hear, to see what you think."

"What kind of a pitch?"

"A business pitch. You and Madeline did well with your business ventures, I know, and I could use some advice."

"Lou, it was mostly Madeline, and you know it. She had a gift for business. I don't. But I'll come along. What is he trying to sell you?"

"He's acting as an agent for some outfit called Hoffman in New York. They import Volkswagens, and he's got a dealership already in Los Angeles. He wants to set one up in San Diego. I'm considering buying into it. It would be a good place for my boys to work."

Lou had four sons; none of them had lived up to Lou's high standards since they had returned from the war.

"A Volkswagen, Lou? One of those tiny little Bugs? I don't think they could climb the hills around here."

"No, you'll see, they are pretty good little cars, and they tell me they are catching on. I'm glad you'll come along."

They rode to Anthony's Fish Grotto in the comfort of Shannon's Cadillac, with Shannon mentally comparing its ride, its automatic transmission, its luxury, with the pictures he had seen of Volkswagens. Neither man referred to the last time they had been to Anthony's together, when their children had married.

In the old days, patrons had to walk through a little grocery store to get to the restaurant, but Mama Ghio had revamped the place, and now the two men walked into a beautiful waiting area, with a bar to the side.

The headwaiter surged forward. "Ah, Mr. Capestro, your guest is already here. I took the liberty of seating him at your usual table."

At the table, Lou introduced them. "Mr. Obermyer, this is my old friend Vance Shannon. I hope you don't mind, but I've asked him to come along and listen to your proposal. Vance, this is Mr. Fritz Obermyer, who owns the Volkswagen dealership in Los Angeles."

Shannon had a sudden mental image of the last—and only—time he had seen the Volkswagen plant, in 1945. The place had been completely destroyed, there was no sign of a Volkswagen car anywhere, but the open bays were lined with machine tools and, at one end, big presses. He knew that the Federal German Republic was counting on the plant to revive the similarly bombed-out German economy.

Obermyer managed a simultaneous heel click, handshake, and bow and said, "Mr. Shannon is well-known to me. And I believe we have not one but two mutual friends—Dr. von Ohain and Mr. Robert Gross."

Obermyer was wearing an expensive suit, and his hair, gray and cropped, gave him the look of a New York executive.

Taken aback, Shannon mumbled, "Yes, of course, and how is Dr. von Ohain?"

"I last saw him in Dayton, just a few years ago, and he was doing extremely well."

Obermyer elaborated on his friendship with von Ohain back at the Heinkel plant. "He was so young, just out of college, and so polite. But he knew how to get things done—and his jet engine was the first to fly." As he spoke, something of the old Nazi in Obermyer showed through, and he visibly reacted, suppressing it, changing the subject.

"I've not been in contact with Mr. Gross for some time. I hope he is well."

"Yes, he's fine, taking it a bit easier now, and is grooming his brother, Courtlandt, to replace him. He's earned a little rest."

As they were ordering drinks, it hit Shannon. Obermyer must have been Gross's clandestine contact in Germany. Years before, during the war, Gross had confided in Shannon, telling him that he was getting amazingly accurate information from a contact inside Germany. Gross was ashamed of the fact, but the information was too valuable not to use. To protect himself, he had informed J. Edgar Hoover about it. Hoover had encouraged him to continue the contacts, promising to protect him if there were any difficulties in dealing with an enemy agent in wartime. Once, when very worn down by other problems, Gross had confided in Shannon, his old and trusted friend.

Shannon looked at Obermyer with new interest. "And what brings you to San Diego, Mr. Obermyer?"

"Will you call me Fritz, please? In Germany we were always so formal, always using the titles and the ranks. I like the American way of using first names. More friendly."

The waiter came with the three martinis and the menus. They toasted and Obermyer said, "Do you mind if we talk first, and then eat?

I'm so sure you will like this idea that I won't enjoy my food until you hear me out."

Capestro said, "Go ahead; we're listening."

"As you know, I have a Volkswagen dealership in Los Angeles. Last year we sold only a few hundred cars. In the United States, Volkswagen sold more than fifty thousand cars, but most of those were on the East Coast, where the big dealerships are. But Volkswagen is going to concentrate on the U.S. market. Our studies show that the American public is dissatisfied with the quality of their cars. When they drive a Volkswagen, they are surprised at first because it is small, but when they see how well it's built, how it doesn't rattle, how it parks so easily, and how it gets so good gas mileage, they become enthusiasts, and sell their neighbors."

He paused, sipped his martini, and went on. "We are going to have a huge advertising campaign over the next few years. We believe we can sell millions of cars in the United States. And we need a strong dealership in the San Diego area. I want you, Mr. Capestro, to have the first chance at owning a Volkswagen dealership."

"Do you have some numbers to show me? The investment you need, the sales projections, when you expect I'd be able to make a profit?"

Obermyer pushed across a thick packet of papers, sealed in a brown envelope.

"Everything is in here. Let Mr. Shannon look at it, take it to your accountant, call my people in New York, talk to your lawyers, do whatever you like to check it out. You'll find that it is a very sensible proposal, a real opportunity. In brief, I'll tell you what it says. If you put up fifty thousand dollars in capital, you will break even in two years and in three you will be earning a substantial profit, far in excess of the usual car dealerships. You'll have complete support from me, from the Hoffman organization, and from Volkswagen itself. You just cannot believe how much the Volkswagen company and the Federal Republic of Germany want this to succeed."

Shannon felt impelled to say something, even if it was inane.

"You'll be getting in on the ground floor, Lou."

Obermyer beamed.

"All right, take the package, look at it, call me tomorrow; I'm at the Coronado." Then switching gears, he said, "I understand that there was quite a ceremony this morning for the new Convair passenger jet?"

Lou nodded. "Yes. You would have enjoyed it, given your experience at Heinkel. Did you work on the Heinkel jet fighter, the He 280?"

"Yes, a little, because it had the von Ohain engines in it at first, and I worked on it then. Later, when we had problems with the von Ohain engines, they substituted Junkers Ju 004 engines, and I was moved to another program."

Obermyer spoke as if he were an engineer. Actually, he had been an excellent machinist, a shop foreman, but he also had political influence. He had been a storm trooper with Adolf Hitler in 1934, on the famous "Night of the Long Knives." Rumor had it that Obermyer had killed one of Hitler's top enemies, and Obermyer never disputed it. Obermyer ingratiated himself with Ernst Heinkel, the head of the firm, by keeping him posted on the internal politics of the factory. Obermyer also had good contacts with many of the other aircraft firms and was able to provide Heinkel with good, solid information on how the Messerschmitt firm was doing.

Lou signaled for another round of drinks; Shannon declined, but Obermyer accepted with obvious pleasure, saying, "Thanks so much. By the way, I learned something a few weeks ago that may be of interest to you. You'll recall how startled everyone was when the Tupolev Tu-104 visited London last March?"

Both men remembered well, for the entire aviation world had been shocked when the Soviets became the first to put a passenger jet in service. Some had scoffed at its old-fashioned Orient Express style furnishings, all heavy mahogany, brass, and lace, but no one could scoff it out of existence. There were some attempts to downplay it, saying it was just a Tu-16 bomber with a new fuselage, but realists knew that it was a triumph for the Soviet Union.

Obermyer went on, "Well, Aeroflot is putting it into regular line service, with flights from Moscow to Irkutsk beginning in September this year, with international flights to Prague starting in October."

Both Capestro and Shannon leaned forward, stunned by the news. "Regular service, or just introductory flights?"

"My informant tells me regular service, and he is seldom wrong."

Vance asked, "How long does it take the Tu-104 to fly from Moscow to Irkutsk?"

Obermyer smiled.

"In the piston-engine Ilyushin Il-14, it was almost fourteen hours. The Tu-104 carries more passengers, and does it in five and one-half hours. It is perfect for the long-distance routes."

"At what speed does it cruise?" Capestro was obviously worried about this new and unexpected competition.

"Top speed is about eight hundred and seventy kilometers per hour—five hundred and forty-five miles per hour. But it cruises at four hundred and seventy, for economy."

They had been using first names for an hour by now, but Shannon still felt uncomfortable with it. "Fritz, am I correct if I recall that you used to furnish Bob Gross with information on various companies in Europe?"

Obermyer smiled. "Ah yes, that was in the old days, when I had to make ends meet. Now I keep my contacts just for old times' sake; there is much more money in the car business than in clandestine work."

Capestro pressed him. "Well, Fritz, if it's not too nosy to ask, what do you think Tupolev has coming down the line?"

"Well, sooner than you think, Tupolev will fly his turboprop Tu-114. It's a passenger version of the Tu-95 bomber. It will be very long-range, able to fly from Moscow to New York, and it will be just as fast as the Tu-104."

Shannon looked at Capestro and shrugged.

"We don't have anything like it. I don't think you'll see any long-range American turboprop airliners, not for a long time. We just aren't there yet. The Air Force was trying, but it gave up on turboprops and went with jet engines on the B-52."

Obermyer laughed and said, "And watch for Ilyushin, too. He's going to trot out a whole series of jet airliners, large and small, over the next few years. Or so they tell me."

Shannon toasted Obermyer with his empty glass and said, "Fritz, I get the feeling that what they tell you is pretty generally correct." Then turning to Capestro he said, "Lou, how about letting me go over those papers with you this afternoon? If it looks right, maybe we could go in as partners."

Capestro smiled in agreement and signaled the waiters that they could, at last, bring the food.

CHAPTER FOUR

September 4, 1957
The Lockheed Air Terminal,
Burbank, California

Lockheed always scheduled early-morning takeoffs for the first flights of new aircraft, but there were invariably delays, and today was no different. The beautiful new Model CL-329, the JetStar, had been rolled out promptly at 7:00 A.M., and it was still sitting by the side of the hangar, mechanics swarming over the port engine, a Bristol Orpheus jet with 4,850 pounds of thrust.

Harry Shannon stood in the small crowd of engineers and technicians who had worked on the aircraft. He always felt comfortable at the Lockheed plant, home to so many great designs, from the wooden Vegas, to the twin-engine P-38s, to the steady flow of modern jet fighters and trainers.

The JetStar was fully in the tradition of those thousands of airplanes. Sleek, with its low-swept wing and tail, it looked more like a fighter plane than a twelve-seat executive transport. It was another product of the Skunk Works, and a rapid one at that, being built only 241 days after the design was approved. Kelly Johnson and his small, dedicated team had worked swiftly, even though for the first few months no one knew which engine would be used.

Kelly, for once, was relaxed. It was as if this aircraft was so within the Skunk Works' competence that it was not a challenge. He was as much on the scene, supervising, as ever, but he wore a jovial, collegial air, encouraging people with jokes rather than the iron-hard curses that gushed like bitter rain from him when he was tense. His behavior was unusual, because like all Skunk Works projects, this was his baby, and he and Bill Statler held the patent on the airplane. But Kelly knew something the others did not. The only major competitor for the contract was McDonnell, and he had word that they were about eighteen months behind in their design. It looked like a cakewalk.

Harry Shannon stayed in the background, not wishing to attract attention to himself. He had only the most peripheral contact with the project, running a comparative analysis on available jet engines for Ben Rich, another of Lockheed's genius engineers and Kelly's heir apparent. Nonetheless, Harry felt awkward because his father was still involved with Bill Lear in his long-delayed attempt to build an executive jet. Harry knew that there was no real conflict of interest—his work on engines was not transferable because the Learjet, as Vance Shannon was already calling it, was a much smaller airplane, built to less demanding standards. Still, someone with an ax to grind could claim at least an appearance of conflict of interest, and Harry would have to defend himself. He preferred to avoid it altogether.

The JetStar had come about as a result of an Air Force competition for a UCX—utility transport, experimental. There had been hints that there was interest in buying up to three hundred of these utility transports for transporting high-ranking officers, congressmen, and even the President. There was also a competition for a UTX—utility trainer, experimental. This was a substantially smaller airplane, and if Lockheed had been competing for it, Harry would have recused himself. It was smaller than the JetStar and closer in size, range, and performance to the projected Learjet. The Air Force did not really intend to use the UTX as a trainer in the conventional sense. Rather, it was to be used as an executive transport for rank-and-file officers who needed flying time in a modern jet to remain current but were not assigned to any operational organization.

The JetStar was radical in appearance, for Kelly had mounted the engines aft on the fuselage, as the French had done with their Caravelle transport—and, as Shannon knew, had been planned for the Learjet. The JetStar's unencumbered wing was very efficient. Mounting the engines in the rear also made the cabin much quieter and reduced the danger of damage from foreign objects. Shannon had heard through the grapevine that the McDonnell competition looked like a scaled-down DC-8 and its low-slung, podded engines would be a magnet for foreign objects. No wonder Kelly was happy! It was just like the old saying: it is not enough to be a success; your best friend must also be a failure. McDonnell was hardly Lockheed's best friend, but its failure would serve.

Harry looked up and saw Johnson striding over to him, parting the crowd like a surfer riding a wave. When Johnson arrived, he slapped his arm around Harry's back and yelled, "Hello there, Harry! Good to see you! Tell me again why you are here instead of your dad?"

"He's all wrapped up in the turboprop transport project, Mr. Johnson, you know; I think they are calling it the Electra II."

Johnson nodded vigorously, a wry, almost contemptuous look crossing his face. "Yeah, the C-130 derivative. I think it's a bad idea. It's hard to believe Americans will be willing to fly a turboprop when there will be jets available. We'd be better off stretching the JetStar here, and making a bigger aircraft from it."

"Well, the turboprops are hard to beat on seat-mile costs. That's probably what's driving the thinking."

"Bullshit, Harry, and you know it. Your dad has been against the Electra II project since the start, but once the decision was made, he's been a good soldier and not said anything about it."

A reporter rushed up to Johnson to ask some questions, but he waved him off to the Lockheed press officer. Johnson turned back to Harry and said, "Is your dad still fooling around with Bill Lear and his little executive jet?"

"It's sort of on hold right now. I think they are having some trouble getting investors."

"Yeah, it's tough, but the JetStar will create some interest, and you know that North American has virtually made a little executive jet out of their F-86, don't you? I think they're calling it the Sabreliner—pretty catchy."

"I've heard about it—I haven't seen any illustrations or anything. It should be easy for them to make the transition."

"Yeah, well, it's going to be about one-half the gross weight of the JetStar here. I figure the Sabreliner will come in at around twenty-three thousand pounds. That's still probably twice as big as Lear is planning, if he's got any sense."

Harry didn't know and said so.

"Well, lookie here, Harry. I don't much care for Lear, but I like your dad. He's always been good to me and to Lockheed. You tell him to think about what North American did with the Sabre, and have him look around for some European fighter he can use as a starting point. They tend to make smaller airplanes than we do, and I think the Swiss are working on an indigenous fighter that might fill the bill. It would save your dad's company a lot of money to do it that way."

Harry was struck by Johnson's evident consideration and concern. Here he was, at the first flight of his own design, and he took time to come over and pass along something that might mean a lot to Vance Shannon.

"Thanks, Kelly, I really appreciate it. I hope you'll call on me if I can be of service."

"Count on it, Harry; count on it."

CHAPTER FIVE

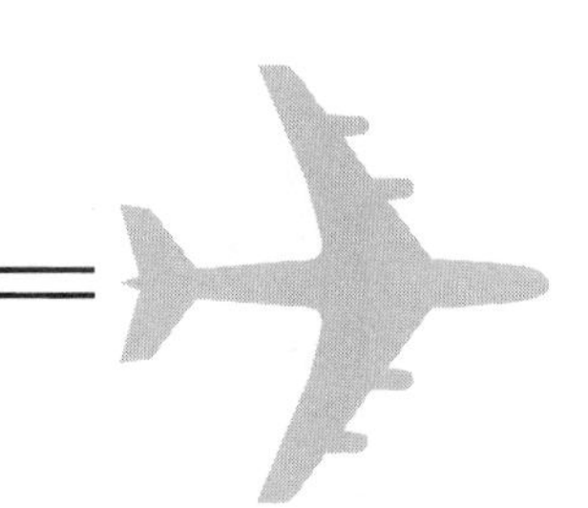

October 4, 1957
A desert base near Tyuratam in the
Kazakh Republic, USSR

Sergei Korolev moved about the "space room" like a man possessed, walking from one console to the next, constantly checking figures against the little black notebook that was his constant companion. Square-jawed and physically impressive, Korolev dominated his white-smocked staff with the power of his personality. So strict that he demanded that even the mock-up of the *Prostreishiy Sputnik*—simple satellite—be polished to perfection, he was also capable of the greatest kindness and understanding.

It was Korolev's style always to urge his people to work faster and better, using a combination of tyrannical threats and softhearted concessions to make his case. A brilliant engineer, he pleased his staff most with his simple, elegant designs. This space-bound *Sputnik* was a thing of beauty, with its four antennae dancing back like the legs of a racehorse in full flight. Designed and built in less than thirty days, the eighty-four-kilogram silver sphere was equipped only with two radio transmitters. They would enable ground stations all around the world—and particularly in the United States—to chart the course of its epic flight and, with it, the progress of Soviet science.

Korolev's inspirational leadership enabled his small team of scientists to bridge the enormous gap between nuclear ICBMs and experiments in space. He had in fact created the world's first intercontinental ballistic missile as a means to facilitate his real interest—space travel.

An astute politician, Korolev had that most valuable of gifts, the ability to manipulate those above him to do what he wanted to be done, often against clear party guidelines. His scientists and technicians knew this, watched him with admiration, and were devoted to him, despite their primitive living conditions and the ever-present threat of condemnation for failure. They were as dedicated to his dream as Korolev himself.

As chief designer, he was responsible for every element of this experiment, from the living conditions of his people to the mammoth R-7 rocket—Korolev called it Semyorka, Little Old Seven—that he had built to place the silver sphere in space that day. To pave the way for this first orbital venture, Korolev had on August 21 sent the sixth R-7 on a successful six-thousand-kilometer flight to the target in Kamchatka. The R-7 carried a dummy nuclear warhead designed by Andrei Sakharov. With this incredible triumph—the world's first successful intercontinental ballistic missile—in hand, Korolev then pressed with all the political subtlety he commanded for using the R-7 to launch a satellite. He arranged for his superiors to ask the Presidium of the Central Committee of the Communist Party if the USSR should try to be the first country in the world to launch a satellite into space. There was no way to say no, and approval came forthwith.

Now the gigantic R-7 rocket stood on the launching pad like an enormous question mark, symbolizing the high risk it involved. Korolev had long since broken free from German V-2 technology, and his rocket looked like no other. It used parallel staging and was composed of a cluster of five identical rockets that ignited simultaneously at liftoff. One hundred and eleven feet long, the five-unit rocket packet weighed 274 metric tons. Four strap-on boosters were attached to a core stage, and the fuel tanks for all stages also served as structural elements. The R-7 took more than twenty hours' preparation before a launch, its volatile cryogenic fuels a hazard during the entire process. Of its six previous flight attempts, only the last had succeeded. All the rest had ended in roaring explosions from one malfunction or another, bringing forth a personal promise from Premier Nikita Khrushchev to shut down the program if there was another failure.

Today's flight was more hazardous than the previous six, for the R-7's usual warhead was simple compared to the satellite, which required precise thermal control and reliable vacuum sealing of components. So many things could go wrong, and any one of them would mean the end of the careers of all who worked on it. Five years ago, in Stalin's day, it would have meant their lives.

Korolev and his men held their breath as the clock ticked steadily down to zero and the five rockets ignited simultaneously in a hellish blast that turned night into day. After an agonizing wait, those interminable few seconds while the rocket seemed to balance delicately between lifting off and blowing up, they saw almost four thousand kilonewtons of thrust blast the R-7 skyward. Its roar shook the staff like white reeds before rumbling out across the surrounding desert in thundering concentric waves, blowing dust, bending trees, and sending animals scurrying to their lairs.

As they watched the R-7 accelerate swiftly out of sight, the spontaneous cheers died off slowly, to be replaced by a mortuary silence. One hundred and twenty seconds later there was a little rustle of approving excitement—they knew that if all was well, the boosters were jettisoned. Two hundred seconds more, and another little murmur filled the room with the knowledge that—perhaps—the core engine had now exhausted its fuel. They could only hope that it reached the design speed of 8,000 meters per second so that the satellite could be placed in orbit some 250 kilometers above Earth.

To the right of the launch control panel, the scientists crowding the small radio room melted away as Korolev walked through their ranks, his face drawn. The hushed room, stifling with the rank odors of unwashed bodies, ill-digested cabbage, and the blue-black smoke of cheap cigarettes, now resonated to heavy breathing and the slight static from the receivers. Stress built up as each man considered what he might have done—or left undone—that could cause a failure. Suddenly there was a very quiet sound, a faint *beep-beep*, a mere alteration in the static. No one spoke until the sound was repeated, stronger this time, and the room erupted in a shouting screaming mass of almost hysterical delight. Sputnik *was in orbit!*

They seized Korolev and raised him to their shoulders. Smiling, he acknowledged their cheers for a brief moment, then motioned for silence, saying, "Our satellite is in Earth orbit. I have been waiting all my life for this day." It was typical of Korolev to say "our satellite" rather than "my satellite." Silver foil tops were torn off vodka bottles as the normally austere scientists, even the most bitter career rivals among them, embraced and kissed in the sweet joy of their triumph of science over the bureaucracy.

Korolev forced his way down and out of the room, hurrying to his private office to make two telephone calls. The first was to the State Commission for the R-7 ICBM. As he expected at this early hour, there was only a duty officer on hand. He took Korolev's message that "the USSR has placed the world's first artificial satellite in orbit" with gruff, uncomprehending condescension.

His second call was to his former prison-mate Andrei Tupolev, who was waiting for his call. There was a long delay before Tupolev's voice crackled through the phone. The connection, like those of most Soviet long-distance calls, was terrible.

"Andrei Nikolaevich, my friend, my mentor. I wanted to tell you personally. Today we have placed an artificial satellite into orbit."

"Congratulations, Sergei Pavlovich! You have sent the world a message about Soviet science! And what an immense amount of work you have put into this triumph."

Korolev filled him in quickly on the size of the *Sputnik*, its orbit, its equipment. Even as the heartfelt congratulations tumbled from his mouth, Tupolev remembered their gulag days together, condemned as spies and traitors by Stalin. All aeronautical engineers were suspect during the mid-1930s, and a system of *sharashkas*—prison design bureaus—was set up to exploit the jailed talent.

"This would never have happened if you had not saved my life."

Tupolev certainly had done just that when he requested Korolev to serve with him in the TsKB-39 *sharashka* in Moscow.

"Nonsense. You would have survived; we are both survivors; we will prevail. It is our stubborn Russian nature."

Stalin's death in March 1953 gave them a new lease on life and now they were relatively secure in their positions. Strangely, like most *sharaska* survivors, the two men were not bitter. Just being alive was an incredible stroke of luck—being alive and able to work at their professions was a miracle.

"Andrei Nikolaevich, I will have a flood of newsmen here tomorrow. May I ask them to have their colleagues call on you for comment?"

"Of course you may, but why? I had no part at all in this grand experiment."

"I want them to ask you what effect this will have on aviation."

"Let me think about it until tomorrow, and I'll have a fine story for them."

"May I suggest something, to start your giant brain turning?"

"My giant brain is already working, but you go ahead."

"Tell them that someday, not too far in the future, satellites far bigger than this first one will be used for communications, for meteorology, for navigation."

"And how about for intelligence work? Shall I tell them that?"

Laughing, Korolev joked back, "Yes, tell them that there will be no more U-2s in the future, that Soviet satellites will cover the world with an all-seeing eye."

Tupolev laughed and said, "I think I'll stick with communications, meteorology, and navigation. Then the KGB won't come after me for mentioning the U-2."

They talked briefly, asking about each other's families, then made their good-byes, Tupolev closing with, "Take care of yourself, Sergei Pavlovich; you know that it is always the tallest nail that gets hammered. I worry about your health."

Before going back to the festivities, Korolev went outside to gaze upward where his precious satellite was hurtling around the Earth. He considered Tupolev's warning carefully. Korolev's health was precarious, but glancing upward to the moon, he knew that there was so much more to be done and little time in which to do it. He also knew how much he owed his staff, particularly Mikhail Tikhonravov, who had pushed the artificial Earth satellite concept from the beginning. It had taken years, but when Korolev finally became intoxicated by Tikhonravov's idea, he managed to keep his enthusiasm hidden behind his work on the R-7 missile. Either the satellite or the missile could shape the destiny of the world—and Korolev hoped it would be the satellite.

CHAPTER SIX

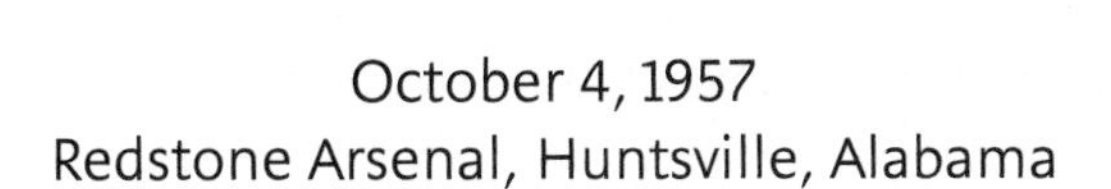

October 4, 1957
Redstone Arsenal, Huntsville, Alabama

October was a blessed time in Huntsville, with the temperature dropping twenty degrees from the scorching high nineties of the summer and the humidity declining from a steaming hot-towel embrace to a healthy 40 percent. The weather more than anything else had shocked the German scientists brought over by Operation Paperclip, that great capture of German scientific talent at the end of World War II. The enervating humid heat of summer was unlike anything they had ever experienced, even the very few who had served in the North African campaigns. It overshadowed the other discomforts such as the strange food, the sense of alienation from German culture, and the longing for family. But all of these things were minor. No one was bombing them now, they were safely out of Germany, and if they had a Nazi past, it was ignored, if not forgotten. And just not to be working for the Russians was an inconceivable blessing. Best of all, the opportunities at Huntsville to go into space exceeded by a thousand fold those they had left behind in the ruins of Peenemünde.

No one was more aware of this than Wernher von Braun as he dressed to attend a reception at Redstone Arsenal. There Major General John Medaris, commandant of the Army Ballistic Missile Agency, was hosting Neil McElroy, who in a few days would be succeeding the current Secretary of Defense, the cantankerous "Engine Charlie" Wilson. In American parlance, the red carpet was rolled out.

The phone rang in von Braun's bedroom, and as he reached for it he marveled at another of the seemingly endless series of luxurious American conveniences—a bath every day with plenty of soap, wonderful cars, freezers, television, and, just imagine, two telephones in the house.

"Von Braun here." He had not yet adopted the simple American "hello."

"Dr. von Braun, this is Lieutenant Allen, duty officer at Redstone. We tried to reach General Medaris, but he must be en route to the reception. We thought you would like to know that the Soviet Union has launched an artificial satellite. It is in orbit around the Earth, and apparently sending radio signals, although we have not picked them up as yet."

Von Braun sat down on the bed, speechless.

"Dr. von Braun? Are you there?"

"Yes, sorry, I was stunned. Do you have any more details?"

"No, sir, but I'll feed them to you as soon as they come in."

Von Braun dropped the phone without even thanking Allen and rushed out of the house, his tie still untied, shoes unlaced, coat slung over his shoulder, heading for the reception and a word with Medaris. On the way, von Braun thought of all the rebuffs he had received since 1954, when he had tried to convince the government to use the Jupiter missile to place a satellite in orbit. Instead, the Navy's proposed Vanguard launch vehicle was chosen to launch a small satellite, one that was to serve as the United States' contribution to the International Geophysical Year to be observed in 1957–58. The Vanguard was still not ready, but his Jupiter C rocket had proved itself. With a few modifications, it could place a satellite in orbit.

His tie tied, shoes laced, and coat safely tucked around his shoulders, von Braun paused outside the austere Redstone Arsenal's Officers' Club to gaze upward at the skies now ruled by Soviet hardware, the first man-made satellite ever to orbit Earth. Five minutes later he had the swarthy, mustachioed Medaris bent over a table, sipping a Coca-Cola, listening intently. Von Braun often joked to his wife that he seemed destined to work for men with mustaches, but Medaris was a totally different boss from Hitler. Distinguished-looking, soft-spoken, and a devout Episcopalian, he had literally created the Army Ballistic Missile Agency out of whole cloth. Medaris had induced the sleepy town of Huntsville, with its seventeen-thousand population, to annex the land around Redstone Arsenal and then provide it with the services it needed but the Army would not provide. Medaris had told an unbelieving city council that in ten years Huntsville's population would exceed one hundred thousand, and now it looked as if he had been conservative in his estimate.

An imposing figure, Medaris valued von Braun, and recognized all that he had done for the Army's ballistic missile program. Nonetheless, Medaris was reluctant to let him speak to the next Secretary of Defense without formal preparation and without clearing the talk through the Secretary of the Army. Von Braun was insistent. The two men had arrived at an easy understanding: von Braun was a genius who was to be given a virtual free hand—but ultimately, Medaris was boss.

"General Medaris, we have no time. If we allow Secretary McElroy to go back to Washington and face an army of reporters with no answers about an American satellite, he will never forgive us."

Medaris finally agreed, and the two men sequestered the bewildered, somewhat apprehensive McElroy in a small office away from the ballroom.

"Tell me again, Dr. von Braun, what the Russians have done."

Medaris nodded and von Braun said "Mr. Secretary, the Russians have placed a small satellite into orbit around Earth. This is the first time this has ever been done. We do not yet know for sure the size of the satellite, or what instrumentation it has, but if it is just a bowling ball, it is an incredible achievement. And its implications are frightening."

"What are the frightening implications?" McElroy was not skeptical, just bewildered and a bit embarrassed at his own lack of knowledge.

"Well, if the Soviets can put a satellite into space, it means they have rockets that can power an intercontinental ballistic missile. And that means they can put a nuclear weapon on a U.S. target in thirty minutes. It is an incredible capability."

"Do we have a similar capability?"

"No. We do not have an intercontinental ballistic missile. We can put a satellite in orbit, however, if we modify the Jupiter C with another stage."

McElroy stroked his chin, distressed at being forced to make an important decision before he was even sworn in. It was not good form.

Von Braun was unrelenting. "Mr. Secretary, when you get back to Washington, you'll find that all hell has broken loose. We can put up a satellite in sixty days—once you give us the go-ahead."

Medaris interjected, "Make it ninety days, Wernher."

"OK, make it ninety days," said von Braun.

McElroy snapped his head up, extended his hand, and said, "Agreed."

Von Braun started for the door, but Medaris stopped him. "We'll start tomorrow, Wernher. Tonight we have a guest."

Impatience flooded von Braun's face, but he understood and flashed the smile that would soon become famous.

CHAPTER SEVEN

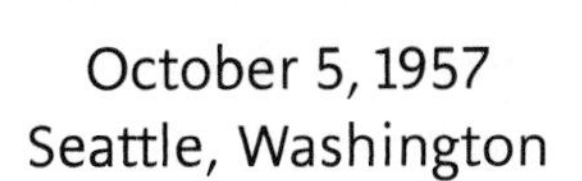

October 5, 1957
Seattle, Washington

A depressed and weary group of Boeing engineers sat staring at the television set, brought into the conference room to show them the firestorm of interest that the *beep-beep-beep* of the *Sputnik* had generated around the world. Daphne Perry, George Schairer's new secretary, came in pushing a cart laden with coffee and rolls. Usually she had something bright and saucy to say, but this Saturday morning she sensed the deep emotion of the room and moved quietly to serve the men.

Schairer was not sitting at his usual position, deferring to the chief engineer, Wellwood Beall, but had called the meeting and was running it with his customary crisp efficiency. As always, Schairer was wearing a well-fit off-the-rack suit and white shirt, but today his tie was undone, his sparse hair in disarray, and his glasses smudged. Around the table, showing similar signs of fatigue, sat eleven of Boeing's finest engineers and Vance Shannon. All were equally dismayed by the Soviet triumph.

"Talk about getting caught with your pants down. It is incredible that they could have pulled this off with so little warning."

Ed Wells, older, shorter, and with considerably more hair than Schairer, nodded in agreement. "There were some hints. The Soviets had said that they had intended to put a small satellite into orbit soon. But the problem is that we just don't have any worthwhile intelligence sources in Russia. We keep getting fed garbage, and I don't think that even our newest sources could have picked this out."

Shannon, a longtime intimate of both Schairer and Wells—he didn't know Beall as well—had been a consultant to Boeing for more than thirty years. He picked up his ears at Wells's comment, assuming that he was referring to the covert U-2 flights over the Soviet Union. It surprised Shannon. A few, a very few, people were aware of the U-2 and its capabilities, and none of them ever talked about it in an open forum like this.

Wells went on, "Well, they've got a new term for it—'humint,' short for 'human intelligence.' We must have a few people on the ground over there, but they are not giving us much help."

Shannon was relieved and troubled at the same time. He was glad that Wells had not slipped up and talked about the U-2 in front of his engineers, many of whom had no knowledge of the program. But the reference to human intelligence—jargon for "spying"—made him squirm, reminding him of what had happened with Madeline eight years earlier.

Beall turned wearily to Shannon and said, "Vance, what does it mean to you? Is this as big a threat as some of the newspapers are making it out to be?"

Shannon waited for a moment before speaking, deliberately taking a swallow of coffee.

"Well, it shows they have rockets big enough to use intercontinental missiles to deliver a nuclear warhead. It doesn't show how many they have or how reliable they are, but it is a definite threat. But I also think it is the biggest and best thing that ever happened to the American aviation industry."

Almost as a man, the Boeing engineers straightened up in their chairs and stared at him, waiting for him to go on. Shannon did, saying, "President Eisenhower cannot take this lying down, and the American people won't let him. You can expect to see funding for experiments with satellites and missiles to explode, pardon the pun. There will be a requirement for us to get our own satellites into the air as soon as possible. It will have an impact on aircraft production, too. The Strategic Air Command will be built up. General LeMay will want to have his own fleet of ICBMs—that's what they call the long-range missiles—as soon as we have any."

Beall nodded approvingly. "That's the way we have to look at it. Convair is way ahead of us on this one. They've been spending development money on an ICBM for years, since 1946. Lots of problems with it, but they are too far ahead of us to compete for the first generation of ICBMs—but there will always be new ones coming down the pike."

The conversation became general, and it was soon apparent that Schairer had invited the engineers carefully for their specialties.

Finally, he said, "Well, gentlemen, it looks like we've got our work cut out for us. We've got a lot of experience already with the Bomarc, thanks to Bob Jewett here."

The Bomarc was a Mach 3.0 surface-to-air missile intended to defend against hostile aircraft. Launched with a rocket booster, it used ramjets for power and had a sophisticated radar homing system. Only three days before, it had completed its first really successful test, but the Air Force was going to buy them in quantity, and it looked as if Canada would, too.

Schairer went on, "We can translate that experience into an organization to explore the production of ICBMs, satellites, and maybe more. Let's meet here again, a week from today, and let me have your thoughts on how to approach it. But before you go, let's just toss some ideas out on the table; maybe it will stimulate our thinking."

Wells started it off, "I've always thought Convair was barking up the wrong tree, using liquid propellants for an ICBM. You really cannot waste the time it takes to fuel and erect a rocket using liquid fuels, and they are much too dangerous. We need to think about a solid rocket, one you can store in the ground for years, then fire with a push of the button."

Jack Steiner, tall, dark haired, and utterly intense, was next. "Well, you can talk about satellites all you want, but what the public will demand is something more Buck Rogers, space planes, rocket ships, and the like. If you can put a satellite in orbit, you could put a man-carrying aircraft in orbit, too, and just let it glide back down when you are ready."

Schairer raised his hands. "That's enough for now—Ed and Jack just outlined twenty-five years of work. I'd like everyone to come back next week, same time, same place, prepared to discuss these two ideas, and in the meantime send me a memo on any other ideas you have. And as far as the press goes, the official word is that Boeing congratulates the scientists in the USSR for their achievement, and looks forward to the forthcoming competition in space."

CHAPTER EIGHT

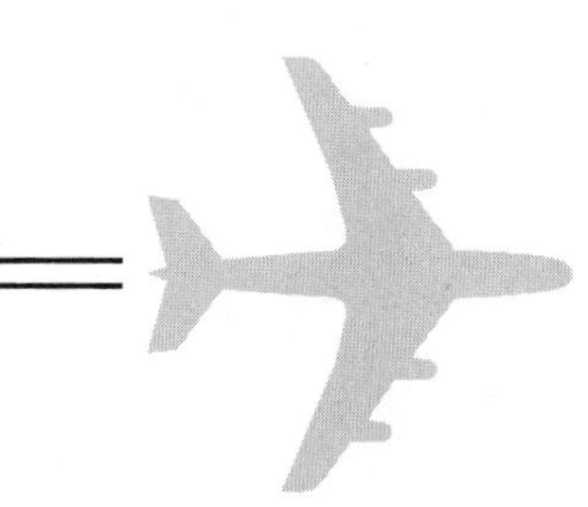

November 4, 1957
Palos Verdes, California

The three Shannons were glued to the television set, watching the grainy photographs of Laika, the dog being carried in orbit by *Sputnik II.* Tom reached down and scratched the head of Poppy, the lovable golden retriever that never left his side when he was home.

"We'd never let them do that to you, Poppy."

The atmosphere was dour from the weather outside and the news of another Soviet triumph inside. This was the first time the three of them had met together for more than two months. Vance had been flying back and forth between Seattle and Burbank, Harry had been spending most of his time at Vandenberg Air Force Base, and Tom's time had been divided between Burbank and the Lockheed plant in Marietta, Georgia, where production of the Lockheed C-130 transport was booming.

"How do these guys do it, Dad? They can't feed their people, they can't make a decent car, but they've completely outstripped us in space."

"Well, they are smart, no doubt about that, and they are tough; look how they polished off the Germans. But the main thing is that they are focused. They've got enough government funding guaranteed over long periods of time. We'll get there, but it better be soon, 'cause they are making laughingstocks of us."

Harry didn't comment for a while, then asked, "Where is Bob Rodriquez?"

"Bob's off back east, in Cambridge, Mass., working with Ed Land on some camera projects. Land is the guy who invented the Polaroid process, you know, and now he is creating some incredible cameras for reconnaissance work."

The answer satisfied Tom, not so much because he was interested in Rodriquez's work as because he was content to have him out of the immediate area. Despite all of his father's explanations, Tom had never accepted the agreement and continued to regard Rodriquez as an outsider. Tom was polite to him and worked well enough with him, but if Bob ever left to take another job, he would be pleased.

Vance Shannon walked over and turned the television set off. "I've seen enough about that poor dog and the blasted *Sputnik II.* Harry, I want you to tell me again exactly what Kelly said to you about designing the Learjet."

Harry recounted the story, emphasizing the need to look at small fighters as a possible platform to launch the new jet.

"It makes sense. The manufacturer would have done a lot of the wind tunnel work, the stress analysis, and so on. It would be overbuilt, to take more g's than an executive jet would require, but if it's light enough, that wouldn't be much of a problem, might even be a plus. Did he mention any types specifically?"

"Yes, he mentioned that the Swiss were working on a fighter of their own, and of course, there are Saab and Dassault to consider."

Harry regretted it the instant he said "Dassault," which was one of the firms that had been given information Madeline had stolen from Vance. It didn't bother him, as he laughed and said, "Well, maybe we have a contact there—Madeline might still be working for them."

He turned to Tom and asked, "How is your project in Marietta coming?"

Tom had been hired to dispose of the surplus tools and fixtures that Lockheed had used when it was building the Boeing B-47 under license. It was a pretty boring job, but it was cheaper for Lockheed to have him handle it than to devote someone from their own workforce, shorthanded now as C-130 and JetStar production began to increase.

"It's in pretty good shape. I'll be winding it up in a couple of weeks."

"OK, you've been hitting it pretty hard. Why don't you take Nancy and V.R. and make a little tour through Europe—hit some of the foreign plants making smaller fighter jets or trainers. There's Folland, in England, and you mentioned Saab and Dassault, and there's Fiat in Italy. Probably some more, if you get out your *Jane's All the World's Aircraft* and see what's cooking. We can set up an itinerary; we know people in most of the plants, or if not, we know people who know people. You won't tell them what you are doing, let them think you are looking in order to recommend a trainer for some foreign government or something."

"I don't know, Dad. Harry's been working hard, too; this doesn't seem fair."

"Go for it, Tom—Nancy deserves it. Anna and I are planning a trip to Hawaii later in the year, so don't feel bad."

Vance looked on his sons with pride. They were finally growing up, becoming more friends and less rivals. It was about time, but he wished he could tell if it was maturity or the Rodriquez factor that made it so.

CHAPTER NINE

December 18, 1957
Venice, California

At sixty, Fritz Obermyer did not get as excited as he did in his youth, but today was different, with an old friend long thought to be dead suddenly calling him out of the blue. The hair had stood up on the back of his neck as he heard the familiar guttural voice of Gerd Müller, his comrade in the trenches of World War I, his friend and bodyguard during the interwar years, and his close companion until the very last day of World War II.

Müller, sounding conspiratorial as usual, had talked only for a few minutes, long enough to arrange to meet that night but not nearly long enough to explain what had happened to him in the twelve years since they had been split up on a Berlin street, trying to avoid capture by the Russians.

Obermyer spent the rest of the day in his apartment. There were absolutely no similarities, but Obermyer always felt as at home in Venice, California, as he had at his favorite hotel, the Bayerischer Hof, in Friedrichschafen. The air, scenery, people, and food were all vastly different, but both gave him the same strange dual sense of anonymity and belonging. He had leased a small second-floor apartment, two blocks from the beach and almost ten miles from his office in his booming Volkswagen dealership. There the pressure was great, even though he had good people working for him. He was just too set in his ways to delegate much decision-making power. He let his best used-car salesmen decide on the value of the trade-ins, but other than that, he approved every deal that was made. He even watched the receipts from the maintenance department. That was one little secret Volkswagen kept from the public. The purchase price and operating costs were relatively low, but maintenance costs were higher than American customers were used to and generated a good percentage of his total profits.

Despite his urge to see Müller, Obermyer was glad to have time to clean up some paperwork relating to his new business colleagues in San Diego. Six months before, he had gone down for the grand opening of Capestro Motors. Capestro and Shannon had done it correctly, buying their land far out on El Cajon Boulevard and putting in more money than the parent firm required to make sure they had a top location, plenty of space, easy access from downtown, and a huge maintenance bay, half again as large as prescribed by Volkswagen.

It was the first pure Volkswagen dealership in the area. A few VWs had been sold by other dealers, whose lines usually included Hillman and Jaguar. But Shannon and Capestro had done things right again by announcing they were going to specialize, and they had already captured most of the repair business for VWs already in the area.

In their early negotiations, Obermyer had not told them about the profits to be made from the higher maintenance costs—it would have alarmed them, as they were both painfully honest men. Now they were finding out for themselves and had to be pleased by the development.

The bigger maintenance bay was probably Shannon's influence, he thought. *He has had a lot of operational experience with aircraft, and it carries over to cars. And he probably learned a lot from Mademoiselle Behar.*

Obermyer flipped through the thick dossier in front of him. In it virtually every event in Vance Shannon's life was recorded, from being an ace in World War I, through test-flying in the years between the wars, to the great success his firm enjoyed during World War II and afterward. It covered details of his family life, the death of his first wife, Margaret, his long affair with Madeline Behar, and his current apparently happy marriage to the former Jill Abernathy.

What impressed Obermyer most was Shannon's list of gold-plated clients. Obermyer knew about Lockheed, Convair, and Boeing, of course, but Shannon was also in demand from Douglas, Martin, McDonnell, Pratt & Whitney, General Electric, and a host of others. Remarkable! It was a good thing he had two sons to help him.

Obermyer paused for a moment to reflect on his own state. He would have liked to have had a family, to have sons of his own, but his life had always been too perilous, too uncertain. Instead he had contented himself with strictly professional relations with expensive women who were never in short supply. There were some advantages to this—he was his own man, could make his own decisions—but nonetheless, in reading Shannon's folder he felt a pang of envy.

The dossier even contained copies of recent flight physicals that showed that despite his sixty-three years, Vance was still in good physical condition. Obermyer noted that Vance was still flying his own airplane, a war-surplus Beech C-45. Although not a pilot himself, Obermyer had been around aviation long enough to know that the C-45 was a demanding aircraft and that Shannon must therefore be quite proficient.

There was a similar, but much thinner, dossier on Lou Capestro. His health was not as good as Shannon's—he was overweight and there was a history of heart trouble. Obermyer made an entry in the little logbook that he always carried, writing: "Insist that they get big insurance policies with the firm beneficiary."

Financially, Capestro was not quite as well off as Shannon was—his sons were apparently a bit of a drain on his resources—but was very comfortable, easily able to afford the investment in the car dealership, and more than able to sustain it during the early months when the earnings would still be low.

The two men had put in seventy-five thousand dollars, forty thousand dollars from Capestro and the rest from Shannon. Obermyer knew from experience that they would need to invest another one hundred thousand dollars each over the next year. After that the business should become increasingly profitable—if the sales projections held up. He was sure that they would. Then the two might be ripe to take on a Porsche dealership, just as he was going to do.

The ease of obtaining personal information in the United States never ceased to amaze Obermyer, who had once prospered by providing such data. Under the Nazis, it was impossible to have access to such information unless one was, as he had been, an operative of the state. Here in California, there was a private investigator on virtually every corner and for a minimum investment one could, quite discreetly, obtain all the information needed on anyone.

The same was true of the aviation industry. Publications like *Aviation Week* generated an incredible amount of detailed information every week. If the articles were analyzed and one did some snooping around, one could easily guess what might be going on in projects that were still veiled in secrecy.

Unable to concentrate, Obermyer returned to thinking about this morning's phone call from Gerd Müller. He had arranged to meet him that night in the only German restaurant he knew of in Los Angeles, the Hofbrau Haus.

After Gerd had disappeared, Obermyer had tried to reach him but failed. There were rumors that Gerd had been killed by Russian soldiers and it was not improbable, so Obermyer had presumed him dead, along with so many others. In those days, death was not only more likely for people on the Eastern Front; it was also preferable. The separation had been quite a blow, as the two men had saved each other's lives more than once in the First World War and had fought together in the Roehlk Friekorps afterward. After Hitler had taken over in 1933, both men had been prominent in local Nazi politics, with Gerd serving as a bodyguard to Obermyer. In return, Obermyer obtained a good-paying job for Gerd at the Heinkel company and shared with him some of the income he made from providing insider information to aviation firms.

Obermyer drove his Porsche 356 Speedster to the Hofbrau Haus, located only four miles away from his apartment. He still enjoyed driving the Beetle, as it was now known almost universally, but felt that as the proprietor of a car dealership he should drive something upscale, and what better than a Porsche, even though it was twice as expensive as the average sixteen-hundred-dollar Volkswagen. Johnny von Neumann had the West Coast dealership for Porsche cars, but Obermyer intended to slice into his business in time.

At the Hofbrau Haus, the German food was of indifferent quality, but they managed a good selection of German beer, all served by cheerful, busty, and sometimes lusty waitresses. No one went there for food, drink, or even sex, for that matter. The Hofbrau Haus's charm was its unapologetic nostalgia for the Third Reich. There were no overt signs, no swastikas or photos of Hitler, but its ambience brought the German émigrés now flooding into Los Angeles together to reminisce about "the good old days" and feel comfortable about it. There had even been one official reunion of former members of the SS. The meeting had been small and low-key, but Gustav Lieberich, the owner, a thin, unjovial penny counter, the very opposite of the stereotypical German barkeeper, was concerned that such meetings might draw fire from local Jewish groups, so he kept things as informal as possible.

The walls were lined with large oil paintings, some ten by fourteen feet, that would have been praised at any Nazi-era art show—strong, scantily clad young men and women harvesting, working together in industry, or seen at home in tender situations featuring golden-haired children. None of the paintings had a military connotation, and yet they fostered the martial air that was the restaurant's real theme. Toward the back, where the restrooms were located, there were some kitschy renditions of monks chasing nuns or sampling wine in monastery cellars, all adding to the homey feel.

Early in the evening, the Hofbrau Haus was quiet enough, with couples sitting decorously at tables and a few men drinking at the long bar. But by eleven o'clock, the building began to ring with German drinking songs that within the hour would turn into marching songs. Lieberich was a canny businessman, and he operated two shops as buffers, one on either side of the restaurant. At its left was a quite profitable dry cleaner, flashing a big "One Hour Martinizing" sign. On the right, there was a newsstand where dirty magazines could be purchased under the counter. It barely broke even, but it served the real purpose of isolating his gold mine of a restaurant from neighbors who might complain about the Nazi overtones.

As was his invariable custom, Obermyer arrived early, excited about the prospect of seeing Müller again. He ordered a double Johnnie Walker Black straight up and two Steinhagers, Müller's preferred drink. Obermyer drank the Scotch quickly, had them remove the glass, and glanced at his watch. Unless Müller had changed, he would be exactly on time, seven o'clock.

And he was, marching through the door in the rambling fashion that Obermyer would have recognized from several blocks away. He stood up, opened his arms, and they embraced, tears running, both embarrassed by it.

They toasted each other with the Steinhagers, signaled for two more, and launched into a long and friendly sharing of memories from the hard days of World War I, through the terrible post-war years, to the few good years they had under the Nazis.

"You know when it was best, Fritz? It was when we were working with Heinkel on that jet that young von Ohain had invented. We had the best of all worlds then, plenty of money, a car, nobody breathing down our necks. I wish it could have gone on forever."

"Remember how we made fun of him—and today everybody flies in jets. It was a privilege to be there—we just didn't know it."

But after the old stories had been covered, at least in part, they settled down to a rapid-fire series of questions and answers, trying to catch up on the last twelve years.

After brushing off probes about how well he was doing, Obermyer asked, "Did the Russians wound you?"

"No, they just captured me—no way out. You remember there was a barrage of mortar fire and we both dove in opposite directions. I went into a cellar filled with dead soldiers, then wandered about in long, dark tunnels, passageways between the buildings."

Obermyer recalled them well. The Berliners had built tunnels interconnecting the cellars of virtually all the building in the city, to supplement the air-raid shelters and to provide a quick way out of a burning building.

"When I came out, I was on another street and four Ivans collared me, took my watch, my wallet, jerked the ring off my finger, practically cut it off. I expected them to shoot me, but instead they took me into what looked like a company headquarters and threw me in a cell. The next day was May 8, the day of the surrender, and they were celebrating. But the kicker was that they introduced me to a German officer, Hauptmann Reinhard Wachter. He was in Russian uniform of course, but he had been captured at Stalingrad, and had worked with the von Paulus committee."

Obermyer snorted in disgust. Members of the von Paulus committee were traitors. Adolf Hitler, the man who had made Friedrich von Paulus a field marshall, expected him to die fighting. No German field marshall had ever surrendered, but von Paulus did, saving his own skin while hundreds of thousands had died. Worse, he not only surrendered; he also helped form a committee of officers denouncing Hitler and his conduct of the war.

"Wachter was there to recruit Germans to work with the Russian authorities after the war. The next thing I knew, I was a block leader in the east of Berlin."

"Why did they pick you? You didn't speak Russian or anything."

"It was my age. They wanted older people, not from the 'Hitler generation,' and it didn't take me long to learn Russian, because it was learn Russian or not eat. Pretty soon I was acting as a translator, and got one political job after another. Then, when the German Democratic Republic was formed in 1949, I was recruited into the Stasi—the East German counterpart to the KGB."

Obermyer chuckled. "I should have known, Gerd, you would bounce out of the frying pan into a soft job. No wonder I couldn't find you when I asked around about what happened to you."

"No, I knew you were looking, but I couldn't respond; they would have fired me on the spot, maybe even killed me. It's a little dangerous for me still to be talking to you, even now, but I need your help."

"Anything you want, Gerd, you know that."

"OK, now what can you tell me about the Lockheed U-2?"

CHAPTER TEN

February 1, 1958
Above the San Joaquin Valley, California

Vance Shannon felt wonderful as he always did when flying the bargain of a lifetime, a Beech C-45 that he had picked up at a war surplus sale in 1946 for fifteen hundred dollars. It was a steal, for the airplane had less than two hundred hours' total flight time when he bought it and was in perfect shape. And despite Jill's undertone of complaints, there was no finer time to fly than early Sunday morning, when his was virtually the only aircraft in the sky.

The Beech had an autopilot, but Vance rarely used it. It was old-fashioned and rather difficult to set up. He preferred flying the Beech himself anyway, enjoying the continual sensual interplay between the air, the controls, and his hands that had given him both challenge and contentment for more than forty years.

Passing over Fresno, he could see Merced in the distance and knew he should deviate a bit to the right to stay out of the B-52 traffic at Castle Air Force Base. It was Sunday, but they'd be flying anyway. As he cranked in a shallow turn to the right, it dawned on him why he was feeling so well. The previous day, the U.S. Army had launched the *Explorer* satellite. After the fiasco of the *Vanguard* blowing up on its pad, he and his sons had watched with pride as the *Explorer* roared off into the night sky in a blaze of glory. Ninety nail-biting minutes had followed until the California track station announced, "Goldstone has the bird"—they were tracking it in orbit.

The early-morning news reports indicated that the United States was reacting with the same patriotic pride shown by the Soviet Union when *Sputnik* was launched. The space race was on, and it was up to Vance to determine how his firm, Aviation Consultants, could help. He decided on the spot that a name change was necessary, perhaps to "Aerospace Consultants" or maybe "Air and Space Consultants." The firm's leadership and direction had to change, too, and the best instrument for that would be Bob Rodriquez, who was already dabbling in things so esoteric that Harry was the only other member of the firm able to understand him.

One thing was for sure—to sustain the interest of the public, they'd have to do more than put satellites up into space. Americans were brought up on Buck Rogers and Flash Gordon and, unless there were people in the spacecraft, would lose interest fast. And the people had to be doing thrilling things that challenged the imagination. You had to sell space just as Tex Johnston sold airplanes, doing things that made the public stand up and cheer.

Vance's mind flashed back to August 7, 1955. He was on the beautiful Boeing company boat, a guest of George Schairer, at the annual Seafair Gold Cup Hydroplane Race at Lake Washington. The entire shoreline was dotted with every kind of vessel from rowboats to multimillion-dollar yachts, and the shore itself was lined with spectators.

His old friend Russ Schleeh, a Boeing test pilot, was just becoming interested in racing the fast boats, and he and Vance were leaning against the bridge. As they stood there, crystal glasses filled with champagne, Vance thought, *I've got to get Schleeh to arm wrestle Kelly Johnson. That would be a match.*

As big as Kelly was, Schleeh was still the strongest guy Vance had ever known, with hands the size of hams, a powerful build, and a big grin—a natural pilot.

In front of them, Bill Allen, Boeing's gutsy president, was entertaining some airline executives, potential customers all, with his usual courtesy and wit.

Schleeh nudged Vance with his elbow and pointed over Allen's head to the north end of the lake.

"It's Tex Johnston. He's going to make a pass in the 707 prototype."

The Seafair announcer came on and alerted the crowd that the new

Boeing jet transport would be passing overhead in just one minute.

Everyone grew quiet as Johnston neared the lake, about four hundred feet off the ground and hitting at least 400 miles per hour. There was an audible gasp from the crowd as the big Boeing began to roll, its left wing going up, its nose lifting a little. To the experts it was obvious that the Boeing had gone out of control and was going to crash right there in front of them. Instead, the roll continued, and then everyone gasped again, none louder than Bill Allen, as the beautiful cream, reddish-brown, and gold-painted airliner rolled smoothly over on its back, looking absolutely outrageous with its engines facing up rather than hanging down. This was the crisis moment when pilots expected to see parts flying off and the nose dropping in a headlong plunge into the lake. Instead Johnston continued his impeccable majestic sweep, rolling out into level flight.

Then to make his point to the still-astonished crowd, to convince them that it was not a fluke, Johnston executed another flawless roll before speeding away to land at Boeing Field.

The crowd was stunned at first, and then there burst forth a roar that seemed to shake the waters—no one could believe what they had just seen, least of all Bill Allen, who turned to a friend and asked for nitroglycerin tablets for his heart.

Vance knew that no one would have authorized a demonstration like that—but he also knew that it was the single best advertisement Boeing would ever have. Even so, Johnston would catch hell for it.

Nudging Schleeh, Vance said, "Tex Johnston just sold a whole bunch of airplanes—no one will ever forget this—I hope they don't fire his ass."

Schleeh nodded and asked, "Would you call that a barrel roll or an aileron roll?"

"I don't know; all I can say is that he probably kept it at one g all the way around and the people inside didn't spill a single drink."

That was a lot more than could be said for the people watching, who collectively had dropped their jaws, their drinks, and their disbelief before the second roll was finished.

Vance began his descent checklist, heading for McClellan Air Force Base, trying to think of something that would sell the public on space as Johnston had sold them on the 707. Putting a man in orbit was one thing, and the Soviets would probably beat them to it. They probably had something lined up already, dangerous as it was. No, it would take something grandiose, something that von Braun and the others had talked about for years, putting a man on the moon. Trouble was, that was at least twenty years away. They needed something now.

CHAPTER ELEVEN

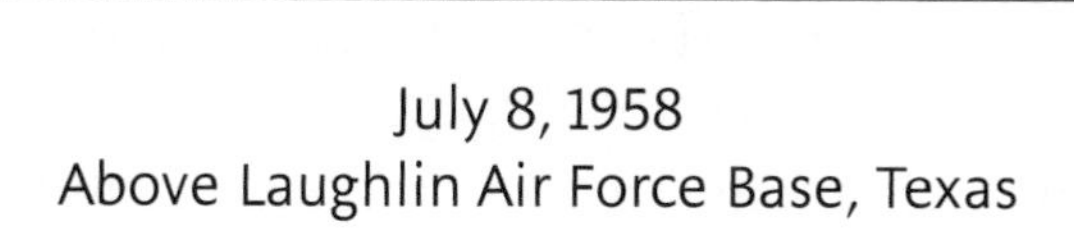

July 8, 1958
Above Laughlin Air Force Base, Texas

Squadron Leader Christopher Osborn pressed his back against the seat of his U-2, trying vainly to suppress an itch that had developed three hours ago. Itching was just part of the package of wearing the MC-3 partial pressure suit, necessary because of the altitudes at which the U-2 flew. He was content, nonetheless, for he was at the controls of the most advanced reconnaissance plane in the world, one of four Royal Air Force officers to be accorded the privilege.

Dark-haired and so hook-nosed that his colleagues joked about the need to fit his helmet with a custom faceplate, Osborn flew with his customary precision, recording the events of the flight as if he were over Mother Russia. His last assignment at the Royal Air Force experimental establishment at Boscombe Down had prepared him perfectly for this mission, and he looked forward to the following year, when he would be making overflights of the Soviet Union.

He picked up a heading of 270 degrees, carefully maintaining his altitude of 67,000 feet. To his left he could see far into Mexico, a place he intended to visit before returning home. To his right he saw the endless Texas plains stretching to the horizon. He had come to love the state in spite of the strange mixtures of its cuisine. Suddenly he wondered, *How many square miles can I see from here, horizon to horizon?*

He had the aircraft perfectly trimmed and reached down to figure out the area on the small notepad on his knee. The radius he estimated at about 150 miles and jotted down "π^2." Pi was easy enough, 3.145, and squaring 150 should be . . .

For some reason, the numbers did not come. He stared at the notepad and sensed that he was breathing a little too rapidly. Glancing up at the instruments, he saw that they registered a thirty-degree bank to the left.

Thinking, *That's definitely off*, he glanced outside for a visual check, realized that he was now in a steep, diving turn, and instinctively pulled back hard on the stick. The airplane was descending through 60,000 feet at 130 knots indicated and the g-forces from his stick pressure caused the U-2 to shed its wings just as the hypoxic Osborn shed his consciousness.

At 13,000 feet, hurtling downward in the wingless, tailless fuselage, Osborn regained consciousness enough to try to use the Lockheed-designed ejection seat. It failed and he was fumbling with the canopy release when the U-2's fuselage dug deep into the hard Texas earth.

CHAPTER TWELVE

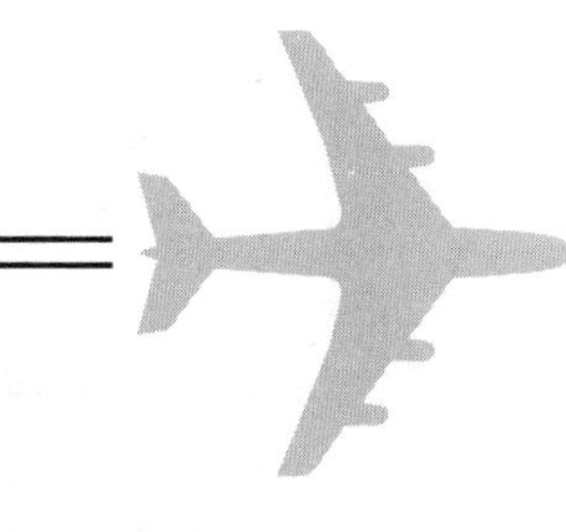

July 15, 1958
Central Intelligence Agency Headquarters,
Langley, Virginia

Richard Bissell, the U-2 project chief within the CIA, had backed Kelly Johnson from the start of the program but never hesitated to butt heads with him on matters of principle. Osborn's death, followed the next day by the fatal crash of Daniel Chaplin in an almost identical accident, had created a crisis.

"Goddamm it, Kelly, we've had ten accidents with the U-2, two in the last week. Everything points to the oxygen system. The first autopsy reports show that both Osborn and Chaplin were hypoxic."

Johnson's face flushed. He was used to doing the yelling in any argument like this, but he wasn't going to do any today.

Bissell went on, "We only ordered twenty aircraft—twelve of them have had accidents. If this doesn't stop, by God, I'll pull the plug on the program unless we get a fix."

Kelly knew this was a bluff. The U-2 overflights of the Soviet Union had already brought back priceless information that revealed that the Soviet bomber force was not nearly as formidable as feared, but that their ICBM program was further along than thought. Nor was that all; flights over Indonesia and China had provided information that allowed the United States to assert its diplomatic efforts with authority. Besides, the Air Force had ordered thirty aircraft, with a provisional order for five more.

"Rich, we've known from the start that flying at extreme altitudes required extreme measures in controlling weight. I've been lobbying for weeks to get a dual oxygen system installed, and every proposal I put in has been kicked back as too costly."

"They have been. I've reviewed them myself, and it looks to me like you are trying to make excessive profits on the engineering-change proposal. That's not like you, Kelly."

Johnson glowered, veins pulsing in his neck and forehead, hands gripping the table to keep from pounding on it.

"You're damn right that's not like me! I brought that goddamn airplane in on time and under budget, and I'm going to be giving you a big fat refund, near ten percent, if things keep going like they are. But the kind of reliability you want in a lightweight oxygen system is damn difficult—and damn expensive—to obtain."

"Well, let me tell you this. We found moisture in Osborn's oxygen system, and ran a fleet-wide check. Moisture in all the systems! Worse, it looks like Chaplin's system had a fire. Talk about contradictions! Moisture in the system and it burns up. And poor Osborn attempted to use his ejection seat, but couldn't get through the sequence in time. Probably too groggy from hypoxia."

Bissell, wanting to cool off and particularly wanting to cool Kelly off, turned to Vance Shannon. "Vance, what do you think?"

As always, Shannon waited a second before replying. It was a ploy he had used over the years, making sure that he understood the question, considering what the implications of the answer were politically, and, most of all, making sure that people were listening to what he said instead of talking among themselves. "Well, it won't affect training too much. We can restrict flights to no more than twenty thousand feet. If the President lays on an absolute must-do mission, we'll just have to accept the risks. No problem with that; this is the greatest bunch of pilots I've ever seen."

He paused, letting it sink in, then said, "The moisture in all the oxygen system, that tells me that it's a quality control problem with whoever is supplying the oxygen or with the storage techniques on the bases. It's a pain, but it should be an easy fix; we've had this in the past on other airplanes, the B-52, for one."

Again he paused, letting Bissel make notes.

"But the fire in the oxygen system is a real worry. Can I have a complete pressure suit, oxygen lines, and all, to study?"

Kelly spoke up, "We'll have one delivered to your office," and Bissell nodded agreement.

Vance went on, now getting a little out of place but determined to make the point. "I think we have to start upgrading the autopilot. It's still too demanding, especially long into a mission, when the fuel management gets even more important."

Bissell jumped on his remark. "You're damn right we do. And a better ejection seat. We've got to get it down to a simple one-step process that is still foolproof."

Johnson stood up, saying, "Send me some proposals on the autopilot and the ejection seat, Vance." Then turning to Bissell, he said, "Do we need Vance for the next part of the discussion?"

Bissell replied, "No, but I suspect we will before too long. Would you excuse us, Vance? We've got something that's still so sensitive and so uncertain that I just want to talk to Kelly about it. You'll be briefed on it sooner or later, I know, but right now, I have to ask you to excuse us."

Shannon stood up, glad to be released, glad that the fireworks had not been any worse. "No problem, I have plenty on my plate right now as it is. Good luck to both of you."

CHAPTER THIRTEEN

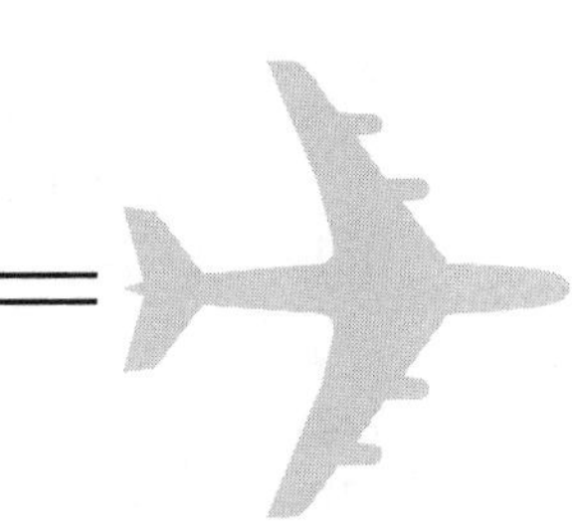

August 1, 1958
Palos Verdes, California

All four men had gone over the MC-3 pressure suit several times. Rodriquez had brought home an oxygen cylinder and the necessary hardware, and Tom had suited up. There was nothing obviously wrong that could cause a fire.

Harry spoke. "We should probably be looking at it in place, in the cockpit. There may be something there that interacts with the suit that we are not seeing."

They mulled this over for a while, using the photos and manuals Kelly had supplied to see if there was anything obvious that might be the problem.

Rodriquez asked, "How old were the suits worn by the pilots who crashed?"

Vance moved to the phone. "I don't know, but Kelly can find out for us. If I called the base at Laughlin myself, they would probably be reluctant to pass on any information."

Vance's call to Kelly took, as usual, some time to get through, and Tom asked, as he was removing the pressure suit, laying the components on a table, "Bob, how is your work back at Cambridge coming?"

Rodriquez was embarrassed. "Don't be angry, but I just cannot tell you. It is top secret, need to know, and I signed a statement that I would not discuss what we were doing with anyone, not even my partners."

Tom cringed at the word "partners." He didn't need to be, didn't want to be, reminded that Rodriquez, a new man to the firm, no relation, was already a partner.

Harry saw the wince and jumped in. "I understand you were down at the RAND Corporation a couple of months ago. How are they to work with?"

"Terrific; they are more Air Force than the Air Force. They should be, of course, the Air Force is paying the bill, but they were really helpful. And they got me tickets to the rollout of the Douglas DC-8."

Vance, done with his call, said, "Kelly's going to call for me. How did the DC-8 look?"

"Well, it's the same formula as the 707, you know, just a tiny bit bigger all around, and they say a little faster. If you saw them parked side by side you might be able to tell the difference, but there's no way you could spot them in the air and decide. To tell you the truth, I think the DC-8 is a prettier airplane, but they've got a long way to go. They're eighteen months behind Boeing now, and it's hard to make up that much time in the airline industry."

Vance shook his head. "Never forget how loyal airlines are to their manufacturers. I'll bet Pan Am will order more DC-8s than they will 707s, just because they've always done business with Douglas. Same with United and KLM; they practically cut their teeth on Douglas products."

Rodriquez replied, "I hope you're right, Vance, but I got a bad feeling down there, talking to the engineers. They seemed concerned about the management, about production costs. They are already talking about stretching the airplane, and they haven't even delivered one to an airline yet."

The phone rang and Vance ran to it, shouting, "It'll be Kelly," over his shoulder. It was, and Vance walked back to his group, shaking his head. "They told Kelly that Osborn's suit was virtually brand-new, but that Chaplin had accidentally ripped his own suit and was wearing one that another pilot had used for about a year. They said it was perfectly sound, and that the two men were virtually identical in size."

They all reconvened at the table where Tom had laid the pressure suit. Suddenly it was obvious. The radio leads to the pilot's helmet ran alongside the oxygen tubes, pressing against them at several spots, but now bound tightly to them.

"All it would take would be a short circuit, particularly near one of the spots where the oxygen tubes bend, and that would be all she wrote."

"It wouldn't even take a short circuit—they are pumping one hundred percent oxygen; just a spot of grease would do the same thing."

"You're right, Bob, but they'd probably be very scrupulous about checking for any oil or grease stains. They might not even see the frayed wiring, but at altitude, in an unpressurized cockpit, the spark could leap right across the fabric. Any tiny leak of oxygen would burn like a welder's torch."

Harry spoke. "Well, at least it is an easy fix—they can reroute the radio wires easily, so that they aren't in proximity to the oxygen tubes. Also they can probably get a change to the suit that puts the wiring into some kind of a rubber conduit, to insulate it. The actual work won't cost much, but the engineering and the testing will be expensive."

"Let's hope Kelly agrees. He's awful sensitive about the oxygen system. Have you done any more work on an inexpensive dual system, Tom?"

Vance's second son had made a trip through Europe earlier in the year, talking to foreign manufacturers of lightweight fighters, with a view to getting information on a building a small executive jet aircraft with Bill Lear. Tom had also taken time to talk to the foreign suppliers and picked up a half-dozen products and ideas for systems for the aircraft.

Tom rustled in his briefcase and brought out a small stack of drawings. "Take a look at this. I picked the idea up from Messier, in France, but this is my own design."

The drawings showed a completely redundant oxygen system, main and backup, in a package no larger than the standard pressure demand system.

"This will cost about ten percent more than a standard system if they only build it for the U-2. If they run the production numbers up, and use it in some other airplanes—like I think they should—it would not cost any more, maybe even cost less. It will weigh less, too."

Rodriquez asked, "Have you applied for a patent, Tom?"

"Not yet, but I will; you can be sure of that."

The two men looked at each other, each wondering what was behind the other's remarks. Vance saw the interchange and thought, *Uh-oh. There's going to be trouble here someday. I wonder if I did the right thing after all.*

CHAPTER FOURTEEN

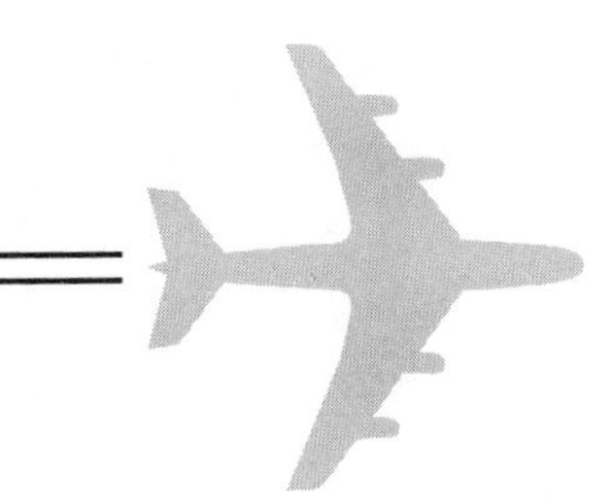

November 8, 1959
The Kremlin, Moscow, USSR

A wan winter sun glinted through the tall golden curtains lining the narrow windows, the freezing weather outside a perfect complement to the chill in their souls. Four men sat at the huge, magnificently carved table, gleaming in the light of elaborate chandeliers and precisely set with tablets, pencils, and silver water carafes. They were waiting, they believed, for the arrival of the new Premier of the Soviet Union, Nikita Khrushchev. Though he was long the power behind the throne—he had been First Secretary of the Communist Party since Stalin's death in March 1953—it had taken Khrushchev five years to consolidate his position sufficiently to also assume the mantle of Premier.

All hoped it would be not be Khrushchev himself, but one of his aides. If Khrushchev came in person, the meeting would not be pleasant. It was not like the old days, of course, when Stalin's whim could send you to a gulag or have you shot. But Khrushchev, full of himself now as an international figure, could make things extremely difficult. If he sent someone else, it was possible that the news was not all bad.

They had been waiting for almost forty-five minutes, and apart from their silent nods of acknowledgment when they were ushered in, not a word had passed among them.

Part of this was the normal caution of any participant in a Kremlin meeting, for they knew that all of their conversations would be recorded and were probably being actively listened to. But the greater reason was mutual antipathy, for on one side of the table sat the two designers largely responsible for the future of Soviet fighters, while on the other sat their implacable rivals. One of these was an aircraft designer from the past who was now fully invested in creating surface-to-air missiles. The other was his chief designer, the architect of the missile defense system that surrounded Moscow.

All four of the men had intuitively arrived at the reason for the meeting. American reconnaissance aircraft, Lockheed U-2s, were flying over the Soviet Union with impunity. There had been official protests, of course, but these were kept secret. No one in the Kremlin, least of all Nikita Khrushchev, could admit that the Soviet Union could not defend its skies. For their part, the Americans arrogantly denied the intrusions or attributed them to errors in navigation.

To the left sat Anushavan "Artyom" Ivanovich Mikoyan and Mikhail Iosifovich Guryevich, whose design bureau created aircraft bearing the MiG designation. The MiG team had not distinguished itself during the Great Patriotic War against Germany but came into its own in the jet age, and its fighters now formed the hard core of the Soviet defense system. The two men, colleagues for more than twenty years, had totally different personalities. Mikoyan was open and convivial, a man who enlivened every gathering and gave encouragement to his workers. Guryevich was modest and retiring, mousy in appearance, and, next to the dapperly dressed Mikoyan, somewhat disheveled.

On the right sat Syemyen Lavochkin and Petr Grushin, both looking apprehensive. Lavochkin, wearing his wartime uniform with all its many decorations as if to ward off evil, had designed a series of successful piston-engine fighters during World War II. He had done less well in the jet age, losing competition after competition to the MiG bureau. At his side, quiet, reserved, was Grushin, the man many credited with saving the Lavochkin design bureau with his series of surface-to-air missile designs. He had started work on his S-75 surface-to-air missile in 1953. It was specifically designed to attack high-altitude bombers such as the U.S. Boeing B-47 and B-52. Current Soviet plans called for more than one thousand S-75 missile sites to be built around the country.

The four men sprang to their feet as the door opened and Premier Khrushchev sprinted in, followed by two aides carrying a mound of reports.

There were no preliminary comments. Khrushchev waved at the two piles of documents and said, "These are reports on the flights of foreign aircraft over our country. The Americans and the British are flaunting international law. And we have not been able to stop them."

He paused for dramatic effect, looking deliberately into the eyes of each of the men at the table.

"Sometime in the next year I am going to have to meet with the American President, Eisenhower. When I meet him I will tell him that he must stop sending his spy planes over our sovereign territory." He paused again. "When I tell him that he will agree, and he will laugh up his sleeve."

Khrushchev bent over the table, looking surprisingly vulnerable. "That is why you are here. I don't want to ask him to stop sending airplanes. I want his airplanes shot down, no matter how high they are flying. I want you four gentlemen to assure me that you will create the weapons that will shoot down these intruders, and do it within the next six months."

He waited again, then spoke in a coldly savage, utterly believable tone, saying, "If you cannot do this, I will have the lot of you shot. Don't think that because Stalin is dead the Premier of the Soviet Union has no teeth. I will see you executed, your design bureaus broken up, and your families sent to the gulags to work until they die."

The four men were silent. Khrushchev jabbed a finger at Mikoyan.

"Speak, Mikoyan; speak! Can you guarantee that you will create a MiG aircraft that will destroy the U-2?"

Mikoyan looked at Guryevich and said, "Yes, I can."

Everyone at the table knew Mikoyan was lying, but there was nothing else for him to say.

Next Khrushchev pointed at Lavochkin. "And you? Can you create missiles which will bring these invaders down?"

Without a word, Lavochkin nodded to Grushin, who rose and said, "We can do it in three months."

Everyone at the table, including Mikoyan and Guryevich, believed him.

Khrushchev snorted, "Very well, we will see. And we will see where the Soviet Union will place its trust in the future."

With that he whirled and left the room, his aides gathering up the documents before dashing after him.

Lavochkin turned to Mikoyan and spoke for the first time that morning. "You will see that you cannot win every competition. In this one we will grind you into the dust." Then, realizing that his remarks were being recorded, Lavochkin put his hand over his mouth.

Mikoyan, irrepressible as always, laughed, saying, "And now you are on record, my friend. We will see who grinds who into what."

CHAPTER FIFTEEN

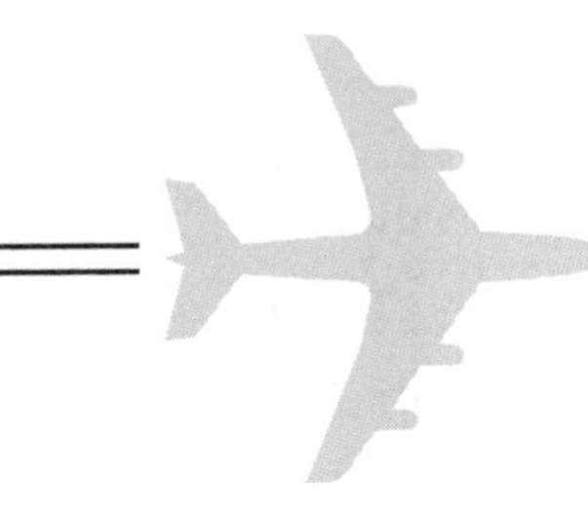

December 20, 1959
Paris, France

The two old friends had visited Paris once before, and oddly enough, that visit had been in December as well.

"Remember that week, Fritz? Nothing but drinking, fucking, and working the black market all week long."

Gerd Müller unbent like a jackknife, struggling to get his not-very-long legs out of the door of the blue Renault Caravelle that Obermyer was driving.

"Do I remember? It was the best time of the war. We were still whipping the Russkies, we'd whipped everybody but the British, and we were down doing business for Heinkel with Renault, setting them up to build parts for the He 111. Now we're back with Renault, trying to do business for ourselves."

The doorman at the George V sprang forward. Obermyer had tipped him a hundred dollars on the day they arrived and twenty dollars every day since. Another attendant darted forward, but the doorman cut him off and took the keys, opening the door as he did so. Obermyer and Müller walked straight to the bar.

Fritz had become more sophisticated over the years, and wherever he went, he experimented with the drinks and the food. He asked for a pastis, but Müller, trapped in the stifling bureaucratic poverty of East Germany, remained the earnest, hard-drinking soldier he had been in World War I and settled for a beer without even specifying that it be German.

"We were young fools then, Gerd. We didn't sightsee, we drank continually, there were whores in the room day and night, and then we wasted some time working for the good Dr. Heinkel."

His partner nodded, half his glass of Tuborg already gone. "How did this morning go?"

Obermyer had been to the Billancourt factory to talk with Renault officials about importing the 1960 Renaults. The Dauphine was already a moderate success in the United States, and he thought the Caravelle—basically a Dauphine with a sleeker body and convertible top—would bring even more people into the showroom. His Volkswagen and Porsche dealerships were doing well, but there were a lot of people who remembered the war and didn't want to buy German products. For them, the Dauphine could be a VW replacement.

"It was a little sticky at first. They took care to remind me that the Germans had taken over the plant in 1940, and that as a result the Allies had bombed it almost out of existence. But they want to sell more cars in America, and they think that with my Volkswagen experience, I can do it."

Gerd nodded. "It's a beautiful car."

"It's a piece of shit compared to the Volkswagen. You are comparing it to East German trash like the Moskvich."

His partner grinned sheepishly. "That's true. I'm lucky to have one, but it always needs repair."

"So will the Renault. Their quality control is laughable. But it's more stylish than the Volkswagen, and that will count with the Amis. In any event, I'm signing on to import them, not many to start, but enough to set up a couple of dealerships. In case you decide to defect."

Müller blew a long column of smoke into the air and finished his beer. "You know that I never stop thinking about it, and yet I know I can never do it. I like what I'm doing now; it's the best work I've ever had." Then, realizing the import of what he had just said, he continued, "I didn't mean working for you—that was a good time. I mean since then. I've become somebody. Working with the intelligence people lets me have foreign contacts. I'm able to travel. They watch me and check on me, I know, but it is all right; I'm doing a good job and they know it. But if I came to America, even if you let me have my own business, I'd be back at the bottom of the pile. I guess I'm getting too old to make big changes."

He signaled for another round of drinks; this time he took a taste of Obermyer's pastis, grimaced, and said, "I'll stay with the beer."

Obermyer grinned and then settled down to business. They were going to meet the woman in forty minutes, and they had not really discussed her yet.

"How did you get in contact with this woman?"

"I didn't. She was in contact with my people in East Berlin, and they called me and briefed me from a dossier that went back twenty years and more. She had started out in the American embassy in Paris; when we knocked France over, she went to England and held the same job in the American embassy there. Then your pal, your protégé, Vance Shannon, came along, and she seduced him, went to America with him, lived with him. All the time she was spying for France, and at two levels. On the one she was reporting back to French intelligence. On the other she was working for Dassault."

Obermyer nodded. "Dassault is a made-up name, you know. Marcel Dassault was Marcel Bloch before the war. He was sent to Buchenwald, but somehow he survived. His brother, Paul, was in the resistance, had the code name Dassault, the French word for 'attack.' Bloch had his name changed after the war. Gets away from his Jewish roots and plays on his refusing to collaborate. Pretty smart."

Müller nodded abruptly. He knew all about the name change and a lot more. It bothered him that Obermyer didn't seem to see the change in their relationship. He was no longer a subordinate; they were equals. It would take some time to get Fritz to see that, but Müller was going to be sure that he did. Then Müller resumed his talk. "She stayed with Shannon, lived with him, ran his businesses for eight years; then she was called back to France. It says in the dossier that it broke Shannon's heart and almost ruined his business."

Obermyer sensed the strength, the new sense of self, in Müller's remarks. It was a different style, something he realized he would have to adjust to. But just because Gerd had more self-confidence didn't mean that he had more brains. Obermyer was confident that he could control Gerd, as he always had, if it came to that. He decided he wouldn't interject any more comments, just ask questions and let Müller talk himself out. "What kind of a woman is she?"

"She's still very good-looking, in her mid-fifties, short dark hair, dresses like an executive secretary of a big firm, a little mannish on the surface, but just a hint of a flirt, too. I'd love to take her to bed, but she's too high-class for me." He waited a minute, couldn't help himself, and added, "Or you, too."

Obermyer laughed. "I wasn't going to try. You know my philosophy—pay for the best whore you can find, fuck her, then forget about her in the morning."

Looking up, he was embarrassed to see a beautiful woman, short dark hair, full figure, smiling at him, obviously pleased to have caught his remarks about expensive whores. It gave her the upper hand right from the start.

Gerd was on his feet, blushing, Obermyer thinking, *He's some kind of intelligence agent, blushing like a schoolboy because I said "whore" in front of his new girlfriend.*

The introductions were quick and muddled, and Madeline Behar asked if she could have some coffee. The waiter left them, and the three sat for a moment, studying one another casually, without any concern.

She broke the silence saying, "I understand that you and a very dear friend of mine, Vance Shannon, are in business together."

"Yes, in the sense that I helped him secure his dealership. And I try to pass on to him what I've learned."

"Be sure to give him my very best wishes when next you see him. He is a fine man."

She spoke coolly, without any evident emotion, but Obermyer thought that he caught a hint of sadness in her manner. Somehow the remark struck him as unprofessional, as did her attitude. Still, what could she say? She must have had a dossier on them; she would know that they had one on her. Maybe it was a ploy, to gain their confidence.

"I'll do that. He's doing very well as a partner in a Volkswagen dealership, along with all his other interests."

Madeline smiled inwardly, thinking, *A Volkswagen dealership! I never would have invested in that.* Then she went on, her German flawless, "Has Herr Müller discussed with you the subject of our meeting?"

Gerd interjected, "No, I did not. I wanted you to explain it."

She nodded and went on, "There is going to be quite a race to create a supersonic transport. The Russians, the British, and the Americans are all going to compete, and so will the French, of course. We would like to be kept abreast of our competition's research."

Obermyer was about to say that he was no longer doing intelligence work but could not bring himself to do so. It was not just Madeline's charm, although that would have been enough. He felt the old lust within him, the desire to be on the inside of major events, to have information that others wanted, and to sell it at a satisfying price. So, instead, he temporized, "I wonder if we are the right team for you? I've been out of the business for many years now, and though I've maintained some contacts, I'm not really active. And as Gerd has no doubt told you, there is not much work on the SST going on in East Germany."

Madeline had sized the situation up. Two old comrades, their relationship changed by time and events. Gerd Müller was obviously anxious to prove himself to Obermyer. Obermyer was obviously trying to preserve the old order.

"I'm sure your friend would surprise you. Tupolev has many projects going, and he reaches out for help where he can. I know personally that he has contracts with Hans Wocke."

Obermyer looked blank and waved his hands uncomprehendingly. She continued, "Wocke was one of the principal engineers behind the Junkers Ju 287 during the war—the six-jet, forward-swept-wing bomber. He's still working on forward-swept wings, and on an ogival wing as well. We would like information on that, and of course on what Lockheed and Boeing are planning."

Müller looked triumphant and Obermyer dissembled, "Well, I doubt if I can be of much help, but I'll try, to help my old friend here," thinking to himself, *I can feed them enough from* Aviation Week *to keep them happy for a while, and maybe, just maybe, I can run some ideas past Vance Shannon.*

Madeline leaned forward. "There is something else. I not only want information; I want to feed the others misinformation. What the Americans call a 'red herring.' Anything that will lead them astray—a new kind of fuel, tire compounds, information on composite materials, anything, as long as it's bogus and will cost them research time. It is important to our people to be first. There is not going to be much of a market for supersonic airliners. First of all, they will be too expensive, and second, they'll be too efficient; you won't need as many of them."

Obermyer felt the chill again; she was talking too much, telling them more than she should have. And she was no amateur. More than that, she had completely fooled Shannon for years. So there was something up.

She stood up. "I've discussed payments and ways to transmit information with Herr Müller. I hope you will find them of interest."

As she left the bar, Obermyer noted that heads still turned after her.

He turned to find Gerd staring after her. *Fine*, he thought. *She's spinning a web, and Gerd has already landed in it.*

CHAPTER SIXTEEN

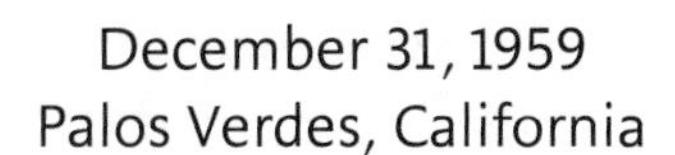

December 31, 1959
Palos Verdes, California

Vance Shannon sat slumped in his favorite chair in the library, three carefully placed piñon logs crackling in the fireplace, a snifter of Courvoisier VSOP on the table beside him.

For years, Vance and Madeline had celebrated New Year's at home, quietly going over the books and reviewing the events of the year, then, at midnight, drinking most of a bottle of champagne. When she left, Vance tried it once more, alone. It was too utterly sad, and he gave it up.

Six months ago Jill suggested that it would be a good thing to resume the practice, but instead of making it a private affair, they should invite all of the family in to participate. He had not agreed, but she took silence as consent and had made all the preparations. It always amazed Vance how carefully Jill walked the line of his memories of Madeline, always speaking pleasantly and courteously of her, never trying to outdo her in things where Madeline excelled but instead filling in all the areas in which Madeline had shown no interest.

He could hear Jill moving in and out of the kitchen, creating what she called her New Year's table, a long festive board filled with bowls of shrimp, cold cuts, a ham, a bowl of non-alcoholic punch—for Anna and Harry—and a copper bucket that held six bottles of Korbel champagne. As his wife, Jill might well have been jealous of Madeline, for Vance had made no secret of it that she had been the great burning passion of his life. Instead, Jill recognized that without Madeline she never would have met Vance, much less married him, and that Madeline had all along intended her to become Vance's wife, to take her place when she left. So Jill was grateful rather than jealous and careful not to try to compete in matters like the choice of champagne. She was sure that Madeline would have had more expensive French champagne, Veuve Cliquot or even Dom Perignon, but California champagne was good enough for her, and she knew that Vance would not even notice the taste, much less the label.

Tom, Harry, and Bob were coming over in about an hour, with Bob bringing a date for the first time. She and Vance had joked about it earlier, saying that his date was probably a six-foot-tall blond surfer—just what the five-foot-six-inch Rodriquez needed. Jill sighed and said, "I just hope she is not a movie star type; it won't bother Nancy, but it will kill Anna."

"If I know Rodriquez, she'll be a knockout. I've seen how women react to him when he walks into a room—he just mesmerizes them."

Vance turned back to the desk, where the balance sheet and profit and loss statements the accounting firm had prepared for his company were laid out. It was just a preliminary statement, but it made nice reading. In spite of his policy of paying top dollar to his partners and employees—there were twelve of them now, incredible for what not too many years ago had been a one-man band—the firm had shown a considerable profit, thanks in large part to new contracts that Rodriquez had secured for the U-2 and for some other even more highly classified programs that he could not disclose, even to Vance. Lockheed was always in a hurry, and their contracts usually carried with them incentives for swift completion—and stiff penalties for delays. In a small outfit like Aviation Consultants, such contracts could get priority and be executed in the minimum time, so the incentive clauses really added to the bottom line.

The accountant had prepared another portfolio, on Vance's personal financial status, and this year it was not quite as satisfactory. Madeline had handled all his financial matters for years, growing his estate in remarkable fashion by farsighted investments in real estate and, to a lesser degree, in the stock market.

"Pretty smart businesswoman for a spy," he mused.

He had not done well in the stock market this year. He couldn't get interested in it, even though it was his money, and his financial adviser,

Cliff Boyd, never seemed to have a suggestion that paid off anything but commissions for Boyd. Then there were two real-estate deals that unexpectedly had been tied up in court. Vance had begun trying to sell off some of the older, more difficult to maintain properties, and in each case the purchaser had reneged and gone into bankruptcy.

The only thing that brightened the day was Vance's 45 plus percent of ownership in Capestro Motors. He was particularly pleased because he had made the decision to join Lou Capestro in the deal without consulting anyone else—it was just a gut feel, and it was paying off. The Bug was wildly popular, and this year Volkswagen's clever advertisements had sold more than 120,000 cars in the United States. People were lining up to buy them at the dealership, and the thing that amazed Vance was that no one was objecting to the high routine maintenance costs. The Chevrolet and Ford dealers were furious—they charged less than half as much for an oil change and people protested. Somehow, the Bugs were treated as pampered pets by their owners, who seemed to take pride in the amount of money spent on them.

Fritz Obermyer had been absolutely right. The Volkswagens sold on their perceived quality, and, judging from articles in *Motor Trend*, even the Big Three were beginning to take notice. Yet Vance had noted that the VW's greatest appeal seemed to be to young up-and-coming people, usually liberal in their politics and free in their thinking. It amused him that two old-line conservatives such as Capestro and him were making money from left-wing Californians.

Vance closed the books, shaking his head. He was far better off than he ever could have imagined and more than able to keep reinvesting all the profits from Aviation Consultants into the business. Boyd, the wizard financier, kept telling Vance that he ought to consider incorporating and taking the firm public, but he didn't like the idea. For years he had exercised a majority control, and for all practical purposes he still did, although his percentage had declined from 52 to 42 percent when he decided to take Bob Rodriquez in as a partner. If he took it public, who knew what could happen?

He was stacking the papers when he heard the usual cries of greeting as Harry and Tom arrived with their wives. Jill was very close to Nancy, as they had worked together for so long, and always tried to be equally welcoming to Anna, but it wasn't easy. It struck Vance again, as it had so many times, that Harry was a good son and a good husband, giving up a promising Air Force career to stick with Anna through all her problems with alcohol. Harry was never a heavy drinker, but he abstained completely to keep her from temptation. Now he was facing a new situation affecting her health—her escalating weight.

The chimes of the door rang again, and Vance thought, *Must be Bob and his date. I'll have to get out there and see how she looks.* There was another flurry of greetings, but somehow they sounded strange, off-key, to Vance. Just then the door burst open and Anna literally ran into the room, not easy for a woman of her size. She stared wild-eyed at Vance for a moment, then half-whispered, half-shouted, "Bob's brought a Negro, a Negress, I mean, to the party."

Vance stood up in a welter of irritation. Sometimes this woman was just too much to stand, no matter if she was married to his son. "Please, Anna, be quiet! You are going to cause trouble with talk like that."

Eyes welling with tears, Anna flounced out of the back of the room, toward the kitchen, beginning the sobbing she used to win most of her arguments with Harry.

Vance sighed and walked rapidly down the hallway to the living room, where the noise had recovered to a normal volume, with Nancy's silky laugh overriding all. He bounded through the double doors to come face-to-face with one of the most beautiful women he had ever seen, a dark-haired beauty with a dazzling smile that seemed to send fireworks cascading through the room.

Bob Rodriquez grabbed him, saying, "Vance, may I present Mae Wilson; she's a big fan of yours."

The group coalesced around him, as he stood almost helpless, fighting not to say something stupid and blowing it with, "Bob, any fan of mine is a friend of yours."

Then he stopped shaking her outstretched hand and kissed it, saying simply, "Mae, Happy New Year, and welcome to our home."

He glanced around quickly, registering the reactions to the meeting. Bob and Jill looked proud, Nancy happy, and Tom annoyed. Harry had gone to look for Anna.

CHAPTER SEVENTEEN

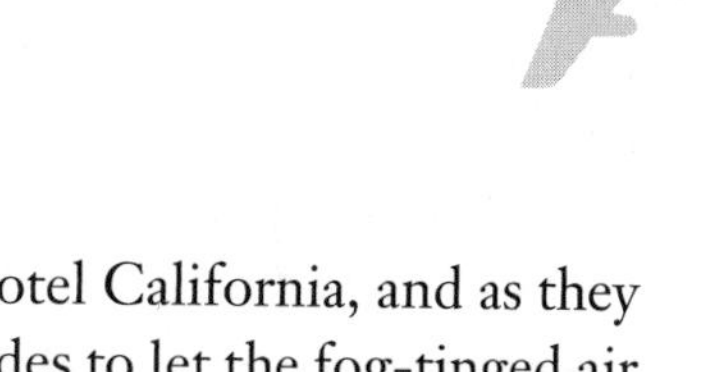

February 14, 1960
San Francisco, California

As usual, they had a corner room at the Hotel California, and as they always did, they opened windows on both sides to let the fog-tinged air waft through.

"Cold?"

"Yes, but let's leave the windows open just a bit more. I love the sound of the foghorns and the feel of the mist."

They sat on the edge of the bed, arm in arm, still happy from their meal at Des Alpes, a Basque restaurant on the Hill. Bob Rodriquez had been impressed when the waiter turned their wineglasses into coffee cups, and Mae had been delighted by his reaction.

Each time they came to the city, they tried to duplicate, as far as possible, everything that had happened on their first visit, two years before, a romantic preference of Mae's. Bob was too pragmatic to really understand it, but he understood that pleasing her was all he cared about.

They had met at a seminar in San Diego, fallen almost instantly in love, but Mae had delayed their lovemaking until she felt sure about Bob. When she had decided she was sure, Mae had suggested that they have a little "honeymoon in San Francisco" to celebrate the event. They had been back three times since, each time as good as the last.

"Wonder what the rich folks down at the St. Francis are doing?"

She stood up to close the windows and said, "They're not having the fun we're going to have."

They had made love in the morning and again before going out for dinner, so they were not in any hurry but undressed companionably, brushing teeth, doing all the domestic things that lovers do when they have time and knowledge and assurance.

Lying next to him, she ran her foot up and down his leg, then asked, "Do you suppose Tom Shannon is over the New Year's party yet?"

"Tom's all right. He's just a little old-fashioned. I don't think any of the Shannons are bigoted; Vance and Harry certainly are not. I'm not counting Anna as a Shannon—she has her own problems."

They were reflective for a bit and he went on. "To be honest, I think I might have been too dark skinned for him to accept as a junior partner. I wonder how he would have felt if I had showed up at the party with a blonde?"

"Well, I'm practically blond compared to you."

He laughed. She was right; her skin was much lighter than his.

"Is it, I mean, am I going to cause trouble?"

"No, you saw how Vance reacted. He's the only one that really counts. His boys are great pilots and pretty fair engineers, but he runs the place." Then unexpectedly he said, "For now."

She understood exactly what he meant but asked, "What does that mean?"

Bob sat up in bed, tossed the covers back, and began talking excitedly. "None of them really realize what's happening in aviation. The impact of what is going on in electronics, in propulsion, in new materials, is going to revolutionize aviation. We're going to be talking about the aerospace industry rather than the aviation industry, and sooner rather than later. None of the Shannons have a feel for this yet. I do, and I'm going to prove myself to them."

"What are you planning, some sort of corporate takeover?"

"No, no, I'd never do that to Vance, not even to Tom or Harry. They've been good to me. But they will see the need and they'll want me to run things. I can see it coming just as clearly as I see a little bit of passion in the corner of your mouth."

"What? Where?"

He kissed the corner of her mouth and they resumed the replay of their honeymoon in San Francisco.

CHAPTER EIGHTEEN

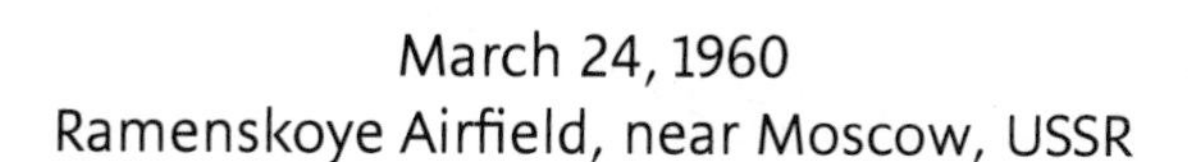

March 24, 1960
Ramenskoye Airfield, near Moscow, USSR

The Lavochkin team had already arrived and set up its easel bearing a stack of charts, each one meter square and prepared of good white paper bonded to cardboard. The top chart showed the S-75 in flight, resembling nothing more than a finned telephone pole with a jet of fire issuing from its base.

Artyom Ivanovich Mikoyan nodded to Syemyen Lavochkin and Petr Grushin, then walked briskly around the table, greeting his colleagues from his design bureau in his usual outgoing manner, blandly ignoring their solicitous looks of inquiry.

Mikoyan was in fact quite ill, his face drawn, with dark circles around his eyes, all clear signals that he was working too hard, that his heart was troubling him again. Glancing up at the huge clock on the wall, he smiled and said, "The Minister is late," just as the door opened and the Deputy Minister for Defense, Marshal Dmitry Ustinov, strode in. He looked dour, with his wire-rimmed glasses perched on a coarse, globular red nose and his forehead reaching far up in perpetual surprise. They all knew one another; there were no pleasantries, no introductions, Ustinov simply barking, "Let's get started. Your team first, Mikoyan."

Mikoyan had selected his deputy for this project, Viktor Aleksander Arkhipov, to do the briefing. Arkhipov was exceptionally articulate, a brilliant briefer who could think on his feet. He had already prepared charts that would show exactly what had been done in the best possible light and in a manner that Ustinov could readily understand.

Mikoyan sat silent in the knowledge that their briefing would fall short, revealing their latest aircraft's inadequate performance. There was no way to fool Ustinov; he was smart and tough. Fortunately, he was not irrational, as Khrushchev sometimes seemed to be.

Arkhipov pulled the cover back on the first chart, a drawing of the MiG-19, the world's first operational supersonic fighter.

"Comrade Ustinov, I present the MiG-19SV."

The drawing was of the typical production MiG-19S. Underneath the drawing, printed in large letters, was one word, "Visotniy," meaning "altitude."

"Here are the principal changes."

The next chart listed:

- wing area reduced by two square meters
- two NR-30 wing cannons removed
- pilot's armor plate removed
- engine turbine inlet temperature increased to 730 degrees C
- flaps deployable to twelve degrees above 15,000 meters

"We've reduced weight, reduced wing area, and increased engine power. Here are the results."

The third chart said simply:

- with zoom climb, 21,000-meter altitude capability
- without zoom climb, 19,000-meter altitude capability
- top speed, 1,420 km/h at 10,000 meters

Ustinov shook his head, asking, "What is a zoom climb?"

"It is a standard tactic. The pilot climbs to a high altitude, builds up the maximum speed possible, and then climbs at a carefully calculated rate, trading the airspeed for the altitude."

Ustinov frowned. "This is not enough, if the U-2 comes over at its maximum altitude."

Lavochkin and his team looked pleased. But Ustinov went on, "But the Americans cannot solve everything; they must have problems, too. I know that our engines have more difficulty at altitude. If the U-2 pilot has engine problems, he may come in at twenty thousand meters or less. If so, we have a chance."

Mikoyan spoke for the first time. "Exactly right. And we also hope that our colleagues from Lavochkin might put up some missiles that might force him to a lower altitude."

It was an ingenious ploy, seeming to praise the archrivals but shifting the burden of responsibility to them. Ustinov understood it exactly for what it was and approved. Given the inadequate performance of the MiG-19SV, Mikoyan was doing the only thing he could do.

"What do you say to that, Comrade Lavochkin?"

Flustered, Lavochikin stood, saying, "We hope to do better than force them down to MiG-19 altitudes. We expect to destroy the U-2 with a direct hit, or perhaps even with a near miss."

He motioned to Grushin, who pulled back the cover concealing his first chart. It showed the S-75 surface-to-air missile on an articulated trailer hauled by a ZIL-157 truck. The second chart showed the missile erected for launching, its cruciform fins prominent on the nose and the tail. Without a word, Grushin went to the third chart, which showed the S-75 streaking skyward toward a distant target, no more than a dot.

The fourth chart was the key to the briefing. A U-2 was seen being struck in the fuselage just behind the cockpit. Other S-75s were shown exploding nearby. Underneath the drawing, in large print, was:

A KILL AT 25,000 METERS

The last chart was simply numbers, showing the S-75s' range (50 kilometers) and the warhead weight (130 kilograms) and launch weight of 2,300 kilograms.

Mikoyan looked at the chart, admiring its understatement. He turned and saluted Lavochkin, a risky maneuver, given that Ustinov had not yet commented.

The Deputy Minister was making some notes in a cordovan leather case. Finally he looked up. "Mikoyan, I am disappointed in you. We need better performance, and we are not getting it from your bureau. Lavochkin here has done his job well. Let me tell you how serious this is. The Americans are operating with impunity. If we do not stop them, and soon, your heads will roll. Unfortunately, and this is the tragic part, so will mine. So there is no point in my threatening you; my fate is bound up with your success. If you fail, I fail. I cannot threaten you with punishment—that is implicit. I can only wish you—for my sake—good luck."

It was a surprisingly gracious, slightly humorous statement from a man not known for either grace or humor.

CHAPTER NINETEEN

May 1, 1960
Over the Soviet Union

The U-2 pilot was busy all the time, carefully watching the heading, the altitude, the instruments, the autopilot, and, above all, the sky, to keep the fragile Lockheed on course in its long haul from Peshawar, Pakistan, across the endless Soviet Union. But there was still time to think as the immensity of the Russian nation rolled beneath, slowly to the eye, but at the rate of 7 miles per minute.

My God, what could the Germans have been thinking of?

Gary Powers shifted in his seat, trying to improve the circulation in his pressure suit–constricted veins. *Hitler must have been crazy. How could eighty million Germans have expected to conquer such an enormous country?*

Today's mission was to gather information on Soviet progress in the intercontinental ballistic missile race, as well as to note anything new of interest—bombers at new bases, new factories, new missile sites, anything with military potential. His 3,788-mile flight path took him across the Soviet Union far beyond the farthest German penetrations, north-northwest over the secret base at Tyuratam, with the Aral Sea gleaming thirty miles to the west, on to a quick curve around Chelyabinsk and Sverdlovsk, and then a dogleg on to cover Plestetsk, Archangel, and Murmansk. He would exit Soviet air space shortly after Murmansk and then make a sweeping turn to land at Bodø, in Norway. A brief thought of the simple but unbelievable pleasures waiting there comforted him—easing out of the cramped confines of the cockpit, having the clutching helmet and pressure suit stripped off, a cold beer, and perhaps a shot with it, the utter freedom of being able to move, to breathe fresh air voluntarily, without the pressure of the oxygen system. It was almost worth it to suffer for hours to reach such bliss.

Like when it feels good when you stop hitting yourself in your head, he mused.

The MC-3 partial pressure suit was an uncertain life belt, uncomfortable as it squeezed its seams into your skin, extracting a flow of perspiration that partially compensated for the inability to urinate. The suit was dangerous because it restricted movement and visibility, turning sensitive hands into unfeeling claws that fumbled at every switch. The suit had to be worn because the U-2, essentially a jet-powered glider, flew at 70,000 feet. Air bled in from the engine brought the cabin pressure down to about 28,000 feet, so the pilot always had to breathe supplemental oxygen, drying his lungs and throat. If the plane depressurized, the suit would pressurize, preventing the body fluids from exploding and vaporizing as it would if unprotected at altitudes above 63,000 feet. When the pressure suit functioned as designed, it enabled the pilot to get down to an altitude where he could survive. But pressure suits had fatal failures in the past and everyone regarded them with distaste before, during, and after a flight.

Powers was of part of an incredibly skilled volunteer pool of pilots, all men of strong character, carefully selected and trained to use this delicate instrument of espionage that the genius of Kelly Johnson and his Skunk Works had created. The challenge of flying the U-2 was irresistible to military pilots, who had to pretend to drop out of service and become employees of Lockheed to disguise their real relationship with the Central Intelligence Agency. The process was called sheep dipping and the pilots were supposed to retain all of their promotion and career opportunities. "Supposed" is the operative word, as many served as U-2 pilots but subsequently lost out in the competitive race for rank.

Despite separation from home and the difficulties of the mission—this was Power's twenty-seventh operational sortie, with several of them overflights of the Soviet Union—there were many compensations. Oddly enough, the least important of these was the extraordinary pay, twenty-five hundred a month, several times what Powers had received as an Air Force captain and an unbelievable sum to a boy brought up by a Kentucky coal miner.

Yet the real motivation that captivated the pilots was the mission's exclusiveness. This small band of U-2 pilots was privileged to fly the newest, highest-flying reconnaissance plane in history, and they were laying open the secrets of the Soviet Union as if they were mounted on a slide in a microscope. It was a cliché, but it was rare for a U-2 pilot, no matter how tired, how uncomfortable, or how hazardous the mission, not to think, *I cannot believe they are paying me to do this*, at least once on every flight.

Powers was a little uneasy today, sensing that he might be pushing his luck. First of all, the aircraft, Article 360, had a long history of maintenance problems, including a previous forced landing in Japan. None were sufficient to ground it, but cumulatively they were more than enough to worry about. Second, the takeoff had been delayed an insufferable hour, keeping him sweating in the suit, waiting for the personal approval of President Eisenhower to make the flight. The delay was not just inconvenient; it had also destroyed the utility of Powers's pre-flight navigation computations, thus rendering the sextant useless. Now navigation was going to be time and distance, just as it had been in the North American T-6 in which he had learned to fly. Finally, there was the timing. The U-2 missions over the Soviet Union first began on a great American holiday, July 4, 1956, and had been expected to last for only one or two years before Soviet countermeasures stopped them. Today was May 1, 1960, International Labor Day, a great Soviet holiday—and the missions had been flown for almost four years, plenty of time for the inventive enemy to devise countermeasures.

Curiously, the U-2 had become a symbol of both American and Soviet power. The incursions of the spy plane demonstrated American technical genius, as did the internal cameras and sensors. But the Soviet determination to respond and retaliate fueled enormous research efforts that improved their science, technology, and tactics. This incessant race for superiority brought the Cold War to its penultimate level, the crucial but indeterminate point just before nuclear bombs were dropped. The difficulty was that the margin for error was nil. One single miscalculation on either side about the U-2 could cause World War III, which would truly be the war to end all wars—and all living things.

The gathering undercast of clouds opened obligingly as he passed over Tyuratam at the customary Mach .72, and he flipped the switch for the cameras. If he had been lucky, he might have caught an ICBM being launched. Instead, looking down he could see swarms of interceptors climbing up toward him. He knew they were no problem; they could not climb to his altitude, and even if they could, he would be out of range before they could arrive.

Radar had picked up the U-2 before it had intruded into Soviet airspace, and as the U-2 flew its implacable course, a sea of activity coursed along ahead of it, as radar stations, fighter bases, and missile sites went on a wartime alert. The frenzied activity flowed all the way to Moscow, where Defense Minister Marshal Rodion Yakovlevich Malinovsky, following his orders, had Nikita Khrushchev awakened and informed of the intruder. Khrushchev's instructions were simple: shoot down the U-2 at all costs.

Malinovsky, who had succeeded the four-time Hero of the Soviet Union, Georgi Zukhov, as Defense Minister, ordered that all air traffic within the Soviet Union be grounded, with all resources focused on the U-2, a single amber dot crawling across dozens of radar screens. Interceptors were scrambled from every base along the route as soon as the U-2 came within nominal range, but these were standard MiGs and Sukhois, without the modifications that Mikoyan had built into the MiG-19SV, and unable to get within shooting distance of the U-2.

Khrushchev began blasting Malinovsky with complaints that were, in traditional military fashion, duly passed on down the line, soon reaching the sharp end of the stick, the pilots vainly attempting to flog an aircraft capable of climbing to 60,000 feet all the way to 70,000. So far no missile batteries had been engaged, in part because of the U-2's route, in part because they were still relatively primitive and the Soviet Air Defense Forces were not yet familiar with their operation.

Lavochkin's staff had worked hard in the field, coordinating with the radar units and trying to speed up the five hours of checklists needed to bring an S-75 battery to operational status. The tie-in with radar sites was crucial, for there had to be sufficient early warning. The typical radar could reach out to about one hundred miles to acquire the target. Then, as soon as notice was received, the missiles had to be brought to the correct firing attitude and its own radar system had to pick the target up. Essentially, the U-2 had to be acquired at least eighty miles away by the S-75 site, or there was insufficient time to fire.

Some three hours into the flight, about 0800 Moscow time, the U-2 passed over Magnitogorsk, clearly heading for the heart of the Soviet nuclear weapon–building facilities in the Urals. When Khrushchev was told of the probable target he went white. This was the worst possible development—if the aircraft got through, it would have film of the most secret area in the Soviet Union. His mind began to drift from firing Malinovsky to being fired himself. He knew how strong his opposition was, how much they would love to dispose of him.

Looking at the horizon, Powers saw for the first time that day a clear sky unencumbered by any clouds. *Maybe my luck is changing*, he thought, and immediately cursed himself for tempting fate.

Fate responded with the nose pitching up violently. Powers disconnected the malfunctioning autopilot, retrimming the airplane so he could fly it manually. When stabilized at altitude, the U-2 was not unpleasant to fly. It was demanding, because there was very little margin between its low-speed stall and its high-speed buffet—the so-called coffin corner. He reengaged the autopilot, his hands still light on the controls. The U-2 flew normally for a few minutes and then pitched up again. Powers disconnected the autopilot and stopped the motion and knew it was trouble. He couldn't risk trying the autopilot again—it wouldn't take many g's to shed his wings. Analyzing the situation, he saw that he was thirteen hundred miles into Russia and had almost twice that distance to go. Common sense told him to turn back, but the lure of the clear sky ahead of him ruled against it. The prospect of hand flying the airplane for another six hours was daunting, but he knew he could do it. He just might need more than one beer after he landed.

In Moscow, Khrushchev had both Malinovsky and Lavochkin on the phone. "He's nearing Chelyabinsk. Are the missiles there ready?"

There was the slightest hesitation before both Malinovsky and Lavochkin replied simultaneously, "Yes, Comrade Khrushchev."

But they were not, and the U-2 sailed over the S-75 battery, with Powers unaware of how close a call it was. Frantic workers determined that the battery radar had malfunctioned. When he heard this, Malinovsky knew immediately that this was something he would have to withhold from Khrushchev, who constantly screamed that the air defense system got everything it asked for but could not defend the country. In his current mood there was no telling what the Premier might do. Instead, Malinovsky called him and said that a last-minute turn by the American had placed the U-2 outside of the missile radar capabilities.

Powers had been a great reader in his youth, and he remembered a Richard Halliburton book that told of the murder of the Czar and his family in Yekaterinburg—now called Sverdlovsk. It was an hour away, and despite concentrating on the instruments, maintaining as smooth a flight path as possible to conserve fuel, he wondered about the last days of the Romanovs and the Anastasia story.

On an air base to the south of Sverdlovsk, ground crew men swarmed around two MiG-19SVs and two Sukhoi Su-9s, topping them off with fuel and preparing them for launch, the mechanics taking special care with polishing the cockpit canopies. Both the MiG and the Sukhoi aircraft had pressurized cockpits, but the MiG pilots had pressure suits, while the Sukhoi pilots did not. All four were under orders to bring down the U-2, by ramming if necessary. Only the Sukhoi pilots thought they would get close enough for shooting, much less ramming.

Utter confusion now reigned in the ranks of the missile batteries. It was a national holiday, and many of the senior staff were on leave. At the district headquarters where the command post controlling the Sverdlovsk missile batteries was located, the battery commander was away, and his deputy, Major Mikhail Voronov, was new to his job and terribly hungover from last night's drinking bout.

Hunched over their sets, three radar operators watched for the first appearance of the U-2, now traveling at more than 9 kilometers a minute along the periphery of their radar signal.

Voronov sat behind the technicians at his own complex, staring at the screen, perplexed, wishing he were anywhere but there. If he fired the missiles and they missed, he would be in enormous trouble. If he didn't fire the missiles, he'd be court-martialed and probably shot.

One of the operators called, "Automatic tracking," then, moments later, "Missile-tracking mode." Another technician leaned over Voronov's shoulder, pointing a grubby finger at the screen where the amber dot was now enclosed in a phosphorescent circle that followed it relentlessly. The U-2 was 24 kilometers away at an estimated altitude of 21,000 meters. His mind made up, Voronov yelled, "Launch three missiles."

The launch control officer looked at him stupidly. They had practiced this many times but never actually fired.

"Fire!"

A sheet of flame burst from the booster rocket of one S-75 missile. The other two missiles remained on their launch pad.

Powers continued on, checking his map for the next set of cameras to be used at Kirov, unaware that the deadly missile with his name on it was now at Mach 2.0, its second-stage rocket exhausted, homing directly in on his U-2, ready to explode its 130-kilogram fragmentation warhead either on a command from its guidance system or from a proximity fuse when it closed on the target. When the warhead blew, it would send thirty-six hundred pellets ahead of it in an expanding ball of steel.

Four Soviet fighters struggling for altitude watched the long trail of smoke from the first S-75 they had ever seen fired. None of the planes were in striking distance, but each pilot hoped to be in on the kill if the missile damaged the U-2 and forced it down from its ungodly height.

Powers was dutifully recording his instrument readings when a huge explosion thrust the U-2 forward like a ball hit by a bat. A garish red sheet of flame surrounded him, lighting up his cockpit like a torch.

His reactions were automatic—shove the throttle to cram power on, level the wings with the control wheel, pull back on the column to bring the nose up. The wings leveled, but the nose wouldn't come up, and the frail U-2 pitched down, accelerating swiftly past its structural limitations and shedding its wings exactly as Kelly Johnson had predicted a hard landing would cause it to do. Now Powers was inverted, spinning in a wingless, tailless fuselage, his once-despised pressure suit inflated and keeping him alive. He fought to eject, realized he could not, jettisoned the canopy, and was flung, still spinning, into the cold Siberian sky, suddenly blind as his faceplate, his blessed, life-saving faceplate, frosted over.

On the ground, Voronov guessed uncertainly at his triumph—the radar indicated no forward movement of the target now, and the technicians cheered, sure that the U-2 was destroyed. Neither they nor Powers, free-falling above them, had any idea that their swiftly concluded battle was the future of jet aviation in microcosm: surface-to-air missiles versus ever more sophisticated aircraft.

CHAPTER TWENTY

September 6, 1960
Burbank, California

The gloom at Lockheed headquarters was as thick as the day was beautiful. The year had been a series of shocks one after another. The first and most visceral was the apparent failure of Lockheed's reentry into the commercial transport field, the sixty-six-passenger Electra II. Too busy to compete with Boeing and Douglas in the jet transport race, Lockheed had decided to take a leaf from the success of the Vickers Viscount turboprop airliner. Drawing on its experience with the C-130, it had created a low-wing four-turboprop airliner. Much faster than the Martin 404s or Convair 240s it would replace, the Electra was perfect for American and Eastern Airlines to use on the short-haul sections of their lines where a 707 or DC-8 was not economical to operate. But three Electras had crashed by March 17, 1960, the first one just a week after it entered airline service. The first crash was probably caused by pilot error, but in the next two the Electra had broken up in the air, killing all aboard, with no obvious reason for the catastrophe. Lockheed fought the Federal Aviation Administration's attempt to ground the aircraft. Elwood Quesada, a famous pilot and military commander, was the FAA Administrator, and he compromised—the Electra could continue to fly, but he limited it to a 295-mile-per-hour cruising speed. Sales of the aircraft immediately dried up, but the worst part of the story was still to come. Today Bob Gross was going to have to make a decision about how Lockheed would bear the expense of modifying the aircraft, including all those already in airline service.

Next in the seeming unending series of disasters was the shock of Gary Powers's being shot down, imprisoned, tried, and sentenced. It was now general knowledge that a surface-to-air missile had destroyed the U-2, with consequences far greater than were being admitted to the public. Nikita Khrushchev had played his cards carefully, not announcing the shoot-down until May 5 and not revealing that Powers was alive until two days later. Khrushchev went on to meet with Presidents Eisenhower and de Gaulle at summit talks in Paris and, in a masterpiece of showmanship, declared that the Soviet Union would not take part in the talks unless the U.S. government immediately stopped all flights over Soviet territory, apologized for those already made, and punished everyone responsible. Eisenhower was embarrassed by the fact that the United States had lied about Powers's flight and promised to suspend all future flights while he was President. This was exactly what Khrushchev wanted—a chance to shore up his failing regime. He declared that Eisenhower's response was inadequate and stormed out of the Paris summit conference, returning to the Soviet Union as a hero who had humiliated the United States.

Everyone at Lockheed and in the CIA knew from the start that ultimately the Soviets would shoot a U-2 down, and work was already under way on a replacement with far greater capability. But Eisenhower's promise to suspend overflights put the replacement program in the same jeopardy as the U-2 program.

George Mulliner, Bob Gross's executive assistant, came into the outer office and said, "You can come in now, gentlemen."

Vance always made it a point to defer to the Lockheed staff. When he stood up, he waved Willis Hawkins and John Margwarth, Lockheed's director of safety, on ahead of him. They were followed by the other Lockheed executives, the senior men in every discipline in the company. Everyone in the room was an old friend and Gross nodded to Hawkins, saying, "Let's have the bad news, Willis."

Hawkins, small, direct, economical in his speech, began his analysis with a brief sentence: "It's the whirl mode phenomenon."

At that moment, only he and Margwarth knew what he meant. But using charts and drawing freehand on the huge blackboard that had been brought in, he gave them a quick engineering analysis of the catastrophic results of a sudden force being applied to the gyroscopic characteristics of a swiftly rotating propeller.

Shannon was an experienced engineer, but it was difficult for him to follow Hawkins's discussion, even when Margwarth jumped in with explanations. When Hawkins finished, Margwarth summed it up in layman's terms for the non-engineers in the group, concluding with the key statement: "Essentially, the flaw was in the three-member structure connecting the gearbox and the engine. It failed and put a precession force on the propeller, which in turn placed an impossible stress on the wing."

Gross's face lit up. "But that means it was not a Lockheed design error."

Hawkins nodded, obviously comforted, but showing no other emotion. He might have been expected to be a little triumphant, a little pleased that his design was vindicated, but he was thinking now of the passengers, victims of a wildly improbable circumstance.

Gross asked, "What is the fix?"

"We can modify the wing to accommodate the stresses," Hawkins replied. "Allison will modify the structure that connects the gearbox to the engine. Without any reservations, I can guarantee to you that there will never be another accident like this on the Electra II."

There was a long silence as Bob Gross hung his head, deep in thought. Finally he looked up to Carl Kotchian, his vice president for production.

"Carl, how much will it cost us to modify all of the aircraft we've sold, or have waiting for sale?"

Kotchian was surprised at the question. Hawkins had previously alerted him that it was not Lockheed's design error, and he was already preparing to wage a legal battle to lay the modification costs at the door of the engine manufacturer, Allison. But he had the figures at his fingertips.

"At least twenty-five million."

Gross's face went white. Lockheed had been doing well, but no one had expected an outlay like this. Then he said, "We'll do it. Lockheed stands behind its products. We'll pay every cent, and make it right."

Gross's words spread shock around the room; every man there knew what the huge charge would do to the balance sheet and ultimately to the stock price. But they expected nothing less from Bob Gross.

As they were filing out, Gross called out, "Vance, have you got a few minutes? There are a few things I'd like to fill you in on."

When the door closed behind the last person, Vance said, "That's a pretty noble gesture, Bob. Not many company chairmen would think that way."

Gross shook his head wearily, reached up, and ran his finger along the fuselage of a model of the U-2 that now occupied a place of pride on his desk.

"It's tough, Vance, but we have to do it. It will pay off later, I know; the airlines will remember this, even if the traveling public never hears about it. They wouldn't understand if they did."

He called for some coffee, then motioned for them to move over to the green leather sofa. Vance remembered when Gross had purchased it, many years before. He had agonized over the cost, worried that people would think he was being extravagant with company money. It was as well-worn as the two old friends were now and seemed to enfold them as they sank down in it.

"Vance, you've been a friend for a long time, and I know how you've been suffering with us through the U-2 problem. I thought I'd give you a couple of pieces of good news for a change."

"I'm all ears, Bob. Glad to hear you have some." And he was. Gross deserved whatever good was going his way.

"How much do you know about the Discoverer program?"

"Bob, security here at Lockheed is good. I know you are involved in it, but all I know is what's been in the papers. Eisenhower's called it a scientific program, it had a whole bunch of failures, and the public is pretty disenchanted. They'd like to see a success."

"Well, we've had one, but we cannot tell anyone. The only reason I'm telling you is that I want to borrow Bob Rodriquez for about six months to work here full-time on the project."

Gross saw the shock in Shannon's face. Gross knew how important Rodriquez was to his firm.

"Before you say anything, let me brief you on Discoverer. That is just a cover name. The real project name is Corona, and it is not for scientific research; it's a photoreconnaissance satellite. We've just had our first successful mission—number fourteen, can you imagine?—and we got more useful intelligence on the Soviet Union in that one mission than we did in all the previous U-2 missions combined." He paused to let this sink in.

Shannon was stunned. The ramifications were incredible. First of all, there was the sheer magnitude of the success after fourteen failures. It was amazing the program had not been canceled long ago. And what an advance! A spy satellite avoided all the problems of overflying the Soviet Union's borders, there was no pilot to capture or kill, and once in orbit it was invulnerable to any attack or interference.

He was about to congratulate Gross but didn't speak for another minute. Shannon also saw that Corona diminished the U-2 at a time when it had already run its course, at least as a spy plane. Even worse, Corona reduced the probability that there would be a follow-on project. He knew that Kelly Johnson had been burning up his slide rule on a new aircraft, but beyond that he knew nothing. Nor should he have. Lockheed was deadly serious about its security.

Finally he said, "Bob, this is wonderful news. For an outfit that has been building airplanes all its life, this is a real triumph for Lockheed."

"Thanks, Vance. It's just the beginning, too. I can see our missiles and space side outgrowing our aircraft side, and in ten years or less. But we're not done with airplanes, not yet, and that's really the main reason I had to talk to you."

Shannon had stood up and strode around the room while he was thinking about Corona; now he came back and sat down again on the couch.

"Vance, you know that Kelly's been working hard on another project. It's a spy plane, too, but one that will have incredible performance—long range, continuous Mach 3.0 speed, altitudes above ninety thousand feet. And it will be built like a battleship, too, nothing like the U-2, all lightweight and delicate."

"Mach 3? Is it manned? And what kind of power plants will you have? I don't know of any jet engine that could produce enough thrust to fly Mach 3 for long periods—or, for that matter, fly Mach 3 at all."

"Yes, and it will be a handful, but we have pilots who can fly it. The first customer is the CIA, naturally, and they've picked Kelly's last proposal to go with. We're calling it the A-12. There are already a dozen variants, including a two-placer for the Air Force, but that's all downstream. You mentioned the engines—that's why I want to talk to you. You've been in jet engines since Whittle was a pup, and we've got a problem we've never even contemplated before. We want to fly at

Mach 3, but we want the aircraft to be invisible to radar, and two big engines make that almost impossible. That will be your task, if you are willing to take it on. You'll be working directly with Ben Rich, of course, and it was Ben who asked for you."

Ben Rich was Kelly Johnson's heir apparent in the Skunk Works. The two men could not have been more different in their size or their managerial approaches. Where Kelly was always hurtled down a hallway, too preoccupied to greet people, Ben's style was hail-fellow-well-met. Where people dreaded Kelly popping into their office—it could only be bad news—they often looked forward to seeing Ben.

"Of course, Bob, I'm flattered—Ben is a genius, and if he thinks I can help, I'll do it."

"It looks like I'm gutting your business, pulling Rodriquez in for Corona and you in for the A-12, but we'll make it up to you. You draw up the contracts, tell me exactly what you need to cover everything you might have made in the next year, and you come to work for us. And you can do it part-time, give us thirty hours a week; that's all I'm asking."

"Bob, you are putting me on the spot. I've already signed a contract with Boeing, guaranteeing them twenty hours a week. It's secret, too, just company secret, but it's a commitment."

Gross laughed. "What's the problem? You work twenty for them, thirty for us, that's only fifty hours a week, and you haven't worked less than sixty hours a week for the last thirty years. And as for Boeing's secret, I won't put you on the spot, but I'd bet five dollars that it has to do with a supersonic transport."

Shannon grinned sheepishly, and they shook hands. Gross walked him out, his arm around his shoulder, asking about Jill and his family. As they walked, Vance took a closer look at his old friend. The stress was telling on him.

"Bob, we ought to chuck everything and take our families on a month's vacation. It would do us both a world of good."

"It surely would, Vance, but you know and I know there are no more vacations in this business, not with the progress the damned Commies are making. We are at war again, or still, and you and I are still on the front lines."

CHAPTER TWENTY-ONE

January 16, 1961
Moscow, USSR

Even at seventy-two, Andrei Tupolev could never rest easy. Memories of how quickly he had fallen from a height few Russian engineers ever reached hung around him in a shroud, as ominous and ugly as the "black dog" of depression that Winston Churchill complained of in his writings.

As he was the founder of the TsAGI, the Central Aero-Hydrodynamics Institute, a member of the USSR Academy of Sciences, and a holder of the highest award of the motherland, the Order of Lenin, his position seemed unassailable. One successful aircraft after another flowed from his design bureau, including the largest in the world, the *Maxim Gorky*. His aircraft made long-distance flights, set records, were used by the Soviet Air Force. Yet on the morning of October 21, 1937, four members of the dreaded NKVD arrested him. In an absurd cover story, he was charged with selling the plans of the Messerschmitt Bf 110 twin-engine fighter to Germany. The real charges were far more serious, alleging that Tupolev was leading a mutinous organization within the Soviet aviation industry and personally committing sabotage as an agent of French intelligence.

The last charge had frightened him most, for although it was totally false, there were circumstances that could be misinterpreted. His visits to the United States in 1935 and to Spain in 1936 had included some contacts with both U.S. and French intelligence. It was inevitable that their agents should seek him out. It was easy for them to secure invitations to the receptions held for him by his hosts. They sent their most able and sometimes most attractive agents to find out what they could from his speeches or from casual conversation. There was one young woman he remembered vividly. She was fluent in Russian and had a piercing intelligence. Her seemingly artless questions had gone to the heart of some of his best designs. He often wondered what might have been if he had been courageous enough to try to escape his duty, his family, his honor, and pursue her, as his body had urged. Incredibly, she had contacted him again this year, in the guise of a letter from the Dassault company in France, inviting him to speak at a conference in Paris. He recognized her name at once. Madeline Behar. How strange that she should write, that she should use the same name. It must be that she wished him to remember her.

The bright spot of her memory faded at once with the recollection of the agony of his arrest. They had detained him in his office until three in the morning then marched him out, a prisoner, in front of his loyal staff, who had remained at work at great personal risk. As he was led away, he had no idea of his fate. Stalin was slaughtering people of far greater prominence than he, ruthlessly purging thousands from the top ranks of military and civil life. Numb with fear, Tupolev hoped, at best, for the traditional exile to Siberia, to work under survival conditions in a mine or a forest. He had reason to be afraid. His colleagues and sometimes rivals Konstantin Kalinin and Vladimir Chizhevsky had already been executed, and he knew personally that neither man had committed a crime. They could not have. They were, as he was, loyal to the motherland, no matter which tyranny ruled her.

In a swift show trial by the Military Collegium of the Soviet Supreme Court, he was charged, convicted, and sentenced without being able to make a token defense. Still, he was grateful not to be carted off and shot.

There followed a year in the dark, fear-filled cells of first the Lubyanka and then the Butyrkii prisons, anguishing every day as the projects upon which he had lavished so much care were taken over by the rival Sukhoi bureau.

In 1938, a decision was made—undoubtedly by Stalin; no one else would have dared—to place the many imprisoned aeronautical engineers to work in the Central Construction Bureau No. 29. In late August, after a bone-chilling interview with Lavrenty Beria, the perverted, murderously insane head of the KGB, Tupolev was taken to a rude prison at Bolshyevo, outside of Moscow. It was there that he began his greatest contribution to the Great Patriotic War, the beautiful, deadly, "Aeroplane No. 103"—the Tupolev Tu-2. He remembered with pride that it won the Stalin Prize—and helped restore his citizenship.

Progress on the project was swift, but there were too few people and too little equipment at Bolshyevo, and in April 1939 the group was transferred to his old building on Radio Street in Moscow. It was now a combination prison and factory, with the top staff mostly prisoners and the workers as free as any Soviet citizen was in those terror-filled days. With some wonderment, he went back to work in his old office, where he had been arrested.

Bureau No. 29 was unlike any prison an ordinary citizen would encounter. Soon the cream of the Soviet aviation industry were there—Petylyakov, Myasishchev, Korolev, so many more. They were definitely prisoners, with all the crushingly banal rules of KGB camps, and they worked to a strict schedule of ten to sometimes fourteen hours a day. Of itself this was no hardship; they had always worked long hours. The amazing thing was that they were well fed, from tables draped with white cloths—not carrying a bowl and licking a spoon as ordinary prisoners did. They didn't stay in cells but slept in large dormitory areas where each prisoner had a cot and a shelf for belongings he didn't wish to store in the office area.

Despite the benign treatment, neither Tupolev nor anyone forgot that they might be shot at any moment. Stalin's paranoid whims were sudden, fickle, and usually fatal.

Tupolev worked there throughout the war, mingling with the free and largely sympathetic workers who came in every day as if the prison were an ordinary factory. It was there that he had another challenge from Stalin, one that implicitly guaranteed a death sentence if he failed. Three American Boeing B-29s had landed in the Soviet Union after raids on Japan. In 1944, Stalin ordered Tupolev to copy them exactly, to create duplicates. At first he gently argued against the idea on the basis that Soviet engineers, working from their own material, could create a comparable aircraft in less time. Copying the B-29, with all its complex pressurization and fire control systems, its powerful but troublesome engines, would be a far more difficult task—in fact, he was not sure that it could be done at all.

Stalin sent back an order to copy it in two years, and copy it they did, wheedling some concessions such as using Soviet rather than American engines. But on May 19, 1947, the copy, known now through Stalin's graciousness as the Tupolev Tu-4, made its first flight. It was the start not only of a long-range bomber fleet but also of the beginning of the jet age, for the advanced technology of the B-29 would transfer readily to the new power plant.

There were many more successes, and three years after Stalin's death in 1953 Tupolev was completely rehabilitated, brought back almost to the status he had enjoyed before 1937. Since then he had created the utilitarian but very successful Tu-104 passenger jet, a modification of his Tu-16 jet bomber. Then there was his greatest triumph of all, the remarkable Tu-95, the four-turboprop swept-wing bomber that matched the remarkable Boeing B-52 in performance. From it was derived the Tu-114 transport, not so fast as the American jets but so much longer ranged that it could beat them over long distances because it did not have to land and refuel. And there was more to come. In just six months, at the first Tushino Air Show in five years, his Tu-22 supersonic medium bomber would be unveiled. It should be enough for any old man.

But it was not. Now, when he should be retired, when his son, Alexei, should take over, he had another task, laden with the same threats for failure as the Tu-4 had been. Nikita Khrushchev had mandated a supersonic passenger airliner, and Tupolev and his old prison-mate and longtime rival, Vladimir Myasishchev, had each been tasked to create one.

Khrushchev was not yet a Stalin but seemed to be veering more and more in that direction. Earlier in the month he had thrown down the gauntlet to the United States, proclaiming that he would support wars of "national liberation" all over the globe, specifically mentioning Vietnam, where there was a strong American interest.

Just as with the Tu-4, the supersonic transport seemed impossible. Just as with the Tu-4, Tupolev would do it. Somehow. At least now there was his son to back him, to take over if and when the time came. No matter that his workers called Alexei the Czarevitch. Andrei Tupolev knew that he was accused of nepotism, but he didn't care. Alexei was his son. He would take over.

CHAPTER TWENTY-TWO

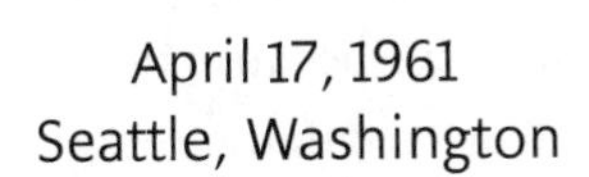

April 17, 1961
Seattle, Washington

George Schairer, noted in recent weeks more for irascibility than humor, looked around the room and said, "As Yogi Berra puts it, it looks like déjà vu, all over again."

Virtually the same group had gathered in the same office, over a similar problem, only forty-two months before when *Sputnik* had blasted into orbit and the hearts and minds and fears of Americans. This time it was an even more significant event. On April 12, a twenty-seven-year-old Russian pilot, Yuri Gagarin, rode a Soviet rocket into space, then made a single 108-minute orbit of the Earth, landing safely. He was the first man to do so, and the Soviet Union justifiably crowed about its achievement. Khrushchev now promised the Soviet people that he would solve their housing problems in ten years and that within the same time their standard of living would exceed that of the United States. Gagarin helped make them believe it.

Vance Shannon responded, "It is exactly like Lindbergh in 1927. Overnight, Gagarin is the most famous man in the world."

Vance immediately regretted the remark. Some of the engineers in the room had not even been born when Lindbergh flew from New York to Paris. Vance hated when his conversation dated him, just as he hated his graying hair, growing paunch, and, too often now, slight lapses of memory. To himself he said, *Next thing I'll be doing is buying one of my own company's Porsches and wearing a gold chain around my neck.*

Harry Shannon watched his father, amused, knowing exactly what he was thinking and knowing that it couldn't have mattered to the Boeing engineers there, all of whom deeply respected him and his work. The fact that the Shannons were invited there proved that. Boeing, despite its size and accomplishments, was still in many ways a small company, and it played its cards close to its chest. Having the two Shannons at a critical meeting spoke volumes for their respect for Harry's dad.

Harry himself had done well working with Boeing. He had been one of the principal architects behind the widespread adoption of in-flight refueling and had conceived the original idea for Boeing's now-indispensable flying-boom in-flight refueling system. In the process he had become close to Schairer, not just because he was Vance Shannon's son—although that would have been enough—but also because they worked well together.

Schairer was the indispensable spark to Boeing engineering. There were literally dozens of stellar engineers at the Seattle firm, but Schairer was always the most inventive, the most unorthodox. He drove his engineers crazy with challenges, and they worked hard to meet those challenges. Today's meeting would have been pointless if Schairer had not fought for the creation of a supersonic wind tunnel many years before. At the time it seemed like an expensive luxury—something that Boeing traditionally did without—but now Schairer's prescience was obvious.

Mild, soft-spoken Ed Wells, a genius and veritable father figure to Boeing engineers, glanced at his watch, a signal that he wanted things to get going. Schairer took the hint.

"As much as we'd like to talk about our cosmonaut friend Gagarin, the business today is the supersonic transport. The question is what do we know and what do our competitors know?"

Wells cleared his throat and said, "We know that our boss, Bill Allen, says that the cost of developing an airframe and engines for a supersonic transport will run from one to two billion. It is too much for any private firm, or any combination of private firms. That means the government has to be involved in financing the project, with all the complications of annual budgets, changes in administration, and all the rest. I think we need to go slow on this."

No one disagreed.

After his last remark, Vance Shannon was hesitant to volunteer another comment. In the past it had been his almost invariable custom to say nothing until asked or, if he had something vital to say, to wait until the very last moment. But shrugging his shoulders, he leaped in now, saying, "I spent two days with Jeeb Halaby last week."

Najeeb Halaby was the personable Administrator of the Federal Aviation Administration, a former test pilot, and a successful businessman.

"Jeeb is absolutely for a supersonic transport, as you know. He says he is willing to go to bat for us with Congress. There will have to be a competition, of course."

He hesitated, shrugged mentally this time, and went on, "And he believes we should go for Mach 3, even if it means using titanium for the airframe. He believes that there's just no way that a smaller Mach 2 transport can pay for itself."

And, in a rush, he added, "He even talked about getting things started by converting Convair's B-58 to use a passenger pod. But I don't think he was serious." The B-58 was the world's first supersonic bomber. Instead of a bomb bay, it carried a weapons pod that was intended to be jettisoned for the trip back from the target.

Maynard Pennell, who had cut his teeth on the Douglas DC-3, was a man of George Schairer's mold, full of ideas. Wells often joked that he got paid just for distinguishing between Schairer's and Pennell's good ideas and their bad ones. Pennell said, "Halaby couldn't have been serious about converting the B-58. But he is right otherwise. For an SST, we ought to establish, as a minimum, a Mach 3.0 speed, a four-thousand-mile range, and at least one hundred and fifty passengers, maybe two hundred if we can find a way to do it."

Harry Shannon whistled to himself. This was an incredible goal, and even more incredibly, the circle of Boeing engineers simply nodded in agreement.

Wells asked, "What kind of a time frame are we talking about?"

Schairer replied, "It depends upon the competition. The Commies have been talking about an SST for a couple of years. They have a bomber prototype, a Myasishchev, or however you say it, looks like a B-58. Maybe they are thinking about doing something like Halaby suggested."

Jack Steiner, who had pushed the successful 727 through against almost incredible engineering and financial odds, was attending the meeting almost by accident, for he was now deeply involved in the 737 project. But he commented, "The Russians are very interested. I've been following this pretty closely. A couple of years ago, June 1959, I think, their fighter guy, Mikoyan, the chief guy at the MiG bureau, told some Brits that they were seriously interested in a supersonic transport. Then about six months later our friend Andrei Tupolev made a speech to the Supreme Soviet, supporting Khrushchev's decision to scale back the armed forces a bit in favor of consumer goods. He said flat-out that they should build supersonic transports."

There was a general silence, everyone thinking much the same thing. Steiner had named some heavy hitters. If Mikoyan and Tupolev were supporting a supersonic transport, one would get built, for sure. Any country that could beat the United States into space could also beat it in the race for an SST.

Schairer shook his head and went on, "How about the British and the French? What do we hear from them? Vance, you are close to a lot of people in Great Britain. What are they saying?"

"They are also interested, for sure. It is the only way they can take the lead back from the United States in transport aviation. They are still smarting from the Comet, of course, and that makes them a little gun-shy. But I know that they've had an official British government advisory committee on the supersonic transport for at least five years. They've got the big airframe and engine builders on it, and spent pretty close to three million dollars in research. But one thing for sure—they are not thinking about Mach 3.0. They are sticking with aluminum structures, so far, and that means Mach 2.0."

"Interesting! Thanks, Vance. Now how about the froggies? What are they doing after the Caravelle?"

Schairer, like most American engineers, had regarded the French success with their first jet airliner, the Caravelle, with something between amusement and disdain. It just seemed improper for France to try to sell transport airplanes to Americans, even good ones like the Caravelle.

Pennell spoke up again. "Send me to the next Paris Air Show, and I'll tell you all about it. Sud Aviation is going to have a model of their proposed SST there."

Wells's quiet voice came through the room. "Good idea, Maynard, except it will be me taking a peek!" He then went on, "Regardless of what anybody else is doing, we've got to do some serious thinking on this. We can use our proposals for the B-70 and the TFX competitions as a baseline."

Boeing had competed for the Mach 3.0 bomber contract that North American had won and also for the advanced tactical fighter contract that General Dynamics had won with the F-111. Many people thought that Boeing had had the best entry in both competitions, but because it already had so much business with the KC-135 and B-52, the contracts were awarded to runners-up. That's what Boeing believed, and firmly.

Wells stood up, saying, "One thing for sure, until the airlines buy enough airplanes for us to recover our costs on the 707 and 727, we cannot spend much money or time on the SST. But George, why don't you subcontract the work out to Vance here, and that way we can keep a tight control, and nobody will be trying to build an SST empire at Boeing."

"Yes, sir, will do."

Meetings never lasted long at Boeing—there was always too much to do back in each man's office. There was a little more discussion, and as the others left the room Schairer waved the two Shannons back to their seats.

"You heard Mr. Wells, George. Do you have the capacity to start the initial studies on the SST for us?"

Vance felt like he was over the barrel. There was absolutely nothing he could tell Schairer about his work for Lockheed—it was beyond top secret. But this was a golden opportunity for Harry.

"George, you know I'm finishing up some work for you. And I've got a contract with Lockheed that is going to keep me pretty busy. But Harry is breaking out from some of his own work with Convair and McDonnell. I can accept a contract on the basis that Harry, not me, will be your primary contact. We'll work together, of course, but it will be Harry's baby."

Schairer nodded. "That's what I expected, Vance. And if Harry does as well on this as he's done on past projects, like the refueling boom, we'll beat the Commies and the Brits and the French on the SST."

Flying back commercial would have been a lot safer and far faster, but Harry elected to fly back with Vance in his C-45. There was something magical about droning along at low altitudes down the Pacific coast, watching the seemingly endless chain of huge mountains pass by on the left. The best part was the communication. The C-45 was far too noisy to hold a normal conversation—you could make yourself heard by leaning over, but it was easier to use the intercom. Then you could stare straight ahead at the horizon, check the instrument panel, or gawk at one of the myriad lakes passing by and still talk directly to the other person.

Vance's voice crackled through the headset, "What do you think, Son?"

"I was just trying to guess who our American competitors will be. Douglas and Lockheed for sure. I think Convair has its hands full with the 880."

"No, I don't think Douglas will be a factor. It's having plenty of problems with the DC-8. But Lockheed will be in there swinging with everything they've got. We'll really have to watch our p's and q's to make sure we don't piss anyone off at either Boeing or Lockheed. Working for both of them like this is murder. I don't think they would do it for any other firm."

"They wouldn't do it for any other person, Dad. It's you that they turn to."

Vance double-clicked the intercom to acknowledge the compliment. He knew Harry was right, and he knew that in time Harry would gain their confidence in the same way that he had.

CHAPTER TWENTY-THREE

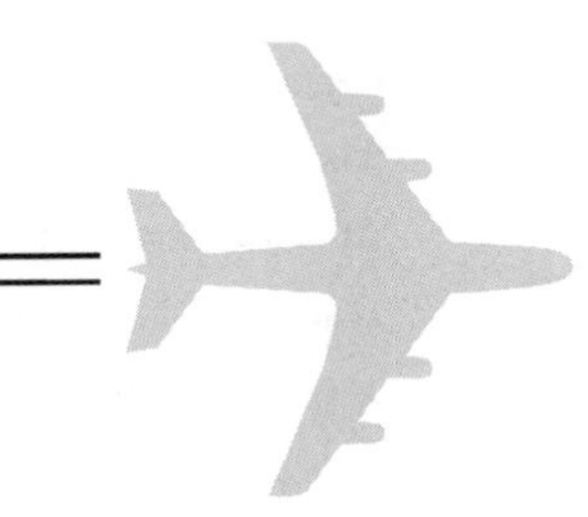

February 20, 1962
Cape Canaveral, Florida

Although the NASA officials had been utterly courteous, making sure that he had all the information he needed and providing him a host to guide him through the launch, Vance Shannon had never felt more superfluous. He tried to put himself into John Glenn's frame of mind, but it was difficult. Shannon had made many test flights in some pretty exotic airplanes, but never had he been in Glenn's position, stuffed into a pressure suit, strapped in a seat, lying on his back facing upward, mounted on a rocket, and, once launched, having almost no control over the vehicle.

His host, Dennis Cunneen, was standing by him, and Shannon pleaded, "Talk me through this, will you, Dennis? It's a little difficult for an old-timer like me to comprehend."

Cunneen, a veteran of the two previous Mercury launches, said, "Sure, I'll try to tell you what is happening as it happens. Sometimes I'll be shouting in your ear, but I'll keep you posted."

Glenn was the third American scheduled to be sent into space, following Alan Shepard's epic first suborbital flight and Gus Grissom's eventful, if trouble-plagued, second suborbital flight. But Glenn was the first American who would attempt to orbit the Earth, a feat Yuri Gagarin had accomplished almost a year earlier, on April 12, 1961.

Shannon had met the charismatic Glenn some months before in Washington, introduced by Shannon's old friend James Webb, the

NASA administrator. After President Kennedy's announcement on May 25, 1961, that the United States was going to the moon, Webb had been NASA's master politician, maneuvering through every congressional or political thicket to push the program forward, ensuring that funding for the lunar missions would be seamless. One of his chief devices was the brilliant use of the seven Mercury astronauts—M. Scott Carpenter, Leroy G. "Gordo" Cooper Jr., Glenn, Virgil "Gus" Grissom, Walter M. Schirra Jr., Shepard, and Donald K. "Deke" Slayton—as front men. When confronted with outstanding, dedicated men such as these, the average congressional staffers melted, willing to trade their members' votes for photographs with the astronauts' arms around their shoulders.

It was an extraordinarily select group, and Glenn was one of the best at reaching out. He had a friendly grin, a sure grasp of the facts, and an impressive military background. Like Shannon's own boys, Glenn was highly decorated, with 59 combat missions flying Marine Vought Corsairs in World War II and another 190 missions in Korea, 27 of them on exchange duty with the USAF flying the F-86. There he had shot down three MiG-15s in the last nine days of the fighting.

Shannon listened to Cunneen as he watched the smooth operation of the center closely, forcing himself to think what Glenn had to be feeling, had to be thinking, as he prepared himself to be the third American in space, flying *Friendship* 7, the Mercury spacecraft that was now mounted on top of a rocket modified from the Atlas intercontinental ballistic missile.

Inside *Friendship* 7, Glenn had to muster all his patience and discipline. The flight had originally been scheduled for January 27, but bad weather had forced a cancellation. Bad weather would also cause scrubs on February 13, 14, and 16 before the flight was rescheduled for the twentieth. Now the Florida sky was a clear blue and the temperature a perfect seventy degrees, but the scheduled 7:30 A.M. liftoff was plagued by a series of minor delays. A bolt had broken when the spacecraft hatch was closed, causing a forty-minute delay. This delay caused another as more fuel was added. Then a valve in the system stuck, and it seemed like there might be a cancellation, and as soon as it was fixed, a tracking station went down. But now the countdown was on and Glenn thought once again about the funny but frightening astronaut joke—

he was sitting on top of thousands of critical parts, all built by a low bidder.

At 9:47 A.M. the countdown was completed and the Atlas belched forth its powerful flames, the vibrations pounding through the ground and air. Shannon felt them in his legs and arms and wondered what it must be like for Glenn strapped inside the very center of the movement.

The room broke into cheers, people shouting, "Go, go, go," when, after an interminable split second, the Atlas launched Glenn, his pulse rate 110 beats per minute, toward orbit. Inside the spacecraft, gripped by his pressure suit and slammed into his seat by g-forces, Glenn vibrated like a reed as the Atlas accelerated the Mercury spacecraft.

Just as Cunnen said, "He's about to reach his max-q—his maximum dynamic pressure," Glenn called out, "It's a little bumpy about here."

Shannon thought, *I'll bet it is,* wondering at Glenn's calm understatement.

At two minutes and fourteen seconds after launch the controllers cheered and Cunneen said, "The booster engines have dropped. The escape tower will be next."

Sure enough, ten seconds later the escape tower, that fragile assembly designed to give the astronaut one last chance if the rocket malfunctioned, jettisoned.

Cunneen said, "Glenn is pitched over now, and will be getting his first view of the horizon."

As if on cue, Glenn's voice came on, saying, "It's a beautiful sight looking eastward across the Atlantic."

Inside the control room, Shannon watched in awe as, only five minutes after launch, *Friendship* 7 was inserted into orbit, its speed more than 17,500 mph, at a maximum altitude of 162 miles. The controllers told Glenn that his trajectory was good for at least seven orbits, and Glenn gave only the standard reply, a short, "Roger."

Cunneen yelled, "Orbital speed is seventeen thousand, five hundred mph."

Shannon, who had once dove to 575 mph in a P-47, just shook his head.

Cunneen edged over to a console that had been prepared for him and they sat down. Until then Shannon had been unaware of how badly his legs were aching. Now as he relaxed in the chair he realized that he had become as fully absorbed in the flight as the dozens of technicians and scientists manning consoles throughout the room. He watched them for a moment—it was like a gigantic human clock, with some of the figures permanently glued to their desks, while others moved from one console to the next. On the wall, the path of *Friendship* 7 was portrayed as a sinuous line arcing about the Earth, passing over the Atlantic, the Africa coastline, and, incredibly quickly, Africa itself.

Time seemed to stand still for Shannon as Cunneen told him that Glenn was having some problems with his instruments. At that moment the astronaut opened his report of his first sunset in orbit with a single word, "Beautiful," then went on to describe it at length. Shannon felt privileged to be there.

The first orbit was almost trouble free, except for the instrument anomaly, with Glenn reporting seeing "fireflies" as he roared over Canton Island. As he passed over North America, Glenn reported that he had a yaw thruster causing attitude control problems.

Someone brought water to Shannon's table and he drank it greedily, not realizing until then just how parched his throat was. He wondered how Glenn was feeling.

Glenn was feeling warm; the temperature in the space suit had climbed and a warning light told him that there was excess cabin humidity. Unknown to him, but apparent to the ground controllers, another problem, potentially fatal, had arisen. Still he was calm enough to joke with controllers about his flight time counting toward getting his flight pay this month. He was earning it for sure, as the autopilot had failed and he was controlling the *Friendship* 7 manually.

Frowning, Cunneen said, "Vance, there may be trouble. The controls indicate that there is a problem with the retropack and it looks like the heat shield may be loose. They are telling him not to jettison the retropack as scheduled, but keep it in place to help hold the heat shield in position."

Shannon understood at once. A problem with the heat shield meant that Glenn would be incinerated on reentry. Shannon glanced at his watch and was shocked to see that four and one-half hours had passed since the launch.

"He's getting ready for reentry now."

Glenn fired his retrorockets, designed to slow him down for reentry, calling out, "Boy, feels like I'm going halfway back to Hawaii."

Six minutes later, Cuneen said, "He's maneuvering the spacecraft for reentry, about fourteen degrees nose-up attitude."

Shannon watched the wall display, knowing that Glenn was descending over the United States, heading for splashdown in the Atlantic. As he passed over Canaveral, Glenn reported that he was flying the spacecraft manually and that there was, "a real fireball outside."

There was a general cheer as Glenn reported that he was deploying the drogue parachute at 35,000 feet. Minutes later he had splashed down in the Atlantic, about forty miles short of the planned spot. The destroyer USS *Noa* picked him up twenty-one minutes later.

Shannon felt absolutely exhausted as Cunneen walked him through the crowd of cheering scientists and technicians.

"I'll tell you, Dennis, I've never been more impressed. What an achievement. Thanks so much for talking me through it."

"It's just a start, Vance. You know if you'd been born twenty years later, you would have been an astronaut yourself."

Shannon shook his head, thinking, *No, much as I admire Glenn and his comrades, I'd prefer to have my hand on a throttle and my feet on a rudder bar.*

But he just said, "Maybe so."

CHAPTER TWENTY-FOUR

April 26, 1962
Groom Lake, Nevada

High-voltage tension crackled through the airfield, shorting good humor and fusing nerves. Every man in the gigantic organization on the field today was holding his breath for this first flight, the riskiest since Kitty Hawk. The revolutionary Lockheed A-12, its unpainted titanium structure gleaming like a modern sculpture in the early Nevada sunshine, not only was different from any previous plane; it also promised the greatest leap in aircraft performance in history—if this first genuine flight went off as planned.

The day before, Lou Schalk's taxi test caused some real worries. The plan was for him to lift off and fly for a mile or so no more than twenty feet off the ground. But as soon as the A-12 parted from the runway, it veered sharply to the right, and Schalk had to boot in left rudder. This set up a series of lateral oscillations that terrified him and everyone else watching. Chopping the throttles, he put the airplane back on the ground but disappeared from view in a cloud of dust. Hearts were pounding, sure that he had gone in, but in a few minutes the titanium nose came poking out of the dust cloud as Schalk taxied back.

Everyone, especially Kelly Johnson, knew that the A-12 was going to be a dangerous airplane to fly—they just had not counted on it being this dangerous on its first hop. Danger was implicit in an aircraft that was going to fly higher and faster than any other and do it for sustained periods. This was no sprint airplane; it was a long-distance Mach 3.0

cruiser, and thanks to Kelly's intuitive genius, the A-12 was intended to be almost invisible to radar. The radical shape was dictated by the totally incompatible need for speed and stealth.

Johnson maintained a notebook in which he entered events on a daily, sometimes hourly basis. Its closely spaced entries, so neatly written that they seemed typeset, were illuminated with his careful drawings. His very first vision of this incredible aircraft was the A-1, rejected by the CIA as too big and too visible to radar. There had been a series of alterations, and now they had the A-12, which, as Kelly noted to all, was almost an exact duplicate of the A-1, only larger.

Kelly decided to use titanium in 85 percent of the A-12's structure to withstand the extraordinary temperatures its skin would reach at a sustained high Mach numbers. Kelly knew that the high temperatures would actually stretch the aircraft more than two inches in flight and had designed the structure to expand and contract. Using titanium meant entirely new standards of quality control—there was only one supplier in the United States, and its product varied widely in quality from batch to batch. It meant new tools, new techniques, and lots of training, but there was no option—titanium kept the weight down. The remaining 15 percent of the aircraft was largely composite materials intended to reduce both the radar signature and the weight.

There were thousands of problems to solve by inventing materials and methods that did not exist. Johnson jokingly announced a prize of fifty dollars for anyone who came up with an easy problem—it was never claimed. A special fuel—JP-7—was developed to handle the variations in heat as the plane went from ambient ground temperatures to more than a thousand degrees Fahrenheit. Aerial refueling presented a special problem—fuel cold-soaked to 60 degrees below 0 in the tanks of a KC-135 would plunge down the refueling boom into tanks where the temperature hovered at 350 degrees at cruise. Ordinary jet fuel, the standard JP-4, would simply have exploded.

The need to compensate for structural expansion meant that the A-12's integral tanks leaked continually on the ground, spawning a huge pool of JP-7 underneath the plane. Fortunately, the volatility of the new fuel was so low that you could throw a match into the pool and it would simply go out.

Lubricants were an even bigger concern, for vital equipment—pumps, control mechanisms, gears—had to work in areas where cruise temperatures reached 600 degrees and every known lubricant simply fried itself out of existence. Hydraulic fluid temperatures soared to 960 degrees, so new fluids had to be invented. The peak temperatures came at the leading edge and at the tail, where they rose to more than 1,200 degrees—while flying in the 60-degree-below-0 stratosphere. Ordinary electrical wiring would not work in the torrid heat, so the Skunk Works produced its own Kevlar wiring with asbestos covering.

The A-12's internal complexities were cloaked in a sinister external beauty. Its huge engines seemed disproportionately large, seeming to gulp in the air even on the ground. Any pilot looking at the A-12's engines, widely spaced on the thin double-delta wing, knew immediately that an engine failure in high-speed flight could create catastrophic asymmetric forces. The slender, sweeping fuselage had its angular cockpit canopy mounted well forward, surmounting the innovative chines that both smoothed airflow and reduced the radar signature.

The entire design was built on risks piled upon risks. Everything had to function correctly, and the pilot's hands had to move the controls as precisely as a brain surgeon moved a scalpel to avoid a sudden catastrophic disintegration. Kelly had insisted on a triple redundancy for all systems, despite the weight and cost. He knew that if everything worked—and not a man on the field believed it would not—the increase in performance would be worth it. When the aircraft went into service, with the J58 engines intended for it, it would have a top speed of Mach 3.3 and an altitude capability of over 100,000 feet. Thanks to aerial refueling, it would have an unlimited range. Carrying a portfolio of cameras and sensors, the A-12 would give the Central Intelligence Agency a reconnaissance capability beyond that of the Corona satellite, which followed a pre-determined path around Earth. The A-12 could be sent anywhere, anytime, and was almost impossible to shoot down.

Vance Shannon felt the ambient tension and found that it helped stifle his sense of personal disappointment. The aircraft had originally been designed for Pratt & Whitney J58 engines, but despite all he, Pratt, and Ben Rich could do, the J58 was running far behind schedule. Vance had spent months shuttling back and forth from the P & W plant to the NASA high-speed wind tunnel at Moffett Field and then down to Burbank. He soon found that Ben Rich was using him as a lightning rod with Kelly Johnson. When there was good news or even just a fairly solvable problem, Ben found ways to tear himself away from the wind tunnel and go to Burbank to brief Kelly personally. But when there was bad news—and there was more often than not—Ben would plead that the wind tunnel work needed him and send Shannon to brief Kelly.

Vance still shivered remembering the day when he reluctantly had to advise Kelly to install the smaller but available J75 engines for this test flight. Johnson, under pressure from the CIA and already concerned about delays, went through the roof. It was hours before he could be persuaded that putting J75 engines in the first five aircraft would not irrevocably damage the A-12 program.

As Vance reminisced, the flight line assumed a familiar geometry. On first flights like this, the area around the aircraft was carefully sanitized and only people vitally needed at the moment were permitted access. Then about fifty yards away were the specialists, experts who might be called in to solve a problem if one surfaced. Finally, another fifty yards to the rear were the hundreds of people involved in the project. Many key personnel were not there—there was still too much to do to allow them time off. But everyone who could get away was there to watch as Lou Schalk set about the business of bringing the A-12 to life.

Only thirty-six years old, Schalk had a remarkable career of test flying behind him. A former Air Force test pilot tutored by Chuck Yeager and Pete Everest, Schalk was as much admired for his engineering analysis as his piloting skills.

Shannon had worked with him on the F-104 program and again during the awful days of the Electra catastrophe. Now Schalk had the most prestigious job in the aircraft industry—chief test pilot for the Skunk Works.

At 7:05 A.M., Schalk made one last survey of his instrument panel, checking that everything was solidly in the green. Then, as he always did, he said a silent prayer, not for safety but of thanks for the opportunity to fly a new airplane. Holding the stick lightly, gazing out the right side of the triangular front windscreen, he advanced the two throttles with his left hand, felt the A-12 roll forward and gather speed swiftly, for it was light and the J75 engines were putting out their combined 50,000 pounds of thrust. The A-12 hurtled down the runway, becoming alive in Schalk's hands, the acceleration amazing him as the aircraft, bronze and silver flashes glinting in the sun, broke ground at

170 knots, precisely the speed he had calculated, the earth trembling with the throbbing power of the engines.

Schalk resisted the almost reflex action to raise the gear—this flight would be made with gear down. He leveled out at 10,000 feet and began checking the stability, hoping that there would be no repeat of the taxi test's problems. He turned one damper off, then another, trying to determine what had gone wrong on the taxi test. Then it hit him. The fuselage was filled with cavernous fuel tanks. Only twelve thousand pounds of fuel had been loaded for the taxi test. He realized that with the taxi-test fuel load, the center of gravity was so far aft that the aircraft was unstable on takeoff. The margin for error was very small. If there had been as little as a thousand pounds of fuel forward, the airplane would have been just been within trim; a thousand pounds more in the aft tanks, and the A-12 would probably have thrown its nose up into a stall and crashed right on the runway.

The thought sobered him. It was a mistake that neither he nor Kelly should have made—and it spoke volumes about the hazards of the future.

By chance, Kelly and Shannon were standing side by side when Schalk brought the A-12 in for a beautiful landing, the long Cobra-like nose kept well up for aerodynamic braking until the speed had dropped off to a minimum.

"Congratulations, Kelly, looks like you've done it again."

Johnson showed no sign of pleasure—his brow was furrowed with his usual look of intense, worried concentration.

"I hope so, Vance, but this aircraft is dangerous. We've lost a lot of people on the U-2 program, and I'm worried about the same thing happening with the A-12. We are pushing the limits on everything here, and I hope we can get to an airplane an ordinary pilot can fly—they are not all Lou Schalks out there."

Schalk taxied into the hardstand, and as they walked forward, Kelly said, "Shannon, I want you to check the engine installation from front to back, inside and out. I'll get ladders out for you and some coveralls, but I want you to check every inch for cracks, abrasions, and anything else you can see as soon as it cools down."

He paused for a second as he considered Shannon's age. "Hell, you may have gray hair, but you are in better shape than I am. You going to have any problem crawling around the engines?"

Shannon laughed. "No, Kelly, I'm sixty-eight, but I can still crawl up and down a ladder. I'll get a flashlight and a magnifying glass from my kit."

It was two o'clock in the afternoon before he was finished. There were suspicious cracks in a half-dozen spots, and he would have to check with Ben Rich to see what he thought of them before reporting back to Kelly. Shannon thumbed down a flight-line pickup truck, asked for a ride back to the operations shack and crawled into the cargo bed amid a clutch of fire-extinguisher bottles and wheel chocks, thinking, *What a year! We put Glenn into orbit in February, and then fly a miraculous airplane like this in April. What will it be like by December?*

Tired from the heat and from inspecting the engines, he wondered if he was getting to old for the business, if things were not speeding up too fast for a man his age to handle. Mach 3.0 speeds, men circling Earth in orbit. Still, what was he going to do, retire and play golf? The thought sickened him. Travel? He'd been around the world so often that there was no place he wanted to go. If Jill wanted to take a trip, he'd go along, but for sure he didn't want to see another foreign country on his own.

The truck pulled to a stop, and the driver, a fresh-faced young man of perhaps twenty, said, "Everybody out, Gramps. I've got to take this thing back to the motor pool."

Shannon eased his way out of the truck bed, thanked the young man, and walked briskly toward the operations shack, anxious to get to his typewriter, where he could get the hastily written notes on the cracks in the engine and nacelles down on paper. Ben Rich was pleasant to work for, compared to Kelly at least. But Rich was undeniably demanding in his own way.

As Shannon rolled the first sheet of paper into his battered portable Royal, a sudden wave of fatigue hit him. "Must be getting as old as Kelly and that blasted young truck driver think I am."

CHAPTER TWENTY-FIVE

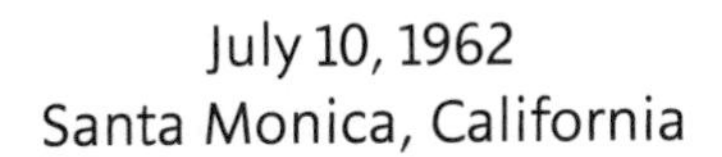

July 10, 1962
Santa Monica, California

Tom Shannon flew the red-eye back from Washington. Rumpled, sleepy, and needing a decent breakfast, he stopped to wash up in the posh executive restroom. The meeting was scheduled to be held down the hall in the gimmick-filled conference room of Lear, Incorporated, Bill Lear's principal moneymaker.

Lear was a brilliant entrepreneur and inventor who had started his career in the U.S. Navy in World War I at the age of sixteen. With an eighth-grade education, he had mastered everything the Navy could teach him about radios. By the time he was twenty, he had his own wireless company. In 1930, he had invented the first successful car radio. As his fortunes grew in a variety of industries he also won the most prestigious awards in aviation, including the Frank M. Hawks Memorial Award and the Collier Trophy.

Vance Shannon and Lear had been thrown together when the latter was building Learstars, souped-up Lockheed Lodestars for executive use. They had a sparkling, sometimes combative but always productive relationship, and Shannon had suggested the idea for building a small jet for executive use. Lear saw the merit at once, adding that the Learjet, as he named it on the spot, would have an even bigger market with celebrities, the same people who bought Rolls-Royce cars and maintained yachts.

Acting on that tip from Kelly Johnson, Vance believed that Lear could save an enormous amount of money if he used one of the new, small European jets being developed as a basis for his new plane. Tom Shannon toured Europe, looking for the right formula.

He found it in Switzerland, where an indigenous fighter, the P-16, was being marketed for use by a Swiss firm. Unfortunately, when two of the four prototypes crashed, the Swiss Air Force lost interest in the project. Both Tom and Bill Lear's son, Bill Junior, flew one of the surviving P-16s and quickly arranged for the purchase of the design rights. Since then, Tom had been working with the P-16's designer, Dr. Hans Studer, to create the Learjet.

The only fly in the ointment was the difficulty of working with Bill Lear, senior. An unpredictable bear of a boss, he was demanding and contentious one minute, easygoing and amiable the next. Lear surrounded himself with the top people money could buy—and then expected them to earn their salaries and more. It was exhilarating being around him, but exhausting if he was challenging your ideas—and he always was.

Tom's assignment today was especially tough, bailing Lear out of a jam with his board of directors. The Learjet was supposed to be Bill Lear's private project, totally unrelated to Lear, Incorporated, but Bill Lear had raided his corporation's resources to fund the Learjet and "borrowed" many of its top engineers. The board was justifiably concerned—they were as liable as Lear, and they had to take action. Bill Lear didn't see it that way. He had created both firms, and the rules be damned!

Ordinarily, his son, Bill Junior, would have represented him, but they were both cut from the same bolt of cloth, and Lear was wise enough to know it. He'd asked Tom to brief the board on the Learjet's potential, in the hope that he could convince them that it was time and money well spent. And he gave Tom a backup position. If the board didn't agree with him, he was to tell them that Lear would sell out his entire stock in the existing organization and build the Learjet with his own funds.

The board had made its position quite clear to Tom in some preliminary correspondence. They felt the Learjet was far too risky and expensive. The money needed to design, build, and certify an executive jet was beyond the capacity of Lear, Incorporated. Many of the board members could remember how much money the firm had lost on the Learstar. They knew it could not survive creating a Learjet, successful or not.

Tom groaned inwardly. The board of directors didn't know the half of it. Things were also not going well in Switzerland, where the workers had a leisurely attitude to the job and were totally unresponsive to Bill Lear's brand of driving enthusiasm. As a result, the Learjet was months behind schedule. The only bright spot was the release of the General Electric CJ610 turbojets for civilian use. They were perfect for the Learjet, powerful, economic, and with a world of military experience behind them.

And that's how Tom started the briefing! "Gentlemen, I'm happy to tell you that the most important element of the Learjet project that was still pending has been resolved. The government has released General Electric's little turbojet for public use, and it is perfect for the Learjet."

This went over well, and he went on. "As we surmised, the competition is simply not there. Morane Saulnier is having trouble selling its Paris jet, and to my knowledge, Aero Commander does not have one order for its new Jet Commander. That, incidentally, is a much bigger airplane, just a piston-engine design with jet engines applied to it. Learjet, on the other hand, has more than a dozen firm orders, and it looks like we will hit one hundred before the first one flies."

He knew this was probably sheer puffery, insisted on by Bill Lear, and while Tom doubted it, he could not say for certain that it was not true.

Talking swiftly, Tom went on to the more painful discussion of the Learjet production, stunning them with the announcement: "Mr. Lear has decided to move production of the Learjet from Switzerland to the United States. Labor costs are higher here, but the workers are far more productive. He has studied several possible venues, and will make an announcement of his choice at the Reading Air Show this summer."

The room exploded in outrage. Tom had been in combat in two wars and rarely felt more in danger. Talk about killing the messenger.

Al Handschumaker, an old friend of Bill Lear since the war, ran the company in his absence and was in the process of trying to rehabilitate its image on Wall Street, where Lear's personal eccentricities had depressed the firm's stock value. Al stood up and called a fifteen-minute recess, grabbed Tom by the arm, and took him into his own office, slamming the door.

"Tom, I know it's not your fault, but this is no way to run a company. What is Bill thinking of?"

Tom couldn't dissemble with Handschumaker, a smart, tough, well-intentioned man who liked Lear and was personally loyal to him. Tom said, "Bill needs ten million dollars to get the aircraft factory started, and he needs it now. He wants to merge the two companies, and concentrate on production of the Learjet."

"There's no way that Lear, Incorporated, can get in the airplane-building business. He knows that better than I do. We don't have the capital, the expertise, the plant, anything. But you tell Bill that if he wants ten million, he can have it. Tell him to agree to sell his shares. I've got a merger cooking with the Siegler Corporation. They'll merge with Lear, Incorporated—but not if Lear is part of the deal. He has to sell out completely."

Tom knew Bill Lear well enough to ask the right question: "Will that get him his ten million?"

"I'm sure it will. Hold on a second."

Tobacco-stained fingers lighting a cigarette in the process, Handschumaker grabbed some papers and went to an old-fashioned crank-style calculator, an anomaly in a business now dedicated almost exclusively to electronics. He checked a few numbers and cranked away.

"Bill has about four hundred and seventy thousand shares of Lear, Incorporated. I think I can get Siegler to cough up at least twenty-two dollars a share. That puts him at a little over ten million. But he has some trust funds, for Moya and the kids, on the books at less than a million. I'll insist that they get the same price, and that will net him another two million, more than a million pure profit."

Tom was scribbling notes.

"Don't bother; I'll write this all out for you. The important thing is that Bill has to realize it will involve selling his name, too; it will be Siegler-Lear, or Lear-Siegler or something. But the big thing is, Bill Lear has to be completely gone from Lear, Incorporated."

Unexpectedly, tears welled in Handschumaker's eyes. "Tom, I hate this. It was more fun when we were making radios and autopilots. But Bill is killing the company. If he goes on, he won't have Lear, Incorporated, or Learjet, either one. He is a genius, but he's impossible to work for in a modern corporation."

Tom nodded and stood up. "I want to send him a wire, with all this down on paper so that's there no chance of his misunderstanding. Too much depends on him understanding it exactly the way you've laid it out."

CHAPTER TWENTY-SIX

August 21, 1962
Cambridge, Massachusetts

The weather was beautiful, the company's campus was gorgeous, green as no factory could be in California, and Vance hated all of it. He would not have come at all, but Kelly Johnson was thinking light-years ahead as usual, and he had a new project that needed attention. Vance shook his head as he considered it—a miniature A-12, unmanned, was going to be carried on the back of an A-12 like a possum carries its babies. The A-12 would launch the miniature—they were calling it the D-21 for some reason—and it would fly a mission over hostile country, take photos, then go to a pre-designated point to drop the camera for retrieval. The D-21 would then self-destruct. It was a dangerous mission. The D-21 was powered by a ramjet and was to be launched at Mach 3.0, a speed where a misplaced rivet could cause a catastrophe, much less a complicated pyrotechnic launch system. Vance had tried to point out the hazards in his first conversation with Kelly but was overruled—there had to be some means of overflying the Soviet Union and China without the risk of the pilot becoming another Gary Powers, shot down and captured.

That's why they were here at the Metaloid Company. The unimaginably expensive concept depended upon the incredible Hycon camera, which in the D-21 in turn depended upon special fasteners manufactured by Metaloid. These were failing at an astounding rate, and there was no apparent reason for it. The Hycon cameras had a great track record, working like a charm on the U-2. It was the best high-resolution high-altitude camera in the world, but the model designed for the D-21 was having one problem after another during testing, and all the problems could be traced back to Metaloid parts.

Bob Rodriquez was lead on the project, but for the first time, he was not achieving what he set out to do. Vance didn't know enough about camera engineering to second-guess him but wanted to meet the Metaloid project officers and get a reading on them and on their relationship with Bob.

Ironically, the flight out had given him more insight into Bob than he had imagined, almost more than he could handle. Although he was young, bitter about the treatment he felt he had received from the Air Force, and socially totally unconventional, Rodriquez had an unusually mature view of Aviation Consultants, the business Vance founded so many years ago. Vance hated the term "visionary." It implied a mystical quality, and he knew that really brilliant long-range engineering like that of Kelly Johnson consisted of the fabled 1 percent inspiration and 99 percent perspiration.

Yet Rodriquez was visionary, laying out a path to the future for the company that was breathtaking, an expansion into technologies that were just beginning to be talked about in the journals. Bob spoke with passion about still having to do engineering with slide rules and calculators when there was a revolution in computers just around the corner. He was using words that he had to define more than once to Vance—like "hard drives," "transistors," "chips," meaningless terms to a man brought up on "horsepower," "wing area," and "speed."

Bob was conversant with the terms, while Vance was barely aware of the companies creating them. He had heard of IBM, of course, and Texas Instruments, but Bob was referring to Digital Equipment, Fairchild Semiconductor, and others that were unknown to him.

But there was another dimension to their conversation, unspoken but there nevertheless. Without saying a single word, Bob made it evident that this new era in the world of electronics was beyond the capacities of both Tom and Harry, so it raised immediately the question of succession.

And succession was heavy on Vance's mind since his episode at Groom Lake the previous April. By coincidence, his annual flight physical came in the following month, and old Dr. Parry damn near took him off flying status, saying that the EKG showed some sort of anomaly. It took all of Vance's persuasive powers, and a promise to check back in for another physical in December, to keep from failing his flight physical.

No one knew better than himself how foolish he was being. He didn't need to fly anymore. He had more than twenty thousand hours' flying time and could easily have given it up. But it was like sex; he was no longer as potent as he had once been, but he was damned if he was going to toss in the towel on that end anytime soon. Laughing to himself, he thought, *Well, with flying, I can always have another pilot along. Can't do that with sex.*

Vance's distaste for the company resurfaced as they went through the process of signing in and getting identification badges for their day in the plant. On the West Coast, the reception desks always had beautiful young women handling functions like this. They were able to laugh or to flirt harmlessly, and they gave a decent start to a day sure to be dull. Here the signing in was handled by an officious middle-aged man, obviously overqualified for the job and resentful at having to perform it. He made the ID badges seem more like passports to prison than introductions to the plant.

The sense of hostility was emphasized when a severely dressed young secretary pounded down the hallway, her low-heel shoes rattling the expressionist paintings on the walls. Expressionist paintings! By God, on the West Coast they'd have pictures of good-looking airplanes on the walls. Sorrowfully, Vance's mind went back to the beautiful young women at Boeing, Lockheed, Convair, everywhere, who were as efficient as they were pretty. One was not necessarily the enemy of the other. Her voice was coolly antiseptic as she told them, "Follow me please. Dr. Peterson is waiting in the conference room."

Vance reacted badly again; the only people he liked to call "Doctor" were medical men like Doc Parry. In Vance's world, engineering doctorates didn't have the same cachet—you proved your engineering merit in your products, not on parchments hung on the wall.

There were half a dozen scientists and engineers waiting for them in the conference room, and as they went through the introductions Vance noted a curious split in their attitudes. Four were genuinely friendly and obviously had a high regard for Bob. Two of these had even heard of Vance and talked about some of his exploits.

Dr. Melville Peterson and his assistant, Dr. Arnold Koenig, were something else. They were cold to Bob, barely acknowledging him, and gave Vance a cold-fish handshake that clearly said, *If you are with him, we are not with you.*

Vance could not fault the briefing, however. They were smart enough to recognize that he was new to the project, and they took it from ground zero, emphasizing the care with which they had modified the basic engineering of the Metaloid fasteners used in the U-2 to adapt to the D-21. They also clearly conveyed that they were not in the habit of being wrong and implied that the apparent failure must be in the Lockheed test procedures or test facilities. This trod directly on Vance's area of expertise, and ego aside, he knew that the test procedures were valid.

There was something else going on. An old veteran of corporate games, Shannon saw that Peterson and Koenig knew something that they were not revealing, and he sensed that it had to do with Bob. Peterson was tall and slim, with a Yankee horse face that belied his southern accent. Koenig was almost the opposite, short, soft, but with a similar accent. Peterson didn't quite say "you-all" but came close enough.

The meeting seemed to be ending inconclusively when Shannon stood up, saying, "I think this pretty well covers all we can do here. But I'd like to have a closed session with Dr. Peterson and Dr. Koenig, if I may."

Turning to Bob, Shannon said, "Wait for me at the reception desk."

Ordinarily Bob might have inquired, but he knew something was going on as well and nodded in acknowledgment.

Peterson demurred saying, "I'm sorry, Mr. Shannon, but we don't have time for a meeting right now. Can we reschedule?"

Shannon asked, "Will you have time for a meeting if I call Dr. Redgrave and ask him to join us?"

Russ Redgrave was the founder of the firm; Vance knew him only slightly, but he knew men like Peterson or Koenig never wanted a scene with their boss that they were not prepared for. Nettled, Peterson sat down in his chair, saying, "Well, if you must, please get on with it."

Shannon did. "I clearly detect an animosity on your part for my colleague Mr. Rodriquez. Please don't try to deny it; it is very evident. Is it because he does not have a doctorate?"

Koenig spoke for the first time, his voice low and bitter. "That's not it at all."

Peterson looked at him with fury as Shannon replied, "Well, what is it? I'm not going to let this lie; I will get Russ here and and I'll have Kelly Johnson fly out if necessary. This program is too important to let personalities get in the way. And before we go any further, delays like this smack of sabotage, not of mere corporate squabbling. So let's have it. Dr. Peterson, what is your beef with Bob Rodriquez?"

Peterson stood up. "Are you aware, Mr. Shannon, that Mr. Rodriquez is engaged to a Negro woman? That is something I simply cannot tolerate, nor can my colleague Dr. Koenig. We find it repugnant to work with him and I think you would be well advised to remove him from the program."

Surprised, Shannon did not respond at once. Then he said, "I'm just amazed. Here in the liberal heartland there are two bigots like you running an important program. Well, I'll give you a forecast. Next week Bob Rodriquez will still be on this program, and you will not."

He turned on his heel, steaming through the door, a little warning sign from his heart tickling his chest, furious at Peterson and Koenig for their stupidity, even more angry with himself for responding to it.

Shannon tossed his badge on the reception desk, grabbed Bob by the arm, and walked with him without speaking to a pay phone. Purely by chance, Kelly was available, took the story in, swore heartily, and promised to call Redgrave that very day.

On the cab ride to the airport, Vance figured he had three problems to deal with on the ride back. The first was explaining all this to Bob without hurting his feelings and keeping him able to go back to Metaloid and work with the people who would be there after Peterson and Koenig were kicked off the project. The second was working out some rules for succession. He knew he could not put Bob in control of Aviation Consultants, not in place of his two sons. Maybe old Cliff Boyd was right; maybe they would have to go public and then split into two divisions, aircraft and electronics. Finally, he had to get back to see Doc Parry; there was definitely something going on with his heart.

About an hour into the flight aboard the gorgeous American 707, they finished their first Jack Daniel's and water, and Vance nudged Bob with his elbow. "Son, you know I think the world of you, and you know that I'm bowled away with your ideas about the future. But we've got to talk now about two problems, and in doing so I may hurt your feelings. I'm going to be direct because that's the only way I know how to be, and I think it's the best way, in the long run."

Rodriquez, who had shot down twelve MiGs and brawled with many more, was a strong man, but he flinched internally, thinking he knew what was coming. He rattled the ice cubes in his glass and said, "Go ahead. I may not agree, but you're the boss."

"Right. That's the first thing to remember and the last, too. But I'm talking to you as a friend now."

Shannon went on to explain Peterson's and Koenig's attitude and assured Rodriquez that Kelly would see that they were off the program. They had withheld some key information from Bob for personal reasons, and they would be lucky if Russ Redgrave did not prosecute them.

"I knew it. They were always impossible to get along with."

Shannon nodded, impatient, and went on. "But Bob, you are going to have to look at yourself. This is a real world. I know you feel that there was some racism involved in your being brought back from Korea just when you thought you might be able to become the leading ace. Maybe there was. But I think you look for trouble now. I'm absolutely sure your feelings for Mae are genuine, and they should be; she is a wonderful girl. But when you cast down a gauntlet like this, an interracial love affair, probably a marriage, you are creating the possibility for trouble."

Rodriquez started to talk, but Shannon cut him off. "No, please be still and hear me out. You don't have to give up Mae, or anything stupid like that. But you are going to have to expect criticism from bigoted people. The world is filled with them, and the business world has more than its share. You are just going to have to pull up your socks and work with them. You cannot make a battleground out of your career. If you want to fight the civil rights battle, go ahead, I'll respect that, but you'll have to do it as a full-time job, not as a part-time addition to being a brilliant engineer."

Rodriquez did not like what he was hearing but had too much respect and affection for Vance to argue. After a long silence he said, "OK. Vance, I get the message. Let me see if I can handle it."

"There's no choice, Bob; you have to, working for me or working for anybody else. It's a real world out there, filled with mean sons of bitches who will say or do anything. You have to rise above them. And here is message two."

He signaled to the beautiful young stewardess who was already on the way with a second round. They popped the caps on the little bottles, poured the whiskey in their glasses, and topped them off with water, using the little ceremony to prepare for the next message.

"On the way out, you opened up some real horizons for me on what is coming down the road in computers and electronics. I wish we had had a chance to talk about it before, and I want to again; I know there is more. But in the process, I could see that when you look to the future, you don't see yourself working for Tom or Harry as you do for me. I can understand that. But there's no way I can put them aside for you."

Rodriquez hung his head, sorry that he had put Vance in this position, sorrier still that he had put himself there with him.

"Bob, I think the best I can offer you is this. We can set up a subsidiary firm, to handle the electronics, with you running it. We can go public, and your share of the electronic firm will be a larger share than the Shannon's. You'll have less of the aviation side of the pie, to compensate. I cannot give you any figures; I just haven't worked them out. But I can promise you that you'll be able to call the shots, develop the products, and so on. But it will be just like any American corporation; you'll be allowed to do that as long as you deliver for the stockholders."

Bob looked up at him. "That's more than fair, Vance. Have you talked about this to your sons? I know my coming aboard wasn't too popular in the first place."

Vance put his drink aside. He could only take about one a day now. "No, I think I've created enough trouble with you today; I'll wait a few days before I stir up my own private hornet's nest."

With that he put his head back and went to sleep. A good pilot can always sleep when someone else is flying the airplane.

CHAPTER TWENTY-SEVEN

October 14, 1962
Approaching Cuba

"Cratology got me here."

Major Richard S. Heyser, the top pilot of the 4080th Strategic Wing, said the phrase aloud, 72,000 feet above Earth, at the controls of a U-2F borrowed from the CIA. With its Pratt & Whitney YJ75-P-13 engine developing almost sixteen thousand pounds of thrust, it was far more powerful than the J57 engine-powered Air Force U-2s that he had been flying for almost seven years. The term "cratology" was coined at the National Photographic Interpretation Center (NPIC) by its director, the fiery, inspiring, hard-driving Art Lundahl. It meant the scientific study of the almost infinite variety of crates, boxes, and shipping containers that the Soviet Union used to protect its equipment en route and on site.

The knowledgeable, eagle-eyed photo interpreters at the NPIC—the use of "PIC" in the acronym was no accident—would study the remarkable photos brought back by the U-2s, the Martin RB-57s, the Boeing B-52s, even the weird aircraft like the C-97 used to carry a huge two-thousand-pound manually operated camera, and analyze the contents. The photos pertinent to Heyser's mission had revealed sixty- to seventy-foot-long crates, and the photo interpreters, looking at every detail—handholds, hooks, straps, bracing—determined that they almost certainly contained intermediate-range ballistic missiles. His job was to delete the word "almost" from their assessment.

Heyser was as comfortable as anyone could be on such a long mission. He had breakfasted on the customary high-protein meal, taken the mandatory sleeping pill at eleven o'clock the previous morning, and slept deeply until eight that night. Thirty minutes after waking up, he was driven to the flight line for a brief, almost pro-forma pre-flight physical examination. The flight surgeons knew him well and would see any anomaly in his physical or mental condition immediately. There was none, so he could enjoy his favorite forty-cent breakfast—steak, eggs, toast, and coffee.

Next he donned long underwear and his flight helmet to begin a two-hour period breathing pure oxygen, to remove nitrogen from his system and avoid the possibility of bends later if he depressurized suddenly. Feeling somewhat ridiculous as always, sitting in long johns and a helmet, he listened to a legion of briefers, all old friends, who told him what it would be like on Mission G-3101, code name Victor. They briefed on the weather (mostly good), how the flight was laid out (long but straightforward, with minimum time over the target) and all the radio procedures (myriad) that such a secret mission had to follow.

After one last trip to the bathroom, they fitted him into his skin-tight pressure suit. The suits had been improved over the years, but there was no way to make them comfortable. All of the connections—pressure, oxygen, radio—were carefully checked.

He climbed into the cockpit at 11:00 P.M. Thirty minutes later he pushed the throttle forward and additional kick of the U-2F's engine power exhilarated him as the aircraft leaped into the air. Night takeoffs were no problem for him, with several hundred hours of experience in the airplane. He jettisoned his tip gear—pogos, they called them—checked the aircraft thoroughly on the climb out, and, with everything working fine, pointed his nose toward Cuba, far to the east. As far as Heyser was concerned, the target might have been Podunk or Paris—it didn't matter to a professional trained to do his job.

Now, just over seven hours later, he saw the Isle of Pines to the north, on a course of 351 degrees.

A quick—but not easy—glance around showed that he was not pulling any contrails. At 0731—one minute past the pre-flight time and not bad for an eight-hour flight—he put the B camera switch on. The time had been selected to take advantage of the twenty-degree angle of the sun. There followed the heart of the mission with the usual noises, a shrill call from the camera motor and the bump of the long lens barrel as it locked into each of the seven positions on its panoramic survey. Far below, out of sight to him but picked up perfectly by the camera, he hoped, were the places laid out on his chart—Davaniguas, Los Palacios, San Cristóbal, San Diego de los Baños, and Los Pozos. The towns meant nothing to him; he assumed there were Soviet technicians there, but there would be Cuban workmen, too, unpacking the crates that the "cratologists" had deciphered. In the villages there would be the families as there had been for centuries, indifferent to politics, worried about their daily work and food, and all unaware that they were being photographed, that they were the center point of a world crisis, that they might be standing on the very ground where World War III began.

Heyser departed Cuba at 0743, heading for McCoy Air Force Base, Florida, on a heading of seventeen degrees. No flak, no SAMs, no MiGs; the mission was the proverbial piece of cake.

As soon as Heyser had landed at McCoy, the two large rolls of film were removed from his U-2F and flown to Washington, where they underwent intense analysis by Lundahl and his top people. Six expert photo interpreters pored over the eight cans of film, frame by frame, working from the negatives, which provided almost one thousand times the contrast—and hence the information—as did positive prints.

Just before 6:00 on the evening of the fifteenth, the interpreters and Lundahl came to an agreement: the shapes were definitely SS-4 medium-range ballistic missiles (MRBM3)—clearly offensive weapons, the very missiles that Premier Nikita Khrushchev had personally assured the President would not be installed in Cuba. Highly reliable, the SS-4s were able to cover a huge swath of the United States with their 1100-mile range. Lundahl informed McGeorge Bundy, the assistant to the President for national security affairs. Bundy decided to delay telling President Kennedy until morning, stating that the President was fatigued from travel and needed his rest.

The next morning, the President was briefed that three MRBM3 sites had been located and saw that what had begun as a minor diplomatic crisis with the Soviet Union had now escalated to a point where war might be unavoidable.

Over the next five days, Kennedy maintained an icy control as the anger toward the Soviet Union mounted within him, an anger compounded by his inability to get a single congruent plan from his civil and military advisers. A whole series of options and courses of actions were offered, ranging from obliterating the threat in a series of surprise bombing raids to arriving at an understanding with Khrushchev on the terms of their withdrawal. There was strong opposition from leading members of Congress who felt that they had been brought into the decision-making process far too late. Many of them advocated invasion. Nonetheless, the President chose the temperate but resolute plan he articulated in a televised address to the nation.

October 22, 1962
Palos Verdes, California

All of the extended Shannon family, which now by habit included Bob and Mae, sat staring at the television image of the young President. Vance's set—an ancient DuPont—was the bane of Bob Rodriquez's existence, but Vance was still so schooled by the depression era that he would not part with it as long as it still functioned. The flickering black-and-white accentuated the serious look of the President, so obviously matured by the nature of the threat. Yet his words conveyed enough of his sense of intelligent restraint and his undoubted assurance of sufficient power to be somehow comforting.

They were silent as Kennedy calmly laid out the unmistakable evidence that Cuba had been transformed into a strategic base of offensive missiles. He made the ultimate use of the missiles clear as he cited the endless lies told by the Soviet Union about their intentions. In clear, unambiguous terms, he stated that the missiles would have to be withdrawn or eliminated.

The Shannons' library was silent except for the sound of young V.R. playing with a Tonka truck. Kennedy went on, seeming to speak to them directly, to say that the United States had placed Cuba under a naval quarantine against the introduction of any additional offensive weapons.

Tom spoke. "Quarantine, but not blockade. Pretty smart."

Kennedy did not mention—he did not have to—that if the quarantine failed, the United States would conduct continuous air strikes until the emplaced missiles and the Cuban Air Force had been destroyed.

The President's speech, transmitted through formal diplomatic channels, threw the Kremlin into panic. Khrushchev had once again underestimated the resolve of the Americans and their ability to react under pressure. And, always and forever, Khrushchev knew that all along the borders of the Soviet Union, Boeing B-52s were orbiting. The long rifles of the Strategic Air Command and fully loaded with thermonuclear weapons, the B-52s posed a threat that Khrushchev could not counter.

On October 27, flying a follow-up mission to determine whether or not all the medium-range ballistic sites were operational or not, Major Rudolph Anderson, Keyser's colleague, was shot down in his U-2 over Cuba, just one day before the Soviet Union capitulated. Frightened by the U.S. military preparations and concerned an invasion of Cuba might take place while the formal diplomatic concession was being decoded, Khrushchev took the unprecedented step of broadcasting agreement to American terms in the clear on Radio Moscow.

Nuclear Armageddon was avoided, but only by the narrowest of margins. The climax was immortalized by Secretary of State Dean Rusk's informal statement: "We're eyeball-to-eyeball, and I think the other fellow just blinked."

CHAPTER TWENTY-EIGHT

June 5, 1963
Colorado Springs, Colorado

"A couple of hotshot pilots shouldn't be puffing like this."

Tom Shannon paused on the stone steps, looking back at the distance they'd traveled and looking up at the distance yet to go.

Harry responded, "It's a damn good thing Dad didn't come; his ticker wouldn't take the high altitude or the long walks."

They could see the crowd beginning to swell at the entrances to the new football stadium. Security was tight because President Kennedy was to speak, and both men patted their pockets to be sure their passes were on hand.

Overhead, the sky was a jet blue, a perfect backdrop for the imposing spires of the beautiful Academy Chapel. To the west, the jagged hills of the front range of the Rockies looked placidly over the endless plains that stretched below.

The Shannon twins were Air Force veterans, and both understood the Academy mystique. Tom had graduated from Annapolis in 1940 and Harry from West Point in the same year. Well-aware of the Air Force penchant for economizing on anything not involving a weapon system, Tom mumbled, "For once they did it right. It doesn't look like they spared any expense on the campus."

Once on level ground the breathing was easier, and they quickly reached the gate where two sets of guards, one Academy and one Secret Service, were vetting each person. As the brothers passed through, the underclassman checked his list and said to Tom, "Colonel Shannon, I've got a note for you here from the Commandant of Cadets."

Looking surprise but pleased, Tom read the note and passed it to Harry. It read: *Tom, you old warhorse, glad you could make it. Stand by near your seats after the President speaks; I want to chat with you, and I want to introduce you to a fan.*

It was signed "*Bill Stone.*"

"Well, I'll be damned. Bill and I flew together in Korea."

They reached their seats, and for once a long wait was actually enjoyable. The magnificent Air Force band kept up a continuous refrain, and it was impossible not to be impressed by the quality of the cadets surging around. They were simply first-rate, the best human material that the United States could produce.

An electric buzz swept through the stadium, and, preceded by the inevitable phalanx of stony-faced, eagle-eyed Secret Service men, President John F. Kennedy swept onto the stage to a spontaneous standing ovation.

Tom whispered, "Does Dad know we voted for him?"

"No. I never talk politics with him. He has some bug about JFK's father, and insists that the election was rigged. But talk about charisma—look at the man!"

The introductory speeches were short. President Kennedy took the podium and immediately seized the hearts and minds of the assembled cadets. He spoke in his usual manner, intimate, friendly, and of course gave amnesty to all the cadets with disciplinary infractions. But his message became serious and no one even laughed when some unfortunate band member dropped his cymbals with a clang. The cadets stared at the President with something approaching awe, honoring him for having successfully steered the United States through the Cuban missile crisis and avoiding nuclear war.

During the speech, the President touched on a visceral matter to the Shannons, calling on the government and industry to work in partnership to build a commercially successful supersonic transport, superior to that being built in any other country in the world.

Harry nudged Tom. "Good thing Dad isn't here. You know how he feels about the SST."

Kennedy went on, his voice gathering timbre. He was obviously in his element, his audience with him as he closed with a statement that gripped the Shannons, both Cold War fighters: "When there is a visible enemy to fight, the tide of patriotism runs high. But when there is a long, slow struggle with no immediate visible foe, your choice will seem hard, indeed. Your choice, ladies and gentlemen, to take on the problems and possibilities of this time, to engage the world, not to run from it, is the right choice."

The Thunderbirds blasted by in full burner overhead as the President acknowledged the roaring applause, then enthusiastically greeted the graduating cadets, congratulating them as they proudly walked up to receive their diplomas, conveying with a word, a smile, a nod, a clap on the back, that he was personally happy for them. It was a psychological tour de force, adding the complete class to his political base. He gave the last man in the class—the proverbial "tail-end Charlie"—a special grin and almost a hug.

Tom said, "We called the last cadet the 'anchor man' at the Naval Academy."

When it was over, the cadets tossed their caps high into the air, signaling that four years of agony had come to an end—they were now second lieutenants, and, they believed, with a little luck they would soon be off to war. The President swiftly said good-bye to the Academy dignitaries and was whisked away to his next talk a few hours later at White Sands, New Mexico.

Tom and Harry stood by, letting the deliriously happy newly commissioned officers in the United States Air Force drift past them with their beaming parents, talking excitedly, embracing classmates, kissing sweethearts. Then Brigadier General Bill Stone showed up, bringing with him the newly minted second lieutenant Steve O'Malley. The strongly built young officer was only about five foot nine. Not handsome but rugged, his short-cropped blond hair topping a square face that merged exactly with his neck, O'Malley had a confident, engaging grin.

As part of the introductions, Stone put his arm on O'Malley's shoulder and said, "Tom, Steve here was our ace quarterback for the last three years, but he's had you for a hero ever since Korea. He's researched your World War II service, and in general heads the local Tom Shannon Fan Club."

"It's an honor to meet you, Colonel Shannon, and I hope that I can have a combat record half as good as yours."

"The honor's mutual, son. Let me know if I can ever be of help."

They talked briefly before O'Malley's proud parents frantically signaled him to come on and he ducked away with a quick salute.

Tom and Bill talked about old times for a while, before Stone had to leave to get to a faculty party.

"Tom, keep your eye on young O'Malley. If we get in another shooting war—and it looks like Vietnam is going to be it—I swear that Steve will be an ace. And after that, who knows—someday maybe Chief of Staff. He's the brightest, toughest, most aggressive kid I've ever known, and still has all the manners in the world."

"I'll watch for him, Bill. And you take care of yourself."

On the long walk back to the parking lot, Tom was quiet, unusual for him on a day like this. Harry finally said, "Tom, from the look on your face, I'd say that you're having pangs of regret about leaving the regular Air Force."

Tom smiled. "Yes, of course, who could come here to this beautiful campus, and see all of this tremendous material, and not feel a touch of sadness?"

"Well, we had some good years, and you had some great ones. How many people have shot down as many planes as you have? Damn few." He paused for a second and laughed, saying, "And nobody resents it more than me."

"For a long time, I thought being an ace was the most important thing in the world, Harry. I must have been a royal pain in the neck. I'm still proud of it, but that's not what I miss. What I miss is the camaraderie, the life in a squadron, the constant testing of your abilities. Flying with the Guard is fun, but it's not the same as life on base. That's really a wonderful way to live."

"It has to be, or they couldn't get all of these people to do it, to face all the danger and the inconveniences they do, at the low rates of pay. Did you hear what your friend Stone said about Vietnam being the next war? That's what Dad has been saying for months now."

Tom paused to survey the beautiful campus once more. "Yes, and I'm afraid he's right. China and Russia are backing the North; it could be Korea all over again."

"I can see the muscle in your face twitching there, Tom. You better forget about it. You're getting older, just like me, and you've got a wife and kid. I know you've kept current in the Guard, but you've got responsibilities to your family now and to the firm. Besides, I thought Nancy set you straight the last time."

Tom grimaced. "That she did. But she's not pregnant now. The baby is coming along well, and I've been conditioning her to the fact that if the Guard is called up, I'll have to go. Besides all that, Dad has Rodriquez to run things now."

Suddenly it was clear to Harry. Tom didn't want to go to war so much as he wanted to get away from Rodriquez.

"Come on, Tom; get over it! There's nothing wrong with Bob. He's doing exactly what Dad hoped he would do. I tell you this: he's doing a lot for our bottom line, more than you and me added together."

"That's another reason for me to go. It would cut down on the overhead."

Harry shut up. When Tom was in a mood like this, it was better to let him stew in it for a while. They would have a real argument later, probably on the way back, and that would get it out of his system. Maybe.

CHAPTER TWENTY-NINE

September 7, 1963
St. Louis, Missouri

Harry Shannon was exhausted. His old friend Dave Elliot, one of McDonnell's top test pilots, had just taken him on an exhaustive tour of the massive McDonnell plant where the Navy's hottest fighter—the hottest fighter in the world—the F-4 Phantom II, was being built in ever larger numbers. Now they were headed back down to the flight line to see the first USAF Phantom, the F-4C, make its first flight.

Elliot slapped Shannon on the back, saying, "You and Gordie Graham did the best selling job I've ever seen on this airplane. If it hadn't been for you two bouncing from base to base, collaring generals, and kicking up your heels, I don't think the Air Force would ever have agreed to buy a Navy fighter."

Graham had "borrowed" a McDonnell F-4B from the Navy and decked it out with Air Force markings. The Navy required a pilot for the front seat and a weapon system operator for the rear, so Harry had no trouble checking out for the series of round-robin trips. They'd gone to Langley Air Force Base first, then hit other Tactical Air Command bases, each time demonstrating that the Air Force had nothing to compare to the Phantom in terms of speed, range, maintenance ease, or anything else. The best fighter in the Air Force inventory, the Convair F-106, simply didn't measure up.

"It was always a hard sell starting out. You could see their backs going up about buying a Navy plane, but when they saw the numbers, and when Gordon would put on that crazy aerial display of his, they came around quick enough. The thing that amazed me was that when they did come, they took the airplane almost as is. I was thinking they'd want a lot of changes, you know, no wing folding, no arrester gear, et cetera, but they were smart."

The biggest change had been the installation of flight controls in the backseat, for the Air Force planned on having both crewmen be pilots. They changed the refueling system, the tires, and a few other things, but in the main, they bought a Navy airplane.

"Were you here five years ago for Bob Little's first flight in the prototype?"

"No, but my dad was. He and Jim McDonnell go back a long way, and he was in the box with Jim."

"How is your dad? We sort of expected him to be with you."

"He's taking things a bit easier these days. It's about time; he's had a little problem with his heart, and he's backing off a bit. Hard on him, but he's doing it."

"Give him my best. He'll know that when the first prototype flew, McDonnell was expecting to sell maybe three or four hundred airplanes. Now with the Air Force coming in, and with the prospect of some foreign sales looking good, we're thinking it might be closer to three or four thousand."

"Dad is clocking this pretty close, and he told me that he'd never be surprised if you sold more than five thousand. That's a hell of a number!"

They were running late, and the gull gray and green F-4C was already rumbling toward the end of the runway, placidly following in the wake of a TWA 707. McDonnell shared Lambert Field with commercial traffic. There were relatively few test flights compared with the number of transport landings and takeoffs, and the only problems occurred on the rare instances when there was an emergency and traffic had to wait for an ailing fighter to land.

"Who's flying?"

"Abe Gentry; he's a new man, one of the production test pilots. I doubt if you would have met him. I don't even know the name of the guy in the backseat."

Gentry applied power, smoke boiled from the two J79 engines, and in a hurricane of noise the F-4C accelerated down the runway, lifting off at the mid-point and climbing straight out.

"He'll be gone for the better part of an hour. It's not like this is the first flight of a prototype. The Air Force is champing at the bit for deliveries, so he'll wring it out, they'll fix whatever he finds is wrong, and it will be on its way to Langley as soon as possible."

The two men walked back toward the hangars and Harry asked, "Who do you think your foreign customers will be?"

"Well, Great Britain for sure, and Germany. Israel, too, if they play their cards right, and oddly enough, Iran is probably going to place a big order. After that, it could be anybody."

"Are you talking to anyone about putting a gun in the airplane?"

Elliot shook his head. "No, and it makes me uneasy. The airplane was designed as an interceptor, mainly, intended to shoot down Russian bombers. It's going to carry the Sparrow and the Sidewinder missiles, but I don't know how good they'll be in air-to-air combat."

Harry snorted. "I'll tell you—they'll be lousy! If we get in a war we are going to be fighting MiGs, itty-bitty little airplanes that can turn on a dime. They are not going to sit out there and let a missile get them, not when they can outturn it. You really ought to get them working on a gun installation."

"Maybe we'll have better luck with the Air Force. The Navy's adamant; this is the missile age, and they are not buying any guns for the Phantom."

"They've got them on the Vought F8U, and the pilots love them. They carry Sidewinders, too, but for the close-in work the pilots prefer the four twenty-millimeter cannon."

"I know, Harry, I grew up firing guns, but there's a whole missile lobby out there, and nobody's interested in spending the money to retrofit guns on the Phantom."

"Well, what about hanging them on as external ordnance? You could make up a pod of machine guns or even cannon, and hang it on the wing like a bomb. At least you'd have something to shoot with."

Elliot stopped for a minute and said, "Let me think about that one. We could do that on the side, not related to the airplane, wouldn't even need to get Navy approval to build it. Then they'd probably test it if we offered it to them."

"I'll tell you what. You build a little 7.62 minigun pod, and I'll guarantee that the Air Force tests it. A flat guarantee!"

"Harry, you are on. After the way you sold the Air Force the Phantom, I'm sure you can sell them a piddling little minigun!"

CHAPTER THIRTY

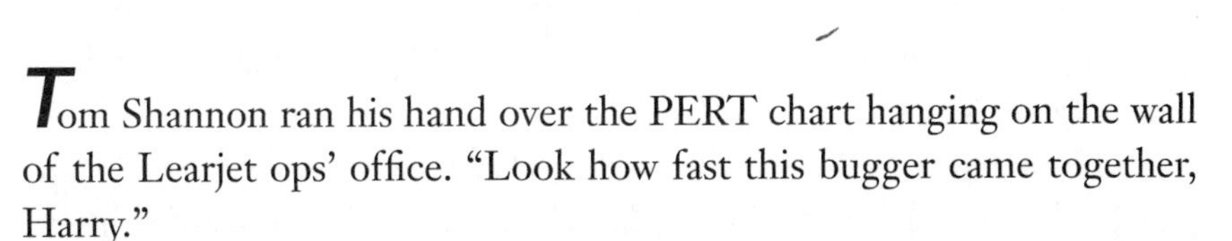

October 7, 1963
Wichita, Kansas

Tom Shannon ran his hand over the PERT chart hanging on the wall of the Learjet ops' office. "Look how fast this bugger came together, Harry."

Vance was back at the hotel, resting; they'd promised to come pick him up as soon as it seemed probable that the Learjet would take off. Tom started signing off the key points on a chart started by his dad earlier in the year. "February 2, 1963, assembly of number one starts; June 7, first fuselage leaves its jig; August 2, forward and aft fuselage sections mated—it's still like a kit, so far, in August! Then August 16—fatigue tests passed. We sweated that one; you can never forget the Comet on a deal like this. Then September 15—roll out. Now today—touch wood—we'll make the first flight."

"How come they had to redesign the tail?"

"It was too much of a good thing, the GE engines were putting out more power than expected, and they needed a new tail to take advantage of it. It drove Bill Lear nuts, it took forty days, twenty-four hours a day, to do it, but it had to be done. You know what he said when it was finally mated to the fuselage?"

"No, but I'll bet it's ribald."

"Right you are. He said, 'That's the best-looking piece of tail I ever saw.' "

"There's more rolling on this first flight than just proving the engineers right, Harry. Bill Lear is in hock up to his eyeballs, and unless he puts on a convincing demonstration today, he might be forced out of business. The fiasco yesterday really hurt."

The day before, a nosewheel problem on a taxi test forced them to cancel the test flight before a disappointed audience of press and stockholders. Vance had been there the entire day, and it had tired him.

"Well, everybody is unhappy; the creditors are yipping; the investors are groaning. If they don't have a spectacular first flight today, he'll never get the money he needs to mass-produce it."

"Is he going to do the test flight?"

"He was, but Dad talked him out of it, told him that if he crashed in the first one, there would never be another one. That did it. They hired Hank Beaird—you remember him from Republic; he was chief experimental pilot there for the late-model F-84s and the F-105. And Bob Hagan, the Cessna chief of flight tests, will make the takeoff."

"Hagan? I remember him from the old Massey Quad Four days. The airplane's in good hands."

The day ground by slowly until 3:00 P.M., when to a flurry of applause the first Learjet, 801-L, slowly taxied down toward runway fourteen. Hagan made a series of high-speed taxi runs, then brought it back into the hangar to be fueled for the test flight.

It was now 5:40 P.M. and growing dark. The tarmac was crowded with workers from the factory. The boys had picked Vance up and he was standing near Bill and his wife, Moya, among a little knot of loyal friends. Everyone was quiet, almost afraid to speak, as Hagan lined the little jet up on runway nineteen. Lear was perspiring profusely; he'd been down with a bad cold earlier in the day, but now all the symptoms were gone, sweated out of him by the sheer excitement of what might happen in the next minute.

Hagan advanced power, the little GE engines responded, and the Learjet moved swiftly seventeen hundred feet down the runway, lifting off at 103 nautical miles per hour at the exact spot predicted.

There was a cumulative cheer from the onlookers as Hagan climbed out at 170 knots to 5,000 feet, where a Cessna chase plane was waiting to give it a visual check, to see if there were any leaks, if the gear doors were sealed, if there were any panels missing.

Bill Lear slapped Vance on the back, grabbed a microphone, called Hagan, and said, "By gosh, you've got her up!"

Bill turned and hugged Moya and began pumping hands of his employees as Hagan took the Learjet to the north, out of sight of the airport, where he could do some practice stalls. Vance, Tom, and Harry moved to the edge of the crowd.

"Boys, do you remember how all this got started?" Tom and Harry looked embarrassed. It was not something they would have brought up.

"Well, I'll tell you. I was down in the dumps about Madeline leaving, and you two were trying to figure out a way to cheer me up. I think it was you, Tom, that suggested a little executive jet, just because I was working on those Learstars at the time. Well, it took a while, but there it is. I'm not going to mention this to Bill; you know him, it's Learjet now, pure and simple, and that's OK with me, but I wanted to be sure you boys remembered."

Word had gone out that the Learjet had made a successful takeoff, and Highway 42 into the airport was already jammed with cars, people coming from the Piper and Cessna plants, Wichita, from everywhere, to watch the first landing.

Beaird didn't disappoint anyone; he brought the Learjet low and fast across the field, then pulled up, made a perfect pattern, and landed, touching down at ninety knots. It was over; Bill Lear had shown everyone, once again, that he was a maverick genius ahead of his time.

That night, at a small party he threw for close associates—the big party for the plant employees would come a week later—Bill had a word for the reporters that crowded in, telling them, "They said we'd never build the Learjet. We built it. Then they said the Learjet would never fly! We just flew it. Now they say we won't sell any. I tell you, they'll be wrong again, we are going to sell these like hotcakes, and owning a Learjet will define whether you are a celebrity or not."

Vance leaned over across the table and shouted to Tom, "We better order one for the firm, Tom; we're getting big enough now that we could use our own jet. Besides, I'd like to check out in one more airplane before I check out for good."

"Don't talk like that, Pop; you'll be around for a long time. You'll be checking out in rocket planes before you get your harp and wings."

"Or shovel and tail."

CHAPTER THIRTY-ONE

October 28, 1963
Weybridge, Surrey, United Kingdom

The two old friends stood with their hands clasped for several seconds, neither man saying anything, each taking the measure of the other, ignoring the cold wind blowing rain-laden clouds on the horizon, their minds flashing back to other airfields, other rollouts, and long-forgotten first flights. They had seen the debut of many new aircraft and engines and they knew intimately both the promise and the hazard of each one. If Frank Whittle and Hans von Ohain were the fathers of the jet engine, it was fair to say that Stanley Hooker and Vance Shannon were its able godparents. Both men had facilitated the growth of jet aviation, Hooker by his direct hands-on approach with Rolls-Royce and later, if somewhat under protest, with Bristol, Shannon by acting as an apostle for the new power plant in the United States, working with both General Electric and Pratt & Whitney to further its development.

Over the years they had met at conferences and seminars, but now it was like the old days, waiting for the company's press people to go through a hokey opening ceremony, as if it were a Broadway show being previewed rather than a powerful new weapon.

As Vance's son Harry looked on, they talked of mutual friends, Whittle, Alan Cobham, and others, before going into the dreadful litany of the recently dead that inevitably defaces the conversations of older people.

Hooker asked him directly, "And how about you, Vance? I've heard some talk that you were not well. I'm glad you could make it for this rollout."

"Yes, I had a little problem with my heart, but my physician has me on some new medicine, and Jill has me on a diet and makes sure I rest. Actually, I feel better than I have in years. Harry insisted on accompanying me, more to see the competition than to be with me, I think."

Harry had taken over some of Vance's consulting duties with General Dynamics, just as he had done with Boeing. At both places Harry met the same reception—a genuine acceptance based on his previous performance but also an unmistakable sense of loss in having him as a substitute for his father. It annoyed Harry at first, but he had grown used to it, realizing that it might take another decade of effort before he was evaluated purely on his own merit. It was both tough and a pleasure to follow in his father's footsteps.

The two older men were talking about Hooker's experience at Rolls and his reasons for leaving when the Englishman said suddenly, "British Aircraft Corporation, Vance! Isn't that a bastard name for you?"

Shannon knew his volatile, voluble friend was off on a rant and merely nodded approvingly.

"For God's sake, we had great names like Vickers, English Electric, Bristol, and the blasted government chops them up into a faceless mess with a symbolic acronym, BAC."

Faced with the prospect of an expensive new weapon system, the British government had merged the three venerable firms to undertake this project, a new fighter, giving Vickers and English Electric a 40 percent share each, with Bristol getting 20 percent. The aircraft was called the TSR.2, for its tactical strike and reconnaissance missions and its Mach 2.0 speed. The design was derived from earlier efforts proposed as replacements for the venerable English Electric Canberra.

"It's all your fault Vance, you and your American friends, with all your so-called efficient management. The British government took over and is imitating you, and they've created the worst damned bureaucracy you can imagine."

Hooker, bigger than ever, weighing close to 250 pounds, leaned over and grabbed Shannon by the shoulders.

"Listen to this, Vance; you won't believe it. When we delivered the first engines, they would not fit inside the airframe! There had been engineering changes in the airframe that the government forgot to send us while we were making the engines."

His indignation was real enough to force him into a coughing spasm. Hooker had reluctantly left Rolls-Royce in 1949, angry with the management there. At Bristol, he had created a world-beater, the Olympus, which put out 10,000 pounds of thrust on its very first trial run. Since then he had brought the engine along, redesigning it as necessary, and two of the latest version, the Olympus 320, putting out 30,000 pounds of thrust each, powered the TSR.2. It was an engineering masterpiece.

There was a sudden cascade of trumpets, and they moved with others to the front of a hangar cloaked with blue and gold curtains. A spokesman for BAC took the podium and announced in his best BBC voice that there would be a short film program. The first set of curtains was drawn back, a screen was lowered precariously on two ropes from the top of the hangar, and the spokesman nodded to the cameraman.

Vance watched with some amusement. They did things like this so much better in the United States. Any public relations man there would have been fired on the spot for arranging to show a film in a setting with so much ambient light, and then they would have fired his boss for not introducing all the dignitaries who were on hand.

The crowd settled down in their seats, and the film began with a series of historic early Vickers and English Electric aircraft, ranging from a World War I Vickers "Gunbus" down through Spitfires, Canberras, Vulcans, and the latest mark of the English Electric Lightning, with its unorthodox mounting of its twin engines, one on top of the other. Then the film shifted to rather primitive animation and the TSR.2 was presented flying a typical mission, going out at altitude to save fuel, penetrating at low altitude and high Mach to avoid radar, popping up to release four bombs, thousand-pounders, they looked like, to streak back home. The animation showed vortices curling back from the wingtips at high speeds.

Hooker poked him in the ribs. "It doesn't show the smoke from the engines. I'm fit to be tied, but I cannot get the test engines to stop smoking at high power settings."

Even though the animation was crude by American standards, it was evident that the airplane was not. With its delta wing, equipped with downturned wingtips for stability, the TSR.2 was clearly a radical advance in aviation.

Vance and Harry found the performance numbers more than impressive—they were troubling. BAC was claiming a speed of Mach 2.0 at altitude and a combat radius of 1,000 nautical miles. The TSR.2 was supposed to be able to carry up to six tons of bombs. This was on a par with the performance promised by their client, General Dynamics, for the new F-111A. While the TSR.2 would never find a market in America, General Dynamics was hoping to sell the airplane to Great Britain as well as Australia. Hooker was talking animatedly with a passing friend, and Harry whispered, "Looks like I'll be making a quick trip to Dallas as soon as we get back. General Dynamics won't be happy with the TSR.2's potential."

His dad whispered back, "And it's no small matter that the TSR.2 is a far better-looking aircraft than the F-111A. Say what you will, many an airplane has been sold on the basis of its looks, and on that score, there is no contest."

Harry had to agree. The F-111A, with its long drooping nose and complex swing-wing arrangement, was an ugly duckling.

There was another flurry of trumpets, the movie screen was hauled up, and, as the final set of pale gray curtains were drawn, a small tractor emerged, connected by long tow bar to the pure white TSR.2 prototype. It was even better looking in life than on the screen. The tractor towed the aircraft to a spot painted on the tarmac and stopped. The driver raced back, disconnected the tow bar, and then drove away, leaving the gleaming TSR.2 standing amid a still-silent crowd. A few seconds later, a spontaneous cry rang out, and the group surged around the new aircraft, huge for a fighter, standing so tall on its undercarriage that most could walk under the nose or tail without doing more than bending their heads.

The three friends joined the crowd, walking around, mentally taking notes. Deceptively simple looking, the TSR.2 had a shoulder-mounted delta wing with a tiny span, no more than thirty-seven feet. Its fuselage was huge, eighty-nine feet long.

"It is absolutely stunning, Stanley! Tell me all about it."

"Vance, it is beautiful, is it not? But the real beauty is not just skin-deep, but in the avionics it carries. This thing can go in at two hundred fifty feet or less, at night, in bad weather, on autopilot. It has a forward and side-looking radar, inertial navigation, and all the information is fed to both the pilot and the autopilot. The terrain-following equipment is incredible—I've made test flights with it in a Canberra, and it will make your skin crawl."

"With all that wing area, it should be able to maneuver pretty well."

The crowd had begun to thin, moving toward the tables where BAC had laid out a very nice tea, and as they sat down, Vance said, "It looks like a winner, Stanley, but will they let you take the time necessary to get it operating right? You remember what happened to the Avro Arrow."

When Avro Canada's Arrow had first flown in March 1958, it had been by far the most advanced fighter in the world, with a speed of Mach 2.5, incredible avionics, and the long range Canada and the United States needed for an interceptor. But a change in government and political infighting canceled the program in February 1959. The new government ordered all ten of the airplanes built so far to be utterly destroyed, along with their tooling, engines, drawings, even their models. It was government vandalism, an engineering and an economic outrage, strangling Canada's position in the aviation market. Then, adding insult to injury, the government purchased Boeing Bomarc missiles as a substitute.

"Vance, you are exactly right. Everybody expects missiles to be the weapon of the future, and there are already politicians at work claiming that the TSR.2 is an expensive dinosaur that needs to be killed at birth."

A BAC engineer spotted Hooker and came up with a special set of expensive-looking brochures. A far less technical example had been prepared for the reporters and the rest of the crowd. These, bound in a faux leather, were prepared for the knowledgeable, and he pressed one into Hooker's hands. Then with a sudden glance of recognition he said, "Mr. Shannon, it's an honor," and gave him one as well.

"Ah, Vance, it's wonderful to be an international celebrity."

"He's probably the only man, besides you, in a hundred-mile radius who would know who I am."

But even as he said it, he felt a glow of pride. He was old, he'd been through the wars, but he still had a little clout, and Harry was there to see it, to be proud of his old man.

Harry excused himself from their dinner engagement. He spent the time in his room analyzing the thick, fact-filled brochure that BAC had provided them, preparing a wire to send to General Dynamics in the morning. In the dining room, Vance and Hooker ate with their usual gusto, while Hooker went on and on about the imminent downfall of the British aviation industry.

"They are trying to force the old firms out of business. Whereas in the old days they tried to keep everybody alive with a few contracts, nowadays they are telling us to merge or die. Pretty soon we'll be down to one firm, making one airplane, and then *pffft*, it will be over."

"What about the Concorde? How is that coming along?"

"It's an amazing cock-up as well, but somehow both teams have a passion for the project, and they overcome the difficulties of language, of measurement standards, of politics with effort and money. Lots of money. The airplane will cost billions in development before one ever flies, but when it does, it will be a treat. I keep telling myself that it has to be done, just to keep up the momentum on research. But I know I'm lying to myself, because it's using my engines, bigger versions of the Olympus."

Hooker said, "Now that you've pumped me, let me pump you. What's going on in America on the SST?"

Vance bit his tongue. He should never have asked about the Concorde, for now he had to level with his old friend. "Boeing and Lockheed are competing. Harry is working directly with Boeing, but he keeps me informed. Against his solid advice, Boeing is opting for a swing-wing configuration. Harry kept telling them there is no way that they can sustain the weight of the swing-wing mechanism, but, as usual, they don't listen. You know how it is with consultants; we have to give our opinion, but once the client's mind is made up, we salute and follow orders."

Hooker nodded. "It is the same over here. And what about Lockheed?"

"All I know about Lockheed is that they are going with a delta-wing setup. There are just the two competitors; everyone else has backed out. It is much too expensive to propose an SST, much less build one."

"Any chance of them teaming up?"

"No, I don't think so, not this go-around. But that's coming. Our industry is melting down, too, and there will be some big mergers in the future. Our problems are the same as yours; neither the government nor the airlines are buying enough new airplanes to keep all the companies in business. Airplanes are getting more efficient, so you need fewer, and they are getting more expensive, so you can afford even fewer than you need. One of our leading thinkers, Norm Augustine, has said that if this keeps up, the Air Force will ultimately spend its entire budget to buy just one airplane. Same thing can be said about the airlines."

Hooker signaled the hovering waiter for another round of cognac, and even though he knew he would pay for it later that evening, Shannon agreed.

"Tell me about your boys, Vance; I was glad you brought Harry and I am sorry to miss Tom."

"Tom wanted to come, but he's so busy and traveling so much that he couldn't. He sends you his best regards. I didn't want Harry to come, but he insisted. The boys are concerned about me; they think I'm a lot worse off than I am health-wise, and do their best to protect me. They are both doing well in the business, and I've brought in a new man that I regard almost as a son, Bob Rodriquez. I'll send him over to you soon; you would like him."

Hooker moved his chair closer to Vance and said, "How about sending Harry back over to see me in a few months? There is a strange bit of business going on with the Tupolev bureau; they are asking too many questions about what we are doing with the Concorde, and we are fixing up a poison pill of information for them."

"What would you want Harry for?"

"He's got your name, Vance, and he's got a terrific personality. We'd like to have someone like him, not directly connected with either the British or French firms working on the Concorde, to supply the information to the Russians. Do you think he would be willing?"

Vance thought for a moment. Harry was perfect for a job like this and would enjoy it. "Let me ask him."

CHAPTER THIRTY-TWO

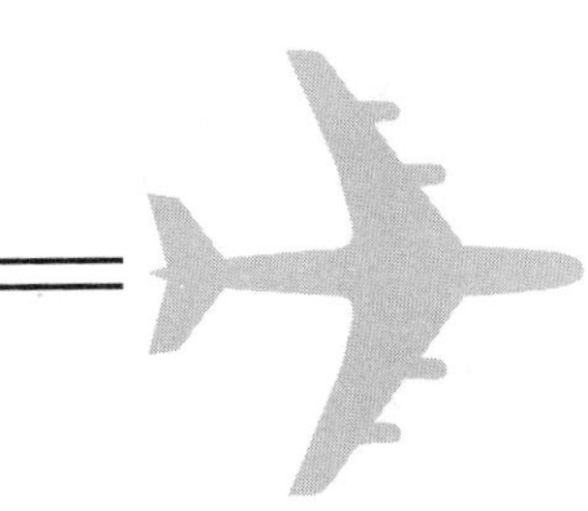

November 26, 1963
Palos Verdes, California

The atmosphere of shock and disbelief was swiftly supplanted by one of suspicion bordering on paranoia in the Shannon household. It seemed impossible to Tom and Harry, who had watched him master the Cuban crisis and then saw him at the Air Force Academy less than six months before, that the vibrant, inspiring John F. Kennedy was dead. To Vance, increasingly irascible and opinionated as his health declined, Ruby's shooting Oswald made it obvious that there was some sort of conspiracy involved.

"Dad, you may well be right, but who is in the conspiracy? You don't think that Lyndon Johnson had anything to do with this, do you?"

Vance grunted. "I don't know. I'm more inclined to think it's the Soviet Union, working with Cuba somehow, trying to avenge the Cuban debacle. Khrushchev will never forget that he had to back down, and Castro will sure as hell never forget the Bay of Pigs."

The three of them worked the theories over for an hour before the two boys saw that Vance was getting agitated, and knew it was time to go.

As they walked out the door, Vance said to himself, *Gad, I'm getting to be an old man, screaming at my boys over something I don't know anything about, something nobody really knows about, nobody but the bastards who did it.*

He moved over to the desk and pulled out the bottle of cognac. It was only 10:00 A.M. and he rarely drank, but he felt he needed something. George Schairer was coming down for lunch, and it wasn't going to be easy talking to him, for Vance was smack in the middle of a building confrontation. A few months before he was killed, President Kennedy was alarmed by Pan American's Juan Trippe placing a "protective order" for six of the British-French SST—they were calling it the Concorde. As a result, he backed the United States building a competing aircraft. Under Jeeb Halaby's aggressive and enthusiastic leadership, the FAA had put out requests for proposals, and Boeing, Lockheed, and North American had all responded.

This put Vance on the spot, because his firm was working on proposals for all three firms. He had been working with Harry on some preliminary ideas for the Boeing SST, as well as continuing to work on the Bomarc. But Vance was also helping North American with their magnificent Mach 3.0 XB-70 and of course was continuing work at Lockheed on the A-12/F-12/SR-71 programs. All of the programs involved supersonic flight, and he would have to be extremely careful not to give anything away. Normally he would have just excused himself on a potential conflict of interest basis, but he couldn't do that now, not when George said he needed him.

Vance walked into the bathroom, kept perfectly hospital neat as always by Jill, brushed his teeth, and rinsed with Listerine.

"Never do for George to smell cognac on my breath, especially in the morning."

Schairer had agreed to come down from Seattle to see him for lunch today when Vance asked to delay the meeting because he didn't feel like flying up. That meant the meeting was important, for Schairer's time was too valuable to be spent flying back and forth from Seattle.

Jill flew in, her arms full of flowers.

"What are we giving George for lunch?"

"You said keep it simple, and I did. There's just fresh shrimp cocktail, two different kinds of sandwiches, ham and cheese and corned beef, and a salad. And ice cream for dessert."

"Good—I was afraid you might fix one of your Mexican specialties, probably too spicy for George."

The doorbell rang, and Vance moved to greet his old friend. As soon as the first pleasantries were over, Schairer said, "Do me a favor, please. Let's not talk about the Kennedy assassination. I'm just heartsick; when I think of it, my mind goes off track and I cannot concentrate."

Vance agreed, and the two men reminisced through lunch, talking about their trip to Germany before the war had ended, about the Cuban missile crisis, painful as it was with its memories of JFK, and about cars—but they left anything skirting the issue of supersonic flight alone.

"I see the Russkies have another first in space—what's her name, Valentina Tereshkova?"

"Brave woman! They seem to have a better grasp on what catches the public's eye. Putting a woman in space is a public relations master stroke, even if it doesn't do that much for advancing space science."

Jill had opted out of eating with them, but as she swept in with the coffee and ice cream she said, "I think you're wrong, George. Even if she doesn't do much up there to advance space science, she's going to get women interested in it, and that generates another fifty percent of the population using their brains about space. It's bound to help space science in the long run."

"Touché, Jill—you are right as always."

The two men moved back to Vance's familiar library, stocked almost exclusively with books on aviation and engineering.

Schairer looked around. "It's a long time since I was here, Vance, but I just noticed something. You don't have an 'I'm a Hero' wall."

Vance laughed. Most people kept at least one wall for their plaques, photos with dignitaries, diplomas, and so on. It was a standard feature in dens and libraries around the country. "No, I've got an 'I'm a Hero' chest—I just toss all of them into a big shipping trunk in the basement. The kids can sort them out when I'm gone."

"That's not going to be for a long time."

"I don't know, George; I get the feeling my time may be running out. My doc says I'll be fine if I take it easy, and take my medicine, but I don't know; I've got a funny feeling. But let's talk about something else. You didn't come down here to listen to me bellyache."

"Vance, I know you have a problem keeping everybody happy and not stepping on anybody's toes. This may seem crazy at this late date, but I want to talk to you about the SST, not what you've been doing, not anything technical, just some generic stuff on how you feel about it. I've got some misgivings, we're not reaching any kind of consensus at Boeing, and I need your opinion. You've got more common sense than anybody I know. I've seen you pull an intuitive thought right out of your gut, time after time, and it's almost always right. So let me have it straight, without regard to our contract or to anything else. What do you think the prospects are for a viable SST?"

Vance considered this for a minute. It was something he could talk about safely to anyone—the FAA, Boeing, Lockheed, it didn't matter—and he had strong feelings. "I can do that, George, and just to be fair, I'm going to have to tell what I tell you to Lockheed and North American. Is that OK with you?"

Schairer nodded agreement, and Vance sighed, then went on, "The truth is, I am a bit of a crank on this, George. I think the supersonic transport is too risky and too expensive to pursue for any valid economic reason. As a matter of national pride, that's different. The Soviet Union will put one up for almost the same reason they put *Sputnik* up, to show the world they can do it. Great Britain and France have made a colossal mistake. They put their countries' pride on the line and launched into something that will be impossible to back out of and will cost a fortune that will never be recovered. The market is just too small to support enough SST transports to recover their costs on a production run."

Schairer nodded, then said, "Do you mind if I make notes?"

"Go ahead; we can tape it if you want. Bob Rodriquez built this for me, he's an electronic whiz. I know you have some Ampex equipment back at Boeing that will be compatible with it."

"Let's do that, but I'll make notes, too."

Vance fiddled with his recorder, tested it twice, then turned it on and began in the professorial voice the instrument always induced in him, "The first thing to realize is that the productivity of a supersonic transport is so great, if it is used as intensively as present jet airliners, only a few of them will be required to handle the traffic. Therefore the production run for whatever company—or combination of companies—that builds them will never generate enough income to cover the tremendous research and development costs, which will amount to fifteen billion dollars or more. The airplanes themselves will be expensive, perhaps fifty to one hundred million—if you try to amortize fifteen billion in development costs over a fleet of even one hundred aircraft, the total costs skyrockets to an impossible number.

And the fleet will never be one hundred. At the outside, it might conceivably be fifty; I think it will be far less, no more than twenty-five.

"The second thing to recognize is that the utility of a Mach 3.0 airliner, or even a hypersonic airliner, is limited by the implacable differences in time zones. To talk, as some are already talking, of a hypersonic 'Orient Express' to fly people from New York to Tokyo in a few hours is utter nonsense, because you could leave at breakfast to arrive in the middle of the night, or vice versa. The difference in time zones makes it virtually impossible to have compatible working days.

"Then there is the matter of the environment. We are only beginning to hear the beginning of objections of people to the daily—or, if the great dreams are realized, the hourly—sonic boom that would be destroying windows, shaking walls, and startling grandmothers. There is also ominous talk about what it might do to the ozone layer.

"Proponents of the SST point to the continual growth in traffic as an argument, citing that annual traffic increases at the rate of five percent per year. And it does—but not in the rarefied atmosphere of people who can pay the high prices that supersonic travel will command. Airlines will have to charge at least ten thousand dollars for a roundtrip between New York and London. The base of the number of people in this upper bracket is small, and even if it grew at a rate of five percent also, it would not be sufficient to fill the seats of a fleet of SSTs.

"In short, while it will be technically feasible to build a supersonic transport—difficult but feasible—the costs involved are going to be impossible to recover commercially."

Vance shut the machine off, rewound it, and handed the tape to George along with a sheaf of papers.

"Here's some mathematical backup for my opinion—predictions on urban concentrations, growth of international travel, passenger miles flown, world airline fleet numbers, airliner utilization—the usual stuff. It's valid for jet airliners, and even if you plug in a Ford Trimotor, it's valid. It will be valid for the SST as well. George, there is just no way to make money on an SST, and there are probably a thousand ways to lose your shirt."

"It's a good thing you taped it—I stopped taking notes halfway through, amazed by what you were saying. But what if we get pushed into it for reasons of national pride, you know, not wanting the Brits or the French or the Russkies to show the world they are ahead of us?"

"If the government is willing to subsidize the effort, pick up the research costs, help with the operating costs, it becomes much more attractive. But I don't think you are going to see the government putting that kind of money into a risky prestige project when there are so many social programs that need funding. Not the U.S. government, I mean; I can't speak for what will happen to the Concorde or to the Soviet efforts."

"Well, Boeing is going to have to keep putting development money into the program until the government declares its hand. We can't afford to have it become a national prestige project and not be in the forefront. I just wish it would dry up and go away."

"That will happen, but not for a few years. In the meantime, you'll learn a lot from the experimentation. Not enough to justify the costs, but since you have to compete, you'll be making some breakthroughs that apply somewhere else. It's always like that."

As they were walking to the door, Vance said, "What did you think—" and bit his tongue. He was about to ask Schairer what he thought about the first flight of the Lockheed YF-12, an interceptor version of the A-12 and a top-secret item. It had flown on August 27 and Kelly Johnson was absolutely delighted with the results.

"What?"

"Nothing, George. I almost spoke out of school."

Schairer grinned his small grin. "I was hoping you would."

CHAPTER THIRTY-THREE

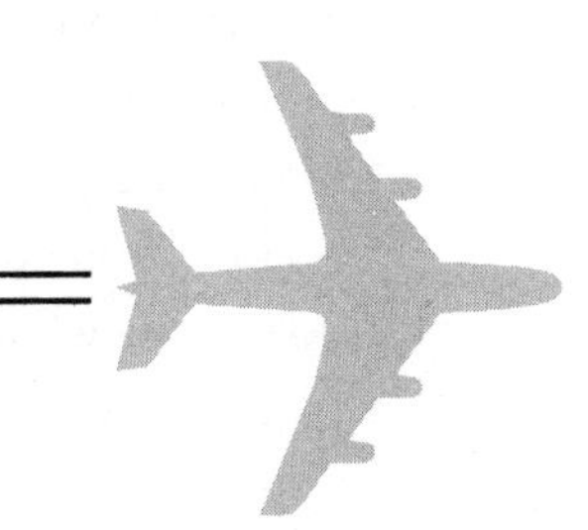

December 31, 1963
Palos Verdes, California

By pre-arrangement, Jill had hauled Vance off to do some last-minute shopping for the night's festivities, leaving Harry, Tom, and Bob ample time to discuss their current problem: how to always be on hand when Vance wanted to fly his C-45. The company pilot, Ray McAteer, was off on three months' leave because of some family problems back east. And Vance, feeling his oats under his new health regime, was flying more and more often. He never went solo—he was too considerate of others to do that, not wishing to become ill and crash into someone's house. But when he wanted to fly, he wanted to fly, and it took time out of everyone's tight schedule.

Harry led off, "I don't want to discourage his flying. I think that it is doing him as much good as his medicine or his diet. But we've got to talk him into making some sort of advance schedule, so we can accommodate it."

"You say that, but you know damn well that's not the way Dad operates. More and more, he just picks up the phone and announces that he's going to Sacramento or San Francisco or San Diego and he wants somebody at the airplane in an hour."

Rodriquez always maintained a low profile at the family gatherings, conscious that Tom had never approved of him as a partner, but now he said, "Can we hire an interim pilot for Mr. McAteer?"

"No. You cannot believe the amount of time it took for us to get Pop used to the idea of an outsider flying with him at all, even though he knew Mac for years, flew with his father, for that matter. It would take forever to get him used to another pilot, and by that time, Mac will be back. I hope."

Tom spoke for the first time. "Well, this is something that we cannot delay on. I say we just make sure that someone is always here, that all three of us don't get away on trips. If there is more than one of us here, we can take turns, but we'll always have him covered."

Tom turned to Rodriquez and said, "I guess you know that this is going to be your big night."

The tone in his voice offended Rodriquez, but he only said, "I don't know what you mean."

"You damn well do know what I mean. You know that you are going to get what you've been shooting for all along. Dad's going to announce that Aviation Consultants is going to incorporate, and that he's dividing it into two divisions, aviation and electronics. You'll be running the electronic side, of course, and we'll be divvying up what's left of the aviation side."

The steel in his tone was unmistakable and Harry said, "Easy, Tom. We don't have any beef with Bob. He's been doing his job just like Dad wants him to, and he has made us all a lot of money."

Tom bridled but grew silent when they heard the front door slam, and Jill and Vance came laughing down the hallway. They had picked up Nancy, Anna, and Mae on the way back, and something had set them off.

The women came in, Nancy excited as usual at the prospect of a party, Anna looking uncomfortable and ill at ease, conscious of her extra weight and embarrassed as always by the contrast with Nancy's lithe figure and Mae's Lena Horne beauty.

The evening passed relatively smoothly until ten o'clock, when Vance said that he was going to bed early, as he always did lately, but that he had an announcement to make.

"Ladies and gentlemen, I want you to be the first to know that within the next three months, Aviation Consultants as you know it will no longer exist. Instead, there will be a new firm, a corporation, Aerospace Ventures, Incorporated. I'll be chairman of the board, and all of you here tonight will be board members. There will be two divisions to the firm. The first one will retain the name Aviation Consultants. Tom is going to be president and Harry will be a vice president and chief executive officer. We've done very well with it in the past, and I want to keep it going. Aviation Consultants will continue doing pretty much as it has done, and we've already got more work than we can handle. And that's pretty good, considering the state the aviation industry is in."

He paused, letting his eyes sweep around the room and bringing back so many memories. Madeline had worked with the architect to create this library next to Vance's office, and very few changes had been made in it over the years. He stood with his back to the centerpiece of the room, a huge stone fireplace with mantels that stretched to the wall on either side. The mantels were covered with models of all the aircraft he had worked on over the years, arranged in a chronological order, and extending from the Douglas World Cruiser on the left all the way around to one of the latest versions of the supersonic transport on the right.

Huge sofas surrounded the fireplace and his family had parked themselves in the same spots that they always used. He glanced at them, taking in the many different expressions. At the far left, sitting on the arm of the sofa, something she would have yelled at him for doing, was Jill, apprehensive about his little talk, not sure that he could pull it off without a family fight. Harry and Anna were next, holding hands, Harry sitting bolt upright and Anna leaning back, trying to disappear into the sofa, eternally self-conscious about her weight and appearance and just as eternally unwilling to do something about it. A magazine rack, filled with ancient aviation magazines, was next. Three feet away was the matching sofa, with Tom and Nancy sitting on the edges of the cushions, Nancy grasping his arm, clearly frightened that Tom would react badly to the news. Tom looked defiantly hostile—being named president meant nothing to him, and he knew very well what was coming next.

Mae stood by Bob Rodriquez's chair. She was strikingly beautiful as always, watching Bob with pride, knowing what was going on in his mind, hoping that Tom would not make a scene, but nonetheless happy to be there, wondering when, if ever, Bob would agree to set a date for their wedding.

Bob's face was a dark Latin mask. He just hoped that Tom would not spoil things. It should be a good night. It could be a great night if Tom just didn't fly off the handle.

Vance went on, "The other division is going to be Avionic Consultants. Bob will head it up, as he has the expertise, and in a minute, I'm going to let him make an announcement himself. Two announcements, in fact. We'll all work together as closely as before, but I think that before the year is out we'll have to expand again. Right now, all the stock is being held in the family."

He looked at Tom, then at Bob and Mae. "And Bob and Mae are part of the family."

Tom muttered something and walked out of the room, slamming the door. Crying, Nancy ran after him.

Vance shook his head. He didn't do this right. He should have worked it out with Tom in detail well before tonight. But Tom was always so abrupt about Bob, it was almost impossible to talk to him.

"Well, boys and girls, that sort of puts an end to the party. But Bob, I still want you to make the announcements you were going to make. It's sad that things are like they are, but they will straighten out."

Rodriquez was on the spot. He had to conceal the natural elation he felt at Vance's honoring his promise as he did and look as if he were not annoyed with Tom—difficult to do when all he really wanted was to punch Tom in the nose. Mae moved with him as he stood up to speak.

"First of all, thank you so much, Vance, and Jill and all of you. I'm sorry that Tom is upset, and I'll do anything I can to make it up to him. I know how he feels. . . ." He stopped, choked up. Mae squeezed his hand, and he went on, "Vance said I had two announcements. The first is that the first new program that Avionic Consultants will embark on is in the synthetic trainer business. Ed Link took synthetic trainers pretty far, and there are several firms making flight simulators today. I think the future of aviation, and ultimately of space, will be bound up in simulators, and we will be starting a new concept, operating our own simulators under lease to airlines. But that's the unimportant news. The important news is that I want to ask Mae to marry me as soon as possible."

Mae buried her face in his shoulder, the other women screamed with joy, and Vance left to look for Tom and talk some sense into him.

CHAPTER THIRTY-FOUR

August 1, 1964
Wichita, Kansas

Tom Shannon had missed the party the night before, and from the debris around the pool—empty glasses, tattered napkins, the top of a woman's swimming suit—it looked like it had been a good one to miss. He walked through the lobby of the Diamond Inn to take a short morning walk and pulled up short. At the top of the motel's flagpole was a pair of men's white underwear, huge shorts that must have been at least an Extra Large. On the shorts was painted, in red letters, "FAA CERTIFICATION."

Shannon turned around and headed back into the restaurant—there were a few Lear employees there and he had to get the story behind the shorts on the flagpole. To his amazement, Bill Lear himself was there, eating an enormous breakfast. As Tom came in, Lear stood up, yelling, "Get over here, Tom; you missed the damnedest party of your lifetime! You know the FAA certified the Learjet yesterday, ten months after the first flight!"

"I saw the news on the flagpole outside."

Lear laughed again. "Yeah, I was skinny-dipping and some smart-ass stole my shorts. I'm going to leave them up there as long as the motel lets me. You know Aero Commander is months away from certifying their jet; this was a big deal, worth lots more than a pair of shorts!"

Tom sat down and ordered as Lear boomed out greetings to each of his employees as they began filtering in for breakfast, many of them looking the worse for wear.

"Goddammit, Tom, you'd never believe it, but a crash saved us! We'd never have made it if the FAA test pilot hadn't fucked up and crashed old number one on takeoff!"

The month before, the FAA pilot, Don Keubler, and the Learjet test pilot, Jim Kirkpatrick, had been testing the Learjet's single-engine performance. After one landing, Keubler forgot to retract the wing spoilers. He took off but couldn't control it and crash-landed in a field off the end of the runway. He did a good job of setting it down, and he and Kirkpatrick evacuated the airplane without any problem. But the landing had broken some fuel lines, and the prototype Learjet burst into flames.

"That goddamn insurance money for the prototype was the only thing that kept us in business, Tom; we were flat on our ass; we'd never have been able to get this airplane certified without the dough we got for it. I'm going to build that into future test programs; we're going to crash and burn one every once in a while, just for cash flow."

Tom laughed with him—Lear had every right to be cocky, to be on top of the world. The FAA had no rules for certifying a small jet weighing less than 12,500 pounds, and so Bill Lear had to fight the agency every step of the way, proving his point time after time.

"You outfoxed the FAA! Good for you!"

"They just got exhausted and gave in."

"Well, just seeing the airplane at the Reading Air Show should have been enough."

Tom had been there and witnessed the public debut of the sleek twin jet, heard the crowd roar, seen the mechanics actually drop their tools and run to the edge of the taxiway to watch the white beauty pass by. There was nothing like it in the world—it was the start of a whole new species of jet aircraft.

"How do you stand for orders, Bill?"

"Orders we got, Tom; it's cash that's short again. I've spent every dime that I've raised, and more. I need another six million to start production, and the only way I'm going to get it is to go public. I hate to do it, I'd like to keep it all in my hands for a while, but there's no way out. I've got sixty-three firm orders, and I'm going to try to convince the Securities and Exchange Commission to go public as soon as possible."

"What are you doing in the meantime?"

"Hunkering down. My guys are all taking salary cuts; I'll pay them all back, they know that, but it's tough. Hell, I'm not even going to pay you until next year."

Tom had been expecting this. "Don't worry about it. You can pay me off in stock when you go public."

"Your dad is going public, isn't he? That will work out pretty well for you."

"Financially, it will be a godsend. I never expected to have as much capital. But it's not the best; you know that, Bill. It's best when you own it all yourself, when you don't have any goddamn board of directors looking over your shoulder."

Lear stood up suddenly, put his hand on Tom's shoulder, saying, "Keep your seat. You know your dad has ordered a Learjet, don't you? He's about thirty-fifth in line to get a production version. Don't you go letting him fly it by himself, Tom. It's a sweet airplane to fly, but it's no C-45, and he can bust his ass in it if he's not careful."

Tom was stunned. His father had joked about getting a Learjet, but no one thought he'd ever act on it.

"You bet, Bill; we'll both come out here and take your qualifying course, Harry, too."

"And send along that Rodriquez feller; he and I have a lot to talk about, simulators and stuff."

Lear whirled and walked off, missing the exasperation on Tom's face as he thought, *That blasted Rodriquez, he's the fucking bride at every wedding and the corpse at every funeral.*

Suddenly he laughed at himself. Rodriquez had just been not the bride but the groom at his own wedding to Mae. What the hell was he doing still angry with the man? This was something he was going to have to beat, and as he watched a B-47 fly overhead, from McConnell Air Force Base, he realized that the only way to beat it was to get back into the Air Force. He had connections; he could do it. Maybe when he got out this time, he'd not be so pissed about Rodriquez.

CHAPTER THIRTY-FIVE

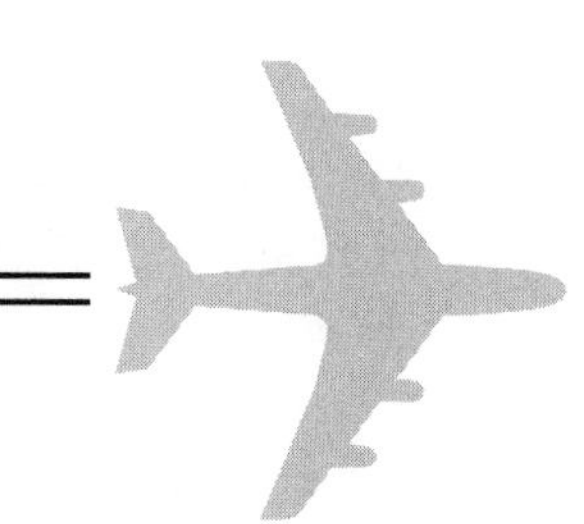

December 22, 1964
Palmdale, California

Vance Shannon watched the long, sleek Lockheed SR-71 roll toward the runway, its sinister beauty sometimes masked by the waves of heat pouring from its twin J58 engines. Kelly Johnson and Ben Rich had led teams that developed the CIA's A-12 into the USAF's SR-71, a two-seater whose existence had been announced to the world by President Lyndon Johnson on July 24.

Shannon had been the midwife on the births of hundreds of new airplanes, but none had ever stirred his emotions as this airplane did. There was an unusual harmony in its appearance, its performance, and its unusual stealth, a harmony that he knew personally came from the intense hard work of Kelly Johnson's team as they distilled their U-2 and A-12 experience into this new phenomenon, already being called the Blackbird from its jet-black radar-reflecting exterior.

An old friend, Bob Gilliland, a veteran Skunk Works test pilot, was at the controls. Gilliland had lots of experience in the A-12, and although there were significant changes in the SR-71, none of them would significantly alter the flying characteristics of the extraordinarily capable aircraft.

"Harmony." Vance said the word aloud, letting all the changes, all the developments, run through his mind, recalling how each one seemed to affect five others. It was like juggling magnetic balls, all leaping to displace one another. The positioning of the engines was a typical point. After thousands of wind tunnel hours and hundreds of arguments with Ben Rich, the two men had finally arrived at the point where the engines had as low a radar signature as possible. The point itself was totally improbable—it was where the shock wave occurred as the aircraft passed Mach 1.0. The materials used in the aircraft were examined and evaluated in the same incredibly painstaking way. Lockheed had made over 13 million individual titanium parts, and records were kept on all of them, despite Johnson and the Skunk Works's inveterate hatred for paperwork. The history of each piece could be traced back to the mill pour of the material, and a record had been made even of the direction of the grain of the titanium sheet from which the part had been made. Records like this helped when problems occurred with the titanium wing panels on the A-12, some of which were failing very early in their life cycle and some of which lasted seemingly forever. A check of the records showed that the panels that failed had been made in the summer. Further checking revealed that in the summer the Burbank water system added chlorine to cut down on the growth of algae. The solution was to use distilled water all year long.

None of the thousands of problems solved were evident in the SR-71, serial number 17590, as it rolled out onto the runway at Palmdale. Gilliland advanced the throttles, and the beautiful aircraft accelerated rapidly, breaking ground at the precisely calculated point and climbing away to the cheers of the crowd. The test pilot flew for over an hour, coaxing the speed to 1,000 miles per hour before coming down to make a perfect landing.

Vance missed Kelly Johnson's debriefing Gilliland after the flight, because Ben Rich had reams of downloaded data on the engine that he wanted to go over with him.

Sitting in the cool, antiseptically clean Skunk Work offices, Rich was distressed, clucking to himself in the oddly annoying manner he had when absorbed in his work. He would examine a page of the printout, sometimes pull out his slide rule to make some calculations, then hand the sheet over to Vance without any comment, other than a sigh, an "oy vey," or a "Holy Christ."

Vance had lost his reading glasses somewhere and was still poring over the first sheet using a tiny handheld magnifying glass when Rich said, "Well, there it is, our worst fears. The damn thing is thirsty! It's eating up twenty-five percent more fuel than we had counted on, and it hasn't even gone to Mach 2.0 yet. God knows what it will use when it hits Mach 3.0."

The words *at least it's not the engine* flashed through Vance's mind. The later A-12s all had variants of the same Pratt & Whitney J58 engines, and they cruised routinely at Mach 3.0, staying within their predicted fuel consumption rates. The difference had to be in the slight redesign of the aircraft.

The SR-71 was longer and heavier than the A-12. Vance went into the classified storage area and pulled out some wind tunnel data on the A-12, then tried to correlate what he found with the SR-71. After about four hours, he gave up. There seemed to be no obvious reason that the SR-71 would demand so much more fuel than the A-12.

As he was leaving the storage area, he saw some profiles of the two airplanes done on celluloid, for use with an overhead projector. Idly he put the latest SR-71 drawing over that of an A-12. The difference leaped out at him. The SR-71 was not only longer; its nose had a slight upward turn, compared to the A-12.

Vance studied the two drawings and then got two more, of other A-12s, to be sure he wasn't seeing things. There—no doubt about it, there was a slight difference in the geometry of their noses. It was not evident on the ground—the aircraft were so goddamn breathtaking that you'd never notice it, and besides, no one had seen SR-71s and A-12s tail-to-tail or nose-to-nose.

But on the drawing it was clear. There were wind tunnel models of the aircraft standing on the shelves, and he put them side by side. They were identical—no help.

Back in Ben's office he asked, "Ben, how accurate are the wind tunnel models compared to the real aircraft?"

Annoyed at the interruption, Ben yelled, "How the hell do I know? Go ask the wind tunnel guys."

"Wait a minute, Ben; take a look at these drawings. Look at the difference in the nose between the A-12 and the SR-71. But the models are identical."

Rich's eyes lit up. "The damn wind tunnel models didn't reflect this! I've spent months up there with models that were feeding me the wrong data."

He grabbed the drawings again, saying, "The difference in the angle of the nose is less than one percent, but that would be enough to affect airflow all along the fuselage and the inboard wing sections and could have a hell of an impact on fuel consumption."

Rich's voice assumed its normal kindly tone. "Vance, could you call down to the flight line and ask them to set up a flight to Moffett Field tonight? I'm going to run home, check on my wife, and grab my getaway bag."

He shot out the door and then reappeared, asking, "And could you have somebody carry the models and drawings over to the ops section?"

Vance smiled and picked up the two models and the associated drawings. He'd take them over himself. If he were twenty years younger, he would have insisted on going along. As it was, he'd made his points, and Ben would credit him for it. That was one thing about the Skunk Works—there was plenty of credit to go around.

CHAPTER THIRTY-SIX

December 31, 1964
Palos Verdes, California

Einstein is completely wrong about this time/space continuum thing. He should have noted that time is asymptotic, and as you get older the curve goes straight up. It seems to me that we were all here yesterday, having a big fight about something, everybody angry, and then suddenly everybody was happy. I say all this as if I know what the hell I'm talking about."

Vance Shannon was standing in his customary position in front of the fireplace, looking around the room with his usual benevolence. For once the whole damn family was here, and for once everybody was getting along.

Tom spoke up. "Come on, Dad; don't ruin it. I made a horse's ass out of myself last time, and I apologized, so don't rub it in."

Anna spoke up, most unusual for her. "And don't forget me. Instead of trying to hide behind the cushions, I'm right out here where you can see me."

She stood up and made a model's turn, showing off her new figure, not yet slim but far from too heavy. "You've all been wonderful to me, supporting me all this time, and I won't forget it."

In the previous years, Anna had gone to various clinics, trying to kick her twin problems of drinking and overeating. In February, she had gone back to her parish priest, who was running a soup kitchen for alcoholics down on the seedy side of San Diego. He had put her to work, given her a diet and exercise regime to follow, and the change had been almost miraculous.

"New Year's Eve is a time to celebrate, and I don't know any better way than to go over the past year's business. We've had one hell of a year, better than anyone could have expected with the industry in a slump as it is, and I want to thank all of you. I know you've all seen the numbers in the draft annual report, but let me just tell you a few things that you might have missed that aren't in the numbers."

He put on his bifocals and peered at his hand-written notes. "First of all, our international business has gone up considerably—it amounts to about thirty percent of our gross income now. That's just phenomenally important, because it means we can ride out some sinking spells in our own economy if things do well overseas, and vice versa. And I have to thank both Harry and Bob for that; working with the Concorde people and leasing the simulators has done a lot for us.

"Second, Tom has expanded our business with the executive jet people way beyond Learjet. His idea about setting up a custom interior shop is paying off with big dividends. I don't think any of the ladies have been out to our new shop at Lambert Field, in St. Louis. You'd be amazed; they bring green Learjets, Sabrejets, Lockheed JetStars, Jet Commanders, in, all stripped inside and primed outside. When they leave, they're like the Taj Mahal, gorgeous woodwork inside, beautiful paint jobs outside. And the profit margin is incredible. I don't know how Tom was working his slip stick on this one, but we are making a fortune on every aircraft we customize, and there are no complaints. It's the damnedest market I've ever seen; nothing is too good for our customers, and they don't even inquire about the prices.

"Third, we are just going crazy with orders on the avionics side. Mae, we need to find another Bob Rodriquez, so I want you out there looking. Seriously, between the new instruments we're developing and the simulators we're building, there doesn't seem to be any end to our growth."

There were pleased murmurs from his family. They all had reasons to be proud of themselves, and that made it easy to be proud of one another.

"And that brings me to something I always thought I would hate, but which I just cannot avoid. We are going to have to go public, because we are going to have to grow, and we are going to have to get outside talent to man some very important posts."

A rustle of excitement swept through the room. Everyone there knew that going public meant a sudden acquisition of substantial sums of money. They had always lived comfortably, even luxuriously by most standards, but now there was the prospect of a totally new level of wealth, something that none of them were used to but all looked forward to.

"This has taken a lot longer than I expected. It's been fun to run a family business, to know exactly what was going on all the time in all the departments. But times have changed, and I think our involvement in Vietnam is going to escalate. The United States is buying into the worst possible situation, a ground war in Asia, and the only way we'll be able to survive is with a tremendous growth in airpower. So we'd have to expand anyway, even if we didn't want to. Any questions?"

"When is all this going to happen, Dad?"

"Son, I'm putting it in the hands of our old financial adviser, Cliff Boyd. He's moved up in the world, and he knows the ropes for a company going public. He tells me that it will take about six months of due diligence, and then about three months of promotion effort, so he's talking September 1965."

Vance looked at the women and smiled. "It will mean a totally new board of directors, and I suspect that not all of us will remain on it. We'll need to reach out to industry and get some heavy hitters to be on the board, to support the initial offering of stock. But we'll all be substantial stockholders, of course, and you can all come to the annual meetings and complain about our leadership."

He stepped down from the raised hearth and headed for the bar, where Jill had a very weak Jack Daniel's and water waiting for him.

She reached out and put her hand on his cheek. "This was so much better than last year. Thank God Tom came to his senses, and got over this business about Bob breaking into the family."

"Honey, there was no way he could disapprove of Bob's performance. The man has simply been a dynamo, taking us into fields we need to be in but didn't have the talent for. Tom finally accepted his good fortune."

There was no evidence of past animosity as Tom, Harry, and Bob gathered around the table in the kitchen, talking business as they always did.

"What happened with the sonic boom tests you were helping the FAA run, Tom?"

In February, the FAA had launched Bongo Mark 2, an operation that used Convair B-58 bombers and Lockheed F-104 fighters to make supersonic speed runs to test the effect of the sound barrier, using Oklahoma City as the main target.

"It was pretty comprehensive. They made more than twelve hundred supersonic runs, and when they polled the public, they found that seventy-three percent of the people didn't object—but this meant that twenty-seven percent did. The tests were so regular that one woman said she used the sonic boom to wake her up instead of an alarm clock. There was not much real damage, some broken windows and cracked plaster, but there were more than eight thousand complaints and more than five thousand claims for damages. So it pretty well spells the end of supersonic airline operation over land areas in the U.S."

Tom chimed in, "If we prohibit transports operating at supersonic speeds over land here, every other nation will follow suit. The governments will be afraid their people will think they are indifferent."

And Harry said, "Not in the Soviet Union. The distances there are so vast that an SST makes more sense, and they don't give a damn about public complaints."

"How are they coming along?"

"I understand that they are doing very well, and are determined to beat the Concorde into the air. But they've got some technical problems, and they have the gall to write us and ask for advice. One of their problems is tires—they cannot get the right rubber composition for tires that will be landing as fast and as heavy as their SST does."

"What about engines?"

"The usual approach: pure power, and damn the operating costs."

"Anybody had a look at a model or a drawing?"

"Not yet, but the Tupolev people are hinting at an unveiling at the next Paris Air Show."

Vance walked by the door to the kitchen, en route to his bedroom, his Jack Daniel's still not tasted. A quick scan of the room made him swell with pleasure. All three were talking animatedly. It was evident that Tom's animosity toward Bob had evaporated, and Bob showed no signs of resentment, as a lesser man might have. And there was Harry, big, strong Harry, always the tower of strength. God, Anna had put him through hell, and he had stayed with her the whole time. If she stayed on the wagon, if she took care of herself, it would be a fine thing for Harry, a real tribute.

They were good boys. Tom had something on his mind, he could tell, but seemed at peace with himself, so that was OK. The three of them could handle the incorporation, and then it was time for Vance to retire, maybe restore an old airplane or his favorite car, a 1937 Cord. Maybe.

CHAPTER THIRTY-SEVEN

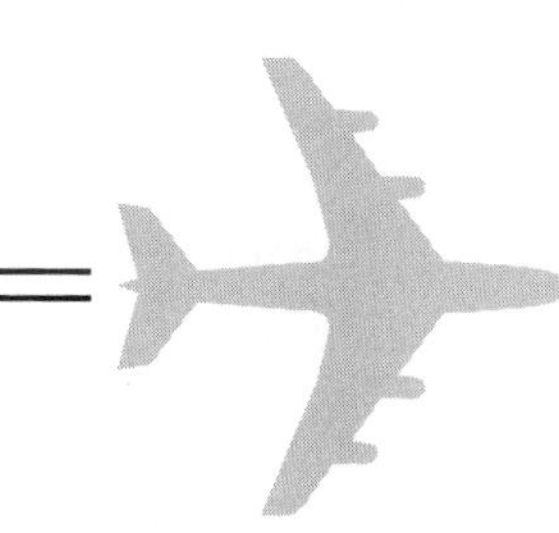

January 6, 1965
Meudon, outside Paris, France

Edged with ivy, the lovely old stone building was located near the fields where Alberto Santos-Dumont, Louis Blériot, and other early aviation pioneers had flown. In its early years at the turn of the nineteenth century, it was the École Nationale Aérostatique, the world's first school for training balloonists. Balloons and airships were built there, a few setting records, more going up in a ball of hydrogen flame.

Military ballooning waxed and waned over the years, but Meudon remained the linchpin of French aviation research. Now the compound at 91 Boulevard Pereire housed the Musée de l'Air, a collection of great French aircraft that began with those of Clement Ader and went on to include warplanes and record setters. They were scattered around an interior so cavernous that it had once allowed balloons to be built and tested. The aircraft, some world famous, others utterly anonymous, were propped above cases lined with equipment and models or suspended from the ceiling on rusting cable. A half century of dust had turned them all into a uniform gray, their once-bright insignias vainly peeking through.

Madeline Behar had chosen the meeting site deliberately. Her Soviet contacts—two Russians and an East German—had complained that restaurants and bars were too easily compromised and wanted to meet some place where they were certain not to be recognized. The museum pleased her, and she hoped it might spark some reaction from them as a symbol of their countries' long and troubled relations. During the 1870 Franco-Prussian War it had served again as a balloon factory. The French Air Force pressed it into service during both world wars. But most of all, she chose it because Marcel Dassault contributed heavily to the upkeep of the museum, especially with the limited restoration work that was done. He headed the firm that served as cover for her intelligence work, and his influence made it easy for her to gain access for a private meeting.

Madeline's Russian was far more fluent than Gerd Müller's and much more stylish than that of either Sergei Pavlov, the official head of Aeroflot's Paris office, or the hulking Sergei Fabiew, who might as well have had "KGB" tattooed on his forehead.

She paused near a SPAD XIII, still in its original fabric with its squadron's stork emblem emblazoned on the fuselage. From above, a suspended Fokker D VII seemed to be fixed forever in a diving attack on its old enemy, the SPAD.

"Do you remember these planes from World War I?"

Müller nodded quietly, pointing up to the Fokker, saying, "Our best fighter. It came too late, but it was good."

Madeline spoke confidently, quietly, as with an old friend. "I've often wondered why the Germans did not seize this collection during the occupation. They could have made a case that the scrap metal was needed."

Müller bristled. "We were not always ruthless. The world remembers only Hitler now, and the slaughtering of the Jews, but the ordinary German had a regard for culture."

Fabiew stared at Müller, obviously displeased by the tenor of the conversation. He did not say a word, but his look was enough to galvanize the East German.

"This seems to be a secure area, unless you are having us watched."

The museum was cluttered with airplanes, and a hundred agents could have been hidden behind them, the exhibit cases, the engines, or the piles of anonymous parts.

"You are too suspicious. If I wanted us to be watched, I'd have insisted on going back to the hotel bar. We are alone. The museum is only open by appointment, and the director assured me that there would be no other visitors. He has no staff to speak of, and all of the museum work is conducted in the shops outside. We are alone."

"Then what do you have?"

Madeline pressed an ordinary brown envelope into his hand.

"This contains a sample of tires that are being tested for the Concorde. They are made from the same material, but are smaller of course. They are testing the special tires on a Vatour."

She paused, her memory going back to Vance. He had brought the design specifications for a lighter version of the B-47 home from Boeing to work on over a weekend. She had copied them and sent them back to her patron in French intelligence, who had passed them on to the manufacturer, Sud Ouest. The specifications led directly to the Vatour, which had done well in battle.

She resumed, "They load the Vatour up beyond its maximum landing weight, and then land at high speeds and brake very hard. The tires burn their way into the runway, leaving big clouds of smoke behind. My mechanic scraped this material from the runway where they land."

"What is it made of?"

"The tire compound itself? I have no idea. That's a closely held secret. But it's not as complex as an atomic bomb! Your scientists will be able to analyze it, and duplicate the formula. There must be four or five ounces of material there. Don't ask me to get more. It was very risky sending a man out to get this. I had to tell the tower that we were looking for parts that had fallen off the Vatour. They let my man go out there because they didn't want any foreign-object damage to the next plane to land."

"How do you know this is from the Vatour? It might come from any airplane."

"Open the envelope, and look at it. You'll see red and green fibers. They were put in the test tires on the Vatour to monitor wear. No other airplane has tires like that."

Pavlov poked through the mound of shredded, burned rubber dubiously, shrugged his shoulders, and handed the envelope to Fabiew, who did exactly the same thing. They nodded to Müller, who suddenly smiled, saying, "This is fine; thank you very much. And I'll have payment for you within a few weeks."

Madeline feigned anger. "What? A few weeks? And in francs or dollars this time, or don't bother; it will be the last business we do. I'm putting my job at risk every time I deal with you, and you are always late with the money."

The Russians turned and started to walk out. Müller grabbed Pavlov by the arm and turned to Madeline again. "What about taking us around and showing us the rest of the airplanes?"

"Do you think I am a tour guide? It's time for you and your friends to go. Who knows when somebody might come in? I don't want to explain what I'm doing here with you."

The four walked rapidly to the double entrance door. She pushed it open for them, Müller bowed, and they went to their parked Citroën.

She watched them through a window next to the door.

"Müller *would* have a Citroën. He always tries to be more like Jean Gabin than Jean Gabin."

CHAPTER THIRTY-EIGHT

July 4, 1965
Palos Verdes, California

Sunday was a perfect California day for a backyard picnic, the sun warm enough to encourage shorts and halters for the ladies, the breeze cool enough to keep everybody comfortable. Anna was so pleased with her new figure that she joked about the little bundle of fat that still lapped over the top of her shorts—it was nothing compared to a year ago, and she was determined to shed it with exercise and an even more stringent diet.

It was the first time in months that everyone was home. It hadn't been planned this way, but it worked out perfectly, for there was a lot of catching up to do. The men of the family—Vance, Tom, Harry, and Bob—took bottles of Budweiser and sat down at the big kitchen table, moved onto the porch for the occasion. Jill turned out her usually dazzling platter of sandwiches—thin-sliced roast beef, pastrami, ham and cheese, and, for Vance, turkey breast on rye, no mayonnaise. An array of condiments surrounded the sandwiches—sliced onion, dill pickles, mustard, catsup, Worcestershire sauce, and even, for Bob, some salsa from the market in Old Town.

Vance, who also loved the salsa but had to watch his intake nowadays, had made a mental laundry list of the things he needed to talk to his boys about, either passing along information or prodding them for the tidbits that never went into their official company reports.

"Let me bring you up-to-date on the TSR.2. The blasted British government has done it again. Stan Hooker—and you know how tight he is with a shilling—has been calling me on the phone regularly. I think spouting off to me keeps him from having a heart attack."

Vance went on to tell the sad story. On April 6, the British Labour government had terminated the TSR.2 program despite strong protests from the British Aircraft Company—some ten thousand workers had mobilized and marched in the streets of London, but to no avail. Then for weeks afterward Hooker burned up the telephone line with reports on the mendacity of the government in ordering completed TSR.2s to be taken to the firing range at Shoeburyness to be used as gun targets. All parts for airframes were scrapped; tooling was destroyed; even the wooden mock-up was dragged out of storage and burned. The avid government agents destroyed photographs, models, and all test reports to make sure that no succeeding government could revive the project.

Harry spoke up. "It's just like the Avro Arrow fiasco!"

Tom added, "Well, to look on the bright side, they say they are going to buy General Dynamics's F-111 aircraft as a replacement. Their Defense Minister, Donald Healey, claims that the F-111 will be less expensive and delivered more quickly than the TSR.2. Man, are they in for a shock!"

Rodriquez, who always had his eye on the bottom line, said, "It's a big mistake on their part. They could have recouped most or maybe all their research cost on export sales. Vance told us early on that the TSR.2 was far more capable than the F-111 was projected to be. It could have generated a fortune in sales to other governments."

Tom chimed in, "If the F-111 is as bad as I think it is going to be, the United States might even have bought some TSR.2s."

All four men were conscious of how fragile the aircraft industry had become. Killing the TSR.2 did not affect just the British Aircraft Company building it—it would disturb the engine manufacturers, the component builders. A ripple effect would reach out, and for the ten thousand BAC people who lost their jobs another thirty thousand workers in other industries would be affected.

"What's happening with the F-111, Tom?"

"Not much good. The whole thing has been screwed up from the start by McNamara and his insistence on the TFX."

Secretary of Defense Robert Strange McNamara was trying to manage the defense department as he had managed Ford, using quantitative techniques that reduced everything to dollars and cents. He advocated the TFX as a single aircraft that would serve the Air Force and Navy with minor modifications, just as Ford, Mercury, and Edsel had shared components. The idea, of course, was commonality. If the same basic airplane was produced for both services, there theoretically would be larger production runs, with the resulting economies."

Tom went on, "The Navy is having nothing but problems with the F-111B, which they never wanted in the first place. I'm sure they will cancel it pretty soon. It's just too damn heavy and too high-drag. It was crazy to think it could ever operate off a carrier."

Vance nodded. "Did you know that General Dynamics actually invited Kelly Johnson out to review the high-drag problem? He took one look at it and said it was the way the engine inlets were mounted, close to the fuselage and under the wing. He got a big kick out of it because he knew there was nothing much they could do to solve the problem. He likes nothing better than seeing his competitors stewing in their own juice."

Vance turned to Harry. "What's up with Boeing, Harry? Are they still pushing a swing wing for their SST?"

"Yeah, but their heart isn't in it. If they could find some face-saving way to switch over to a delta wing, like Lockheed is using, they would. But right now, they are toughing it out, insisting the swing wing is the way to go. But I know damn well if they win the contract, they'll switch to a delta in nothing flat."

"What do they think about the Concorde?"

"Well, first of all, they know it's a Mach 2.0 aircraft, so they discount it. But they hate the thought that both BAC and Aérospatiale are already building the prototypes and all Boeing has is a mock-up. It's a beauty, but it's mostly plywood."

"And the Russkies? How are they doing?"

Harry was on the spot. Boeing had permitted him to respond to a BAC request to do some clandestine work, slipping the Russians disinformation. Incredibly, the covert activity had brought him face-to-face with Madeline Behar, looking strangely sad and unwell.

For an instant he was back in Paris, shaking Madeline's cool hand. Strangely, he was most affected by her voice, the rich French accent,

"Hello, Harry. How is your father, and how is Tom?"

"We're all fine, Madeline. And you?"

"I've had some rough spots recently—some minor health problems—but for the most part I am fine. And how are the women of the family?"

Harry had told her that his father had married Jill and Tom had married Nancy, and she laughed.

"It doesn't surprise me about your father and Jill, but I had not planned for Nancy and Tom. My last plans for Tom had not worked so well."

"Well, it worked well for me and Anna."

Vance's voice broke through his reminiscence, "What the hell is wrong with you, Harry? I'm just asking about the Russians and their Tupolev."

"Sorry, Dad. My mind wandered."

There was no way in the world he could ever let his dad know about his meeting Madeline. He had no idea how Vance might react. He was happy with Jill now; there was no point in raising the ghost of Madeline—it might well break his heart. Harry finished his bottle of beer in one long gurgling gulp before answering.

"The Russians are cutting metal, too. I understand Tupolev has orders to get his SST in the air before the British and the French—a matter of prestige. Khrushchev has ordered that it fly in 1968. They had a great model of it at the Paris Air Show, claiming a Mach 2.3 cruise and a four-thousand-mile range. It looks so much like the Concorde that they are calling it the Concordski as a joke."

Vance smiled, saying, "People always believe that if any two airplanes look alike, it means that one designer stole the idea from another. Everybody said that the designs of the Japanese Zero and the German Focke-Wulf FW 190 had been stolen from the Hughes racer. The truth was that faced with similar design problems, the designers came up with similar solutions. No doubt that's how it was with the two SST projects."

Harry cautiously went on, "Well, Dad, in this case, it's the truth. The KGB, and some people from the East German secret police, the Stasi, they call it, actually got Concorde blueprints and technical data. They pretended to be working for Aeroflot, and found some Communist sympathizers at the factory in Toulouse. French intelligence arrested a guy named Pavlov, supposed to be the head of the Paris Aeroflot office, caught him with drawings of the Concorde's brakes, gear, and airframe. Caught his East German colleague, too. They tried to do the same thing in England, trying to learn about the engines, but the Brits were on to them."

Vance said, "Stan Hooker would kick their ass if they tried to steal secrets from him!"

They laughed and Harry went on, glad to change the subject, "The big surprise for Boeing is their uptick in B-52 maintenance and modification. They are reaping a totally unexpected fortune out of the Vietnam War. SAC has deployed B-52s to Andersen, to use in South Vietnam, mainly. Can you imagine that, the big nuclear long rifle is going to work as an iron bomb dropper. They've got a modification going on with the B-52Ds, called Big Belly. They'll be able to drop more than a hundred bombs, all five hundred pounders, in a single salvo from one bomber. Imagine what a formation of them will do!"

Bob whistled, then said, "This Vietnam thing is a cancer that won't go away until we get serious. It is going to drain our life's blood to fight a ground war over there. I can't imagine what McNamara is thinking of."

The same man who had forced the TFX on the Navy and the Air Force had insisted on building up the Army to fight a ground war in Vietnam.

Tom laughed. "You got to remember, he's the man who gave us the Edsel."

Harry went on, "Boeing was really upset that Lockheed won the big Air Force transport competition. They swear they had the best design, but they think Lockheed might have won because the C-141 is working so well. And they swear that Lockheed has better lobbyists in Washington and more powerful people in the Congress."

"More powerful than Scoop Jackson? That's hard to believe!"

"Well, that's Boeing's story and they are sticking to it. But they are trying to make lemonade out of the lemon—they are converting their design work so that it applies to a big civilian transport, one that will meet Juan Trippe's demands for a huge airliner."

A reflective quiet spread over the table. Decisions on big contracts had a tremendous effect on Aerospace Consultants—Aerocon, as Rodriquez called it. If Boeing had won the design competition for the Air Force transport, there would be lots of work for Aerospace Consultants, because so much new ground would have to be plowed. Lockheed's winning meant that Aerocon probably wouldn't get much play, because the new aircraft would be based on the well-proven C-141.

Rodriquez said, "Maybe there is a bright spot. Aerocon is already making C-141 simulators for the Air Force. It won't take us much effort to update the basic design so that they can serve as C-5 simulators, too. And if Boeing brought out an airliner as big as the C-5, it would certainly need new simulators, too."

Vance asked him, "How are you coming on the idea of establishing our own simulator facility and renting it out to the smaller airlines?"

"We'll have one in Colorado Springs by the first of the year. We will have to run it twenty-four hours a day to accommodate the demand. The little outfits have been making do with stationary simulators, not much better than the old Link trainers. They are chomping at the bit to get at our simulators."

Vance watched Tom, saw the customary mixture of anger and distaste in his face. He'd managed to get along with Bob for a while, but the success of the simulator company seemed to infuriate Tom. It didn't make any sense, but there it was. Time to change the subject.

"Tom, how is the McDonnell F-4 working out for the Air Force?"

Tom turned to him, the relief obvious in his expression. "Man, you would think they had invented the airplane all over again. They are really bringing it into the inventory fast. They already have squadrons over in Vietnam, with more on the way. It's amazing, given that they were refusing to even look at the airplane when it came out. Of course, McDonnell is a wonderful outfit, they have the best tech reps in the world, and they are over in Thailand and Vietnam, working to make these airplanes airworthy one hundred percent of the time."

"What is its safety record? Seems like a lot of airplane for anybody to handle."

Tom nodded his head slowly. This was a good opening. "I can give you the firsthand scoop on that. Harry, you remember that young cadet, Steve O'Malley, that we met at the Air Force Academy?"

"Yeah, your fan, he called himself. What about him?"

"He promised to stay in touch, and he has, with a vengeance, calls me every two weeks. He graduated from flying school last year, and went through the fighter training school at Nellis. They kept him as an instructor, which means he must have been a pretty good pilot. Anyway, he tells me that they are losing a few of them. The F-4 suffers from adverse yaw—in hard turns, you cannot roll it with ailerons; you have to center the stick and boot it around with the rudder. If you don't watch your airspeed in a turn, the aircraft will depart, go into a wild stall, and maybe you'll lose ten or fifteen thousand feet before you recover. And some of the guys have not recovered."

Vance grunted, "Hell, all airplanes will do the old stall spin! They've been doing it since Orville and Wilbur."

"Not like this, Dad. It's not a simple stall; the damn thing goes wildly out of control, gyrating around the sky, even bangs you around the cockpit. And it is inhibiting in combat—if the battle slows down, the adverse yaw gets worse. It's tough. But they have Jerry Gentry down at Edwards doing spin tests on the airplane, and he says you have to work it hard to get into a spin-stall situation. Gentry says that if you keep the airplane trimmed out and maintain your airspeed, it won't happen. But too many young pilots let their airspeed go, the airplane departs, and they fight it all the way down trying to recover. Then they wind up too low to eject. It only takes a few seconds to get from stall to smash."

There was a general silence and Tom surveyed the room. This was as good a time as any. "There are some other problems surfacing as well—the engines smoke, so the MiGs can see them miles away, and the climate is hell on the electronics, turns the damn potting to mush. But I'll be in a better position to tell you all about this in a few months. I'm going to get a reserve assignment as an F-4 pilot, then apply to be brought to active duty. With any luck, I'll probably be in Vietnam before Christmas."

Tom's combat record and his status as an ace gave him plenty of clout, and the Shannon name gave him access to the top four-stars. Few other people could have worked their reentry on to active duty as he had.

There was a dead silence before Vance asked, "And what does Nancy say about this?"

"She understands, Dad, and I hope you do, too."

Vance was furious. "Dammit, Tom, you are leaving her and V.R. in the lurch, and us, too! Who the hell is going to take your place here? And what the hell are you going to do over there? You are forty-seven years old! You'll be flying with kids half your age. When are you leaving?"

"You'll find someone to take my place easily enough, Dad. This is something I have to do. Nancy understands, and I think you will, too, as soon as you think about it. You know me; you know how I feel about flying in combat. I won't be leaving right away and I'll have to go through a complete F-4C checkout. Maybe I won't cut the mustard anymore."

Despite his anger, Vance did understand, and so did Harry and Bob. They recognized the phenomenon, a compulsion for combat. There was something about air combat that insinuated itself into some people's psyches and made them yearn for it as an addict yearned for a fix. There were other elements, of course—patriotism, the fear of getting older, and more. But the main thing was the need to be in combat, to put your life on the line against an enemy of unknown capability and prevail. Bob was a veteran combat pilot, too, he'd shot down twelve MiGs in Korea, and that was enough for him; he never wanted to go back to the Air Force or back in combat. But he understood Tom's need.

Vance was relentless. "Tom, believe me, I understand only too well why you want to go. What I don't understand is why you don't have the brains and the discipline to control your desires. It is irresponsible. I wish you had talked to me about this."

Tom stood up and put his arms around his father, kissed him on the forehead. "And if I had done that, you would have talked me out of going. You still run this family and this company with an iron hand, Dad, even though you keep it pretty well gloved. I didn't tell you because I was determined to go—but knew you could talk me out of it."

Vance shook his head and turned to Harry and Bob. "I guess you both knew about this, and just kept me in the dark."

Tom broke in, "No, Dad, neither one knew, unless Nancy told them, and I'm sure she wouldn't do that. I had to keep it quiet until I went through the physical and got all the paperwork cleared up. If things hadn't worked out, I wouldn't have said anything, wouldn't have let you know that I'm still such a half-wit."

"Well, Tom, you've done well in two other wars. You'll do well in this one. Just don't get the ace syndrome going. You don't have to shoot down any more airplanes; you just have to bring yourself home."

CHAPTER THIRTY-NINE

July 5, 1965
Palos Verdes, California

Tom's bombshell had taken a lot out of Vance. Jill was happy when he decided to get up late and spend the morning at the umbrella-shaded table that had been a fixture on their rear porch for years. He had boxes of paperwork with him, a calculator, and he'd worked steadily all morning. Finally at eleven o'clock he had called to her, "I'm going in to have lunch with Lou Capestro. Come out here for a second, honey."

When she sat down he pushed a sheet of paper to her. It showed that his interest in the Volkswagen dealership had grown to more than three-quarters of a million dollars.

"Volkswagen is doing just what Fritz Obermyer said it was going to do. It's taking off. They sold more than three hundred thousand cars in the United States last year, and we sure sold our share."

"Wow, I had no idea you had this kind of money!"

"It's *our* money, Jill. And I'm thinking about selling out, and just using it for us to indulge ourselves, you know, do some first-class traveling."

"Who are you trying to kid? The last thing in the world you want to do is travel. I've slipped a dozen brochures in your mail over the years, and the first thing you do is toss them in the garbage can. And I don't want to go if you don't want to go. What fun would that be?"

"Well, you be thinking of some way you want to spend the money, and I don't mean just buying stuff for the kids. I want you to figure out how you want to spend it. That's the only way I'll get any fun out of it."

She laughed again. "Let me tell you what you are really thinking about. You're thinking about setting up a trust fund for V.R."

He looked at her in disbelief.

"How the hell could you know that? I've never said a word about it."

"We've been together a long time now. You don't have to spell things out for me to know what's going on in your mind. You were talking about him going to college the other day."

She kissed Vance and said, "Let me put another thought there, something you would think about eventually."

He waited, thinking how lucky he had been the third time around. Margaret, his first wife, had been a wonderful mother. Madeline, his lover, had seemed wonderful—until she left him holding the baggage of her espionage. But Jill was just a gem, able to do so many things, understanding him so well, handling the touchy situation with Tom and Bob. He was lucky to have her.

"Mae is pregnant. I think it would be a nice gesture to include her children in any trust arrangement. Lord knows there's enough money to go around for a half-dozen kids."

"She's pregnant, eh? That rascal Bob, he's a fast worker. How do you think that would go down with Tom?"

"Not too well, but what will we care? We'll both be pushing up daisies before it comes into effect. We'll just keep it quiet, between us, and they can sort it out in a fight at the funeral."

"Let me think about it. I like the idea, but there are some ramifications. Harry doesn't have any kids, and it sort of leaves him out."

"Honey, the money from the dealership is only a part of your assets. You'll have plenty for Harry and Tom, and they are well-fixed on their own, thanks to you."

She walked with her arm around him down to the garage, where a cream-colored 1937 Cord Beverly was parked next to her Cadillac. Vance had acquired it in one of the rare moments when he decided he was going to work less. He'd gone through a long ritual of reading the automobile books, talking to traders, and finally located it in Illinois, stored not in the traditional barn, but on the third floor of an abandoned factory outside of Chicago. The cost of getting it out of the building and transported to Palos Verdes was almost as much as the price of the car. It was rolled off the truck, into Vance's garage, and had sat there ever since. It was beat-up but somehow still beautiful, with its windshield cracked on the passenger side and one of the retractable headlights popped up in a perpetual leer.

"Are you ever going to get this thing fixed up?"

"First thing I'm going to do when I finally retire."

"I'm not holding my breath."

THE LUNCHEON WITH Lou Capestro was more than disappointing; it was frightening.

"I hate to tell you this, Vance, but I'm thinking about selling, too. I know you've been having trouble with your ticker, but I think my problem is even worse. It's colon cancer. I'm lined up for an exploratory operation in two weeks. It doesn't look good."

"My God, Lou, I'm sorry to hear this. I know you'll beat it, but I'm sorry you have to go through it."

"Well it's part of life. I haven't told anyone except you, not even my wife. There will be time enough for them to know when I get ready to go to the hospital. No sense in worrying them any longer than I have to."

They sat quietly together, two old friends who had been through the wars. Lou relentlessly played with the cutlery, drumming a knife against his glass so loudly that he was getting stares from a couple at the next table.

Lou finally spoke. "Why don't we call Obermyer and see if he'll buy us out? He's doing very well in Los Angeles, and he's always been fair to us."

"Yes; I don't want to go through the agony of selling it on the open market. If Fritz would take it over, I'd be willing to make some price concessions to him to do it."

"Me, too. Somehow money just doesn't seem too important nowadays."

Alberto, their waiter for many years, brought them their usual coffee and the special grappa that he kept for old customers. Vance knew for sure that Lou was not well when he pushed both of them away, untasted.

CHAPTER FORTY

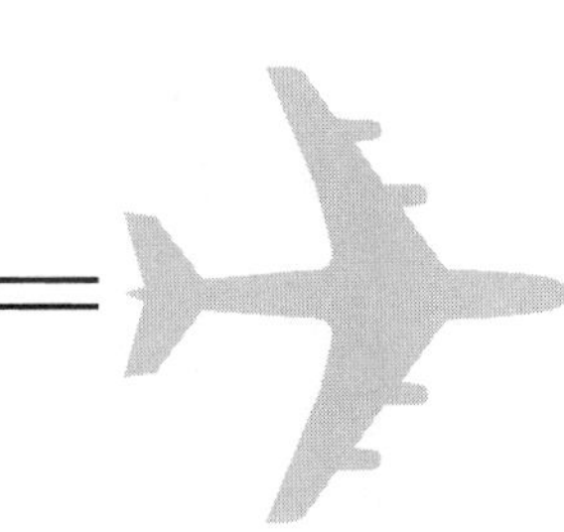

September 7, 1965
Moscow, USSR

Andrei Tupolev was seventy-seven and felt every one of his years. He stared with pride across the room at his son Alexei, now just forty years old and coming into his own despite the snide claims of nepotism made by jealous rivals. "Czarevitch," indeed! Alexei had long since earned his position within the bureau by dint of hard work.

The two men had been at their desks since early morning, scarcely exchanging a word. Alexei was in the midst of a mammoth reprogramming effort, so deeply absorbed that he did not even look up when his father made one of his now too-frequent trips to the bathroom.

The elder Tupolev knew full well that his son did not have that rare spark of flaming genius that would lead him to a brilliant design, a spark that Andrei had possessed in such abundance for most of his life. But Alexei had something more important now, in this age when huge, sophisticated aircraft required teams of designers. He had the ability to integrate a mass of often-conflicting information and plan huge production efforts that involved the aerodynamicists, engine people, the materials group, everyone, in a sophisticated, closely scheduled program. This was a gift that few people possessed, chief among them Andrei himself.

In the eleven months since Khrushchev had been deposed, Tupolev had hoped that there would be some relaxation in the insane schedule that had been ordered for the SST—to fly in 1968 but, above all, to fly before any Western SST flew. Instead, the flighty Nikita had been superseded by a pure technocrat, Leonid Brezhnev, who made a quasi-religion out of the Marxist-Leninist reverence for science and technology.

Brezhnev saw the SST as a personal fiefdom to gather prestige for the Soviet Union and for himself. Worse, he saw it as one of his own toys, no different from his growing fleet of exotic foreign automobiles. Far from relaxing the schedule, he let Tupolev know in no uncertain terms that the future of his bureau depended upon a successful flight in 1968.

Andrei Tupolev had still not recovered from the embarrassment at the Paris Air Show, which had gotten off to a bad start when an Italian Fiat G.91 fighter crashed into a crowded parking lot. One of the many models of the SST was flown in for exhibit, and its sleek shape both stunned and amused the foreign press, which immediately dubbed it the "Concordski" for its resemblance to the Anglo-French transport.

There was a good reason for the external similarity. Industrial espionage agents in France had given Andrei a three-year head start by stealing plans and data on the French research. He disliked the fact that the stolen design drove him to adopt the delta wing, something he had always avoided in the past.

Despite the undeniable external similarities, internally it was a different matter. Western avionics and engineering were far in advance of anything he could command, and so he settled, as usual, for what worked best and was achievable. Soviet designers as a group always tried to keep designs simple, so they could be manufactured, strong, so that they could operate off Russia's rough fields, and most of all workable, so that the designers didn't go to jail.

The most visible difference between the two SSTs was in the air intakes for the engines. The Concorde design had sophisticated sliding ramps that automatically moved forward and backward to smooth out the airflow to its engines. The Tu-144 used an old-fashioned idea, very long inlet ducts, which were heavier and far less efficient than the movable ramps.

Internally, the differences were far greater. The Concorde used its fuel tanks as heat sinks, to absorb some of the heat generated by high speeds. At Mach 2.0, the temperature at the leading edge could rise to more than eight hundred degrees Fahrenheit. The Tu-144 was forced to resort to old-fashioned cooling systems, heavy, noisy, and space consuming.

The most annoying thing about Paris was the press, which constantly pressured him for information and commentary. He kept up a brave front, maintaining the party line that the Tupolev Tu-144 would go into airline service soon, on international routes.

It was hogwash, of course, for unless Alexei came up with some sort of a miracle there was no way that the Tu-144 could fly before 1970—and even then only with a good deal of luck. The British and the French were playing their cards close to their chest, but casual, well-hedged predictions were made that the first Concorde might fly sometime in 1969. Well, good luck to them!

He glanced at the clock. It was almost two and he was hungry. "Alexei?"

Too deeply absorbed to hear, his son seemed to thrash about with papers, moving them from the center of his desk to a table at the side and from there to the floor. He called again, "Alexei, I am hungry; would you like to get something to eat?"

Alexei looked up, smiling. "In a moment. Just give me a moment more, and I'll show you something that will give you an appetite!"

Andrei Tupolev looked at the large clock on the wall, thinking, *If he is not ready in twenty minutes, I'm going without him.*

"Look at this." Alexei put a series of papers before him, charting the flow of components to the factory for assembly. They came from all over the Soviet Union and were as tightly scheduled as a space shot.

"You want to fly in 1968? I'll show you how if you will take the risks involved."

"What risks? The whole program is a risk; life is a risk."

"Yes, but this is the worst kind of risk, engine risk! If you will agree to accept the Kutznetsov KN-144 turbofans right now, and agree that we will not change, no matter what, we just might be able to fly in late December 1968. But it means that we will be able to cruise at Mach 2.0 only in afterburner—and you know what that means for fuel consumption and for range."

Andrei sat, crestfallen. Damn this airplane, with its damnable delta wing and with its primitive engines. It should be a work of art, not something rushed through production like an army boot! There was no need for an SST in the Soviet Union, no need for one anywhere, if you got down to it. Ah, if he had five years to work on it, he could deliver an airplane with the range, the speed, and the safety. Especially the safety—they were exploring a whole new world, and they had no data to rely on.

But he didn't have five years to work on it—he had a little over three, and there was no one who could say that he would even live that long.

"What else? Surely there are other risks."

"Well, you know the story on the tires. The French put one over on us, and that cost us four months of tire development. The fact is, we won't have the right kind of tires, but we'll be able to fly the airplane with what we have, even if we have to replace them all after every flight. The main thing is we can fly in December of 1968 if we commit to doing so now. And that means you'll have to give up some of your prerogatives on changes. Once we are committed, you just have to accept what comes along. There will be surprises, but we'll deal with those. Now tell me, shall we go ahead with this?"

Andrei was hungry and tired. There was very little choice. If they did not fly in 1968, Brezhnev would close down the bureau and everything would be lost, the dacha, the cars, good universities for the grandchildren, everything Andrei had worked so hard for. Alexei would be sent to work in some rival's design bureau if he was lucky, to some gulag if he was not. As for Andrei, it wouldn't matter. He could not survive the failure; he might not even survive the success.

He closed his eyes. How could this be finessed? Perhaps they could fly it in 1968—no one said it had to be a supersonic flight. No one had even said the gear must be retracted. Perhaps they could get it into the air for one trip around the pattern—that would be enough. Then they could stall and maybe get new engines for the next prototype. It was a fraud and a sham, of course, but so was the entire Soviet Union. The Tu-144 would simply be the fastest fraud, the biggest sham.

He opened his eyes.

"Agreed. We will proceed with the Kutznetsov engines, despite their unreliability and their thirst for fuel. No one is going to expect us to fly four thousand miles for the first few years. You really think we can make this schedule?"

"I think perhaps—and I think it's the only way."

Andrei's stomach rumbled.

"Let's go get something to eat. When we come back, we'll put a message together for Brezhnev, telling him what we are doing, asking for his approval. If he approves, and things go wrong, it will be a life preserver for us."

"It will if he's still in power."

They walked out arm in arm, Alexei profoundly happy with the decision, Andrei profoundly worried by it.

CHAPTER FORTY-ONE

December 17, 1965
New York, New York

Jill had insisted on making reservations for them at the Waldorf Astoria.

"If I leave it up to your penny-pinching ways, we'd be in some run-down hotel like the Windsor in Seattle! You are seventy-one years old, you have a lot of money, and you ought to spend it on yourself."

"You didn't have to get a suite, did you? And Harry didn't need a separate room; he could have bunked in here."

Harry laughed. Nothing would ever change Vance, who still watched every nickel spent on himself but was generous with everyone else in the family or the firm.

Vance waved Harry into the sitting room, where he had two tablets put out on the table.

"Harry, this is going to be one of the toughest meetings we'll ever have. We have to go in and tell two of the most powerful men in the industry things they don't want to hear. I'm not worried about Bill Allen, but I don't know Juan Trippe very well, and I understand that he can be pretty willful."

Harry nodded. "Are you sure you want to do this, Dad? You are going to be offending virtually everybody—Boeing, Pan Am, even Pratt & Whitney. From all I hear, both Allen and Trippe have made up their minds to build a big transport, and I don't think there's anything we can tell them that will stop them."

"You're right, there's not, but Aerospace Consultants—I mean

Aerospace Ventures—has made a reputation, and a pretty good living, on calling things as we see them, and that's what we're going to do."

He put his hands together in a characteristic gesture and said, "We're dealing with a lot of emotions here. Boeing is ticked off because Lockheed won the C-5 contract, and Bill Allen wants to recoup some of that engineering investment in an airliner. Trippe is angry because the SST program is getting killed off, and he wants a new airplane to take its place. But he's insisting that the SSTs will come in, and then the big airliner will have to be converted to be a cargo carrier. So he's compromising the design right from the start."

Vance and Harry talked earnestly for the next forty minutes, each making occasional notes before leaving his tablet on the table and departing for their meeting in the glittering Pan Am building. They were pleasantly surprised to find Harold Gray, Pan Am's president, waiting for them on the steps.

"Good to see you, Vance! I remember the day you checked me out in a Sikorsky S-42."

Genuinely touched that Gray had come all the way down to meet them, Vance turned to Harry and said, "This is Harold Gray, the finest pilot Pan Am ever produced! And he's one hell of a businessman, too."

Harry stood by as the two men went through the usual litany of inquiries about mutual friends. Once seated in his office, however, Gray turned serious.

"Listen, Vance, I have to know. What are you going to tell Mr. Trippe about the new airplane?"

"Well, it's not all good—I have concerns about the engine, about its freight-hauling capability, about its weight estimate. I'm going to piss both of them off, I guess, but I have to do it."

"Well, I hope to God you can talk them out of it. If we go through with this deal the way they are talking about structuring it, it will be a miracle if either company survives. It's just too damn risky, especially with the war in Vietnam escalating all the time. We don't need an airplane this big yet."

"I don't have anything against its size, although it will be a problem for the airlines to handle at the terminals, but I am concerned about a number of things. But Harry here tells me there's little or no chance of changing their minds. Half the staff back at Boeing are terrified of what might happen if there's a problem in production. They don't even have a factory to build it, you know."

Gray glanced at the clock and said, "We can go in now."

The office was quietly elegant without being extravagant, with recessed lighting and lots of leather chairs. Paintings, photos, and models of Pan American airliners were everywhere, starting with the early Fairchild and Fokkers and continuing on through the glorious days of the flying boats, down to the latest jets. Vance noted a model of a generic SST had pride of place next to Trippe's desk.

Vance had first met the man who had made Pan American a household name in 1929. Charles Lindbergh was serving as Pan Am's technical adviser and had asked Shannon to come out to evaluate competing aircraft for the mail route that was planned for the Caribbean. Vance had ultimately recommended the Sikorsky S-40 for the route. Trippe had seemed somewhat remote, reserved even, in Lindbergh's company. Vance had come away with the impression that Trippe was a visionary autocrat, who listened only to what he wanted to hear. In later years Vance heard that Trippe was obsessively secretive, that he ruled the company with an iron hand and frugal paychecks. Vance wondered if anything had changed.

Both Trippe and Allen stood when the two Shannons came in, a gracious touch that pleased Harry for his father's sake. Gray made the introductions and, to Vance's surprise, excused himself, pleading a crisis in the accounting department.

Trippe seized the initiative with a briefing that would have been worthy of Boeing's legendary salesman, Wellwood Beall. "This new aircraft—Boeing's going to call it the 747—will revolutionize air travel. Every projection that you see tells you that air travel is going to double or triple in the next ten years. Pan Am is going to lead this revolution, and to lead it, we need a big aircraft."

Trippe had an easel on which drawings and charts were displayed, and he went through them one by one. The aircraft was to be huge, grossing 550,000 pounds and carrying up to four hundred passengers for over five thousand miles at Mach .9. He went on and on, stressing the effect the big jet's capacity would have on airline fares.

"I expect this airplane to have a seat-mile cost thirty percent below every other competitor, even other Boeings. That means we'll see airline fares dropping to the point that everyone will be traveling, not just U.S.

businessmen, but everybody. We'll see airports filled with people from all nations, able to travel for the first time because fares will be so low. This airplane may do more for peace than anything else in history."

Bill Allen was always quiet when a customer was talking, but he nodded vigorously at the right times. It was clear that the two men shared a vision.

Trippe pulled out drawings. "Vance, you remember how popular the lounge was on the 377?"

Vance remembered it well, as did Allen; it was virtually the only memorable element of the Boeing Stratocruiser, an airliner that had failed to compete with the Connies and DC-6s.

"We're going to take that idea and expand on it."

The next drawing showed the upper deck of the 747 converted to a lounge, complete with martini-drinking passengers and laughing stewardesses.

"And look at this—trans-Atlantic travel in full comfort."

Trippe showed the upper deck again, this time configured with first-class seats that all converted into beds.

Always a showman, Trippe concluded with the blockbuster—each new aircraft would cost between 15 and 18 million dollars, with Allen chiming in, "And worth every cent of it."

Trippe moved toward his chair, saying, "Vance, we appreciate you and Harry coming east to be with us. But we know you have some reservations, and we want you to tell us exactly what they are."

Vance nodded and stood up, moving to the easel.

"Thank you, Mr. Trippe. I'd like to say you made a believer out of me, but I do have reservations. First, I'm worried about the drag that's being built in because of the future cargo requirement. If you could accept a smaller fuselage diameter, I'm sure the cost of the airplane and, more important, the cost of flying it would go down dramatically. But I know your views on this. Personally I think it would be cheaper to develop a dedicated cargo version later, rather than compromise the design of the passenger plane. I've got some figures on this that I'll leave with you."

He hesitated for a moment and went on. "Second, I think you are way off on your weight estimations. I've never seen an airplane that didn't grow from the drawing board to the rollout, and the bigger they are, the more they grow. I hope you are right, but gut instinct tells me that you are off by about twenty percent in the empty weight. When it rolls out it will be closer to six hundred thousand pounds than five hundred thousand."

Trippe looked sharply at Allen, who winced and shrugged his shoulders.

"It's the same with seats. You are talking four hundred seats now, but that will grow twenty percent, too, maybe more. And of course, unlike the weight, that will be a net plus when the aircraft is flying."

Vance looked at a drawing of the 747 on the easel, seeming to study it intensely. Then, with genuine diffidence, he said, "Pratt & Whitney has been a client of our firm for many years. Harry cut his business teeth on the J57. But I have to tell you that I'm worried about the development of the JT9D engine."

Allen interrupted him. "Juan, Vance Shannon has been in on jet engines from the very start. He worked hand in hand with Frank Whittle, and later with Hans von Ohain. I don't think there's anyone in the world that has a better feel for jet engines than Vance."

Trippe's brow furrowed. It was clear that he didn't think he would like what he was about to hear.

Vance went on, "And you are sizing the engine for a five-hundred-thousand pound airplane. When it grows—and believe me it will grow—the engines won't have the power you need. But that's the least of it. That's a known factor. What worries me is the unknown unknowns, the inevitable problems that develop with any new engine, but particularly one as powerful as this one."

He looked around, his expression pleading for a little more time, a little understanding. "The Pratt & Whitney JT9D is a magnificent advance, but it hasn't been tested enough to be used as a commercial airline engine yet. They are getting up to about forty-three thousand pounds of thrust out of an engine that weighs only eighty-six hundred pounds, dry, and that is fantastic. But it is also an extraordinary stress on the materials, and most of all on the design. I think you run the risk of having engine problems surface just about the time you are supposed to deliver aircraft to the airlines. If that happens, everybody loses—Boeing, Pan Am, Pratt, everybody."

Trippe had half-risen out of his chair, positioning himself like a linebacker ready to sack a quarterback. "There is always a risk involved in a new airliner, Mr. Shannon; you know that better than anyone."

"You are exactly right. But the risk isn't always one that threatens to bankrupt three companies at the same time. And there is another issue."

"What's that?"

"Oil prices. An airplane equipped with engines like the JT9D can be a bargain at current oil prices, but what happens if there is a sudden surge in prices? What if there's a big war in the Middle East and our sources dry up? Oil prices could triple—and that would more than wipe out all the savings of carrying more passengers."

Allen said, "Vance, can you point to a specific problem with the JT9D that you are concerned about?"

"No, I can't. The kind of problem I'm afraid of won't appear for two or three years after you produce your first 747. The problem won't show up until there are a lot of engines with a lot of time on them. When it comes, it will be a serious one, and you'll be faced with grounding the fleet, and keeping eighteen-million-dollar airplanes on the ground, and not flying is incredibly expensive."

Vance suddenly understood why Gray had left. With his accounting acuity, he probably foresaw the downside of the big airplane much more clearly than Trippe or even Allen could. Fuel prices were artificially low now. Some people were already predicting a big increase in oil prices—you could see it in the futures market.

Trippe had drawn up within himself like a coiled spring. Harry watched him closely, expecting him to explode. Instead, he thanked Vance very courteously, saying, "Well then, Mr. Shannon, what is your advice?"

"I think you should delay a minimum of two years to get more information on the engine. Conduct a really aggressive test program, flying the engine on a fleet of smaller aircraft, and putting on as many thousands of hours as you can. I believe that would greatly reduce your risk. I guess what I'm saying is that the expected value of delaying two years is far greater than the expected value of rushing the program."

Trippe simply nodded, excused himself from Allen, and walked them all the way out to the elevator. There he said, "Mr. Shannon, I remember you from years ago. You were a straight shooter then and you are now. I'll consider what you've said, but I'll tell you both right here—we are going ahead with the 747."

With that the elevator arrived, Trippe gave them a little bow, and the door closed.

"Dad, you were terrific. That was the plainest talk he's had in years, I'll bet."

"I hated to put Bill Allen on the spot. A delay might get Lockheed into the big airliner competition, when they get further along on the C-5 program."

"Well, I noticed he didn't interrupt you. He knew you were right."

"We did what we said we'd do, tell them what we think. It didn't change a thing. I just hope that they have some luck, and that the airplane pans out. With a little luck it could be a winner. And Boeing's always been lucky."

The two men were silent all the way back to their suite at the Waldorf, reflecting on the meeting, on its possible adverse effect on their firm.

On the way up in the elevator, Vance said, "Harry, can you pick a great restaurant for lunch, and another one for dinner? I want Jill to have some fun on this trip."

When they walked in, Jill was standing by the telephone, her face ashen, tears running down her face.

"Honey, what's the matter?"

"You won't believe this. You had two telephone calls while you were out. One was from Fritz Obermyer. He's agreed to buy the dealership at the price you negotiated the last time you met. The other was from Lou Capestro's lawyer. Lou died today during an emergency operation. I'm so sorry to tell you this, Vance."

Vance slumped in a chair. Lou Capestro gone. Impossible.

Harry asked, "Did they say anything about how Anna was taking this? I've got to call her."

CHAPTER FORTY-TWO

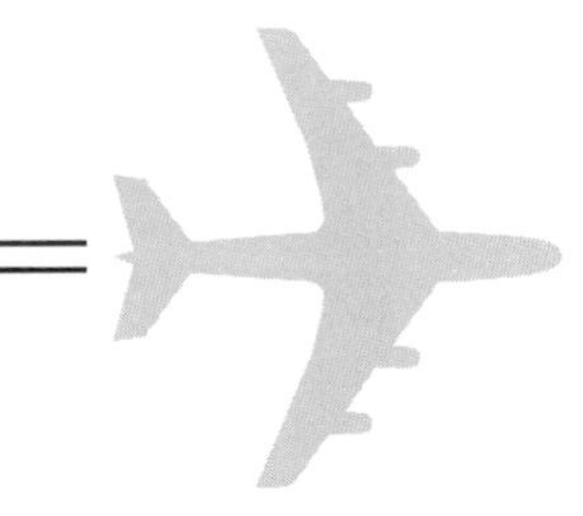

January 27, 1966
Palos Verdes, California

Jill glanced for the twentieth time that hour into the library, trying to see how Vance was getting along. The past month had been impossible. There had been Lou Capestro's death and the huge, almost gaudy funeral. This was followed by a vicious fight with Obermyer over the purchase of the Volkswagen dealership. The price had already been agreed upon, but Obermyer was now contesting the value of the inventory, claiming that it was actually worth several hundred thousand dollars less than Capestro and Shannon had indicated. The draining combination of events, one after the other, was climaxed by the utter deterioration of Anna's health.

Anna reacted to her father's death with an overwhelming grief, blaming herself for having caused him so much pain by her drinking. Then she assuaged her guilt by going on a bender of monstrous proportions. She had left the house one evening, ostensibly to go the drugstore for a prescription, and disappeared for four days. She was finally found dead drunk in a filling station south of San Diego, where a sensible attendant had seen her condition, taken her keys, and called the police. The long-suffering Harry had brought her home, but their physician, Dr. Parry, had sent her to the hospital after a quick examination. Harry spent all his time with her, trying to will her back to health.

Then two days ago, the third Lockheed SR-71 Blackbird broke up in mid-air, with Bill Weaver, the pilot, escaping via the ejection seat. Sadly, the backseater, Jim Zwayer, was killed in the accident. Jill knew how down Vance was when he discussed it with her—normally he would never have mentioned the existence of a super-secret aircraft like the SR-71, much less a crash, but Zwayer had been a friend for years, and he was disconsolate. Typically he blamed himself—the right engine had flamed out when one of his own principal spheres of responsibility, the bypass doors, had malfunctioned.

Vance was a difficult man to comfort. When he was down like this, he wanted to be alone, was indifferent to food, didn't touch a drop of alcohol, but was on the telephone constantly, talking to everyone who might have some insight into the accident. Only Anna's health and the ongoing argument with Obermyer kept him at home, away from the crash site.

And now Obermyer was at the door, pleading to see him, promising that he was there not to argue but to agree to the original deal.

She entered the room so quietly that he was startled when she said, "Vance, Fritz Obermyer is here to see you."

"Dammit, Jill, don't go pussyfooting around like that. If you want to come in, make some noise, bump up against the door, do something, but don't scare me out of what's left of my wits."

He smiled gently and put his arms up to her. She embraced him, asking, "Should I send him in? He says he's ready to come to an agreement."

"Sure, why not? The way things have been going, there's nothing he can say that will make me feel worse."

Obermyer oozed into the room. Prosperity had turned him into a Peter Grosz caricature of the prosperous German businessman, all paunch and white whiskers, elegantly dressed, and wearing glasses that looked as if two monocles had been joined by a slim silver nosepiece.

"Vance, I'm so sorry to bother you. I know it has been a terrible few weeks for you. It has for me, too. I really admired Lou, and I hoped he considered me his friend."

"Fritz, of course Lou liked you; he wouldn't have done business with you if he did not. It has been a good, mutually profitable relationship, and Lou was always talking about how accurately you had predicted the growth in Volkswagen sales. He considered you a friend. As do I."

An almost imperceptible tear glistened in Obermyer's eyes. He was not used to talking or thinking in these terms. Life had always been difficult. In the old country, when he was not struggling to survive he was making others struggle to survive. It had been so different in America. Things had gone beautifully, he had become wealthy, and he was proud of his friendship with men such as Capestro and Shannon.

"About the inventory. I know you think I was being greedy, but I've had another look at it, and I know I'm right. But let's forget it. I'm ready to sign today, just as we agreed, and I'll have the accountants write off the inventory loss as goodwill, or whatever they choose."

"That's good of you, Fritz. I don't agree with your assessment, but I'm glad you are willing to settle. Why don't we have another meeting later this afternoon, here, if you don't mind? We can have the lawyers come in, look things over, and then sign the papers."

"Fine, Vance, thank you so much. And I have another favor to ask. When you are up to it, I need to talk to you about some other things, nothing to do with the car business. Just some things from the past."

Shannon's ears perked up. Obermyer had been an industrial informant in the past, trading secrets around the world for a price. He had a reputation for having solid information early, and Vance knew several U.S. firms that had taken advantage of Obermyer's civil spying. Industrial espionage was always frowned upon but was still always used if it were done in the correct way, that is, without danger to the recipients of the information.

"Sure, Fritz, let's talk about it after the meeting this afternoon."

THE AFTERNOON MEETING had gone very pleasantly. Jill had the foresight to put a few bottles of champagne on ice to celebrate the occasion. The signing took a little over an hour, the time spent mostly in Shannon and Obermyer signing and initialing one set of documents after another. Maury Nunes, Lou Capestro's personal attorney for more than twenty years, was there representing his interests.

Jill was heartened to see Vance take a glass of champagne into the library for his talk with Obermyer. Even if Vance didn't drink it, it was a gesture, a sign that he might be coming out of his depression.

When they were comfortably settled, Vance said, "Go ahead, Fritz. What is it you want to talk about?"

"It is extremely delicate, but I am being pressed by my old contacts in Germany—East Germany to be exact—to furnish them information on the American supersonic transport. I'm not doing this for money, but my old colleague Gerd Müller is being pressured to come up with some data on what Lockheed and Boeing are doing. Since it is a civilian effort, not a military one, I thought you might be in a position to tell me what kind of progress they are making."

"Your friend Müller is working for the Soviet Union, of course? We know that Tupolev and maybe some others are working on an SST."

"Yes, Tupolev is supposed to have an SST flying in 1968—before the British and French fly."

"Let me think about this, Fritz. I consult for both Lockheed and Boeing and I'm not going to tell you anything that is of proprietary interest. But I do think I can tell you something that isn't general knowledge, and that you can say is insider information. Will that help?"

"Yes, sure, but not just something from *Aviation Week.* They research all the magazines. I have to give him something that will be new to them."

Vance put his finger to his lips, closed his eyes, and thought. He wanted to help Fritz but wouldn't compromise himself.

"What if I tell you something that the Russians won't want to hear?"

"If it looks like an American secret, I don't care. It will be up to Gerd to determine whether or not to use it."

"All right, let me write it down for you."

Vance moved over to his old portable, rolled a paper in, and began typing:

1. Lockheed or Boeing believes that a Mach 2.0 to Mach 2.5 transport is not worth building. They are shooting for Mach 3.0 and beyond. This means titanium airframes for the most part. Titanium is very difficult to work.
2. There is no way to recover the research and development cost of any supersonic transport because the production runs will be so low.

He stopped and asked Obermyer, "How many people need to go between, say, Moscow and Vladivostok every day?"

Obermyer frowned and said, "Well, I would think perhaps two hundred? Every day? Well, maybe not so many, perhaps one hundred."

Vance resumed typing:

3. If, for example, the Russian SST will be used on the Moscow/Vladivostok route, one SST could cover the route, assuming that it carried one hundred passengers and made two flights a day. A close analysis would have to be made of the total Soviet passenger requirement versus the production run, but most probably no more than twenty SSTs would ever be needed.
4. The research and development costs for any SST will be in the billions-of-dollars range. The operating costs will depend primarily on the cost per seat-mile, and that in turn will depend upon fuel costs.
5. There is no way to make the SST financially viable. It will be lucky if it can earn its operating costs. It will never recover its research and development costs—but these may have unexpected value in other programs.
6. It comes down to a question of prestige.

He pulled the sheet out of the typewriter and handed it to Obermyer.

"Will this do?"

Obermyer read through it hurriedly, glanced up at Vance, smiled, and then read it slowly.

"This will do it. And I'll tell you something, Vance; this is the last sort of work like this that I will ever do. I came to the United States with very little money, and today I am a wealthy man. I don't need to risk everything on something stupid like this."

He shook Vance's hand and left. Somewhat buoyed by the experience, Vance went in and told Jill about it.

"Vance, what were you thinking of? You shouldn't have given him anything, not even if it's not secret at all."

"Why not? He could have gotten this from *Popular Science*."

"Yes, he could. But he is not Madeline's former lover and you are. You almost lost everything once, when she was stealing your secrets. You just concluded a deal worth almost a million dollars with him, and he waltzes out with your best thoughts on the supersonic transport. What do you think George Schairer would say about this?"

Vance slumped down in a chair.

"My God, what have I done? How could I have been so stupid? I must be senile!"

He looked up at her, whispering, "You better get me my heart medicine; I think there is something going on in my chest."

CHAPTER FORTY-THREE

January 29, 1966
Palos Verdes, California

Vance's longtime friend and physician, Bill Parry, had rushed to his house two days earlier, examined Vance thoroughly on the spot, then had an ambulance take him to the hospital for further tests. Everything checked out, and now he was back in his robe and slippers, talking to Harry, Tom, and Bob.

"Doc Parry said it was not a heart attack at all, but something he called a panic attack. And I can tell you, I had just been so stupid that I was entitled to have one."

He went on to tell them of his conversation with Fritz Obermyer.

"I cannot believe I did what I did. It took Jill two seconds to see how stupid I was. I'm just telling you now so that you won't be surprised if something comes of this."

Tom said, "It doesn't seem to me that anything can come of it, Dad, if Obermyer keeps his mouth shut. Do you think he'll blab?"

"I don't think so, but then you never know. What about his contacts? I was up visiting Obermyer once in Los Angeles, in the early days of the dealership, and he insisted on taking me to a crummy German restaurant. I met some friend of his there, some palooka named Miller or Müller or something. He and Obermyer were friends all the way from World War I, and I could see they had some kind of deal going on."

Harry looked agitated, and it worried Vance. "What's the matter, Son?"

"I don't like it, Dad. I think maybe you are a little vulnerable here. Do we have any hold on Obermyer?"

"No, he said he was through with this sort of thing. I'm hoping he meant it."

"He probably meant it, but these guys play rough, and they might lean on him to get some more information."

Harry weighed the possibilities. He had never told any of them of his activities with BAC, slipping the Russians the wrong information on tires for the SST. But this was close to the bone. Madeline could easily be involved in this; she had used Obermyer's friend Müller as a contact. If things blew up, Vance would be terribly hurt if he suddenly found out that Harry had concealed his meetings with Madeline.

"Look, guys, I've got something to tell you. You've got to keep it absolutely secret. Dad, this may make you angry, but I don't see how I can do anything else but level with you all now."

"What the hell are you talking about, Harry? You didn't have anything to do with this."

"Not this, but Boeing gave me permission to work with BAC. My job was to pass on some bogus information to the Russians on supersonic transport tires. We made up a fake compound—guaranteed to ruin any tires they made from it—and passed it off to them."

Harry quickly filled them in on the details, telling them how the material had been deliberately compounded to appear genuine but to have inherent flaws that would foul up the manufacturing process. All three were laughing when Harry said, "Dad, you won't think this is funny. My contact with French intelligence, believe it or not, was Madeline. She sent her best wishes to you, but because I couldn't tell you anything about the project, I couldn't tell you about her. And I didn't want to; I didn't want to open old wounds."

There was a complete silence until Vance asked, "How was she? How did she look?"

"I think she was fine, Dad. She looked tired and overworked. She smoked continuously, as she always did, and I think that ages a woman. But she was very effective. I understand that she planted the information on the Russians and the East German in January, and then had one of the Russians and the East German arrested in February."

"She was always very efficient. Do you have a contact for her? Somewhere that I could write her if I wanted to?"

"No, Dad, the whole thing was very sanitized. No one told anyone else their names, much less anything like an address. If I had not recognized her, no one would have ever known." He waited for a moment and then said, "But I'm sure that if you wrote to her at Dassault, the letter would get to her. It might compromise her in some way, but you could . . ."

Vance shrugged. "No, I'd never write her. She was part of my life once, but she's gone. I'm just glad to learn that she is well."

He hesitated and said, "We'll keep this to ourselves? Jill wouldn't be too happy if she thought Madeline might materialize someday."

Bob, as usual, was reticent. He always tried to avoid annoying Tom, whose threshold for irritation was getting lower and lower. It was going to be hard to avoid a fight someday, and given that Tom was almost a foot taller and forty pounds heavier, Bob didn't like the possibility.

"Can I change the subject just a bit? Harry's given me an idea, and I want you to think about it. You know that the Soviet Union is buying up our technology anywhere they can find it? They are buying machine tools, radios, television sets, anything that's not on our restricted list. I'm not kidding you; they are buying IBM 360 computers through every blind they can think of. Believe it or not, they even have tried to buy a RadioShack retail outlet!"

Tom was irritated. His father was facing an emotional crisis, and Rodriquez was running off at the mouth, again. "Another time, Bob. I think we've had all we can take for a day."

Vance was eager to prove he had absorbed the shock and said, "No, go on, Bob. What the hell do they do with the stuff?"

Rodriquez shifted away from Tom, then got caught up in his flow of ideas. "They reverse engineer it, just like they did the B-29, then cull everything they can out of it for military use. They are absolutely crazy about anything that has any kind of computer involved in it, no matter how simple."

Harry was distressed by being forced to reveal having met Madeline but could not repress his amusement at Tom's reaction to Rodriquez, thinking, *He's like a jealous lover. He'd like nothing better than to reach over and smack Bob on the head but knows he can't—at least not in front of Dad.*

"Here's my idea. Why don't we monitor what the Soviet Union is buying, and slip them a Trojan horse, just like Harry did with the tire compound? We could manufacture computers that would have defects in them that wouldn't show up until they were given another application. For example, the Russians could be buying computers and using them for numerically controlled tools. We could have the computer we sell them programmed to begin making small errors after a certain period of time. The Russkies wouldn't figure it out for a long time, because the errors wouldn't show up until the equipment being manufactured wouldn't work properly."

Then, in a major mistake, Bob leaned forward with an exultant grin and asked, "Get it?"

Tom blew up, leaned forward, fist cocked, and Bob dove behind Vance. "Get it? Get it? You think we are morons? Of course we get it." Then, embarrassed, he added, "What I don't get is how you think you could ever get anyone to agree to the idea."

Vance said, "Easy, Tom. It's a hell of an idea, but Tom's right, Bob; how could you ever persuade industry to do this?"

Bob emerged from behind Vance and said, "Let me work on this. I know a guy in Washington, Gus Weiss, and he can do damn near anything. He'll eat this up."

Tom leaned forward and said, "Sorry, Bob; I lost my temper."

He turned to his father, said, "Sorry, Dad; I made a jerk out of myself."

Harry couldn't resist. "Nothing new in that, Tom."

CHAPTER FORTY-FOUR

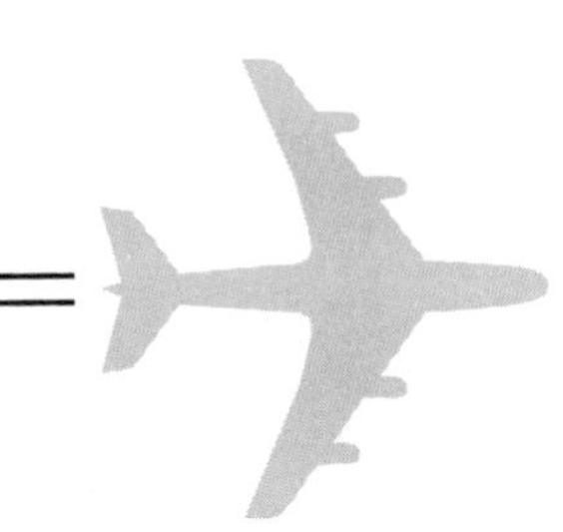

February 14, 1966
San Diego, California

Mae had been in labor for sixteen hours when the nurse came out to see a desperately anxious Bob Rodriquez in the waiting room. Smiling, she said, "It is a beautiful little boy, Mr. Rodriquez, and the mother is doing fine. You can see her in a few minutes."

The nurse gave him the vital statistics and Bob raced to the phone with the good news, getting through to Mae's parents almost immediately but getting no answer at home. Then he called Jill. "Jill, it's a boy, seven pounds, four ounces, and Mae is doing fine. He's got all his fingers and toes, they tell me, and everything else looks fine. It was a tough labor, sixteen hours, but she's fine. I'm going in to see her in a few minutes. I cannot believe how lucky we are to have a boy, first time out of the starter's gate."

"You'd be just as happy with a little girl and you know it."

They talked a little more, and Bob hung up, knowing Jill was wrong. He had wanted a little boy, and that's what Mae gave him. As he walked down the hallway to her room, he thought, *I'd like to call him Vance, but that would be too much for Tom. Maybe I'll call him Tom—no, that's no good; if he ever has a nephew, then he'd be Uncle Tom. No good. Maybe Robert, a junior?*

He raced to Mae's side. She was wet with perspiration; her hair was in disarray. Normally always so perfectly made up, she looked utterly exhausted and never more beautiful. He kissed her, asking, "How do you feel?"

“Better than you look—you better go home and get some sleep.”

“Not until they bring Bob Junior in for me to see.”

“Bob Junior?” There was doubt in her voice.

They talked for a while holding hands. When they brought the baby in, Mae’s joy illuminated her face. She looked at him closely, caressed his cheek with her lips, turned, and said, “You’re absolutely right. This is Bob Junior.”

CHAPTER FORTY-FIVE

March 9, 1966
Nellis Air Force Base, Nevada

The red dawn spread across the desert as the Nellis flight line came alive with the sound of ground equipment carts being started, aircraft being towed into position, and the horn of the roach coach calling mechanics in for early coffee.

Tom stood savoring the gritty desert air, still laden with the dust from yesterday's storm. He was immensely happy to be back in the saddle, marveling at how well things had worked out. Tom had been pushing his return to active service when a requirement came up for an experienced F-86 pilot to take part in a secret project at Nellis. A buddy of his at Air Force Personnel was swift enough to match Tom's skills with the test requirements and cut orders for his return to duty.

He had prepared long and hard for it, dieting and exercising so that he was now down to the same 205 pounds he had weighed when playing football at Annapolis. His Air National Guard assignment had given him lots of leeway in flying, and he had spent a month at his old stomping grounds, Eglin Air Force Base, putting in a lot of time flying both the fighters and the simulators. When he was flying the fighters, he put himself through a rigorous process of building up his g-force tolerance, so much so that he was able to win most of the few pickup dogfights he was able to garner. The Air Force was changing, and the emphasis on safety restricted the aggressiveness of the pilots. Only the older troops and the very young ones seemed willing to mix it up; most of the troops, earnest young captains and majors, seemed more concerned about their careers than their egos as pilots. Tom wasn't sure it was a net gain.

He had repeatedly distanced himself from Bob Rodriquez and his fascination with simulators, and the simulators at Eglin confirmed Tom's opinion. They were almost negative training, for while they were useful for procedures, they lacked everything necessary to re-create the conditions of combat. Tom overcame his distaste for Bob and all his ideas by sending him a long memo, detailing what was really needed in simulators—a three-dimensional presentation of the combat arena, motion simulation, and, more than anything else, a total immersion into the flight. In the simulators they were using, it was impossible not to realize that it was all a game. The simulators Rodriquez should be creating should be so realistic that the pilots would forget they were on the ground but believe they were locked in mortal combat. Tom knew he didn't know how to do it, but he had the feeling Bob would.

Despite Tom's reservations, he spent every hour he could get in the F-4 simulator, learning all the emergency procedures and bringing his instrument flying up to snuff so that when he got into combat he'd not even have to think about routine things—he'd just be there to fight.

When he arrived at Nellis, it had taken him only a few hours to check out in the North American F-86H Sabre that was being used in Operation Feather Duster, an attempt by the USAF to devise new tactics to use against the small and nimble MiGs being encountered in increasing numbers in Vietnam. The idea was to fly the Sabre against a super-secret MiG-19 to find out what kind of maneuvers might work best against it. Then there was going to be a second series of tests, using the McDonnell F-4 against the much more modern MiG-21, to refine the tactics.

Much had already been learned about the Russian-built aircraft. The MiG-19 was very close to the North American F-100 in performance and was more maneuverable. The MiG-21 was reportedly a delight to fly but had very poor visibility. The pilot was so blind to the rear that a rearview mirror was an obvious quick fix. The windshield glass was so thick that the pilot could see only about three miles forward.

Tom would have to check out in the F-4, too, but that was part of his plan. He wasn't sure he understood the rationale for using the Sabre. It seemed to him that the best way would have been to use the F-4 and forget about the F-86H, which was now in service in only a few National Guard and Reserve outfits. But he didn't protest, since the project had landed him exactly where he wanted to be, preparing to return to combat.

Nor did he inquire as to the source of the MiGs. He presumed it was Israel, but they were in use in air forces all over the world, some of them satellites of the Soviet Union, some of them not. Scuttlebutt had it that these were from Syria, but it couldn't have been too difficult to obtain examples from a number of countries.

The crew chief signaled Tom that the airplane was ready. He did a thorough walk-around—he always did, no matter who the crew chief was—and soon was strapping himself in, feeling like he was back in Korea, ready to go to MiG Alley.

Twenty minutes after takeoff, he entered the MiG's operating area ninety miles north from Nellis. The MiGs were maintained at Tonopah, an isolated field, about thirty miles southeast of the town of Tonopah, Nevada. Unlike another super-secret facility, the Groom Lake facility in Area 51, the Tonopah air base was easily visible from public land and there was even a sign pointing to it on the highway. Nonetheless, the MiGs were kept under heavy security to keep their existence secret.

A glint of silver in the sun revealed the MiG-19, orbiting at the edge of the operating area. Tom pulled into formation, admiring the functional beauty of the aircraft. It was painted in U.S. colors, but there was no mistaking the MiG profile, with its portly fuselage, gaping engine intake, and huge slab-sided rudder. Its sharply swept-back wings attested to its supersonic speed capability.

The test was very tightly programmed to extract the maximum information from the limited airtime their fuel allowed. The two planes were to fly programmed paths, checking on acceleration, deceleration, turn radius, and climb speeds. When they completed the prescribed turns, they were free to engage in mock combat as long as their fuel state permitted.

Tom called, "Outlaw One, this is Sabre One."

"My God, is that you, Tom? This is Owen Clark. What's a nice guy like you doing in an old airplane like that?"

Tom recognized Clark's Texas accent as easily as Clark had recognized his voice. They had flown together in Korea, thirteen years before, and then again at an air show two years ago.

"Good to hear from you, Owen. Let's get cracking on these profiles, and then I'll wax your ass in a dogfight."

The two planes moved in unison, the MiG-19 accelerating swiftly past the F-86, its afterburner kicking out a long plume of flame. When it came to turns, it was no contest—the MiG-19 had a much better turning radius. The same was true on the deceleration tests—the MiG would throw its big dive boards out, slowing down as if it had hit a wall, while the F-86 sailed past.

"Owen, I'm damn glad we were fighting MiG-15s in Korea and not this brute. How does it handle?"

"It's about like an F-84F, if you've ever flown one. Not bad, just not like a Sabre. Let's hassle; you must be getting down to fumes."

As the pre-flight instructions had called for, the two planes circled and then made a head-on pass to start the engagement.

The two fighters turned, and Tom broke suddenly, intending to close behind the MiG into a firing position. Instead, the MiG, with its low wing loading, turned inside him, chewing up the distance, getting into a firing position.

"Can't turn with this mother, so I better climb."

Tom heaved back on the stick, converting airspeed to altitude. Feeling the g-forces, Tom looked up through the canopy to see the MiG-19 rolling out at the top of its climb and diving away. Tom pulled through the arc of his climb, rolled his wings level, and settled in on the tail of the MiG, which jinked right and left—but not soon enough to have avoided being shot down.

Clark came on over the radio.

"Good fight, Tom; you haven't lost it. See you at the club tonight."

Feeling pretty good about himself, Tom signaled that he was returning to base. Short on fuel, he throttled back, extending the glide, worrying about the possibility of a flameout but glowing with pleasure from having waxed Clark's ass. He'd have to avoid talking about it tonight at the club—unless Clark mentioned it. When Tom touched down, the fuel warning lights were blinking.

Air Force Officers Clubs were pretty much the same the world over, slightly better than average food, much lower than average liquor prices, and a constant high-decibel level of conversation. The club at Nellis Air Force Base differed only in the higher testosterone level of pilots who put their lives on the line every day, either training or teaching in the hottest aircraft in the world. There were not too many fights but a lot of near fights, tempers growing with the beer intake. Most of the steam was let off with impromptu games that involved a lot of pushing and shoving.

Clark had driven down from the MiG base and was waiting for Tom when he arrived at the club. Tom slid in the leatherette seat beside him, signaled the waitress, and they began the usual endless process of matching names and dates and, always, deaths.

"So what do you think of Feather Duster?"

"So far so good. But I'm scheduled to check out in an F-4 and repeat the entire program in about six weeks."

"I know; I'm scheduled to check you out. They figured that you'd be too much for some fuzzy-faced young instructor to handle. We'll be doing the checkout concurrently with Feather Duster I—it means a hell of a lot of driving for me, but I come down here every night I can anyway. I like to see if there's any action in town; if there's not, I drive back. Kills the evening, and sometimes it's not too expensive."

"That reminds me; I had a friend here, a young guy named Steve O'Malley. Did you ever run into him?"

"Absolutely. He was a phenomenon, just like he was at the Air Force Academy. First in his class as a student, then probably one of the best instructor pilots we ever had. In fact, if he were still here, I'd recommend him to instruct you, but he was fighting to get into combat, so he's on his way overseas, heading to the Sixth Tactical Fighter Wing at Ubon, in Thailand. He's a hot young pilot and knows it, but he has a lot of class, very considerate, a really good instructor; none of this banging-the-stick-around stuff, he would analyze the students' problems and then tell them how to overcome them."

Clark drank his beer and said, "And he was really good to his backseaters. That's unusual nowadays."

Tom grunted. He wasn't thrilled about flying a two-seat fighter, depending upon the guy in back to get them into trouble and then out of it.

"It must be hell for a young pilot to be stuffed in the backseat with a radar set!"

"Tom, it is a hell of a problem. The idea, of course, is that the GIB—short for 'Guy In Back'—learns the ropes from a good pilot, then advances to become a front-seater himself. But it doesn't work out."

"Why the hell are they doing it? The Air Force is short on pilots and has a surplus of navigators—they could fly the backseat as well as anyone."

Clark shook his head, saying only, "Let's eat."

They moved on into the dining room, ordered the inevitable steaks and baked potatoes, messed around with the salad bar, and when they were seated again, Clark continued, "The worst thing about it is when they crew them up overseas, they will put the strong front-seaters with the weak backseaters, and vice versa. Some of the old-time pilots have flown single-seaters all their lives, and they tell the GIB just to sit still, be quiet, and not touch anything unless he's told to."

"Pretty grim!"

"And of course it's no better when they stick a competent back-seater behind some guy who has been flying a desk for years, then gets stuffed into an F-4. There's a lot of retreads out there and most of them are lousy, present company excepted. Then when they get in combat, the experienced young guy in the back raises hell with the senior guy in front. It's no good at all."

"Any solution?"

"The Navy did it right with their F-4s, designed them right from the start to have weapon system operators in the back, same as a navigator or a radar bombardier. No flight controls, no question about who's a better pilot, et cetera."

Tom was thoughtful for a moment.

"And how do they award a kill? Suppose you get lucky and shoot down a MiG, who gets credit for it, the pilot or the backseater?"

"Believe it or not, they both do."

"Holy Mother of Christ! That is bound to be trouble. I can just see it now, some Navy weapon system officer or some Air Force backseater could become the first ace in this war."

"Maybe, Tom; it could happen. Unfortunately, we are not shooting enough of them down to have many aces. Besides, what do you care? You've been an ace in two wars; that ought to be enough for anybody."

Tom was quiet, a reserved look drawing over his face. "That's what my dad was trying to tell me. But, you know, being the only ace in three wars, that would be something. I can't beat Rickenbacker's twenty-six kills, or Bong's forty kills, but I could be the only guy to be an ace in three wars."

Clark's expression changed from deep enjoyment to concern. "Don't even think about it, Tom. You'll wind up getting an Atoll missile stuffed up your ass, and your kid won't have a father. Just go over there and teach the young bucks what you know; let them do the killing and take the risks. You've paid your dues."

Tom nodded, his thoughts twelve thousand miles and five more kills away.

CHAPTER FORTY-SIX

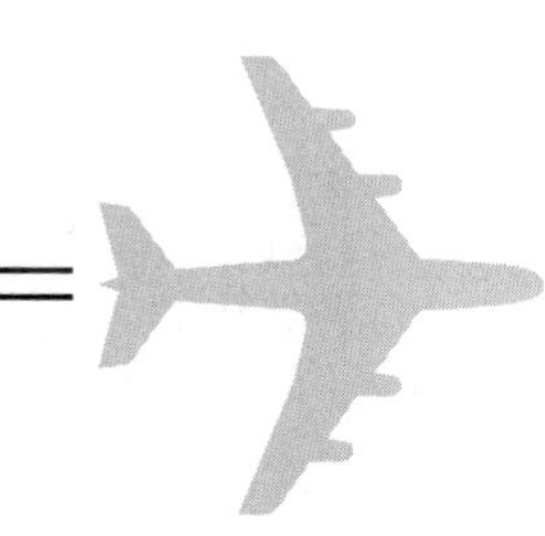

September 21, 1966
En route to Ubon Royal Thai Air Force Base,
Thailand

The pilot on the muddy Lockheed C-130 had apologized to Tom in the operations room on the military side of Bangkok's Don Muang Airport.

"Sorry, Colonel, we've been in country all week, hauling supplies, and the birds needs a bath. I'm honored to be taking you to Ubon, but I wish we'd had a chance to get things cleaned up for you. It's not good to bring in a new wing commander in a beat-up old plane like this."

"Don't you worry about it, Captain; I'm pleased to have a ride, glad to get out of the Bangkok taxis in one piece, and looking forward to the trip."

"You can ride up in the cockpit with us, Colonel. It's not much cleaner, but the view is better."

And the view was magnificent. Tom watched the beautiful Thai countryside roll by. First there were huge patches of forest, some brilliant green, some overlaid with dust from the tapioca factories. The overgrown forest soon gave way to marvelous farms, the rice fields gleaming like mirrors in the sun. Little jumbles of houses, as if someone had spilled a Monopoly board, sprang up along the klongs, the canals that served as combination roads, food and water supply, and sewer. There were small Buddhist temples everywhere, flashing gold in the water and among the palm trees. At frequent intervals large compounds sat astride the few paved roads that connected one village to the next. They had the regularity of a Roman encampment and were almost always surrounded by a miles-long fence of pine trees. Tom spent most of the flight standing between the two pilots, watching the familiar efficiency with which they flew the plane, a cheerful nonchalance that spelled expertise. As the countryside flashed by, he tried to recall everything he had learned in his abrupt, almost savage briefing from General William "Spike" Momyer, Seventh Air Force Commander.

"Shannon, I'll tell you first that I don't like the way you've waltzed in and out of the Air Force at your convenience, making money when times were tough, but coming back in when there was some action. If everybody did that we wouldn't have an Air Force; we'd have a massive Reserve outfit, nothing more, a fucking militia Air Force."

Tom had no rejoinder for this. He had done exactly that—come in and out of the Air Force when it suited him.

Momyer went on, "But I've got no choice. I've watched you over the years and I've read some of the papers you written about going back to basics."

Tom was granite faced. Over the years he had formally protested the emphasis the Tactical Air Command was placing on the delivery of nuclear weapons. He had insisted that this was the job of the Strategic Air Command and that TAC should become supreme in gunnery, in dive-bombing, and in dogfighting. Essentially he said that the key to air superiority was the fighter, not the fighter-bomber. It hadn't made him popular.

"The Sixth is in trouble. It has been coddled too long, and it's not getting any results. The pilots are all pissed off because we are being assigned worthless targets from Washington. Well, we have had a lot of worthless targets, but when we've had a worthwhile target, the Sixth hasn't taken it out."

Momyer's face darkened. "We've lost eleven airplanes and twenty-two people in the last three months, all but a few against junk targets, mostly trucks carrying rice. Now when you take command, you can restore discipline and improve morale if you can. I frankly don't give a damn about that, what I want is results. I don't want any more losses, and I want the targets taken out on the first mission, not after three or four."

Tom did what any sane subordinate would do. He said, "Yes, sir," saluted, and got the hell out of Momyer's office. But ever since then his remarks had weighed on Tom. He was being handed a group of pilots whose training had been all wrong and who were not getting the right support in the field. All he had to do was reverse the process, see that they were trained, and instead of lobbing bombs on rice bags set about winning the war, the air war, anyway. Tom's tour was for a year, but he was determined to shape the Sixth up in six months—and spend the next six months shooting down MiGs.

The C-130 touched down right on schedule at Ubon and was cleared to park directly in front of Base Operations, where a reception committee waiting, backed by a huge sign saying: "Welcome to the Cougars." A group of grinning officers was standing in rank order to greet him, and behind them was a bevy of beautiful Thai girls, each one with garlands of flowers.

It put Tom off. There was a war going on and flowers from Thai girls were incongruous. But he was an old guy, from other wars; he knew these men would be looking at him with suspicion, wondering what an aging crock could contribute to them. He didn't know himself.

The acting wing commander, Lieutenant Colonel Fred Calfey, was genuinely glad to see him. Calfey took him down the line, introducing him to people whose names he forget immediately, as he knew they would always be wearing name tags.

They knew from their own experience that Tom had had a long day, and Calfey took him to his quarters, a double-sized hooch fixed up with air-conditioning and a private bath.

"Will we see you at the club, tonight, Colonel? There's a lot of people who want to meet you."

"Sure, Fred, I'm going to have dinner, but then I'm going to cut out and come back here—I've got some paperwork today, and I want to get an early start tomorrow. I'd like to talk to everybody that's not flying tomorrow at oh eight hundred."

"Nobody's flying tomorrow, Colonel. We knew you'd want to talk to us, so we asked to stand down for one day."

Tom controlled his temper. Standing down for a goddamn briefing! No wonder Momyer was pissed off.

"That's fine. See you later, then."

As Calfey turned to go, Tom asked, "Is Captain Steve O'Malley still with the Sixth?"

"Sure is; he's due back from his mission in about twenty minutes."

"Well, when he's debriefed, and if he feels up to it, would you ask him to drop by my quarters?"

"Sure thing, Colonel."

O'MALLEY SHOWED UP an hour later, showered, shaved, and wearing a luxury, a clean flying suit.

"Steve, I'm going to count on you for some straight answers. General Momyer is dissatisfied with the results the Sixth has been getting. I understand from the grapevine that morale is bad. How does it look to you?"

O'Malley looked miserable. "I don't want to be a fink, Colonel. This is a great group of people; they just haven't had the leadership they need. Our last commander, Colonel Nealon, didn't exactly lead from the front."

"Come on; tell me what's going on. You're not a fink; I know you better than that. But I'm behind the eight ball here; the guys will be watching me to see what I do, and I don't want to make the same mistakes."

O'Malley unloaded. Nealon had flown only twenty-four missions in the previous year, and of these only two were "counters"—missions to North Vietnam.

"And we've got this stupid stuff that comes down from the White House—I mean it, not Washington, but from the White House itself. It comes through channels, of course, and that means it takes so long that the enemy knows about it before we do. They say General Momyer hates it, but has to salute and do what he's told. And the top people, the President, I guess, and the Sec Def, McNamara, are fixated on statistics. They want everything quantified. So when we were short on munitions, we were launching four F-4s, each one carrying half a load, because it increased the sortie rate."

As O'Malley went on, Tom got a clear picture of the problem. Good aircraft, great mechanics, good pilots, but poor morale because of the leadership and the stupid missions.

"You've been briefed, I know, on the rules of engagement—we cannot hit enemy airfields, flak, or SAM sites unless they are preparing to fire on us. Crazy!"

"What about the enemy? What are the North Vietnamese like?"

"Damn clever. They have little itty-bitty airplanes that maneuver like crazy. Even the old MiG-17 is still competitive in its own regime. The MiG-21 is a hell of an interceptor. And they have good tactics—they are not interested in dogfighting; they just want to make the bombers drop their bombs. So they lie low, come in with plenty of speed, pull up, fire a heat-seeking missile, and they are gone. Sometimes they'll stay and mix it up, but not often."

"Why do you think Momyer is so pissed about poor results? He must know the story here."

"I don't think so. He knows that the orders come through from the White House—they go through his command—but he discounts that, saying those orders are a small percentage of what we do. But he is hit by the ground commanders in South Vietnam who see their forces and the South Vietnamese forces getting chewed up by regular North Vietnamese troops as well as by the Vietcong. He wants the supply routes stopped."

They talked some more and O'Malley left, obviously pleased at becoming a confidant of the new CO, a man he'd long admired. Tom sat back, disheartened. There was an obvious solution—you didn't try to stop the flow of supplies by bombing men carrying bags of rice on their backs. You stopped it by bombing the source of the materials in Hanoi and Haiphong. But that was forbidden by the rules of engagement.

Just before he dropped off to sleep, it came to Tom. There was no way to influence what the President wanted; there wouldn't be any bombing of Hanoi or Haiphong in this administration. But Tom could get results if he got the North Vietnamese to engage and he could shoot down enough MiGs. It wouldn't take a lot—there were probably no more than sixty or seventy MiGs in their inventory. But if he could take out a sizable chunk of them, it would make Momyer happy, it would raise the morale of the Sixth TFW, and it just might make Tom an ace in three wars.

At eight o'clock the next morning, all the pilots and most of the staff officers in the wing were assembled in the only building big enough to accommodate them, the Officers Club. Tom called Calfey over and said, "Colonel, have the officers fall in outside the building in open ranks. You and I will inspect them."

Calfey looked at him dumbfounded, almost asking if he was kidding, then realizing that would be a mistake. It took ten minutes, but the men were finally assembled, and Tom and Calfey trooped their ranks. As Tom expected, it was unsatisfactory. He was not a fanatic on spit and polish, but these uniforms, shoes, and shaves were unacceptable.

"Colonel Calfey, we'll repeat this inspection at eleven o'clock. Tell the men to be in Class A uniforms, have their shoes shined, and their faces shaved."

At eleven, Tom and Calfey repeated the performance. The sense of resentment was palpable, but the group was presentable.

Tom said to Calfey, "Now we'll have our meeting."

At eleven fifteen, Tom walked in at the back of the room, Calfey called the group to attention, and they sprang to their feet. Tom strode the length of the room to the podium. He stood there, seeming to gaze directly at every individual before saying, "At Ease."

He spent a full moment gazing around the room, watching the increased annoyance, some faces coloring, others making whispered asides. Then he said, "Pretty chickenshit, eh? Fat-assed old colonel, a crock from World War II, comes rolling into Ubon, doesn't know his dick from a doorknob, and gets everybody into a sweat on their first day off in weeks. 'The poor old bastard probably hasn't flown this year, and he's going to be leading us. God have mercy.' "

Looking around, he asked, "Did that about sum it up? Well, you are right. I am a fat-assed old colonel, and I don't know my dick from a doorknob, but I'm going to learn, and you are going to teach me. I'll start flying tomorrow, number four in the last flight, and I'm going to have you teach me everything you know. I'll move from position to position, from one day to the next, and in two weeks, I'll know as much as you do, and from then on I'll be leading the show, every show, and especially every show that goes north."

There was a quiet murmur, incredulous but approving.

"Now we're going to intensify our flying. We'll fly all the missions they assign us, and we'll fly an additional training mission every day. We'll practice dive-bombing, air-to-air gunnery, and, most of all, how to avoid surface-to-air missiles. Don't tell me we don't have the airplanes to do this, or the fuel, or anything else. If we don't have it, I'll get it."

He stepped down from the podium, hesitated, then climbed back up on the little stage and said, "One more thing. We are going to shoot down one hell of a lot of MiGs in the process."

Like a fast serve being returned, he heard from the back of the room: "What's this we shit, *kemo sabe*?"

Tom stopped in his tracks.

"OK, who is the wise guy?"

A short, heavyset man sent his hand up in the air, his dark face flushed with embarrassment.

"What's your name?"

"I'm Lieutenant Michael Pavone."

"What's your job, Lieutenant Pavone?"

"I'm a backseater for Captain Murray."

"Not anymore. From now on you fly with me."

It was as good a way to pick a crew member as any—at least he knew Pavone had guts. No brains, maybe, but guts.

CHAPTER FORTY-SEVEN

January 27, 1967
Palos Verdes, California

Vance's health had been up and down for the past few weeks and it was unusual for him to hold a meeting at night, but there was a pressing issue and it turned out that both Harry and Bob were available after nine o'clock. Vance hated to impose on them, but with Tom gone, there was more work than he could handle.

Vance knew that Harry and Bob recognized that he was gradually turning more and more control over to them. He did it reluctantly, not because he didn't trust their judgment but because he hated the thought of not being on top of every detail. He'd spent a lifetime building up his firm, and now, when it was at its peak, with offices in three cities, he had to give up the reins.

He felt fortunate that he had Harry and Bob to take over. Tom's return to the Air Force had disappointed him, as much as he understood it, and judging from Tom's letters, he was doing well, shaping his unit up, and even scoring two kills. Imagine that, a forty-eight-year-old man in combat and shooting down airplanes. It was incredible, even if Tom was his son, his favorite son. Vance could admit it only to himself; he'd die before letting Harry even think that was the case. But Tom was so much like his mother, while Harry was just another Vance Shannon. All of Tom's strengths and weaknesses were the very ones Vance had loved in Margaret, God rest her soul.

The only real problem was Tom's antipathy toward Bob. Oddly enough, Vance knew Margaret would have felt the same way. It was something inherent, some sense of turf that they both had aplenty. Tom had made an attempt, not at reconciliation but at least cooperation, a few months ago with some very pertinent suggestions on simulators, based on his experience at Eglin. But since then, it was the same old story, a coldly formal friendship. Tom's wife, Nancy, went out of her way to be nice to both Bob and Mae, but the lines of separation were there, hard and unmistakable and, now, getting more troublesome all the time. Vance knew that Tom was clearly in the wrong, that his views were counterproductive for the family and for the business. Vance also knew that there was nothing he could do or say to make a difference.

Things were not improved by the way business had boomed for the last six months, not always in the manner Vance liked to see. Last December, the German Luftwaffe grounded the Lockheed F-104G, after the sixty-fifth crash of the hot little fighter. The grounding was the result of a recommendation of a committee in which Harry and Bob had both participated. Naturally enough, the Germans were unwilling to admit that there was anything wrong with their training system and wanted to find an inherent flaw in the airplane. The truth was different. The attrition rate for F-104G was no worse than that of other high-performance fighters in other air forces around the world and, in fact, better than in some that also flew the Starfighter.

It was a crisis for the Luftwaffe, as it grudgingly accepted that it had not been as stringent as it might have been in either pilot selection or training. But as was so often the case when Rodriquez was on the job, there was a windfall for Aerospace Ventures. Well-known among the Luftwaffe leadership for his twelve victories in Korea and able to speak German well enough to sell, if not actually negotiate the contracts, the affable Rodriquez had walked away with an $80 million contract for simulators to improve instrument training. The contract had to be shared with half a dozen European countries, but it was a fantastic boost to the Aerospace Ventures bottom line.

Vance thought to himself how strange it was that Bob and Harry got along so well but that Tom couldn't stand Bob. Yet Bob used Tom's ideas for simulators in the proposal he had made to the Germans. All that remained was to build them—easier said than done. It was typical of Bob that he had insisted that one section of the contract specifically spell out that the basic idea for the 3-D simulators he was proposing was derived from Tom's suggestion.

The other bit of bad news was deceptive, for it looked good on the surface. Boeing had beaten Lockheed for the contract for the supersonic transport, somewhat to the Seattle firm's chagrin. Opposition to the SST was building on a number of fronts, but the major opposition was from a wide-ranging coalition of environmentalists. The principal leader was William Shurcliff, who headed the Citizens League Against the Sonic Boom. At the same time, government support was waning. Jeeb Halaby had been a strong and vocal advocate of the SST when he headed the FAA, but he had gone on to run Pan American. Now Bill MacGruder, a former Lockheed test pilot, was running the SST program for the government, and he simply did not have Halaby's clout.

Yet there was another problem, far more subtle, that Vance saw early on. It was not perceived by Boeing, and Vance couldn't point it out without offending a long laundry list of friends. The SST was being designed primarily by engineers from Boeing's commercial aviation side. But because the government was funding 90 percent of the program, these engineers were dealing with the same government representatives who worked with the Boeing military aircraft people. Boeing's commercially trained people were treating the sole government customer as if it were one of several airline customers, a basic error that had to be redressed. As a result, communication was poor and the government was forming a very bad opinion of Boeing's responsiveness.

Just as they had promised, Harry and Bob rolled in at nine o'clock, both men apologizing for being late and both eagerly wolfing down the sandwiches and cocoa that Jill had prepared for them. Jill cornered Bob, made him show her every new picture of the baby, and gave him yet another outfit to take home for Bob Junior.

Vance watched approvingly, then said, "It's a hell of a note that we cannot get together during the day like normal human beings, but there's just too much going on. Thank goodness that Luftwaffe business is over with—I thought you guys would have to give up your citizenship if you didn't get back here."

Bob Rodriquez shifted a bite of sandwich to the side of his mouth, took a sip of cocoa, and said, "If I hadn't come back, Mae was going to divorce me. She's really upset about me being gone so much with a brand-new baby. And it's not really over, Vance, in truth it's just getting started, and that's why I was happy you got us together tonight. When you've gone through your agenda, I want to make a proposal to you both."

"OK. We'll do that. Mine is short and sweet. With Tom gone, we are just stretched too thin, so either we've got to bring some talent on board that we can really rely on or we're going to have to consider selling some of the business off. I hate to do that; everything we own seems like part of the family. But we cannot keep growing like this without expanding our management base. The problem of course is to get people we're comfortable with. Right now, any one of us . . ."

He stopped, then said, "I was going to say any one of us can cover all the bases. That's not true anymore. Bob has projects going that are beyond my ken—especially the simulators."

"Mine, too." Harry didn't like saying it, but it was true.

When he was excited about a project, Rodriquez was like an eager beagle puppy, almost unable to contain himself with the prospect of pleasing someone and very anxious for approval. Vance saw him squirming and waved him to go ahead.

"Look, I've got an old friend at General Electric, Bill Roos. He's in their electronics division and has been experimenting along the same lines I have, introducing the digital computer into simulators. We had a long talk, off-the-record, of course, and it turns out we have an exact fit between what we are developing at Aerospace Ventures and what GE is working on. We both plan to get away from the big special-purpose computers that everybody, Link included, has been using, and use smaller general-purpose digital computers."

He saw that he had lost both Harry and Vance technically.

"I'm sorry. To be brief, I'm proposing that we split off our simulator line completely from Aerospace Ventures and sell it to General Electric. Both our systems are able to generate three-dimensional images, but ours is a better system, easier to manufacture. But they are way ahead of us in using color. It is a perfect fit, and Bill Roos is more than willing to buy. It fits their plans even better than it might fit ours."

Vance looked alarmed. "What about your interest in this? You wouldn't be going with them?"

"No, I've taken it about as far as I can go. We couldn't justify the expense at Aerospace Ventures to do what GE is going to do. But I'll bet we can sell to them at a great price, considering we're bringing the German contract along. Besides, I've got some other ideas I need to work on."

Harry cut in, "Like what? Are they apt to be as profitable as we projected the simulators to be? I'm not sure I like the idea of GE cleaning up on your invention."

"Well, I think the next big field in the military will be what they call smart bombs, you know, precision guided munitions, and I've got some ideas that I want to develop. I think it will be at least as profitable as simulators, maybe more. There's no question in my mind that the volume will be greater—we'll be getting to a point where there will be a surplus simulator capacity in five or ten years, but we'll be dropping smart bombs forever."

Vance and Harry both looked at him with admiration. Rodriquez always managed to be thinking ten years ahead, a vital characteristic that they lacked—and knew they lacked.

"And remember, the deal with GE will have a percentage rider in it; we'll continue to make money from the simulators they sell."

Bob, ever the salesman, turned to Vance for the close. "What this does, Vance, is free up about eighty percent of my and my people's time. We'll devote about half of that to the new projects, and the rest is at your disposal, to help out where you are short."

Vance mulled it over in his mind. No sense in going to Tom to inquire whether he was interested or not; he'd say he didn't care and be pissed off at Bob anyway. The key thing for Vance was that it provided at least a partial solution to the current management crisis, and although he hated to admit it, he was always more partial to munitions than to simulators. Gad, he was tired. Twenty years ago he'd have made up his mind in a second. Now he wanted to think about it.

"Tell you what, Bob, let's talk in the morning by phone. I can tell by Harry's face that he thinks it is a good idea, and so do I, but I want to see the deal you propose to GE first."

He'd always liked General Electric since the days back in the mid-forties when he'd brought Whittle's engine over for them to copy. They'd never looked back and were now one of the biggest jet-engine makers in the business. Maybe this would be the same. He started to tell Bob and Harry a story about the first Whittle engine blowing up, then stopped. He was getting old, but he was not going to be one of those old blowhards, always dredging up stories from the past.

The phone rang and Vance picked it up. "Vance Shannon here."

"Vance, this is Bud Bodie down at the Cape. We've had a catastrophe here, a fire in *Apollo I.* All three crewmen are dead. We're convening a board of inquiry and wonder if you can send Bob Rodriquez down as soon as possible, tomorrow if you can."

Shannon was stunned. He knew all three of the primary crew for *Apollo I*—Gus Grissom, Ed White, and Roger Chaffee—and two of the three men on the backup crew, Wally Schirra and Donn Eisele.

"Which crew was on board?"

"The primary. Can Rodriquez be here? I have a bunch more calls to make."

"He's on his way."

Shaken, Vance hung up the phone. "Bob, we'll talk about your proposal another time. You have to go to Cape Canaveral, first thing in the morning. They had a fire in *Apollo I*, killed all three of the crew members. I guess they want you because of your background in oxygen systems."

They talked quietly for a bit, shaken by the tragedy and speculating on its effect on the Apollo program.

Rodriquez said, "This open policy on the space program is a good thing, I guess, but there are going to be some real turf wars over this. The Russians do it differently—they never let any word out about any tragedy; they only tell about their successes."

"Well, we lost three fine officers in this. And I'll bet we lose six months or a year of time. It might cost us the race to the moon. I hope not."

After a long silence, Vance went on, "It looks like the space age is going to be built on sacrifice, just like aviation has been."

They left him with his thoughts of so many of his friends lost over the years and of the question he had asked himself a hundred times, whether it was worth it or not. He had asked himself that most often when he knew Tom or Harry was flying a dangerous mission.

Funny enough, he thought to himself, *sad as it is, there is something in the human soul that makes it worthwhile. If it wasn't worth it somehow, there wouldn't always be someone willing to take up the challenge after an accident.*

CHAPTER FORTY-EIGHT

February 27, 1967
Over North Vietnam

So far the weather was absolutely perfect for Operation Toro, Colonel Tom Shannon's trap for the MiGs of the North Vietnamese 921st Fighter Regiment. A solid cloud deck covered the ground at about five or six thousand feet. There were some intermittent layers of clouds all the way up to his 15,000-foot altitude, where fourteen flights of four McDonnell F-4 Phantoms each flew at 480 knots, pretending to be bomb-laden Republic F-105s.

He rocked his wings, craning his neck to view as much as he could of the magnificent spectacle, fifty-six superb fighters in the classic Air Force fluid-four formation. From each of the Phantom's two engines there extended the usual telltale columns of smoke that would have been a dead giveaway had there been no cloud cover.

Pavone, his voice husky with excitement, called, "Crossing the Red River."

Shannon accelerated to 540 knots, and the Phantoms assumed the QRC-160 pod formation that the F-105s always used, hoping to lure the North Vietnamese up to fight. If they did, they would be cold meat, for more F-4s from Da Nang were positioned to cut off their route home, catching them with their fuel low and nowhere to go. Shannon felt like an airborne Hannibal, planning his own lofty Cannae.

A glance at the clock told him that the trap would not be sprung for ten more minutes, and he luxuriated in the enforced idleness. All they had to do was stooge along, pretending to be bomb-laden F-105s, until the MiGs appeared. Constantly alert, he scanned the sky, checked his fuel state, set the armament switches, and noted a change in the vegetation near a village that he had flown over the previous day. But even as he watched and set and checked, he allowed his mind to go back and recap the past few action-packed weeks.

Shannon stretched in his seat, thinking how good it was to be back in combat and how impossible it was to explain the feeling to Nancy. She'd never understand what it meant to be accepted as the leader of what he knew was now the most formidable Phantom unit in the world, the Cougars of the Sixth Tactical Fighter Wing. And intuitively, he knew that he loved her better for not understanding.

It hadn't been easy to mold the Cougars into their current from, for the war was being fought on a ludicrous basis. The Secretary of Defense, Robert Strange McNamara, had issued stringent rules of engagement that pitifully handicapped the United States Air Force. Left to follow its own doctrine of air superiority, the Air Force could have cleared the Vietnamese skies of all enemy airpower in one or two days of fierce action. But McNamara was convinced that he could educate the North Vietnamese with a graduated response to their aggression, sending subtle messages to Hanoi to desist or things would get worse.

It was absurd. The people running the Hanoi government had resisted the Japanese and defeated the French. They were not susceptible to hints or persuasion. Nonetheless, McNamara persisted, conferring political air superiority upon the enemy, a historical first of enormous importance. Under his rules, the airfields from which the MiGs flew were off-limits, as were the surface-to-air missile sites that fired the deadly telephone pole–long SA-2s, supersonic surface-to-air missiles that could blow you out of the sky with a near miss. If World War II had been fought the same way, the Germans would have won.

Other rules specified that it was necessary to have a visual identification of enemy planes, to avoid fratricide. This made sense except that it put the F-4s in a hopeless position with their all-missile armament. Their AIM-7 radar-guided Sparrows were designed to reach out and destroy enemy bombers at a distance. The requirement to visually identify the target negated the Sparrows' value, discounting their combat capability.

The heat-seeking AIM-9 Sidewinders were also handicapped by the requirement, but not to the same degree, being intended to work closer in than the Sparrow. But both missiles were designed for use against bombers flying straight and level, not for dogfighting with a diving, twisting, turning MiG fighter. As Tom had said so many months before, what was needed was a gun—but there were no guns on Phantoms yet. McNamara had refused to consider their installation, saying that in the age of missiles they might as well put bows and arrows on the Phantom. Sometimes, when all his missiles misfired, Tom would have settled for a longbow.

Tom had flown this route so often that he knew exactly where he was by elapsed time alone, if the predicted winds were correct, even though the cloud cover continued to obscure the ground. It was sweet flying in this beautiful, powerful airplane, the constant radio traffic in the background, the heavy sound of Pavone's breathing coming in regularly except when he was bending over, grunting, to change some of his settings. Tom's mind went back to his Navy days, to his first fighter, the Grumman Wildcat, with its 1200-horsepower engine and six .50-caliber-gun armament. Now his throttles controlled almost twenty times the power—but he still would have liked to have the guns in addition to his temperamental missiles.

The missiles were excruciating to operate for a fighter pilot used to closing up behind an enemy, pressing a trigger, and watching the metal fly. The F-4 carried four AIM-7 radar-guided Sparrows and four AIM-9 heat-seeking Sidewinders.

Carried partially embedded in the Phantom's belly, the four-hundred-pound Sparrow had a sixty-five-pound warhead. The Phantom's radar would lock onto a target, creating a "beam" for the AIM-7 to follow to the target. But launching the AIM-7 was complex and time-consuming. Once launched, the Phantom's radar had to continue to lock onto the target, or the Sparrow would go out of control.

Launching the Sidewinder was slightly less complex but still nerve-racking, as the pilot had to wait until a tone in his headset confirmed that the missile was ready to fire. Carrying a smaller twenty-five-pound warhead, the Sidewinder used an infrared sensor to seek out the heat from the enemy's engine exhaust. To make a good Sidewinder shot, the Phantom had to fly into a thirty-degree cone within a mile of the aircraft, set up, hear the buzz that said the missile was ready, then fire. Far different from pulling a trigger.

Both missiles had proximity fuses, but both had minimum ranges—you couldn't get closer than three thousand feet to the enemy, or the missile would disarm as a safety precaution. The real problem, however, the one that drove air crews crazy, was that both missiles were extremely unreliable, often going wildly out of control after their launch.

Tom wondered what was going on at the enemy airfields below. The Vietnam People's Air Force (VPAF) had very few aircraft deployed in combat, perhaps fifteen of the modern delta-wing MiG-21s and a mix of fifty MiG-15s and 17s, mostly the latter. They very sensibly did not try to engage the Americans in air combat. Instead their mission was to make the fighter-bombers drop their bombs before they reached their targets. Once that was done, the MiGs would disappear, their mission accomplished.

Their tactics were just as Steve O'Malley had described them. Under ground control, they would track a formation of the F-105s and, whenever possible, attack from the rear with their Atoll missiles, an unabashed copy of the Sidewinder, but with improved performance. Or they might spill out of a cloud bank in a slashing attack, trying for the same goal—to make the 105s jettison their load. It was a very clever, very economical way to fight a war—but it was frustrating to the American pilots who wanted to score victories.

Shannon chuckled to himself. At forty-eight years old he'd come out to Ubon a complete green bean compared to the men in his wing and within ninety days had scored two kills. He wasn't too proud of one of them, a MiG-15b, the two-seat version of the famous fighter. It must have been lost on a training flight, flying in a slight curve, as if it was signaling ground control for assistance. Tom found it quite by accident, coming back from Hanoi, and killed it with one Sidewinder that went right up the MiG's tailpipe.

The other was a legitimate victory. A MiG-17 had tried to lure him down to a turning fight at about ten thousand feet. The MiG was serving as a decoy to another flight of MiG-17s up above them, but the Vietnamese pilot made the mistake of flying straight and level long enough for Tom's Sparrow to guide in and blow him up.

The victories were far more important than just raising Tom's score, for they raised the morale of the Sixth TFW and firmly put him in the saddle as a leader to be respected. As for Pavone, he couldn't contain his elation. He had two victories, too, and he let no one forget it, particularly pilots he had flown with before Shannon's arrival. And the victories permitted Shannon to train his wing harder. The Australian No. 79 Fighter Squadron, equipped with the big-engine CA-27 Avon F-86 Sabres, was based at Ubon. These were hot airplanes, perfect to simulate the MiGs the Cougars were encountering in Vietnam. Shannon asked the Australian commander to scramble two Sabres twice a day to intercept his Phantoms as they returned from combat. Most of the Phantom pilots had little or no air-to-air combat experience, and the education the Australian Sabres provided was invaluable. The Cougar pilots loved it, and the Australians liked nothing better than attacking the incoming Phantoms. Many an argument about who shot down who was settled later in the evening at the bar.

Tom was tired. He worked hard at his job, flying every day if he could. When he wasn't flying he was massaging the squadron, visiting every area from armament to the motor pool, not as a CO on inspection but as a leader trying to learn. Within sixty days of his arrival, he knew virtually everyone in the wing by their first names and he could usually make some mental association to remember their family or their new baby or their last court-martial.

It was so easy to do little things to improve morale. The armament people worked hard and sometimes didn't finish in time to get to the mess hall for a meal. Shannon ordered the dining facilities to stay open until the last man was fed, regardless of the hour. The curious thing was that it not only improved the morale of the armament guys, it made the mess-hall people feel like they were important, and their morale improved as well. It didn't hurt that Tom sometimes went down and drank with the enlisted men. It was strictly against protocol, but you could learn a lot listening to smart young airmen whose inhibitions were loosened by a couple of beers and who were pleased to have their CO tipping one back with them.

The flying was arduous. The rules of engagement made nonsense of targeting. Rice- and truck-laden ships in the harbor at Haiphong, perfect targets for both their missiles and bombs, were off-limits, their cargo having to be picked off bag by bag, truck by truck, on the Ho Chi Minh Trail. Worse, they forced the attacks into a routine pattern of times, routes, and altitudes that removed every element of surprise. In essence the American effort became a colossal school of aerial warfare, with the Americans the instructors, the North Vietnamese the very apt pupils.

Tom admired the enemy for their effective responses to the weak American ploys. McNamara ruled that dikes would not be attacked, because for reasons of world opinion he didn't wish to reduce the North Vietnamese food supply. The enemy responded by promptly moving their formidable anti-aircraft guns to the dikes, where they could operate with impunity. When the USAF revised its tactics, going in low to offset the surface-to-air missiles, the enemy brought up enormous amounts of anti-aircraft artillery, supplied by Russia and China. Then when the USAF came up with electronic equipment such as the QRC-160 pods that effectively jammed radars, they brought in more aircraft to vary the threat.

Shannon's wing was flying with borrowed QRC-160 pods today. The F-105s had adopted the "pod formation" with them, maximizing their ability to jam enemy electronic systems. As the F-4s were pretending to be F-105s, they had to have the QRC-160s as well.

It was one more place where Steve O'Malley had proved his worth. Although the idea of the F-4s masquerading as F-105s had been Shannon's, he had delegated the intricate planning of the mission to O'Malley, Pavone, and two other flight leaders to work out the details.

O'Malley had thrown himself into the project, determining the key points on the routes in and out, the force to use, the refueling points, all the details of radio communications, anti-aircraft suppression, and the electronic countermeasures. When he asked for QRC-160 pods from Seventh Air Force, he met immediate resistance, because they were in short supply. O'Malley flew to Saigon, made the right contacts, and swore on his life that he would have the pods back in seven days. Then he waited until he had personally seen the pods loaded onto a C-130 bound for Ubon before he took off himself. He beat the C-130 to Ubon, of course, and was there to off-load the QRC-160 pods and supervise their installation on the Phantoms.

At one point O'Malley came to Shannon, cautioning him on how narrow the margin for success was. The MiGs were very short-ranged, and if the North Vietnamese committed them to combat, they would be in the air for only about one hour at the maximum. If they launched too soon, they'd be landing before the Phantoms arrived; if they waited, the Phantoms would be gone before they could get there. Shannon decided to stagger the flights of Phantoms, so that they would arrive over the target area in five-minute intervals—at least someone would get a shot if the MiGs showed up.

Shannon glanced at the clock and remembered the three basic advantages they had, besides surprise. First of all, they had altitude, and that meant energy. Second, the silver MiGs would be coming up through the clouds, and that meant they would be visible. Third, and most important, in this environment the Americans knew where all the airplanes were, so he had ruled it a "missile-free" environment. The Phantoms could fire their missiles without getting a visual identification.

Pavone called, "Time over target."

The ground was still completely overcast, with the tops of the clouds around seven thousand feet. They were right on the money on time, directly over the Phuc Yen airfield, but where were the MiGs? Had someone slipped up? Were the call signs too obvious? O'Malley was a car guy, and he had designated the flights by makes of cars. Shannon was lead in Cadillac flight, O'Malley was leading Plymouth flight, and so on. Did that tip the North Vietnamese off?

Shannon began a slow 180-degree turn, calling out, "Visual ID required."

With one flight of Phantoms over the target and another arriving in four minutes, it was no longer a missile-free environment.

Plymouth flight arrived—just as the MiGs began popping up through the overcast, expecting to find a sky full of Republic F-105s but instead finding Phantoms screaming down on them.

Shannon picked up a silver MiG-21, its delta shape shining brightly against the clouds below. Long before, he and Pavone had done the intricate teamwork necessary to set the missiles up, doing the "switchology," throwing the switches in the right sequence, letting the missiles come online so that they could be fired. Pavone was eager but inexperienced, his focus entirely within the cockpit, checking the radar and the warning lights. Tom's vast combat experience now asserted itself. As he pursued the MiG, its pilot probably wondering Custer-like where all the fucking F-4s had come from, Shannon possessed in abundance what fighter pilots called situational awareness. He took in the entire combat situation, from horizon to horizon and from the ground up. His mind picked each of the MiGs, climbing toward them at near supersonic speed, and he automatically estimated where they would be in the next minute. He did the same with the American planes, even though the sky had become a whirling windmill of fighters.

Fighting the MiG-21 required finesse. A tiny airplane with a big engine, it was faster and more maneuverable at higher altitudes than the F-4. The Phantom's great advantage was its colossal energy that it gained in vertical maneuvers, offsetting the MiG's ability to turn.

Just like Wildcats and Zeros, Shannon thought as Pavone, breathing hard, yelled, "We've got a lock."

Shannon hit the auto-acquisition switch, put the pipper on the MiG, and launched a Sparrow. He cursed to himself when he saw the agile MiG disappear into a cloud and the Sparrow begin to tumble wildly.

Shannon thought, *Shit, I'm getting old, my reflexes are off—*

Just then he saw another MiG appear in his ten o'clock position, coming fast. He slammed the afterburner, pulling the Phantom up in a forty-five-degree climb. The MiG was turning to the left and Shannon barrel-rolled to the right. Just as he had anticipated, he was now above the MiG, inverted, and able to keep on turning behind him, closing the range to 1,500 yards and using a twenty-degree deflection angle. Now he passed below the MiG, framing it in his sights, a silver triangle against the sun as he launched two Sidewinders. The first one hit the right wing of the MiG, blowing it off; the second passed through the fireball.

Pavone was beside himself. "Hot damn, we got three now, skipper; let's get another gomer while we're here."

Shannon grunted under the five g's he was pulling as he arced the Phantom around, thinking, idiotically enough, *Get 'em while they're hot*, the old ball-game chant of the hot dog vendor. Exulting in the swift changes in direction, the spinning reversal of sky and ground as he rolled, the g-forces slamming him into his seat, he burned with the adrenaline coursing through him.

As he turned he saw O'Malley's Phantom fire two Sidewinders against another MiG. The first missile tumbled out of control, but the second one blew the vertical surface off the enemy plane, sending it rolling swiftly to the ground. It was O'Malley's first kill and Shannon knew how he felt as he turned on a MiG that had apparently overshot its target and was flashing through the center of the combat, diving down toward the airfield at Phuc Yen.

Pavone yelled, "Get him," and then, "Lock on."

Shannon hesitated—he had the MiG in his sights, but he was too close for the Sparrow and he switched to a Sidewinder. There was an eternity before he heard the buzz and launched it to fly like the maniacal robot it was, straight down after the fleeing MiG, smashing into its tailpipe, just as it was designed to do. The pilot did not eject.

Pavone was screaming, "I got four! I got four! Goddammit, I got four!"

"Shut up, Pavone; we're getting short on fuel—"

And there it was, a MiG-21 following a Phantom down in a course to the southeast. Shannon rolled the Phantom over, acquired the MiG in his sight, and followed it, holding his fire until Pavone yelled that he had a lock.

O'Malley's voice came over the radio.

"Cadillac One, break right; there's two MiG-17s coming behind you; *break, break, break!*"

Shannon heard the warning, decided he had five more seconds, and launched his two Sparrows as the 37mm cannon shells of the MiGs clawed through his wings and fuselage.

The broken Phantom, shedding parts amid a ball of flame and smoke, went inverted, and Shannon yelled to Pavone, "Eject, eject, eject," as he pulled his own ejection seat handle that would eject Pavone first.

The front and rear canopies peeled away, Pavone ejected, and Shannon followed him out, separating from his seat as the rush of air tumbled him until his parachute deployed with a painful but satisfying jerk. The blast of wind tore off his helmet and mask and the sudden eerie quiet was unsettling. Shannon shifted in his harness, turning until he saw Pavone's open parachute well below him and perhaps five miles distant. Too bad—their chances to evade would have been better if they had landed together.

He slipped into the top of the cloud layer, rehearsing in his mind all he had been taught about escape and evasion. Getting rid of the chute was paramount, and then he had to find a place to hide during the day. The clouds suddenly parted and he saw that he was going to land in the middle of a huge North Vietnamese Army encampment—if he survived the rifle shots that were now cracking around him as the enemy troops picked up their weapons and fired.

Shannon slipped his chute to speed his descent, wondering if he would survive to see Nancy and V.R. again.

CHAPTER FORTY-NINE

September 20, 1967
Van Nuys, California

Willis Hawkins stopped his frantic pacing around the low-slung, lethal-looking new Lockheed AH-56A Cheyenne helicopter and walked rapidly over to Harry Shannon.

"How is Vance bearing up, Harry? We were so sorry to hear about Tom being shot down. Have you heard anything from him?"

Harry was touched by Hawkins's concern at a time like this, when the Cheyenne, Lockheed's $150 million foray into the attack helicopter business, was being prepared for its first flight. Things had not been going well for the company lately, and much was riding on the success of the radical new design.

"He's not doing too well, Willis. We haven't heard a word about Tom except that his parachute was seen to open before he entered a cloud deck. They made a reconnaissance over the area where he went down and found that it was a bivouac for an entire North Vietnamese division. No way for him to escape, I guess, but we're hoping that they took him prisoner."

"You give Vance our best, Harry, and we'll all be praying for Tom. Now, if you'll excuse me, I've got to get back to work."

Hawkins had been a stalwart at Lockheed for thirty years now, and he was as active and as aggressive an engineer as ever and fiercely protective of the veteran engineer most responsible for the Cheyenne, Irv Culver. Culver was an intuitive genius who arrived at his designs in totally unorthodox manners, often in ways that other engineers could not easily replicate. Without the usual formal training, he had actually invented his own system of mathematics—and it worked. Hawkins had the utmost faith in Culver and had backed him in a succession of designs that led to the Cheyenne.

It was a bright, sunny California morning, and Lockheed had provided stands for the VIP onlookers. Bob Wachter, an old-time Lockheed engineer, waved for Harry to come sit down. Wachter had invited him to the first flight because he had been designated to develop a simulator for the Cheyenne. Wachter knew that Aerospace Ventures was in the process of selling its simulator division to GE but he wanted to pick up some tips. He'd actually asked for Rodriquez, but Bob was still tied up with the *Apollo I* fire investigation. Harry felt woefully unprepared to talk to Wachter but felt he could at least take questions and get answers.

Wachter started off by repeating Hawkins's conversation almost verbatim. Harry was grateful for the esteem in which they held his father. They didn't really know Tom, but they seemed totally sincere with their concern, for they knew it had affected Vance terribly.

Wachter and Harry's talk then turned to mutual friends, who was where, and, inevitably, the state of business, especially the purchase of Douglas by McDonnell earlier in the year.

" 'McDonnell Douglas'—sounds funny, doesn't it?"

Harry nodded. "It's the start of a trend. Stan Hooker warned my father about it years ago, when all the British companies were drying up. At least they kept both names—it would have been tough just to have it be 'McDonnell.' "

Wachter nodded his agreement. "Couldn't do that—too much history tied up in the Douglas name. It would be like Chrysler dropping the Plymouth brand."

Harry filled Wachter in on all the details of the new Boeing 737, and Wachter gleefully recounted his Moscow-to-Tokyo trip in a new Tupolev Tu-114, a special flight laid on by Leonid Brezhnev for the foreign press and industry people.

"It's the damnedest thing you ever saw, Harry, four huge turboprops, swept wings, and it goes like a bat out of hell. The amazing thing was the service on board. They must have had a special crew of stewardesses, because you couldn't turn around without them offering you a vodka and some caviar. And they were always hinting that if you wanted more of something else, they'd be willing. I don't know if anybody took them up on the something else, but everybody took them up on the vodka and caviar."

Harry asked, "How was the noise level?" Turboprops were notorious for their noise and for their high frequencies, which often made ground crew men violently ill if they were not wearing adequate ear protection.

"On the ground the noise was just impossible, deafening. I don't think the FAA would ever approve it for domestic operations, just way too noisy. But inside, not bad at all. You're conscious of it on takeoff, of course, but in level flight it's quieter than a piston-engine transport, noisier than a jet."

They were silent for a while, companionably watching all the effort—cars driving up, people racing to the sideline for parts, panels on the aircraft being pulled, and an impatient group of executives glancing at their watches. It was all part of the preliminaries for a first flight.

"I'll tell you, Harry, if we don't get a contract for this chopper, there is no justice! It is so advanced compared to anything else in the competition."

"A rigid rotor! That's not just advanced; that's futuristic. Can you make it work?"

"Well, you see that itty-bitty fixed wing?"

The Cheyenne had stub wings, about twenty-five feet in span, into which its wheels retracted.

Harry nodded.

"Well, they off-load the rotor during high-speed flight. It makes the fixed rotor practicable. And the pusher propeller makes it as controllable as an airplane."

"Any problems that you see?"

"The wind tunnel and the slide rules tell us that it all works fine, but Willis is worried about stability at high speeds. You know it's designed for about two hundred and fifty miles an hour—that is performance! Nothing like it in the competition."

Harry nodded. As important as the jet engine had been to conventional aircraft, it had proved to be a lifesaver for helicopters. All the previous piston-engine helicopters had been woefully underpowered, particularly at altitude. The jet changed all that, and the success that

Bell had with its Model 47 seemed to change the helicopter world. Now it looked as if the Cheyenne was the next great advance.

The Lockheed engineer went on, "This bird has everything! It carries a minigun in the nose turret, and can take six Hughes anti-tank missiles under the wing. They decked it out with night-vision equipment that you wouldn't believe, and the helmet has a gun sight built in. It's just phenomenal!"

In time Wachter's enthusiasm for the Cheyenne trailed off, and he began inquiring about the simulator business. Harry leveled with him. "Bob, let's just get right down to what you want to know, and let me get back to you. If I try to wing it, I'll be certain to foul you up."

Wachter pulled a folder out from the briefcase beside him and said, "I thought you'd never ask! Here's about twenty key questions—any information you can give us I'd appreciate."

Harry glanced at the questions and shrugged his shoulders. The first question: "Is three-axis motion feasible for a helicopter simulator?" took him out of his depth.

"Let me get this to Bob Rodriquez. He's down at the Cape this week, but I'll send it special delivery and he'll get an answer back as soon as he can. He's pretty busy there."

Wachter nodded. "I understand they are attributing the accident to the one-hundred-percent-oxygen environment?"

"That's what I hear, too, but not officially—just the usual rumors. Apparently a spark was all it took to turn the entire spacecraft into an inferno, and with the way the entrance hatch was designed, they had no way to get out. It means pretty much of a redesign of the entrance and the pressurization system."

There was a flurry of activity by the Cheyenne where Hawkins was tossing his notebook on the ground in disappointment. He recovered himself and walked to the microphone that had been used to brief the crowd earlier.

"Ladies and gentlemen, I'm sorry, but we'll have to postpone the first flight. There's a small problem with the electrical system. First flight will be tomorrow, and I hope you all can return. We'll shoot for a two o'clock takeoff."

Wachter smiled ruefully at Harry, saying, "That's the breaks. How many times has this happened to you?"

"More than I can count. It's just part of the business. And I'll be back to you on the simulator stuff ASAP."

Hawkins walked over and sat down besides them. "What's the electrical problem, Willis?"

"That's just a cover. All of a sudden the Army project manager, Emil Kluever, decided he wanted to go along on the first flight! We don't have a seat for him, so we have to rig one. I couldn't tell that to the crowd. Kluever is a nice guy; I didn't want to put him on the spot."

The next day, at two o'clock sharp, veteran test pilot Don Segner took off and put the Cheyenne through its paces for twenty-six minutes. Kluever perched on a makeshift seat in the front cockpit.

Harry talked to Segner later. "She looked pretty good, Don; what do you think?"

"I had some control problems, nothing I couldn't handle, but I tell you this. The Cheyenne is too good."

"Too good? How's that?"

"As soon as the Air Force sees the Cheyenne's performance, it's going to start a rolls and missions war with the Army. They don't want any two-hundred-and-fifty-mile-per-hour helicopters out there providing ground support. I got a bad feeling about this, Harry. It doesn't make sense, I know, but the Cheyenne is just too hot to succeed. But don't tell anybody I said this—that's just between you and me."

Harry nodded—rolls and missions were the basis for apportioning the budget, and the services were intensely jealous about them. And as much as he hated to admit it, he knew that politics might prevent the Army from getting the best weapon it could.

CHAPTER FIFTY

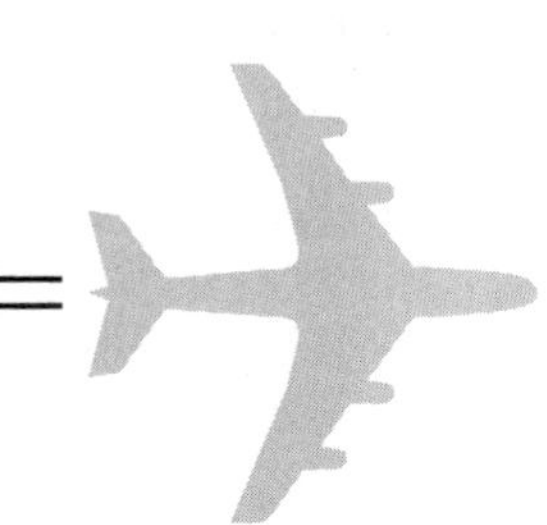

January 8, 1968
Palos Verdes, California

Clad only in his old terry cloth bathrobe, Vance Shannon was reaching for the refrigerator door when the stroke felled him. He stumbled straight ahead, gashing his scalp on the door handle, then crashing to the Mexican tile floor with a thump that brought Jill running from the next room.

She knew what it was at a glance, checking his breathing, then calling an ambulance. Forty-five minutes later he was in the hospital undergoing treatment, Doc Parry at his side.

Harry had rushed to the hospital and now he sat with his arm around Jill, comforting her. Jill had come late in life as a stepmother, but he loved her dearly.

"Anna will be here soon, and so will Nancy, as soon as she gets a babysitter."

Jill was a trooper, no tears, her emotions betrayed only by her death-white face and the constant squeezing of the handkerchiefs she held in each hand. She and Harry sat in the long green hallway, the walls throbbing with reflected fluorescent light, nurses and medics racing up and down, patients wheeled by, the curious combination smell of medicine, illness, and death, all with everyone looking anxious.

"I thought something was coming, Harry. He ate scarcely anything last night, just went into the library, and sat there, worrying about Tom and the business. Every once in a while, he'd talk to himself, and I could see him being agitated. I went to try to comfort him a few times, but he did what he always did, smile, and say he was OK in a way that let me know he wanted to be alone."

An hour later Parry emerged, his hair tousled as usual but his manner unusually grave. Normally almost preternaturally cheerful, Parry sat down with them and said, "Vance is going to live, but I think he will be impaired. I hate to tell you this, and I hope I am wrong, but it's apparent that this was a serious event, and we are going to have to watch him carefully for a few days. Then, when he comes home, he'll need almost constant care for a while."

"Is he conscious now?"

"No, he's sleeping, and that's the best thing for him at the moment. We'll do our best for him. I know what his regular medications are, but has he been taking anything over-the-counter?"

Jill thought for a moment and said, "Aspirin, he's always been a hound for aspirin, but I noticed he was taking them two at a time, several times a day, recently, complaining about headaches."

"That's a break—it may have saved him, that and your getting him to the hospital right away."

Harry and Jill went in to see Vance, frail and drawn, the usual array of drip bottles surrounding him.

Harry made a wry joke. "Too bad Bob isn't here to make sure the oxygen flow is right."

Jill whispered back, "Too bad Vance can't hear you—he'd be the first to laugh."

After a sad, silent twenty minutes, they left to meet Anna and Nancy in the hallway. They arranged to meet back at the house.

On the drive home, Jill cried quietly. She put her hand out on Harry's arm. "You know what this means, Harry. Vance wanted you to take his work over completely, and now you'll have to. I know you are too busy already; do you think you can handle it?"

Harry pulled over to the side of the street, closed his eyes, and thought hard. "I'll never be able to do what he did. He had an immense amount of knowledge and just incredible intuition. But I'll try to cover as much as I can. I think the best thing to do will be to get together with Bob and see what he's willing to take over. We can sort of divvy things up. And if it gets to be too much, we'll hire people. There's a recession going on in the industry now; lots of companies are squeezing their higher-salaried people out, the old story. We should be able to pick up some talent without much of a problem."

Jill said, "You do what your gut instinct tells you. That's how Vance operated, and he did well. He always told me that you would be running the place."

Harry turned and looked at her, flicking on the overhead light as he did so.

"Did he really say that? I'm amazed. Tom was always his favorite; I thought he would be the one to get the nod."

Visibly angry, Jill said, "How can you say that? He loved you both just the same; you must know that."

Harry shook his head, a rueful smile on his face. "No, that's just the way it was, I didn't mind, he never thought he was showing it, he always tried to be super-fair, but there it was. I think he saw a lot of Mom in Tom and that appealed to him. You don't mind my saying that?"

Jill shook her head. "No, I'm not jealous of your mother. Who could be? She did a fine job. I'm jealous of Madeline, but that's another story. But not your mother, never."

Harry drove on. "If I'm clinically honest with myself, I have to say that I'm a better choice than Tom, because I get along with Bob."

"Your dad saw that. That was part of his reasoning, but not all. He always considered you the best businessman in the family, himself included."

Harry put his hand on hers, patted it, and said, "Well, now we'll see. I just hope that poor Tom has survived. If he came back tomorrow, I'd be glad to give him pride of place; he deserves it."

Jill said, "He'll come back. I know it. I just hope it is not too miserable for him until he does."

VANCE'S RECOVERY WAS progressing quite well until he had a sudden, totally unexpected bout with pneumonia. It was three weeks before he was allowed to return home to Jill's loving care. To her surprise, he soon had a regular caller, Fritz Obermyer, who came down twice a week from Los Angeles to sit with Vance for precisely two hours. Vance had not yet regained his ability to speak, but he seemed to like Obermyer's being there. It was an unlikely friendship, given their different backgrounds, but it was evident that Vance enjoyed the companionship and it was a welcome relief for Jill.

It was mid-February when Fritz left Vance's bed and asked if he could talk to Jill. "That old car downstairs, the Cord. It is a favorite of Vance's, right?"

Jill nodded.

"Let me take it. I will have my people restore it. They have connections with the Auburn-Cord-Duesenberg club; they can get all the specifications. They will make it like new. Then we will surprise Vance; we'll take him down and take him for a ride in his new Cord."

Jill demurred at first, afraid that it might be done in a way Vance wouldn't like. But Fritz persisted, and she finally agreed, hoping that it would tug Vance back closer to the real world and perhaps give him an incentive to recover. Something had to be done. It was so sad to see this imaginative, even artistic man bundled up within himself, unable to communicate beyond shaking his head and, when he was feeling really well, making a mark to signify "yes" or "no" on a legal pad with a large crayon that Jill placed in his hand.

CHAPTER FIFTY-ONE

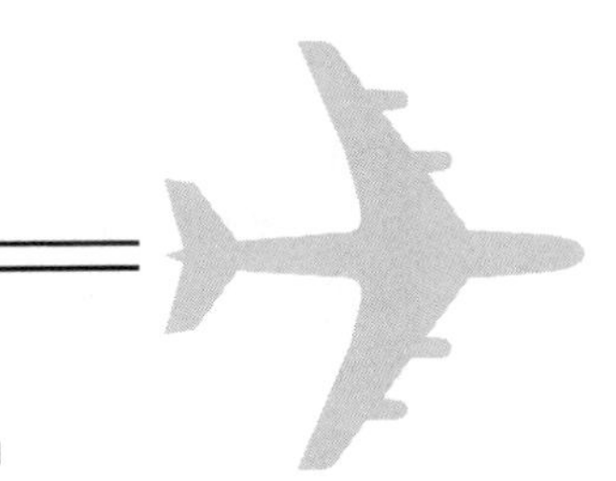

February 2, 1968
On the outskirts of Hanoi, North Vietnam

Pain was the path between consciousness and oblivion. He would submerge into an unconscious state, deeper than death could be, only to be jolted back into a shocked awareness of pain so unbelievably intense that he would lapse back into unconsciousness again.

The North Vietnamese captors had not yet tortured Tom Shannon. He was already so broken that there was no way to inflict additional pain. They knew that he had to recover before they could retrieve useful intelligence from him. Only then he could be tortured profitably.

Shannon had survived so far only because of the almost superhuman ministrations of Michael Pavone, captured simultaneously with him. Both men had ejected successfully, but Shannon had landed in the middle of a North Vietnamese infantry unit. The troops had thrown down their rifles and rice bowls to leap on Shannon, beating him with a ferocious glee. Pavone had landed only a few miles away and was scarcely beaten at all before being taken into custody by an intelligence officer, Võ Trân Kiêt. When Kiêt finally reached Shannon, the pilot was unconscious, his face brutally kicked in, his right eye enucleated, with both arms and his left leg twisted grotesquely. He was scarcely breathing through a foam of blood. Kiêt immediately assigned Pavone to care for him, ordering their escort to allow Pavone to do what he had to do to keep Shannon alive.

Pavone used his and Shannon's underwear to bind up the worst wounds and fashioned crude bamboo braces to immobilize his arms and legs as much as possible, given that he was being manhandled on trails until they reached a point where they were shoved into the back of a rough-riding truck. There was very little food, but Kiêt, conscious that Shannon was a colonel and therefore must know a great deal, passed Pavone sufficient rice to keep them both alive. Shannon could not chew, but Pavone chewed the rice for him, pressing it into his mouth and massaging his throat to induce him to swallow. All the while Pavone talked to him, sometimes as if he were a baby being induced to eat, sometimes screaming at him for not shooting down the fifth airplane for certain.

"I could be an ace and never know it."

Curiously, Pavone didn't blame Shannon for his bitter failure, for fixating on the target so long that he allowed them to be shot down. But Pavone was indignant that they might indeed have killed their fifth MiG and might never know for sure.

Pavone had no illusions. He knew that Kiêt's bounty would end as soon as they reached some place where Shannon could be hospitalized. Then it would be Pavone's turn to be beaten. He was not sure he could take it. It might be better to make a break for it, to be killed, rather than to endure the utter brutality that he had seen inflicted on the other prisoners who joined them on their long march.

On the second day on the trail, Shannon's eyes fluttered and he stared up at Pavone, the glance questioning all that had happened. No one saw Shannon's flicker of consciousness, and Pavone bent down and whispered in Shannon's ear.

"Colonel, you've got to hear me. You're hurt bad, but you'll live if you get a chance to rest for a few more days. I've checked your arms and legs, and I don't think they are broken. They want to question you, but as long as you are unconscious they'll let you be. I think they know you were the man who tricked them and shot down the MiGs. Don't ever let them see that you are coming around. I'll take care of you, but you've got to pretend to be unconscious, no matter what they do."

The North Vietnamese had moved them with a restless energy from one makeshift prison to the next. There was no pattern to the movements; sometimes as many as half a dozen people would be driven along, sometimes only Pavone and Shannon. It took all of Pavone's declining strength to keep Shannon moving. The villages were indistinguishable, the people hostile, the prisons little more than bamboo pens or rooms in the back of some old French government outpost. During the day their legs were freed to allow them to walk, but their arms were tied, further upsetting their sense of balance and causing many additional wounds from branches that snapped back into them as they were hustled along the trails. At night they were trussed, arms and legs, so that they could not move, lying on their backs and soiling themselves.

Then they were back on the truck again, heading north, judging by the sun, when Pavone saw an arrow with the words "Hà Nôi" painted on it. A few moments later he was adjusting Shannon's arm braces when he saw his good eye open and his lips moving.

Shannon gave a slight nod of his head and then lay there, thinking coherently for the first time since he had hit the ground, his parachute billowing around him. He had instinctively understood what Pavone meant about pretending to be unconscious. As long as Shannon could convince them that he was near death, he would probably not be tortured. Sooner or later they would find out, but if he could get a few days he would be stronger, more able to resist. Right now, torture would be easy for them; they would only have to twist one of his arms or kick him in the legs. But if he could get stronger, he could resist longer.

Wondering how Nancy and his dad had taken the news of his being shot down, he sank back into the black hole where pain could not come.

CHAPTER FIFTY-TWO

March 28, 1968
Everett, Washington

The invitation to watch the first 747 wing assembly to be removed from its assembly jig came at a bad time for Harry, but he reshuffled his schedule to be there. Moving the twenty-eight-thousand-pound assembly would signal that the Boeing 747 was on time, on schedule, and on its way to rollout.

Harry wanted to check out the huge new factory that Boeing had carved out of seven hundred acres of Washington wilderness in less than a year. With forty-three acres under one roof, it was by far the biggest industrial building in the world. Boeing had had to build highways and railways so it could construct the $200 million plant. It started assembling 747s even before the enormous structure was roofed over.

As big as Boeing was, it still depended upon individuals to move projects like the plant and the 747 itself forward. Joe Sutter and his team had done a fantastic job in designing the big transport, which posed a lurking danger to the Boeing company. Any major problems in building or selling it and, most particularly, any crash for any reason would almost certainly destroy the company. Everything was riding on the 747, and everyone at Boeing from Bill Allen down knew it.

As a result, Sutter designed the aircraft with many redundant systems, making sure that any problems would be "fail-safe." Harry Shannon had contributed in part to this, creating a new method of anticipating failures that he called fault-tree analysis. Charts recorded the safety relationship of every component to every other component in the airplane. If an element failed, its effect upon every other element could be spotted at once. With this in place, it was possible for the Boeing engineers to create solutions to problems before they occurred.

Sutter's operational counterpart was Mal Stamper, the driving force behind creating the factory and getting the first prototype assembled. Stamper literally lived at the factory, returning home only for an occasional meal and to collapse in bed. The stories about him were legend, but the most characteristic occurred when an unbelievable—even for northwest Washington—sixty-seven consecutive days of rain caused massive mud slides. A hill was washed into the still-building factory area, and it took more than $5 million to clean it up. In the midst of the cleanup, Bill Allen found Mal Stamper down in a ditch, directing how a pump should be installed. In the great tradition of Boeing, Stamper didn't mind getting his hands dirty.

The huge assembly bay was almost filled with spectators, awaiting the removal of the wing assembly. It was not a lengthy process, but not a word was said until the huge assembly, the first really major portion of a 747 to be completed, was moved toward its next station. As it slid effortlessly along, the room burst into cheers.

Gordy Williams, a protégé of Wellwood Beall and fast becoming one of Boeing's most successful salesmen, was standing next to Harry. When the cheers had died down, Williams said, "Got a second? I need to talk to you in my office."

It was a long walk to Williams's office, and Harry was puffing by the time he flopped into the leather chair facing his friend's desk, realizing at the same time how out of shape he was.

Williams had his secretary bring them some coffee, and she said, "Did you hear the news? Yuri Gagarin was killed yesterday. Crashed on a training flight."

The two men discussed the irony of a man surviving being shot into orbit only to die in an ordinary plane crash before Williams said, "Harry, this has to be on the q.t. We're getting some unexpected resistance to the 747 in domestic sales. American and TWA keep telling us what they've been telling us all along—the 747 is too big, and what they really need are smaller, three-engine airliners like the McDonnell Douglas DC-10 and the Lockheed L-1011."

Harry nodded. The name "McDonnell Douglas" still sounded unfamiliar, but he knew that American Airlines had already ordered twenty-five DC-10s. Further, and he could not tell Williams this, he knew that Lockheed had secured orders for almost 150 of the L-1011s from Delta and some other airlines.

"I tell you frankly, Harry, we're not so much worried about the DC-10. It depends too much on DC-8 technology. But the L-1011 scares us; it is a very modern airplane."

Harry wanted to be noncommittal. "I see that they've gone with Rolls-Royce for the engines. It really surprised me."

"Me, too, but it's supposed to be one hell of an engine. Anyway, what I want you to do is do a study, sort of like the one your father did on the supersonic transport, and lay out the merits of the 747 versus the L-1011 and even the DC-10. Tailor it for domestic customers, using domestic routes. We don't have any problems with foreign carriers ordering the 747, they're lining up in droves, but we need to nail down more of the domestic market."

The request both touched and bothered Harry. He was glad that Williams considered him in a league with the legendary Vance Shannon when it came to plans and forecasts, but he had some doubts about his ability to live up to the reputation. Vance had more experience, and he had an intuitive sense that Harry felt he lacked. Yet he knew that Boeing had many strong, experienced people who could do a study like this. Williams obviously wanted an unbiased, unvarnished look and felt that Harry could give it to him.

"I'll be glad to do it. What's your time line?"

"The usual, yesterday morning, but if you can give it to me in six weeks, I'll have it before a tour I'm going to do of all the major U.S. airlines."

Harry thought for a moment. Six weeks was cutting it close. He had to leave Everett and go directly to Fort Worth to the General Dynamics plant. The F-111 had been deployed to Vietnam and been an instant disaster, with three aircraft disappearing on combat missions. The airplanes were withdrawn from combat, and there was an all-out push on to discover the cause. Still, there were always nights and weekends, so Harry said, "Six weeks it is."

Harry started to go and Williams said, "Maybe I shouldn't be asking you, Harry, since I've got my own sources in the company, but how's it going in the great SST race?"

"Ah, Gordy, you know the Boeing team is still working hard, but I can't get the sense that anyone believes there will be an American SST, not even after all that's been spent on it. What do you say?"

"I say you are right. We won't even be ready to start on the prototype until next January. But what are our friends the Brits and French doing, and our old Commie buddy, Tupolev?"

"They've got a real horse race going. I keep getting feedback on it, and the Anglo/French cooperation is better than anyone has ever seen, in spite of themselves. The bigwigs get in major dustups, one crowd walks out of one meeting, the other the next, but the troops on the factory floors are getting along, trading information, making it work."

The Concorde was being created by the French firm Aérospatiale and British Aerospace. The French built the wings and control surfaces and much of the internals. The British built almost all of the fuselage, the vertical tail surfaces, and the engine installation. Four of Stanley Hooker's Olympus engines had been fitted, improved, and enlarged to provide 38,000 pounds of thrust each.

Harry went on, "In fact, even if they never built a single SST, they've forged a pattern for European cooperation that's a real threat to Boeing. And I've heard talk about an international consortium being formed to take build airliners."

Williams snorted. "They've tried that in the past, especially the Brits. Except for the Viscount and the Caravelle, the Europeans have never been a threat. I think they'll lose their shirt on the Concorde and there will be no follow-up airliners. Mark my words."

Harry never argued with a customer but went on, "Well, the first SST to fly will get a lot of press. It will probably be the Concorde, because we hear there's trouble with the Tupolev job. But who knows?"

Williams laughed and said, "Harry, you're just like your dad. Informative, but always politic! One thing for sure, whatever happens, you'll be among the first to know."

CHAPTER FIFTY-THREE

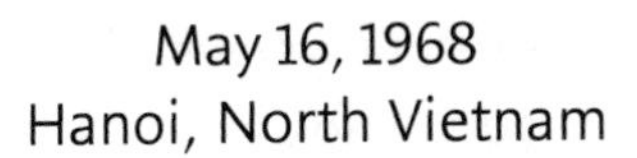

May 16, 1968
Hanoi, North Vietnam

The huge block-square Hoa Lo prison was located virtually in the middle of Hanoi, the shabby, run-down North Vietnamese capital. The prison was built by the French, and the name meant "portable earthen stove," because the hibachi was the principal industrial product of the area. Most of the North Vietnamese government had been imprisoned in Hoa Lo by the French. Now it served primarily as a catch basin for the increasing numbers of U.S. airmen shot down over Vietnam.

With its dirty, cream-colored stucco walls and muddy-red tile roof, the prison was run-down like all the Vietnamese public buildings. Inside, the bottom halves of the walls were painted black, while the tops were the same dirty cream as the outside. Every wall was worn, with the paint stained from the salts weeping through the concrete. When the wind blew, the air was filled with the open-sewer odor that pervaded Hanoi. When the air was still, Hoa Lo generated its own foul smells, a mélange of unwashed prisoners, open latrines, and the decades of filth and mold, a living, breathing petri dish of bacteria that coated the prison's walls, ceilings, and floors.

It had not been difficult to feign unconsciousness at first. Tom's internal injuries hurt so much that he just lay still, minimizing all movement. They knew the prison housed other airmen—Pavone reported hearing one whistling "Yankee Doodle" and at night there was an almost jungle rhythm to the prisoners' communicating by tapping. But

Tom and Pavone were kept completely isolated from the others, living in a damp concrete world of their own.

Their cell—Pavone had noted that it was Number 44, according to the door—was about ten feet square. Their beds were concrete blocks, fitted out with metal and wooden stocks for their feet—in case they needed to be restrained. A battered bucket placed against the wall was their toilet, patiently brought into position and held by Pavone when Tom needed it. A wooden door, so worn that it was reinforced with strap iron, had a peephole. Opposite it was a window with bars. Pavone said he could see the prison wall from it, but Tom had not yet tried to get up to do so.

They listened constantly to the tapping, trying to get in on the communication flow, to let someone know who they were and to find out who else was suffering with them. Both men strained to catch any sound of a guard coming. The slim rations, watery rice with an occasional fish head floating in it, were inedible at first, but by their second week of imprisonment it took all of Pavone's sense of duty to divide the rations equally and not sneak an extra bite for himself.

Two days before, a guard had sneaked up on them and caught Tom whispering to Pavone, and the game was over. The first thing the Vietnamese did was play catch-up with Pavone, who had been almost immune from torture as long as he was taking care of Tom. Two guards, inexplicably led by a vociferously profane brute of a Cuban, pulled Pavone out of the dank cell and carried him away.

For almost forty minutes Tom heard the steady stream of blows raining down on the screaming Pavone until, suddenly, he went quiet. Tom wondered if they had killed him.

Two guards came back to his cell and dragged Shannon down the hall, showing him an unconscious Pavone, trussed up, his hands manacled, ropes tied around his upper arms until they forced his elbows to touch. Another rope was looped around his neck and his ankles and tightened so that even unconscious, on his side, Pavone's back was painfully arched.

They took Tom back to his cell, shoving him to the floor. Not until the next day did they dump Pavone's horribly bruised body in Tom's cell, the Cuban guard saying, "Now you have to take care of him."

There wasn't much Tom could do. After checking Pavone for broken bones, he laid him out on the hard concrete bed. To Tom's surprise, a Vietnamese guard handed him a bucket of water without his asking, and he tried to wash his friend's battered face. Pavone's eyes were swollen shut and his tongue bulged from his mouth. Tom drizzled water on Pavone's tongue, saw where he had bitten almost through it in pain, and stopped, afraid to start the bleeding again.

The Cuban came back later in the day and motioned to Tom.

"Tomorrow it will be your turn. Then you'll learn how we get information in Cuba."

There was nothing to do but wait. Tom sat with Pavone, talking to him constantly. About noon, he seemed to be able to swallow and Tom carefully daubed the water back behind the cut in his tongue. That afternoon Pavone regained consciousness. After a few hours of moaning, he stirred himself to say, "Tom, I broke. Second goddamn day, I couldn't take it and I broke."

Tom stroked his forehead. "Don't worry about it. They can break all of us. It doesn't matter. We don't know anything they don't know."

"It was strange; I tried to give them phony stuff about where we were based and what kind of airplanes we were flying. I said we were flying T-33s. But they didn't seem interested in the military stuff; they kept talking about war crimes."

American prisoners of war were operating under a strict Code of Conduct, established by President Eisenhower after the Korean War when it was learned that some prisoners of war had been broken by fiendish torture. Under the Code, you could tell the enemy only your name, rank, serial number, and date of birth. You were obliged to try to escape. You could not help the enemy, of course, or accept any favors from them. Most importantly, you were forbidden from making any disloyal statements about your country. Korean torture experts had extracted confessions of war crimes from some U.S prisoners, and it had rocked the services. But the Code had no provision for the hard fact that sustained brutality could ultimately break anyone.

The Cuban came back the following morning, with two of the khaki-uniformed guards. They picked Tom up and forced him to walk down the hall, certain that the long-deferred torture was coming. To his surprise, the Cuban abruptly left and Tom was placed on a chair in the center of a room about twice the size of his cell. Opposite him, behind a worn wooden table, were seated two North Vietnamese officers. What followed might have been scripted for a B movie about Nazi interrogators. The Vietnamese on the left was about five foot eight, thin and severe looking. He was obviously the bad cop. To his right sat a shorter man, quite rotund for a Vietnamese, who seemed cordial and concerned—the good cop.

Tom expected them to question him about Operation Toro. He intended to follow the Code of Conduct as long as he possibly could when they tortured him, but he also prepared an elaborate story, totally false, about the mission.

The mission never came up. Instead, the two asked him the same questions over and over again. First it was what kind of a plane he was flying and where he had taken off. Then it abruptly diverged from the military, and they asked where his home was, what political party he belonged to, a whole series of non-military questions.

Tom replied only with his name, rank, serial number, and date of birth, refusing to answer anything else. After a long and boring two hours, he was taken back to his cell. Pavone was sitting up.

"What did they do to you?"

"Nothing. Just some softball questions."

"They didn't hit you?" Pavone seemed almost resentful.

"No, but I figure that's coming soon enough."

The next morning, the two Vietnamese who had interrogated Tom came to his cell with the same two guards. Without a word, he was half-walked, half-carried down to the same room. This time the two interrogators left and only one man was in the room. The Cuban.

CHAPTER FIFTY-FOUR

July 8, 1968
Palos Verdes, California

Jill was in the kitchen preparing lunch, tears of happiness running down her face. It was a miracle. Vance had been almost helpless for months, unable to do more than grunt or to make a stroke on a pad of paper when she put a crayon in his hand.

Then that crazy Fritz Obermyer had showed up with a young amateur historian, Warren Bowers. Bowers was writing a series of articles for *Wings* and *Airpower*, two specialist aircraft magazines for history buffs. He wanted to interview Vance on his early test pilot days. Jill had said no at first, but Fritz had really persisted, and Bowers had been coming faithfully two or three times since early April.

At first it was painful. He would ask questions of Vance, framed so that they could be answered by a grunt for "yes" or a shake of the head for "no." But within about two weeks. Vance began to be able to say individual words, almost always of a technical nature—things like "flaps" or "canopy" or anything related to airplanes. Bowers then began to expand his questioning technique a bit.

By mid-May, Vance was speaking in short sentences. He obviously delighted in being interviewed by Bowers on subjects everyone else had long since forgotten. Bowers had an encyclopedic knowledge of aviation and especially aviation people, and when Vance had a memory lapse Bowers would provide a name or a date that would set him off again.

Now Vance was speaking almost normally—hesitating sometimes but for the most part able to converse, not just with Bowers but with anyone.

Most of the interviews went right over Jill's head, but she could see the pleasure in Vance's eyes when Bowers hit on a subject particularly dear to him. For the most part, they were obscure people or planes of whom she heard—people such as Charles Rocheville, John Nagle, and Jean Roche or strange airplanes such as the Zenith Albatross or the McGaffey AV-8.

It didn't matter to her. Bowers had literally pulled Vance back from the grave, and she would be forever indebted to him.

And to Fritz. He was in with Bowers today, listening with pleasure to Vance's responses and planning a big surprise. While they were talking, some of Obermyer's people were delivering Vance's Cord, fully restored and running better than new.

AFTER THE USUAL two hours, Bowers, a polite and affable curly-haired young man of about thirty, gathered up the photos he used to spur Vance's memory and excused himself.

Fritz said, "Come on, Vance; let me take you to the window. I have a surprise for you."

He pushed Vance's chair to the window overlooking the driveway, where he had parked the cream-colored Cord, its headlights retracted, its long coffin nose gleaming in the sun.

Vance stared at the car, then gripped Fritz's arm.

"Is that my old Cord?"

"Yes—but it's the same as brand-new now."

"My God, it's beautiful. Who restored it? You, Fritz?"

"Some of my boys. It was a labor of love; they really enjoyed it."

"Look at that beauty, Jill; that's my dream car. Can you get me a calendar?"

Fritz shook his shoulders and looked at Jill, who hurried to the study and returned with a wall calendar.

"Today's what, the eighth of July?"

They nodded.

Vance riffled through the calendar.

"OK. Jill, mark the eighth of September. That's the day I'm going to walk down the steps and drive that beauty. Fritz, thank you so much. You've given me an incentive, just like young Bowers did. I tell you, I'm going to be back working by the first of the year."

They both believed him.

CHAPTER FIFTY-FIVE

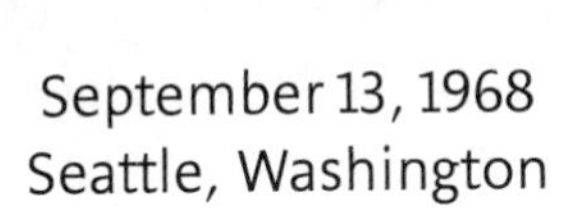

September 13, 1968
Seattle, Washington

Friday the thirteenth was no day for a marketing meeting, but Harry had no choice. Gordy Williams had invited him to hold a little seminar with as much of Boeing's sales team as Gordy could convene at one time. While most were based in Washington, Gordy had asked all the overseas representatives to come as well, and most obliged, delighted to get an unexpected free trip home.

The seminar went well from the start, with Gordy pleasing Harry by introducing him as "the legendary son of the super-legendary Vance Shannon" and telling the assembled group of well-paid, very successful men that Harry was going to start with the basics and would "tell it like it is."

Harry began by giving a general overview of the business and noting the relative positions of the three companies in the airline market. "The first thing I'll tell you is something you all know. The aerospace industry is terribly risky, and the earnings are not adequate for the level of risk. In about ten years, the industry will reach a point where it will be difficult, if not impossible, for a single company to undertake a major new project. We can look forward to more mergers like that of McDonnell and Douglas."

Williams spoke up. "Never at Boeing. We may buy somebody, but we'll never merge; we'll go out of business first."

There was a round of "hear, hears," and Harry smiled. "That's the spirit, and I hope you're right. The reason that Boeing is currently doing well is because it is making several models of each of its airliners—the 707, 720, 727, and now the 747—and tailoring each of them to the individual customer's requirements. McDonnell Douglas has not been able to match Boeing in the number of models, and has some well-known production problems. Lockheed has a credibility problem; its last airliner was the ill-fated Electra II, and it is really starting from scratch."

Using an overhead projector, Harry rapidly put up slides that gave the performance specifications for the DC-10 and L-1011, comparing them to the 747.

Then he got down to cases. "There are a lot of 'good news/bad news' jokes going lately, and this is going to be a 'good news/bad news' briefing.

"The good news is that there is a market for about one thousand wide-bodied aircraft to serve the American market. The bad news for Boeing is that many U.S. airlines—TWA and American for two—are convinced that the 747 is too big for them. That's good news for McDonnell Douglas and Lockheed. The bad news for them, though, is the fact that the break-even point for either airplane is about seven hundred and fifty planes. That means that if they divide the market, they will both suffer tremendous losses. Neither firm may be able to survive. These losses will go up with every Boeing 747 domestic sale."

There was a gasp as the audience understood what was happening. As far as the airliner business went, McDonnell Douglas and Lockheed were like two scorpions in a bottle—they would sting each other to death, and both were certain to die.

Rolfe Anderson stood up and said, "Are you sure about the break-even point?"

Harry shook his head. "Nobody's ever sure about a break-even point, not ever. I'm just telling you what I'm projecting, and even if I am off by fifty percent—which I am not—it spells disaster for your two competitors."

Jerry Bader raised his hand and said, "Do they have any way out?"

"Lockheed had one, but it blew it. It was approached by Douglas on a merger a couple of years ago. If Lockheed had accepted—and it could have—the problem would have gone away. The DC-10 would probably have been dropped, and only the L-1011 would be competing for the sales. But there was hubris at Lockheed, and some of the management wanted revenge, remembering the long rivalry of the Connies and the DC-6s and DC-7s. So they let it pass. A big mistake."

An old friend, Doug McKeon, stood up, asking, "What's it all mean for the 747?"

Harry took a breath and said, "Good news and bad news again. Bad news first—I think you are going to have a rough two or three years. You know there are engine problems, and we're going to see 747s sitting out on your ramp without any engines, maybe for months at a time. It's going to be tough for Boeing to survive, but I'm sure it will. The good news is that there is so much foreign interest in the 747. There are a lot of countries out there establishing state airlines—it's a matter of prestige. And if you want prestige, you have to have the 747. So I say that you'll sew up the foreign market over the next few years, and by that time, the American domestic market will have developed to the point that you'll be able to sell 747s to compete with the DC-10 and L-1011. One of them may have dropped out by then, anyway."

There was an exhausting question-and-answer session following his talk, and Harry was grateful when Gordy Williams at last stepped to the podium and called a halt to the meeting, thanking the salesmen for attending and thanking Harry for his insight.

As they walked down toward the simple but elegant Boeing executive dining room, Gordy said, "I know you have another meeting at one o'clock. What's it about?"

"I'm afraid I can't tell you, Gordy. No offense, I just can't. I wish I could; you'd love it. But I'll tell you in a few years, maybe."

Williams shrugged and they went into lunch, Harry's mind racing with anticipation.

At ten to one, Gordy dropped him off in front of the conference room that was normally used for meetings with the military customers. Completely insulated, checked electronically every day and before every meeting for listening devices, it was otherwise almost clinically simple, with a large oval oak desk in the middle and plain oak chairs spaced equidistantly around it. A heavy green curtain covered a blackboard.

To his surprise, there was only one person in the room. Harry had expected to see George Schairer and perhaps Joseph Arena from the CIA. Instead just one man was at the table, short, dark skinned, reading a folder with furious intensity. He glanced up as Harry came in, nodded, and returned to his reading. Harry sat down close enough to see that the report was written in Russian.

The man tossed the folder over to Harry and said, "I'm Gus Weiss. We've talked on the phone a few times."

Bob Rodriquez had introduced them by telephone. When they had talked, Weiss's booming baritone voice had formed a completely false mental impression for Harry. He had pictured Weiss as a tall, athletic type. Instead, he was just this side of being childlike in appearance.

"Mr. Shannon, since you were in on the first bit of deception we did with the Russkies, I thought you might want to know what was happening with their SST."

Shannon nodded, still nonplussed by the difference between his mental image and the actual person. "I certainly would, particularly the tire business."

"That slowed them down by about six months. It was certainly worth doing, and it taught us a few lessons, too, about how to approach them. But the real secret has been in the programming for the numerically controlled tools that we've officially allowed to be sold to them, and in the computer parts that we've arranged for them to buy clandestinely."

Now Weiss seemed to parody Humphrey Bogart, taking time to pull out a pack of Camels, open it, extract one, tap it several times, and light it, all the while staring Harry in the eyes.

"That's why we are stopping all efforts to hinder their SST development. We think their SST will fail on its own." The word "we" seemed to embrace the whole Central Intelligence Agency. "And we don't care if it flies first. But we do care that the Russians continue to get computer material from us. Sabotaged computer material, of course."

Harry paused to consider this and Gus went on, "It's probably a good thing. The next batch of SST material we were sending was going to alter the stability of the aircraft at high angles of attack. We might have caused an accident."

"Have you told the British or the French of this?"

"Of course not; we would deny whatever we were accused of. We're all for the Concorde, but not to the point that we'll give up our assets to help them."

"Mr. Weiss—"

"Gus," the other man interrupted.

"Gus, please call me Harry. And if I may ask, why are you telling me this? I certainly didn't have any need to know."

"You do in a way, because I want something from Aerospace Ventures. I know you are in the process of selling your simulator division to General Electric."

"It's a done deal; we're just clearing up the paperwork, getting stuff ready to ship."

"Yes, I know." Gus didn't seem to want anyone to believe there was anything he didn't know. Maybe there wasn't.

Weiss went on, "The Soviet Union is trying to buy flight simulators, not for the simulator itself, but because of the computers it contains. We want to sell them the simulators that Aerospace was developing, but we want to do a little work on them first. We believe that they want the computers for new navigation and bombing systems they are creating, and for use on their spacecraft. That's fine with us, if we have the privilege of altering the computers so that they have a latent defect that won't emerge until very late in the various programs, after they have invested a lot of time and effort."

Gus saw the look on Harry's face and smiled. "You really don't like this clandestine work, do you, Harry? I can see this rubs you the wrong way."

"You're right; I don't. I was thinking I'm glad this isn't going to affect things like the SST, where innocent civilians might get killed when things go wrong."

Weiss smiled again. "There are no innocent civilians in the Soviet Union, Harry, believe me. They have missiles targeted on all our major cities, missiles with huge warheads, much bigger than any of ours, and the missiles are there because the Soviet people allowed them to be, created them, worked on them. And if someone told them to launch those missiles, eighty million Americans might be killed in a thirty-minute period."

There was no comeback to a comment like that, and Harry said, "What do you want us to do?"

"You are going to be approached by a friend of yours, a good friend of your father's. She worked with us on the tire material, and she'll be our contact on this as well."

CHAPTER FIFTY-SIX

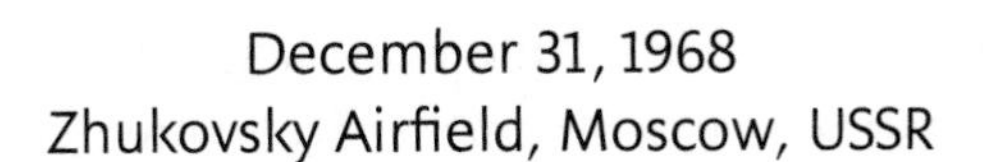

December 31, 1968
Zhukovsky Airfield, Moscow, USSR

The great Soviet Union ran on the basis of bribes and kickbacks, and the key lever in the great corruption game was the end of the year. All over the country, contractors who had failed to deliver material—anything, nails, wash pans, or supersonic transports—dreaded the last day of the year. If you did not meet your mandated goals by the thirty-first of December, everything could be lost—bonuses, rank, pay, prestige. As a result, the last day in December saw a convulsive effort to make formal delivery of hardware, no matter how unprepared its state. Nuclear submarines declared unfit for service by their commanders were nonetheless ordered to sea, sometimes sinking on their first voyage. But no matter—the bonuses would already have been paid.

Andrei and Alexie Tupolev had more to worry about than just the ordinary headaches of the end of the year. No less than two premiers, Khrushchev and Brezhnev, had declared that the Soviet Union would be the first to fly a supersonic transport and, further, that it would fly in 1968.

A huge black Zil 111 limousine carried Andrei to the flight line. This would be the 120th time that he witnessed the first flight of an aircraft bearing his name. He knew that it would also be the last.

His son, Chief Engineer Alexei, greeted him along with the chief designer, Yuri N. Popov, and his team. They were very proud to have brought this gorgeous gleaming white aircraft into existence, overcoming an almost unending series of problems to do so.

Andrei was very familiar with the aircraft, but there were film crews who had to have footage for television, and the old campaigner, smiling, followed his son around the enormous aircraft, making the appropriate gestures of appreciation as each feature was pointed out.

Both Tupolevs knew to an exact degree how much each of these features had challenged the design teams, presented seemingly unsolvable problems, and were finally overcome by a team effort unusual in the Soviet Union. The engines were a case in point. Originally they had been laid out four abreast under the huge double delta wing. Then retraction of the nose gear posed a problem, so the engines were moved to be located in two pairs, with space between them for the nose gear. This made it difficult to retract the main landing gear into the wing, which, despite its great size, was comparatively thin. A gear of incredible sophistication and cleverness had to be designed to permit retraction of each of the eight-wheeled landing gears.

As the Tupolevs finished their circuit of the aircraft, looking up with admiration at the "drooped snoot" of the Tu-144, test pilots Eduard Yelyan and Mikhail Kozlov were going up the steep yellow ladder to the entrance door. At the top, Yelyan turned, sought out Andrei Tupolev in the crowd below, and saluted him.

Andrei Tupolev could hear a member of the film crew dictating into a recorder, saying, "Now the intrepid crew has boarded the Tupolev Tu-144, the world's first supersonic transport. There will be no passengers today, but if there were, they could enjoy the luxury of beautiful carpets, fine wines, and classical music."

Tupolev smiled to himself. It was a Potemkim SST if they described it like this. His *Maxim Gorky*, flown thirty-four years before, had all those things, but this prototype was Spartan. The passenger cabin was not pressurized, and the pilots and flight engineer had ejection seats! Tupolev knew that there was much to be done before the aircraft could be placed in production. New engines, new wing shape, and in a following model they would have to use a crude fix that was an abomination, retractable canards, little forewings that could be deployed to improve low-speed characteristics. But that was all in the unknown future. What was known was that right now, the last day of 1968, Andrei Tupolev would fulfill his orders from the Soviet Premier: the SST would fly.

Despite his voluminous coat and fur hat that fit down well over his ears, the bitter cold gnawed at him. Glancing around the field, Tupolev could see the rooftops of the field's buildings and all the hangars crowded with people eager to see this massive airplane fly.

Andrei was talking to the press now, reciting the formidable statistics of the Tu-144. "The Tu-144 will fly from Moscow to New Delhi in just over two hours. A passenger taking off from Moscow at noon would land at Montreal at nine the previous morning—the Tu-144 will outdistance not only sound, but the sun."

It was all necessary. No one knew better than Andrei the shortcomings of the prototype, but no one but his son, the so-called Czarevitch, could have had a prototype ready on this last day of the year. He had planned, argued, threatened, and cajoled as he traveled back and forth across the country to get the suppliers of the myriad parts to put out the extra effort necessary. This was really Alexie's airplane in every sense of the word.

Now V. N. Benderov and engineer Yu Silverstov were onboard and the four enormous NK-144 engines, which would soon be capable of almost half a million horsepower at top speed, began their roaring rumble of a start.

The aircraft taxied out with remarkably few preliminaries, the controls being exercised and the pilot making one simple S-turn, checking the steering. As it did so, Andrei Tupolev moved along the tarmac to be exactly opposite to the point where he thought the Tu-144 would break ground. He stood there with Alexei watching, as he had watched so many of the products of his genius in the past.

The Tu-144 turned onto the snow-covered runway and applied power, lurching forward, followed by huge snow vortexes that blanketed it from the crowd as it gained speed. Then it was off, at the spot Andrei had predicted, and climbed, the nose drooped for visibility.

Alexei turned and embraced his father. They had done the impossible. The Soviet SST was flying, the first SST in the world to do so.

The Tu-144 flew for twenty-eight minutes, its landing gear never retracted, just as had been planned those many months ago. The unpressurized fuselage was filled with hundreds of recording instruments, all telemetering their information back to the ground. The pilots' and engineer's voices were heard plainly and were taped—if anything went wrong, the engineers on the ground wanted to know what was happening.

But it was an uneventful flight for an airplane that would ultimately exceed 2,500 kilometers per hour. Andrei knew what would follow, joyous celebrations in *Izvestia* and *Pravda*, boastful comments from the Kremlin on the coming prosperity of the Soviet Union, and a general national euphoria about yet another technical success.

Andrei shook his head. The Tu-144 had flown before the Concorde, but other things were happening. The Americans were making amazing progress in space, doing much more now than the Soviets were. Only a few days before this flight, the American *Apollo VIII* had orbited the moon with three men aboard. Think of it! Orbiting the moon with a manned spaceship. He knew from his contacts that the Soviet Union was years from being able to do this.

He turned once again to look at his Potemkim SST before climbing back into the welcome warmth of the Zil. It was a beautiful airplane but not yet a good one. With time, however, it would be both.

CHAPTER FIFTY-SEVEN

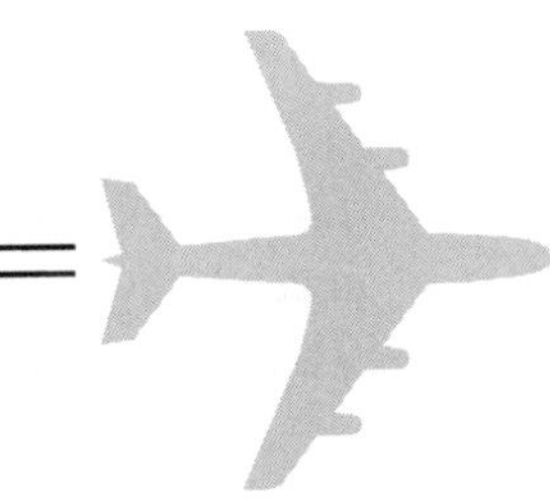

April 14, 1969
Palos Verdes, California

Jill Shannon stood with her arms wrapped tightly around a sobbing Mae Rodriquez. Mae's three-year-old son played in the corner with the enormous set of smoothly finished blocks that Tom and Harry had played with many years before.

"Take it easy, honey. Bob will be all right, and one of these days he won't have to work so hard or travel so much."

Mae gulped and said, "I'm so embarrassed to do this. I should be tougher. But in the last year he's only been home about thirty days, total. It's not fair."

"It's this crazy business they are in, Mae. Men get wrapped up in aviation, and it becomes their life, and their families get short shrift. It happened to me, you know."

Mae nodded. More than once Jill had related the story of her marriage at eighteen to a young pilot, Jimmy Abernathy. They were happily married for six years before he was killed, not in an airplane but in a stupid car accident, smashed by a drunken driver on Highway 1.

"Jimmy loved me, I know that, but flying is demanding. He was gone for months at a time, trying to sell airplanes in South America. The competition is tough, and there's something about it that screws up men's minds."

"Why did you marry Vance, knowing that?"

"Honey, when I married Vance, I was totally in love again, and he was older and more settled. If I had ever had daughters, I would have taught them not to marry anybody in flying. The wife always winds up second-best to the airplane. They cannot help it, they are good providers otherwise, but when that damn engine starts, they are gone, off to fly."

"But Bob's not doing much flying himself anymore; it's just business, always going down to Florida, or off to Houston, or overseas. I can't go along because of Bob Junior."

"He's not flying the airplane, but he's in aviation, and the passion carries over. These guys only know one way to operate, full throttle, be there fast, be there first, and stay there until you get the job done. In a way it's admirable, even when we know they are not doing it for us; they are doing it for their own goddamn fascination with flying. So we have to be admirable, too, and put up with it and support them, even though it's tough."

"You're describing Bob exactly."

"Worse, I'm describing Vance even now. Every day that he is better, he tries to do more in running the business. It's tough on Harry, because Vance sometimes steps in and overrules him, or interferes. And apparently his judgment is not quite what it was. Harry often has to go back and mend fences, make changes, and somehow keep Vance from knowing about it. But Vance is even worse about Vietnam. Since Tom has been shot down, he has been steadily getting more rabid about the way the war is being fought. Not hearing from Tom, not knowing whether he is alive or dead, is a nightmare. Vance wants to tell the government to bomb North Vietnam until the war is won, and I think it is because he secretly believes Tom is dead. He claims to be sure that he knows Tom is alive, but if he really believed that, he wouldn't advocate bombing Hanoi."

"I've never seen this side of him."

"No, he conceals it from most people, and only lets go with Harry and with me. He knows that he sounds a little round the bend, but with us he doesn't care."

Mae carefully folded her handkerchief, put it in her purse, and looked straight into Jill's eyes. "Jill, I'm being honest with you. I don't know if I can go on."

"Are you talking about getting a divorce?"

Mae looked horrified. "A divorce, never. But Bob's got to give in a bit on this. He wants me to have another baby, but I couldn't handle two of them by myself, being alone so much. You are a godsend, but I cannot off-load my family on you."

Jill wouldn't have minded if Mae had off-loaded her family permanently. She had never had children, always wanted them, and adored Tom's little V.R. and young Bobbie.

"I know it doesn't help, but look at Nancy. Tom's in Vietnam, we don't know if he's dead or alive, and she's coping. She's even helping Harry with Anna, making sure she stays on the wagon."

Mae felt ashamed. There was no comparison. She knew where Bob was, he called every day he was away, and he was safe. Poor Nancy. Mae pulled herself together, gathered up Bobbie. Jill walked her out, patting her on the back, picking up the just-delivered mail in the process. It was the usual big bundle of letters, bills, and magazines. Vance still subscribed to every aviation magazine in the country and a few from Europe, though he rarely took time to read them anymore. Most of his time was spent in front of the television set, ranting at the news. When he felt up to it, he had Jill drive him to the office for a few hours.

Carrying the mail on her way into Vance's study, Jill riffled through the envelopes. She came to a sudden halt when Madeline's familiar handwriting leaped out at her like a cobra striking. The letter was postmarked in Paris and addressed to Vance.

Without a moment's hesitation, Jill tucked the letter into her apron pocket and brought the rest of the mail in to Vance, who was reading the proofs on yet another article on his test work by Warren Bowers.

"Anything good, like a check?" he asked.

"No, just the usual bills and advertisements. There is one good thing, a letter from Bob."

She realized she had never lied to Vance before, not ever, not about anything, and Madeline's letter was suddenly a time bomb ticking in her pocket. Anxious to get away, she asked, "Would you like some cocoa?"

Ripping open Bob's envelope, he replied, "No, but how about some tea? With a couple of Oreos on the side?"

She walked rapidly from the room and ran down the hallway to the bathroom, locking the door behind her. Madeline had inflicted enough harm on Vance; Jill was not going to let her do it again.

There was a scissors in a basket near the sink. Jill carefully opened the envelope, shuddering at Madeline's precise, ornate, almost calligraphic handwriting. She read:

> *Dearest Vance,*
>
> *It must be so strange to get a letter from me, but I have to write you this one last time, and tell you why I was so heartless as to leave the man I loved.*

Jill's stomach contracted as she thought, *The man she loved! She means the man she deserted, the man she almost ruined. What nerve!*

The letter went on:

> *You'll remember that I never spoke of my family? It was because they had been collaborators—my father and brother, I mean, not my mother. I was the only one to serve the Free French. After Dunkirk, I made it to England on a fishing boat, and they got me a job in the American embassy to work in intelligence. You'll remember that's where we met, and how lucky I was.*
>
> *But I remained in intelligence—call it being a spy; that's what it was—all my life, as you know to your sadness. You are a patriot, and you must understand that I was a patriot, too.*
>
> *But now it is over, not because I wish it, but because I am terribly ill with cancer. The doctors say that I have not long to live, and of course I am frightened. I did not want to die without writing you and telling you that despite my actions, I truly loved you. Not just when we were together, but always, to this day.*
>
> *Give my best love to Tom and Harry; they were like sons to me, even though they did not think of me as their mother. Forgive me for having hurt you, forgive me for leaving you, but most of all, remember that I loved you until the end.*

It was signed simply "Madeline."

Jill took the scissors and methodically cut the letter and envelope into narrow, curling strips. Then she hurried down to kitchen, banging pots to indicate she was brewing tea. She put the butchered shreds into a frying pan and lit them with a match. They burned poorly and she used half a dozen matches to get them truly lit.

She knew she should feel guilty, but she did not. This was the right thing to do, for Vance and for their marriage. She knew how Madeline's memory affected Vance and was uncertain what the image of a dying Madeline would do to him. As unwell as he was, he still might have picked up and gone to Paris, to find what?

Jill heard him moving down the hall, moved the frying pan to the sink, dowsed it with water, and threw the soggy residue into the flip-top wastebasket.

Vance walked in beaming, then asked, "What's that smell? And what's the matter with you? You look terrible."

Jill sat down at the table and began crying uncontrollably. Vance stood behind her, rubbing her neck. Jill got up, saying, "Make your own tea," and ran from the room.

VANCE SHOOK HIS head. It was unlike Jill, but Mae must have said something to bother her. That was strange, for it was usually Anna who got Jill upset.

He had enough worries of his own. Rodriquez was off again, down at Eglin Air Force Base, running a series of tests on the new bombs he and his team had devised. One was television guided; the other used a reflected light of some kind to guide the bomb. Fascinating as it was, it was beyond Vance's knowledge. Worse, it meant Bob would be away for another month. Worse still, Vance was still not sure how they would make any money from it. It probably was a mistake to sell the simulator business off—but he didn't understand that, either. It was better when things were simpler. When he was hired to test-fly a new airplane, he would look it over, fly it cautiously for a bit, then put it through its paces. When he landed, he'd write a report, they would pay him, and it was over. Now when they did something it involved contracts, partial payments, quality control, safety inspectors, a thousand ways to fill up paper.

Still he felt the routine pang of guilt that he was no longer pulling his weight, even though he tried to help Harry, who, as always, was overworked. They had a chance to catch up during the second week in February, when the two had gone to Seattle to see the first flight of the Boeing 747. On the way up, Harry briefed him on the problems the 747 was causing Boeing, Seattle, and Pan Am, all things that he had shielded Vance from while he was convalescing.

"Dad, just like you predicted, they kept revising the airplane and the gross weight kept going up until now it's more than seven hundred thousand pounds. The Pratt & Whitney JT9D-1 engine was putting out the power it was supposed to—but that's not enough anymore, and Pratt is advising Boeing to let them add water injection to boost power, at another one hundred thousand dollars per engine."

Vance listened thoughtfully. It was all so predictable, all so normal. How could they not have anticipated this? He had warned both Trippe and Allen, told them to wait a bit, let things mature. If only he had not fallen ill, he might have been able to prevail on them a little.

Harry went on, "The orders for the 747 dried up, and when they did, Boeing had to start laying people off. And so, of course, did all of Boeing's suppliers, most of them right there in Seattle. It was an economic disaster for the city. Some joker put up a billboard sign saying: 'Will the last person to leave Seattle turn out the lights?' "

Shaking his head, Vance asked, "And what has been going on at Pan Am?"

He had been following the problems through *Aviation Week*, the only magazine he still read regularly, but he didn't read everything, and his retention was diminishing.

"It was just as bad there. They bought the 747 thinking that airline travel was going to increase by maybe twenty percent by the time they are delivered. Problem is that more people are traveling but only about five percent more. So they will have 747s hanging around, full of empty seats."

"And then there's the new overseas carriers."

"Right, Dad, for the first time, there are other American carriers flying transoceanic routes, and every one of them has domestic lines to hook up to. Pan Am doesn't. Your old pal Jeeb Halaby said Pan Am was an airline without a country and he was right.

"What's Jeeb doing?"

"He's being groomed to be president of Pan Am, probably within a year or so."

Vance was feeling pretty bad by the time they got off the airplane, but his reception by old friends at Boeing buoyed his spirits. And it made him feel good simply to walk around the huge transport, aware of his and Harry's contributions to it. Planes had come a long way from the Curtiss Jenny Vance had trained on in 1917.

The takeoff was watched by thousands of spectators lining the airfield, but the forty-five-minute first flight was a bit of an anti-climax. A flap malfunction forced Jack Waddell, the pilot, to make the entire flight with the flaps down. Still, there it was, the world's largest, fastest airliner, a mammoth airplane intended to change air travel forever.

In Seattle, Harry had tried to persuade Vance to go to Toulouse, to see the first flight of the Concorde. He was tempted to go, but Jill talked him out of it—she wanted him where she could keep an eye on his health and, he thought, she probably didn't want him traipsing around France, where he might run into Madeline. Good thinking on Jill's part!

Madeline. He wondered how she was doing after all these years. He hoped she was well. She was probably better than he was, for sure.

CHAPTER FIFTY-EIGHT

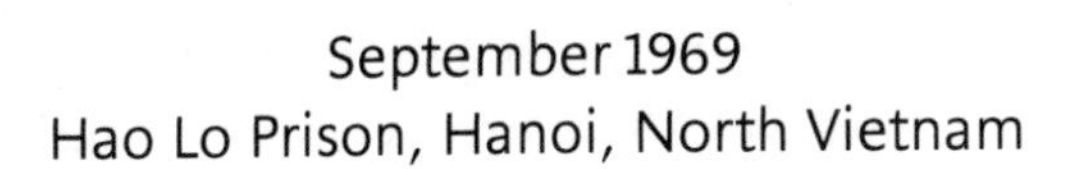

September 1969
Hao Lo Prison, Hanoi, North Vietnam

The North Vietnamese catalog of cruelties included starvation, systematic torture, and crude but continuous attempts at brainwashing. In many ways it was strictly business to the Vietnamese, who had an ordered hierarchy for dealing out punishment. At the top were officers and civilian officials whose task it was to gather information for either military or propaganda use. Below them were less well-educated guards, who handed out pain and punishment in part as prophylactic discipline, in part in response to any slight, real or imagined. Underlying their efforts was the unreasoning, frightened hatred of small, uneducated men for large, professional men.

There was an almost irrational insistence that the prisoners of war have no verbal communication. A prisoner speaking a language their captors could not understand was a mammoth affront, an insupportable insult. Whenever possible, prisoners would find themselves in a position to talk through a wall or over a fence, but the guards were vigilant and interrupted forcefully.

Tom had feigned illness long enough to gather a little strength as Pavone and he were switched around from one miserable holding pen to the next. He was unable to tell whether he remembered the long, agonizing trips from one squalid "jail" to the next or he only remembered what Pavone had told him about them. They were all similar, either bamboo cages or damp concrete cells, and all were liberally populated by rats that seemed invisible to the Vietnamese. As Pavone recalled it, the jails all must have been within twenty or thirty miles of Hanoi. They learned later that the Americans gave the jails popular names that the Vietnamese sometimes used themselves—"the Zoo," "Alcatraz," and so on.

Pavone had long since confirmed that the North Vietnamese suspected that Shannon was the author of the trap over the Phuc Yen airfield. On one occasion three men had come to stare at him, one apparently a MiG pilot, judging by his gear and the fact that he surreptitiously left behind a small package wrapped in newspaper that contained aspirin, a grainy bar of chocolate, so old that it was chalk colored, and a small stone image of Buddha.

The long deceit gave Shannon just enough strength to survive the indiscriminate serial beatings that the North Vietnamese inflicted on all the prisoners. Yet hunger overrode even the pain from the beatings, and he was weak from a miserable diarrhea that was alleviated only by long periods of constipation.

Still there was change in the air. The relentless beatings and torture had diminished in the last few months, although either could be quickly provoked by something as simple as not bowing as swiftly as a guard thought you should. Tom was now well integrated into the tapping grapevine, even though he had not yet been in a position to talk to another prisoner. He was being kept isolated, and Fidel, as they called the Cuban, promised that he would never have a chance to speak to the other prisoners.

The tap code was utterly simple. Twenty-five letters of the alphabet, with *K* excluded, were laid out in a matrix of five lines and five columns, with *A* through *E* in the first line. One tap indicated the first line; two, the second; and so on. Thus one tap followed by one tap was *A*; two taps followed by one tap was *F*. While they never reached a telegrapher's speed, the prisoners soon could "read" transmissions as fast as they were given. When the Vietnamese cracked down on the tapping, sneezes, coughs, hacks, throat clearings, et cetera, were all substituted for taps. Hand movements, flashing a scrap of paper or a twig, worked equally well. Tom was amazed by the facility he gained in just a few weeks. Still, the other Americans occasionally got a chance to talk to one another. He could not remember when he had talked to another American besides poor Pavone.

There was a lag time in prison news. New arrivals came in but were sequestered for weeks or months. Then it took a long interval to get them into the tap-code circuit. Once that was done, they were pumped for all news of home, not only political events, such as President Johnson ordering a halt to the bombing of North Vietnam.

The bombing halt was inexplicable to Tom. He knew that it was intended to send a signal to Hanoi that negotiations might be preferable to further bombing, but it missed its mark. The halt gave the North Vietnamese an immense boost to their morale. Instead of interpreting it as a gesture of peace, a possible basis for negotiations, they saw it properly as a sign of weakness. The North Vietnamese very sensibly used the "time-out" to vastly strengthen their anti-aircraft artillery and surface-to-air-missile strength, especially along the southern portions of the infamous Ho Chi Minh Trail.

Pavone was not adapting well. Tom feared that his last beating had caused some brain damage. Pavone could do the tap code only if he went so slowly that it was agonizing for the party on the other end and too often interrupted by a passing guard.

The communication, primitive as it was, was essential for security and morale. Just knowing who some of the other prisoners were made a lot of difference. Knowing how long they had been here was not. A Navy A-4 pilot, Ev Alvarez—Alvey, they called him—was the first American shot down, and had been a prisoner since 1964. Most of the names were unfamiliar to Tom. There was no reason to know the Navy pilots, but among the Air Force pilots the only name he recognized was that of Robby Risner, an ace in Korea whom Tom had flown with on more than one occasion. Most of the other men were younger, and he did not recognize their names.

Despite the mindless beatings and torture that had been meted out to him, Tom was still defiant, his resolve stiffened by the painfully tapped-out stories of Alvarez's and Risner's epic resistance to torture. Risner had been tortured continuously for twenty-six days and gave up nothing. Tom swore that if Robby could do it, he could, too.

Tom was amazed by the general optimism of the prisoners. Most of the tap-code conversations related to either resisting or the prospects of going home. There were few complaints about the wretched food and the uncertain length of their stay, although sometimes they give in to describe a fantasy meal. Contemptuous but apt names for the guards were coined, as in "Dipshit," "Eagle," "Cat," and "Rabbit," and these were the subject of usually wry jokes.

Tom learned early on that face was extraordinarily important to the Vietnamese and that it was wise always to be polite no matter how stressful the situation.

Pavone and he had been kept isolated for their entire stay, but he knew from the tapped "office gossip" that they would be meeting some of the others soon. Half the tapped messages concerned this new sense of change, and no one could tell whether it was for good or ill.

With the relaxation of the beatings there came a new phenomenon, the utter boredom of being confined to a tiny cell with nothing to read. Tom knew how much he owed Pavone—his life, for openers—and busied himself caring for him. But it left time for thought and self-reproach. Tom now spent hours grieving that he had been so selfish as to leave Nancy with V.R., not because of the discomfort of being a POW, but because they must be suffering not knowing his fate. He also regretted his attitude toward Rodriquez. Tom's anger had made his father's life much more difficult than it should have been, for no reason other than jealousy, perhaps, or a desire to protect his turf.

But even in prison he could take satisfaction for the way in which he had turned the Sixth Tactical Fighter Wing around, converting it from a poorly performing, low-morale outfit into one that was, in current tap-code parlance, "S.H." for "shit hot." He remembered with pleasure breaking the back of the North Vietnamese MiG-21 strength with Operation Toro, even though that was now long years ago. He didn't dwell on it because of an irrational fear that the enemy might somehow pick up on his thoughts and torture him to reveal details.

Almost on cue, he heard the sound of footsteps in the hall, and the usual visceral fear gripped him. He waited hopefully for the sound of another door being opened, realizing he was wishing punishment for someone else but not able to resist doing so. Then he heard what all prisoners dreaded—the turn of the key in the lock.

It was Fidel, with two guards.

"This time you will talk."

Tom pulled himself to his feet. The two guards grabbed him by the arms and forced him to run down the hallway, the Cuban following slowly behind, knowing that a prisoner's apprehension was a key element of successful torture.

It started simply enough. The cell was about fifteen feet square, with a desk and table at one side. In the center of the room, directly under a suspended electric light, a bare bulb, a white circle about two feet in diameter was painted on the floor.

The guards deposited him on the circle and the Cuban barked, "Stand at attention. Do not move out of the circle." He spoke in a strangely accented Vietnamese to the two guards, who took up positions in front and in back of Tom. Fidel then left the room.

Though nothing had been said, Tom had learned from the tap-code circuit that stepping outside of the circle would be punished by blows from the long thin, round sticks carried by the guard. They were like pool cue sticks but not tapered and operated more as a cat-o'-nine-tails than a two-by-four. Supple, they tended to chew up the flesh rather than break bones.

Like many of the other prisoners, Tom had long since turned to prayer, and never more than when under this sort of acute stress. He ran through the prayers he remembered. The Lord's Prayer, both the Catholic and the Protestant versions. Hail Marys by the score. And most often, most ardently, Acts of Contrition.

Tom kept his eyes focused on a light spot in the paint on the wall opposite him. He flexed his toes and his knees as unobtrusively as possible, tried to move his muscles without obviously breaking the posture of being at attention. Memories of the old Charles Atlas system of dynamic tension came to him, and he tried working one muscle against another internally, without external movements. Pressure built in his bladder and he felt his bowels turning to water.

He put up his hand and said, "Latrine," and the guard on his right jabbed his stick into Tom's belly. He voided, and the guards roared, it was forbidden, and they both picked up a baseball stance, setting their feet, whipping their sticks back behind them, then simultaneously striking him front and back.

The pain ripped through Tom and he staggered back. The guard on the right stepped forward and swung again. Tom sidestepped, grabbed the stick, and struck the smaller man across the throat with it. He turned to hit the other guard, who dropped his stick and ran from the room screaming, slamming the door behind him.

Within a minute, the door burst open again, the burly Cuban leading the way. He charged directly into Tom, slamming him into the wall, knocking the wind from him.

The Cuban then stood over Tom and began kicking methodically, moving up and down his body with his boots as if he were playing a marimba, dealing out the punishment with a fierce gleam of pleasure in his eye. The pain was excruciating. Fidel knew where Tom had been most injured and kicked those places—his back, his arms and legs, with greater ferocity.

Just before he became unconscious, Tom thought, *I'm not going to live through this one.*

CHAPTER FIFTY-NINE

December 24, 1969
Palos Verdes, California

Jill ran to the door. V.R. was beaming in through the glass side panels, and outside Nancy was standing with Mae and Bob, almost collapsing under the weight of their presents.

They poured in, all incredibly happy with the news—Vance's beaming mailman had delivered a letter from Tom. The only thing it proved was that he was alive when he wrote it, and there were dark hints of ill-treatment within the letter itself, but the relief from uncertainty was so great that they could not be less joyous.

"How is Vance taking the news?"

"He's in the library now with Harry and Anna, poring over the letter, trying to figure out what Tom might have meant, but he is deliriously happy; he's been a changed man since the letter came this morning."

V.R. had already run down the hall to throw himself into "Grampaw Vance's" arms, with Bob Junior following close behind him.

"How are you taking it, Nancy?"

"It's unbelievable. I'd almost given up on him. Not a single word since his last letter from Thailand. And now this. It's wonderful."

After the tumultuous round of greetings and laughter, they passed the letter around so that each one could see it. It was obviously written to a North Vietnamese format, seven lines only, and Tom's normally bold script was compressed into tightly spaced printed letters, so that he could jam the maximum amount of information into the space available.

Some of it was obvious North Vietnamese propaganda, but there were some sentences that had both Vance and Harry stumped. Anna, who had taken up photography as a hobby, had photographed the letter, enlarged it, and made it into a transparency. Harry set up the overhead projector he used for contract briefings and shined the letter—more difficult to read now but still legible—on the motion picture screen that dropped down from its roller above the fireplace.

Vance's voice, a little weak and shaky in recent weeks, was strong, and his hands were trembling with excitement. He had already read the letter a half-dozen times, but there was a curious quality to it. He knew Tom was telling them something that would not be obvious to the enemy censors.

The letter was written on a single sheet of paper, with a Vietnamese phrase at the top next to the date, "October 15, 1969." Beneath the seven lines of the letter were some instructions, in Vietnamese and English. The English lines read: "Write legibly and only on the lines" and "Notes from families should also conform to this pro forma."

On the screen, in tiny cramped letters, they could read:

Dear Nancy and V.R.

Nancy's trembling voice asked, "Why did he write to me but send it to Vance?"

Harry replied, "We don't know, but it may have something to do with your security."

> *I love you and miss you. Please write and tell me you are all right. I am well. I am being treated well by the North Vietnamese even though I bombed their innocent villages. The food is unusual but good like at Armenian Joe's. I was wounded when I bailed out but I'm better now, Ollie. They have good medical treatment, just like the Revolutionary War. I hope that the war ends soon the way I know Dad will want it to end. Tell Dad and Jill and Harry and Anna I love them all. I guess V.R. is a big boy now; tell him his Daddy loves him. It's like from Memphis to Mobile here most of the time. Vlad would be right at home. I will endure. I love you all. Tom.*

Vance, his eyes filled with tears, said, "Some of the first lines are just propaganda; they must tell them that they have to say that."

"What does he mean by 'Armenian Joe's'?"

"There used to be a restaurant just outside of San Diego called Joe's Armenian Palace. It was shut down after a series of food-poisoning incidents. The food must be really rotten."

"Poor Tom—and the way he likes to eat."

Harry grimaced and said, "You know how he loved Laurel and Hardy. That phrase 'I'm better now, Ollie,' is what Stan used to say when he had done something else dumb. It must mean that he's not better, that he's not getting the right treatment. And saying that the medical treatment is like the Revolutionary War is a dead giveaway."

Bob spoke up for the first time. "I'm surprised they let that go through. They are probably thinking it means their revolutionary war, so it doesn't sound so bad. But I hate the sound of this. He's been injured, they are not feeding him, and his injuries have not been taken care of properly."

Mae dug her elbow in his side and gestured to Nancy, sobbing quietly, stroking V.R.'s head. Even V.R. was affected by the charged atmosphere that combined glee at Tom's being alive with grief at the conditions he was enduring.

Nancy spoke up. "I think 'from Memphis to Mobile' must mean 'blues in the night.' They must be torturing him at night. But who is he talking about when he says: 'Vlad would be right at home'?"

Bob spoke again, his voice quiet, under control, but seething with anger. "He must mean Vlad the Impaler, the Transylvanian count who is the source for the Dracula legends. He was famous for his tortures."

Mae's elbow dug into Bob's side again.

Vance spoke up, carefully controlling his voice. "We have to look on the bright side of this. I never thought we would ever learn what happened to him. To find that he is alive, even if he's a prisoner, is a godsend. And look at his last line; he says: 'I will endure.' You can bet on that; he's a tough cookie. I just hope we get him out of there soon."

Harry stood up and flicked the overhead projector switch off. "They will, Dad. The country will not put up with having our people being treated like this."

Mae was usually very quiet at family discussions, knowing that Bob was really a latecomer, an outsider in fact, and that Tom resented him in particular. But she could not resist. "Harry, I hope you are right, but I'm afraid that the anti-war movement here is going to stiffen the Vietnamese resistance. I don't think they will ever let our prisoners go unless we pull out."

Vance said, "If Tom were not there, if they didn't have our other prisoners, I'd say nuke them and be damned. But we cannot."

Harry furrowed his brow and responded, "No, we cannot nuke them, Dad, but we can put enough conventional bombs on them to make them surrender. General LeMay tried to stop us getting into the Vietnam War, but once we were in, he wanted to take out ninety-four important Vietnamese targets and win the war. We could still do that."

Vance, angry now, "Then goddammit, let's do it! What's holding us back? These rotten peaceniks, parading everywhere?"

"Sadly, you are exactly right. I don't think the government has the will to do what is necessary."

"Well, God have mercy on us and on Tom."

Jill had stayed in the background for the entire meeting, her eyes never leaving Vance. She stood up, saying, "God has already had mercy on Tom; he's alive when he could so easily be dead! If he's alive, he'll endure, just like he says, and he'll come back to us. Let's be thankful for that. Now, the last thing Tom would want is for food to go to waste! We've got a big spread in the kitchen; come on in and help yourself."

As they filed out, Vance grabbed Harry by the arm. "Harry, you know that ops research contract you have with SAC?"

Harry stopped, concerned that his father's memory was acting up again. Harry had done some consulting work with the Strategic Air Command a few years before, once doing an involved operational research study on targeting in the Soviet Union. "That was some time ago, Dad."

"I know that, dammit; do you think I'm daft? Just a few years ago, you were working with a young guy, a famous ace from World War II, what was his name?"

Harry remembered. "That was John Meyer, Dad. He's no longer with SAC; he's the Vice Chief of Staff of the Air Force."

"Even better! I want you to get me an interview with him. I don't care where it is; I'll go see him anywhere. I've got to talk to him about this business with Tom."

The intensity of Vance's gaze frightened Harry. Was Vance slipping round the bend? Or was this the old fighter, picking up his arms for one last charge? It didn't matter.

"I'll do that, Dad. It might take a little time; he's awfully busy now."

"Tell him to get unbusy. I want to see him."

CHAPTER SIXTY

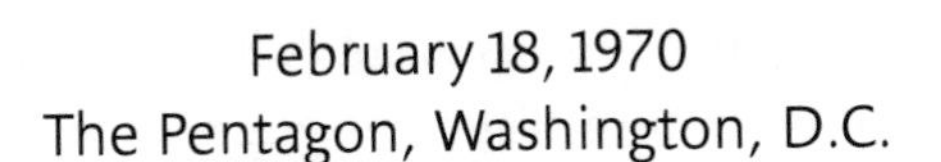

February 18, 1970
The Pentagon, Washington, D.C.

Harry had hoped that Vance would relinquish the idea of talking to General Meyer, particularly since he would not share what he intended to talk about. He had tried for weeks to get an appointment with General Meyer but never got past his staffers until an old friend, Colonel Harvey "Cobra" Connelly, showed up on Meyer's staff and took Harry's call.

"Harry, you have to understand, General Meyer is completely snowed under the pressure of the things going on in Vietnam, getting the budget ready, and testifying to Congress. The poor guy was a lot better off when the Luftwaffe was shooting at him."

Meyer had destroyed thirty-seven and one-half enemy airplanes in the air and on the ground and was the leading American ace in the European theater. Then he had gone on to shoot down two MiG-15s in Korea.

"Cobra, he probably knew my brother, Tom, in Korea, or at least knew of him. And I have to tell you, my dad's dedicated his life to aviation, and to the Air Force. He's asking to see General Meyer about Tom, and it's important to his health."

As it turned out, Connelly had an easy time of it once he told Meyer that the request was from Tom Shannon's father. "Vance Shannon? He's a real living legend. And I knew Tom in Korea, met him several times, flew with him once, a great pilot. I'll be happy to talk with him. I'd go out to the coast to do it if I could, but see if you can set something up here in mid-February."

Jill had not wanted Vance to go, but once Harry had the appointment, there was no holding him back. He insisted on flying to Washington three days early, to be sure that he would be rested and to be sure weather wouldn't keep him away from his appointment.

Now he and Harry were waiting in Meyer's plush outer office, filled with plane and missile models. Vance had flown or worked on most of the planes.

Meyer's secretary, Grace Northrop, was a very proper-looking middle-aged woman with her pure white hair piled in a stylish bouffant. She had come to the Pentagon as a stenographer when it was opened and worked her way up to her current position of real power, able to give appointments with the Vice Chief or deny them. She said, "Please go in now, gentlemen."

Meyer rose to meet them, coming around his huge desk to shake their hands and direct them to a small settee next to a coffee table.

"I've followed your career for years, Mr. Shannon, and I'm pleased to meet you. I remember when you and Ben Kelsey were flying the old Bell Airacuda! And you know that I knew Tom, too. I'm so sorry that he was shot down, but I'm glad that he's alive."

"That's why I'm here, General Meyer. I know there are many political considerations to running the war, and I know the White House has not made it easy for you, but I'm here to plead for an all-out air assault on North Vietnam."

Meyer started to speak, but Vance said what few people did. "Hear me out, please. We've made a big mistake in not using airpower in the North like it should be used. If we are ever going to end this war, we have to take out Haiphong and Hanoi, flatten them. I don't mean nuclear bombs; I mean putting the B-52s over North Vietnam instead of having them bombing the jungle in South Vietnam."

Meyer nodded, a concerned look signaling Vance to go on. "I know it sounds crazy, with my son in a prison in Hanoi, but there's no other way. I've studied this for more than a year, I've analyzed it from every angle, and if you knock out Haiphong and Hanoi, you will break their backs."

Meyer saw that Vance had stopped for a moment. "That's exactly what General LeMay and General McConnell told the administration and the Congress should be done. And they refused, probably because they didn't want to risk China or the Soviet Union being involved."

"They are involved, already! They are furnishing the arms, the airplanes, the food, the trucks. But you know that. They will not intervene on the behalf of North Vietnam! China hates Vietnam, and Russia won't risk a nuclear war for the sake of a tiny country like North Vietnam. They are making fools of us."

Meyer nodded. "Mr. Shannon, it happens that I agree with you one hundred percent. But I won't insult you by glossing over this. There is no chance that this administration will use overwhelming force against North Vietnam unless the United States finds itself in a position where it is going to lose massive numbers of troops on the ground."

"We're already losing massive numbers of troops, General Meyer. You know that."

"Yes, but I'm talking about losing perhaps twenty or thirty thousand in a single action. If that were the case, I believe the White House would authorize the Air Force to do exactly what you say. But believe me, it's is not going to happen, not in the foreseeable future. I wish I could tell you otherwise."

Vance slumped in his chair, defeat written over his face. In a much weaker voice, he said, "Thanks for seeing me, General Meyer. I knew all along that you would have known what to do, but I had to tell you myself. I hope you understand how a father feels."

Meyer walked them both to the door, shook Vance's hand, then turned to Harry. "Thanks for coming, Mr. Shannon, and thanks for the privilege of meeting your father. We are doing everything we can to get our prisoners out, and I hope that the next time we meet I'll be able to do more than I have done today. Believe me, if we ever get the go-ahead, we will drive the North Vietnamese out of the war in a matter of days."

Harry and Vance spent two more days in Washington, allowing Vance to gather strength for the flight home. Harry could ill afford the time away from the office, but he did not want Vance to travel until he had recovered somewhat from the disappointment he so obviously felt. While they were waiting in the crowded terminal at National, Vance tugged at Harry's sleeve.

"Harry, don't think I was just being a crazy old man. I knew that the Air Force knows what to do. It was just that I had to be sure that they did, for Tom's sake. I couldn't rest on the off chance that somehow no one had considered it. It was foolish, I know, a waste of General Meyer's time and yours, but it was something I had to do."

Harry nodded, his arm around his father's shoulders, watching him intently. As Vance talked, he seemed to shrink, seeming to crawl within himself, to give up.

"Dad, it's important that you look to the future. Tom will be coming home, we know that, and he will be coming home to see you. You've got to be sure you take care of yourself, not try to do too much, not worry too much. The main thing is for Tom to come back and tell you personally how it was."

"I'll try, Son, but it's not going to be easy."

"Then think about this. How would it be if Tom came back and you were gone? He'd be devastated. You need to take care of yourself so you can give him the kind of homecoming he deserves. It might be next week, it might be five years from now, but he'll be coming home and he'll want to tell you all about it."

CHAPTER SIXTY-ONE

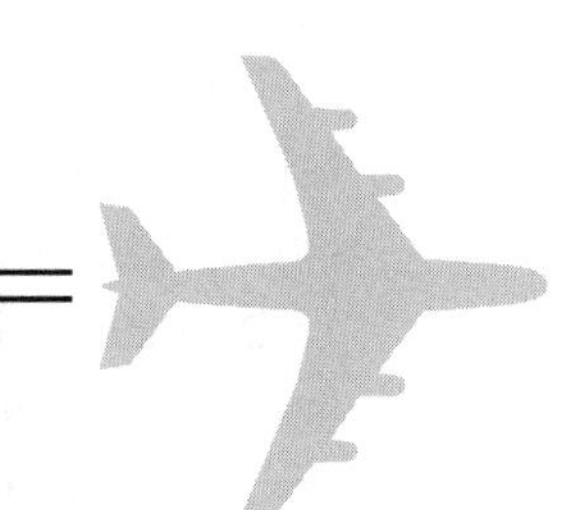

December 31, 1971
Palos Verdes, California

Vance Shannon looked vacantly at the line of pill bottles and for the fifth time in a week could not recall what he had taken or when. Mumbling to himself, he said, "Seventy-seven years old and acting like I'm ninety-seven. Better take these out to Jill."

Jill was preparing the lavish New Year's table that was a Shannon tradition, even though only four other people were coming tonight, Harry, Anna, Nancy, and Warren Bowers, Vance's unofficial biographer. In years past Jill had entertained as many as twenty or thirty people on New Year's Eve, but since Tom was shot down the only entertaining they did was this little annual year-end gathering.

When Vance walked in with his array of bottles she smiled, saying, "Honey, you took everything you were supposed to take this morning. I'll put the rest out for you tonight, after Warren goes."

She knew that the others would eat and run back to their children, but Warren would be there for hours. He was finishing up a book on Vance for which he already had a publisher. Bowers had written a long series of articles for *Wings* and *Airpower* magazines on Vance and virtually every plane he had tested. Now Warren was combining these in book form with a story of Vance's life as a businessman. Tonight he was going to finish up with a review of the past couple of years in aviation and Vance's predictions for the future.

Vance placed the medicine bottles on the sink and left. She ran her hands over them, knowing that the best medicine for him would be news that Tom was coming home. The second-best medicine, oddly enough, was Bowers's methodical search into Vance's past. He had never talked about what he had done, and in listening to the interviews and reading Bowers's articles Jill had learned much that made her admire Vance even more. The process was a tonic for Vance. She firmly believed that it had made the crucial difference between life and death for him.

The front door banged open and she heard Harry's excited voice calling, "Dad, Jill, come on into the library; I've got something that will knock your socks off—it's a movie with Tom in it."

Nancy and Anna quickly set up Vance's old 16mm motion picture projector, a relic of his days of test flying, while Harry pulled down the movie screen and moved in to thread the roll of film into the projector. Warren Bowers hung near the door, looking uncomfortable, so Jill got him a Coke and told him to sit down, that this, too, was part of Vance's story.

Vance came in and after hurried greetings Harry said, "Dad, this is Lieutenant Colonel Steve O'Malley. He flew with Tom in the Cougars, and he's working with Bob now on the smart bombs."

"Welcome, Colonel O'Malley. Tom spoke and wrote of you often."

Unable to contain his excitement, Harry said, "Dad, General Meyer has sent Steve out here with an incredible reel of film. He wanted you to see it as soon as possible. Tom is on the film and he is doing something absolutely fabulous; wait till you see."

Vance exploded. "You mean you looked at it first without bringing it straight over here?"

Harry put his arm around him. "Easy there, old fella; I had to! What if it was the wrong reel or something? You would have killed me. But it's not, and wait until you see it."

Anna went around and switched off the lights as flickering black-and-white images appeared on the screen. Harry adjusted the lens, and the images resolved into the dimly lit interior of the Hao Lo prison—the Hanoi Hilton.

"No sound?"

O'Malley, uncharacteristically quiet, spoke up at last. "No, sir, they've got a sound version, but it's classified until they get the Vietnamese translations done. No one is supposed to have even this silent version, but General Meyer knew what it would mean to you. And you'll see that, silent or not, it says a lot."

The film was obviously done by an amateur. The camera panned jerkily around the bleak room, coming to a halt on a desk, covered with some sort of cloth and bearing a book, writing paper, and what appeared to be a judge's gavel.

The Shannon family held their breath as a figure brushed past the camera, to stand behind the desk. A haughty Vietnamese, dressed in a military-style uniform without any distinguishing insignia, threw his shoulders back, coming to a loose attention.

There was clumsy shift in point of view as the camera was apparently carried around to focus on a prisoner, standing on a white circle painted on the floor, his head hanging down as if he were warding off a blow.

Nancy screamed, "It's Tom!" just as the others perceived that the emaciated, dirty creature in his threadbare pajamas was indeed Tom Shannon. A crude misspelled subtitle, "Colonel Shanon, USAF," then appeared, inserted at about knee level.

Tears sprang to Vance's eyes. "My poor son; may God have mercy on him."

The Vietnamese judge, if that was what he was, read at length from a set of folded papers, the camera going from him to Tom and back again.

Crying, Jill, who never used bad language, said, "He's so thin, and look how he's holding his arm. It looks like he can just about stand up. Those dirty bastards, they've been torturing him!"

Harry and Vance had long known that Tom was undoubtedly being tortured, but they had maintained a fiction with Jill and Nancy that he was being treated according to the Geneva Convention.

Harry said, "Now watch; you are going to see some great acting."

The camera panned toward Tom, then went to a close-up of his face. Nancy moaned, "Look at the bruises. The poor baby, he's been beaten."

Even as she spoke, Tom seemed to weave as he began to talk. They couldn't hear him, but he was obviously talking very slowly and deliberately.

O'Malley said, "Watch his eyes."

Tom's eyes blinked tightly together, held for a second, opened, then repeated. It was as if he were reacting to the bright light, but there was a pattern, a rhythm, to it.

"See that! Look, he's blinking in Morse code! And they don't see it; they think he's too sick to be able to resist; they think he is saying what they want him to say."

Tom was on-screen for a full two minutes. Apparently another camera was in use, and this one shot over the shoulder of the North Vietnamese interrogator. Tom continued speaking the whole time even as he blinked his eyes.

"Dad, my Morse code ability is long gone, but I'm sure you recognize some of it. Colonel O'Malley brought me a translation. I'll read it."

Vance said, "No, dammit, this is my son talking to me. Let me see how much I can figure out; then you can tell me."

The film ended and Vance said, "Run it again."

They played it five more times, and Vance finally said, "Tom is blinking three messages. The first one is just 'SOS'—I guess that was to tip us off to the fact that he was blinking Morse code. The second was 'Bad hurt, will live.' And the third was 'Bomb Hanoi; they fold.' "

"Damn, that's pretty good, Dad, just what the Pentagon decoders read."

Vance, feeling his oats, said, "I may not know what medicine to take, but I can still take Morse code."

They ran the film another three times, with the women crying and the men getting angrier with each showing.

O'Malley, visibly excited, said, "Do you realize how sharp he has to be to be able to speak the drivel they were making him say and at the same time blink out a Morse code message to us? It's like rubbing your head and patting your stomach at the same time, only harder."

Vance pounded the table. "Are they so stupid as to think this is good propaganda for them? It shows them torturing a helpless prisoner."

"Dad, most of their audience is already anti-American; they'll eat this up, sad to say."

Nancy had sobbed almost uncontrollably throughout all the showings, once going up to the screen to touch her finger to Tom's image. She spoke bitterly. "There are Americans who will eat this up. I don't know what's happening to this country."

O'Malley had to leave immediately, and dinner was a quick affair, with Harry, Anna, and Nancy departing within the hour. Bowers asked, "Mr. Shannon, are you sure you want to be interviewed tonight? I know you must be completely engaged by the film."

"No, Warren, you've spent the whole day coming here. I'll have plenty of time tonight to think about the film. Let's go into the library and maybe we can finish this up tonight."

In the library Bowers went through his usual elaborate setup of two voice recorders, put his list of questions in place, and arranged the yellow legal pad in which he wrote so swiftly that he kept pace with the recorders. He always prepared for a meeting by furnishing Vance an advance copy of his questions, along with some follow-up questions from previous sessions.

In all their months together, Bowers's natural diffidence never allowed him to call him Vance, despite being urged to do so.

"Mr. Shannon, as I told you, I'm pretty far along with the book. Tonight, if you feel like it, I'd like you to give me a quick review of aviation for the past couple of years, and then tell me what you think the future holds. Maybe we can break it down to commercial, military, and general aviation, or some other way that is convenient for you."

Vance, his mind still on the tape, on Tom's plight, on his inability to help, didn't respond.

"Sir, would it be better if I came back?"

Vance shook himself and sat up in the chair. "No, Warren, let's get on with it. I don't want to waste your time. Let's take a quick review of the past two years. It has been pretty surprising, some big advances, and some big setbacks. Would you like a cognac?"

Bowers never drank and declined. Vance poured himself a double shot of Courvoisier, saying, "Normally I never touch this stuff anymore, but tonight I need it. It was pretty demoralizing seeing my son . . ."

He stopped and visibly gathered his resources.

"But let's get down to business. I made some notes, and I'll just read them out and you can ask questions if you want."

Bowers fussed with the recorders—he usually fouled up the process one way or another, listening to Vance talk after letting the tape stop recording or forgetting to start it again after a pause. Bowers sat poised to take down the comments in his own brand of shorthand, as a necessary backup.

"Let's do as you suggest and break it down. Let's talk commercial aviation first. It's a mess, as you know, despite the fine airplanes that we are flying.

"One thing you have to remember, Warren, is that industries age, and companies age, just like men do. Douglas was a terrific success as long as Donald Douglas was younger and running it with a few key managers. But when he aged, so did his management and so did his company. They got behind the eight ball with the DC-8—no pun intended—and almost went under with the DC-9 until they got things figured out. But even the DC-9 couldn't save them, and McDonnell took them over. Their new airplane, the DC-10, made its first flight in August of 1970, and it would be a success if the market was there. But the market's not there, and worse, the Lockheed L-1011 is there. Both good airplanes, but airplanes cost too much nowadays."

Warren had heard this before and asked, "How does Boeing compare in this regard?"

"Well, Boeing, much against its general inclinations, diversified better than other companies, better and smarter. Instead of diversifying by building canoes like Grumman tried to do, or a light plane, like General Dynamics tried, Boeing built a whole array of airliners, and that has kept them going. But they are having a hard time, too. The 747 sales have dried up, and the SST program has been canceled, just like they knew it would be, but after they poured millions into it."

Vance was quiet for a moment. Somehow the SST program was really the aircraft industry at its most idiotic. The government forced companies to bid on a plane it didn't really want built. The companies bid on it, knowing they were going to waste a lot of money, and in the end, everything went down the drain. Not like during wartime, when you could decide on a plane you knew was needed, like the B-17 or the B-29, and be sure you built it by the thousands.

"Boeing was damn near bankrupt early in 1970. They had thirty 747s sitting out in front of the plant, white tails, with no engines in them."

"White tails?"

"They call them white tails because they don't have any airline logo on them. But they cost money, sitting there. They owed money to everybody, couldn't get it from the banks, finally got it from the industry—big subcontractors put up enough to keep them going. And they laid people off, right and left—more than sixty thousand of them. They had a running gag that an optimist at Boeing was somebody who brought his lunch to work. It was horrible."

"What happened with Lockheed and Rolls-Royce?"

"Well, that was a terrible mess, too. Lockheed foolishly picked Rolls-Royce as its main engine supplier because the RB-211 fit the S-shaped duct in the tail. You know how the DC-10 has the third engine; it goes straight through—well, the L-1011 is more streamlined, and it needed an engine the size of the RB-211. Rolls-Royce got into difficulties manufacturing the RB-211—some of the materials it wanted to use for the turbine blades didn't work out. The British government pulled the plug on it when it found out the shape it was in. And that almost killed Lockheed. They finally worked out a consortium of bank and government loans to bring Rolls-Royce back to life, develop the engine, and keep Lockheed going with the L-1011. But like I said before, that's a big mistake. The L-1011 will never make a profit and neither will the DC-10."

"Can I quote you?"

"You can quote me. But let me tell you, young Warren Bowers, none of what we just talked about amounts to a hill of beans compared to the problems we face with terrorists. You remember how in September last year the Arab terrorists hijacked four airplanes and blew them up? Well, unless we are careful, that's going to be a way of life, and we'll see airliners being blown up in the air, not on the ground. I don't see any way around it, the way the Middle East is."

This was a little too esoteric for Bowers; he wanted to talk airplanes, not politics. "How about on the military side? Any good airplanes coming along there?"

Vance brightened visibly.

"Yeah, good old Grumman, the Iron Works, flew the F-14 Tomcat last December. It's a hell of an airplane, and Grumman is a hell of a company. You know my boy Tom—" His voice broke momentarily. "My boy Tom flew Grumman Wildcats and became an ace in World War II. And I hear the new McDonnell Douglas F-15 will be a great airplane when it flies. But let's go back to the commercial side for a minute. A new company got started this year, Federal Express—just carries freight, but carries it fast, one-day service all over the country. Mark my words, it is going to make a pack of money."

Bowers came back, "How about foreign aircraft? The French firm Dassault seems to do well, even though it is comparatively small."

Vance shook his head. Dassault reminded him of Madeline, and he didn't want to talk about it. "They are OK, I guess. But no one has the resources of our guys, Boeing, McDonnell Douglas, General Dynamics, Grumman—nobody."

Bowers checked his tapes and asked, "How about the space program? I see where the Russians keep doing well, with the Soyuz spacecraft and the Salyut space station."

Vance looked dour again. "I hate to tell you this; it makes an old man out of me, even though I'm already an old man. I just cannot get excited about space flight. I know it's a great scientific achievement; I know we have to keep up with the Russians, even if they do keep killing themselves."

"What do you mean?"

"You know they keep their space program secret, never tell in advance about a shot, and don't tell about any deaths or anything if they can cover it up. Last January, I think, they had their Soyuz hook up with their space station, the Salyut or whatever it is. That was a hell of a feat, but their guys were killed on reentry. But I understand why we have to compete; even if we are ahead of them now, they never got to the moon, and our guys just brought back a hundred pounds of rock on *Apollo XIV*. But it's not like real flying; you are more like a passenger. You want to talk space flight, I'll have you talk to Bob Rodriquez when he gets back."

Bowers nodded. "I feel the same way, but maybe the Space Shuttle will be different. Do you want to talk a little bit about the future? I don't need much."

Vance thought for a minute. "There are a number of things going on, all interrelated. First of all, airplanes are getting way too expensive, even though they are way more efficient. This means there will be fewer bought in the future, military and civilian. That means there will be fewer contracts, and fewer companies to bid. Pretty scary, but actually good for a company like ours. When they cut staffs, they have to put out stuff for consultants, and that's what we do."

"On the military side, what is the most important factor now, bombers or fighters?"

"Oddly enough, neither. The tanker has become the single most important part of the airpower equation. You can't operate anything, bombers or fighters, without the tankers. You need them for logistics, too; they'll have to get transports with in-flight refueling capability soon."

"What about—"

"Let me finish. Airborne electronics—anti-jamming, radar, and so on—are going to be as important as tankers. What it means is that a few bombers and fighters, especially when they get equipped with what they are calling 'smart bombs,' will be able to do the work of whole air forces in World War II. And it will perhaps permit not using nukes. Although I have a couple of spots I wouldn't mind seeing nukes laid on."

"Tell me what 'smart bombs' are."

"Well, we had a hand in developing them; at least Bob Rodriquez did."

Vance hesitated for a moment. Bob had done exactly the same thing with his smart-bombs ideas as he had done with his simulators. As soon as he got things to the stage where they were ready for production, he sold the idea to a larger firm, retaining a percentage of the profits for Aerospace Ventures. It was working well with the simulators; there were royalties coming in on a scale Vance had never imagined. He just hoped that it would be the same with the smart bombs.

"Bob's going over to Thailand next year, going to the same base that my son Tom flew from, to help in their employment. There are two basic types, one guided by television—they call it electro-optical, but they would be better off calling it just TV. The other is guided by a laser. I cannot explain to you exactly what a laser is—you can look it up in the encyclopedia, I guess—but it's like an invisible light that one airplane shines on a target. Another aircraft, the drop plane, drops a bomb that homes right in on the light that's shining on the target. They have little controls that enable them to fly right to the bull's-eye every time. The old bombs, the so-called 'dumb bombs,' you dropped them after a bomb run and prayed they hit something, but once they were out of the bomb bay you had no control. These you can fly right smack-dab on the target."

This was a little too technical for Bowers, and he shifted his line of questioning. "What about general aviation, you know, the Cessnas and the Pipers and so on?"

"I think it will be tough for years, because we've never figured out a way to make flying less expensive. There's another problem, too. Flying is too much a man's game. We've excluded women, so when you go out to the airport there's no socialization. Look at a yacht club—there's always as many women, maybe more than men. And there's something else that inhibits flying becoming popular—you cannot, I repeat cannot, have any drinking with flying, not even social drinking. On a sailboat, you can go out, everybody has a couple of drinks; it's a party. With flying it's a grim man's game; you go out alone, fly around, have fun—but you don't meet any women—and that's a hell of a drawback for the business."

"What about executive jets? I know you had a big part with the Learjet."

"They are improving all the time, getting more costly, but they will pay for themselves. Companies have to learn to look on an executive jet as a tool, just like a big drill press or something. If they really cost it out, and see that it pays for itself, executive jets will take off. Right now they are sort of toys for the chairman of the board and for movie stars. Ten years from now, they'll be moving mid-level executives around like they were riding a bus."

"And what about just plain-old pleasure flying?"

"There you've hit it, my boy! There is a great outfit out in Oshkosh, Wisconsin, the Experimental Aircraft Association. That's the future of sport flying, believe me. They have already done more good than anybody realizes, and they will be doing more in the future. They have fantastic fly-ins, thousands of aircraft; it is amazing. If you like flying, you ought to join."

Vance yawned and said, "Do you think you have enough for tonight? I'm a little tired. Maybe you could give me a call, and we can finish up, fill in any loose spots over the phone?"

Bowers quickly shut down his recording gear, stowed it, and got up to go. Then he said, "Mr. Shannon, I hope your son comes home soon."

Shannon reacted angrily. "Warren, me, too, but I don't think he'll come home until we bomb the hell out of them. We've been fighting a crazy war; we've dropped three times as many bombs on Vietnam as we did on Germany—but ninety percent of them are being dropped on South Vietnam, our ally; for Christ's sake, we're bombing our ally. It just doesn't make any sense."

Warren was sorry he'd said anything.

CHAPTER SIXTY-TWO

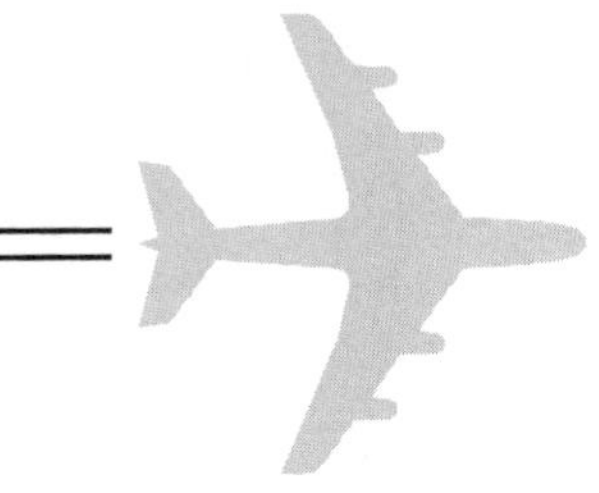

May 13, 1972
Thanh Hoa, North Vietnam

A few inanimate objects project their nature. Gibraltar's size and shape clearly say strength and stability. The pyramids of Egypt evoke a sense of mystery, awe, and deep spiritual experience. The bridge at Thanh Hoa stood as a symbol of North Vietnamese defiance, an arrogant structure, welded into the rock with ingenious architecture more suited to a fortress than a bridge. The number of anti-aircraft guns, surface-to-air missiles, and MiGs defending it had increased in number every year since the first attack on April 3, 1965.

Built in a crash program in 1964, the bridge funneled supplies out of Hanoi to support North Vietnamese units operating in South Vietnam. Used for both rail and road traffic, it was 58 feet wide and 540 feet long, hanging 50 feet above the Son Ma River. The North Vietnamese named it "Ham Rong"—the Dragon's Jaw—and they rejoiced that it had withstood seven years of bombing. American fighter jets had assaulted it 869 times with bombs of varying sizes. Each time the smoke from the exploding bombs, the guns, and the burning wreckage of aircraft had cleared away, the bridge stood undamaged, funneling the lifeblood of the war to the south. Eleven American jets had been shot down, their twisted remains salvaged and turned into weapons, pots, and pans by the thrifty peasants who manned the guns when they were not tilling the fields.

The bridge at Thanh Hoa was a prime example of the utter futility of the bombing-campaign rules set up by the American Secretary of

Defense, McNamara, and continued by President Lyndon Johnson. On March 31, 1968, Johnson had announced that he would not seek or accept nomination for the presidency. He had also announced a bombing halt on all targets above the twentieth north latitude, shielding the bridge and almost all other important targets in North Vietnam for four precious years. In that interval millions of tons of supplies and tens of thousands of soldiers had begun their journey to South Vietnam over the Dragon's Jaw. In that interval thousands of American and South Vietnamese troops had died.

Johnson's goal had been peace talks. The North Vietnamese goal was victory. In the four years of the bombing halt, the Americans had followed a policy of "Vietnamization," strengthening South Vietnamese forces so that they would be able to resist the North Vietnamese without active American assistance. At the end of the fourth year, on March 30, 1972, the North Vietnamese, their roads and bridges repaired, their strength at a peak, launched a full-scale offensive into South Vietnam, with the intent of ending the war with a unified country run from Hanoi. The South Vietnamese, unable to fight without massive American air support, collapsed.

The United States responded with a massive infusion of airpower. Units were sent again to Thailand and naval forces were reassembled off the coast. With only about twenty-five thousand American troops on the ground in Vietnam, only airpower could prevent a complete North Vietnamese takeover. President Richard M. Nixon called for Operation Linebacker on May 10, 1972, allowing air operations against the North and permitting North Vietnamese harbors to be mined. And for the first time, that airpower was going to be supplemented by Paveway One bombs.

Bob Rodriquez stood on the tarmac at Ubon, watching the powerful McDonnell Douglas F-4 Phantom IIs preparing to take off for their strike on the Dragon's Jaw. Rodriquez was exhausted, having spent the entire night going from one aircraft to the next, making sure that the Paveway systems he had done so much to develop were operational. Then he had waited on the flight line, skipping breakfast, to learn whether the bombs he had labored over for so long would work as they should.

In the interval, Bob thought about all he had learned about the miserable conditions of American prisoners of war in Hanoi, and he feared for Tom's life. As usual, Bob felt guilty that Tom had gone back into the service and he had not, even though he knew that he had done far more for the American war effort as a civilian than he could have done as a pilot. Still the guilt was there, made even sharper by the knowledge that Tom disapproved of Bob's place in the business and the fact that he now knew for certain that torture was inevitable for American prisoners of war.

Bob had been to Ubon often over the years and was amazed at the way each succeeding year had seen more U.S. creature comforts in place. When the Americans had first arrived, the base was primitive, with remnants of Japanese hangars from World War II still being used. Each succeeding year saw tactical improvements—a new control tower, bigger, longer runways, and so on. But even more noticeable were the spread of air-conditioned buildings, comfortable quarters, a swimming pool, a twenty-four-hour Officers Club, and so on. Ubon now housed the Eighth Tactical Fighter Wing, commanded by an old friend, Colonel Carl S. Miller. Miller had flown 57 combat missions in Korea, some of them with Bob, and gone on to fly almost 450 more in F-100s and F-4s in Vietnam. Miller told Bob that torture was epidemic in the North Vietnamese prisons.

Rodriquez glanced at his watch. In a few minutes, fourteen F-4Ds of Miller's Eighth TFW—the Wolfpack, it was called—should begin their assault on the Dragon's Jaw.

North Vietnamese radar had long since picked up the fourteen F-4Ds, their place in the sky clearly visible from the long oily-black columns of smoke issuing from their GE J79 engines. The Phantoms were loaded for bear, carrying among them nine three-thousand-pound laser-guided bombs, fifteen two-thousand-pound laser-guided bombs, and forty-eight conventional five-hundred-pound bombs.

For ten square miles around the bridge, anti-aircraft crews slipped on their helmets and assumed their positions, while the missile crews prepared for a sudden launch. When the enemy came in range they would release their customary torrent of fire.

The Phantoms rolled in on the target in a waterfall of lethal metal, each one sending its laser-guided bombs to the target, each pilot seeing the roaring wall of flak reaching up to them, and every one pulling off the target at top speed to avoid the murderous anti-aircraft fire. The first crews could not see any damage, but the last three crews saw bombs striking the bridge, exploding in a roar of fire and smoke. All fourteen aircraft emerged undamaged, with the bridge down behind them.

Later RF-4Cs crossed the target, and their photos showed that the western span of the bridge was blown completely off its forty-foot-thick concrete foundation. Twenty-four laser-guided bombs had accomplished what the full ordnance loads of 869 previous attackers could not do: destroy the bridge at Thanh Hoa.

Ubon Royal Thai Air Force Base erupted in a celebration of the victory. Colonel Miller invited Rodriquez to the party that night, but he stayed in his quarters, analyzing the combat reports of the crews and scanning the photos the RF-4Cs had brought back. He wrote a long report back to his project officer at Eglin, concluding with a passionate paragraph that he begged be forwarded up the chain of command, all the way to the President, if possible:

> In conclusion, the Paveway bombs offer a path to the future that could provide a very clinical victory in Vietnam. It could be applied against North Vietnamese cities with surgical skill, taking out their vital industries and still not causing much collateral damage or killing many civilians. The risk of provoking Red China or the Soviet Union would not only be minimal, it might even be salutary, for I suspect that they would be reluctant to engage the United States after it had demonstrated such technical prowess. Let me repeat this: the Paveway, and the other precision-guided munitions that will soon be available to us, can win the war by the application of airpower alone. This path to conquest can begin at once with the weapons on hand, and it can be followed up by the deployment of those under development, all at a cost far less than that of maintaining a huge ground army.
>
> In simplest terms, with Paveway and its developments, Vietnamization can work, and South Vietnam can defend itself. Without precision-guided munitions and American airpower, South Vietnam will never be able to resist North Vietnam in open combat.

Bob reread what he had written and then copied the report, sanitizing it so that he could send a copy of it back to Vance, who would be heartened by it.

Rodriquez signed his report, then walked it over to the command section for transmission back to Eglin. "This is going to make a lot of people happy—and a lot more unhappy. I wonder if anybody will read it except at Eglin?"

CHAPTER SIXTY-THREE

September 23, 1972
Moscow, USSR

The main party celebrating the fiftieth anniversary of the Tupolev bureau had been held in the new assembly hall, scrubbed operating-room clean for the occasion. It was filled with tables laden with vodka, caviar, and delicacies from all over the Soviet Union, provided by the many suppliers who had contributed to creating the latest Tupolev triumph, the Tu-144. Both Andrei and Alexei had made speeches, and there was a long film specially created for the occasion that showed Tupolev aircraft over the years, from the very first one, the little all-metal ANT-1 monoplane, down to the first takeoff of the Tu-144 SST on December 31, 1968.

The entire party had been created and paid for by the employees, and it included two gleaming examples of Andrei's creation, a beautifully restored Tu-2 from the Great Patriotic War and an operational Tu-22, the supersonic bomber that had startled the world with its debut at Tushino. The company's own model makers had created a lineup of every Tupolev aircraft ever built, from the ANT-1 to the Tu-144. It made an impressive lineup.

Alexei, conscious of his father's fragile health, had made their excuses early, and they were now sitting in his old office on the third floor of the KOSOS building, engaged in one of their customary clinical analysis sessions, not going over the party with its host of old colleagues but instead thoughtfully analyzing the Tu-144 and its magnificent flight three days before.

Andrei caressed the single sheet of paper in his withered old hands, raising it to his lips and kissing it as if it were a love letter. The letter was official notice that the Tu-144 had just flown from Moscow to Tashkent, almost three thousand kilometers, in just 110 minutes. The flight had been made at 18,000 meters. "This is something, Alexei; they cannot take this from us, no matter what."

Andrei Tupolev had believed in the Tupolev Tu-144 because he had to believe in his son Alexei. Alexei believed in it because he had distilled his father's wisdom, his design team's best efforts, and his own administrative skill in the pell-mell rush to have the aircraft fly in 1968, as both Khrushchev and Brezhnev had demanded.

Both father and son knew that the design was rushed, despite the preliminary design information that had been stolen from the French and English. Both men knew that there were faults that had to be corrected before full-scale production could begin.

"Yes, Father, but the thought of the Concorde sticks like a bone in my throat. It is embarrassing that they have been able to do so much in the last year. It will kill our foreign sales."

The preceding June the second Concorde had made a world's sales tour to the Middle East, the Far East, and Australia. Sales were made to China and Iran. It was heartbreaking. There was no way the Tu-144 could be committed to such an itinerary, not yet.

The two men, so devoted to each other, had long since settled their disputes over some of the radical design paths forced on the Tu-144 by time and technology. Andrei Tupolev hated the idea of a delta wing and, more recently, the canard winglets, while Alexei accepted these as a fait accompli of the schedule. On the other hand, Alexei would have preferred a less complicated nose section, using a television system to aid the pilots in landing. His father had insisted on the heavy and time-consuming nose that drooped for takeoff and landing to give the pilots better visibility. Both men still believed in their own ideas, long after there was any question of changing it.

Where they differed most was on the potential for sales of the SST within the Soviet Union. Andrei felt that the design was premature, that another ten years' work needed to be done on improving the passenger cabin and lowering landing speeds. Alexei, knowing how primitive the passenger accommodations were on most current Russian airliners, felt that passengers would endure the noise and the cramped cabin in return for the speed.

For perhaps the hundredth time, Andrei said, "I just wish we had had more time to prepare the airplane for the Paris Air Show. We looked like ragamuffins compared to the Concorde."

At the last Paris Air Show, the Concorde and the Tu-144 had been eagerly compared by foreign observers. With its spotted paint and worn tires, the Russian SST showed the ravages of more than thirty months of test-flying. To Tupolev's acute embarrassment, it looked shabby and worn compared to the sleek, fresh finish of the Concorde. Tired as he was, he had once again led the promotional charge, insisting in briefing after briefing that the prototype Tu-144 was still provisional and that a more sophisticated version would be flown soon. There was more truth than anyone knew or would admit in that statement.

"The French and the English had so many advantages. Their governments leave them alone to conduct their business. No rush to first flight, no demands that certain components be used."

Alexei nodded. "And most of all, they had the magnificent Olympus engines." Both men were silent, contemplating the power, the fuel economy, and the relative quiet of the Concorde's Rolls-Royce engines.

They had known that Tu-144's engines were not powerful enough from the start, but there was no other option. The Tu-144 could fly supersonically only with the afterburners on, and this brought the range down from 4,500 kilometers to about 2,000—almost ruling out export sales.

Andrei's office was filled with photos and models, and on his desk was one of the second prototype of the Tu-144, originally intended for the factory celebration. Some security-conscious bureaucrat had ruled that it was too secret to be seen on open display and removed it from the lineup. Andrei had asked that it be placed on his desk, and now, ever so gently, he extended his finger and ran it over the model, tracing the shape of the wing and the engine nacelles.

Alexei's eyes followed the movements of Andrei's finger. Both knew that it was here that a fundamental mistake had been forced on them. The wing, lovely despite its foreign delta shape, was optimized for flight at supersonic speeds. It was perhaps the most modern element of the design, much more complex than the wing of the first prototype. It now incorporated variable camber, twist, and negative dihedral, and further changes were contemplated. The engines, which had been moved outward ten feet on this aircraft, now had square intakes.

The absolutely crucial error was that the Kuznetsov NK-144 engines were optimized for subsonic flight. This mismatch of wing and engine design was a mistake of colossal proportions, but one that had to be accepted to meet Khrushchev's and later Brezhnev's mandate for a flight in 1968.

The early French and English data had helped enormously, but the final design was by Andrei's own team. They had followed British practice by testing the wing design on an "analog" aircraft, a MiG-21 fitted with delta wings. The veteran MiG test pilot, Oleg Gudkov, flew the analog and found that the delta wing created a cushion of air—ground effect—that would greatly reduce the Tu-144's takeoff and landing speeds. The analog had come along to late to have any effect upon the prototype's design, but it provided insight that enabled them to proceed so swiftly with the redesign of the second aircraft.

The model showed the canards, the forward flying surfaces that Andrei resented so much as a makeshift, an obvious admission that there was a flaw in the design of the wing.

Pointing to them, Andrei said, "My God, Alexei, this is no different from the Wright brothers! We've come sixty-nine years since they first flew and we are still sticking little wings up front."

Alexei did not respond. Advances in technology were forcing the use of canards on many designers. They were complex and they added weight, but they worked. With the ground effect and the canards, the Tu-144 was now spared the hard landings that threatened integrity of the intricate twenty-four-wheel main undercarriage. The canards added lift and further reduced the landing speed, but Andrei hated their complexity, their appearance of being an add-on. He always wanted his airplanes to be simple and elegant. Canards were just the opposite.

At last, just as Alexei knew he would, Andrei ran his finger along the nose of the aircraft, raising and lowering the cockpit. This had been his invention, it was his principal contribution to the design, and he was proud of it. Alexei knew what was coming and deferred to it.

"I tell you Alexei, that there is no substitute for the human in the cockpit. No television set, no computer, no array of computers, can ever replace the best flight computer of all, the test pilot's brain."

Andrei suddenly sat back in his chair, overwhelmed by fatigue. Alexei rose to help him, and the elder Tupolev struggled back, pointed to the Tu-144's nose, and said, "There it is, my son. That is my last contribution."

One day less than three months later, Andrei Nikolaevich Tupolev died peacefully in his own bed.

CHAPTER SIXTY-FOUR

December 20, 1972
Hanoi, North Vietnam

Beating Tom almost to death seemed to have given Fidel the Cuban a proprietary interest in him. Fidel closely monitored Tom's recovery, even arranging for some minor medications. But as soon as he was able to walk, Fidel arranged for him to be sent to a filthy holding pen prepared for the most dangerous prisoners, called Alcatraz by the American prisoners. He and Pavone were thrown into separate underground cells, damp and ruled over by the usual collections of insects and rats. After a few weeks, the agonizing moans from Pavone's cell had stopped. Tom reluctantly assumed that he had died. It was a terrible blow to Tom's morale, for Pavone had done so much to help him and, in the end, he was unable to do the same for Pavone.

Sometime in the fall of 1971, there had been one forced trip back to the Hanoi Hilton to be filmed by news cameramen, and afterward Tom had been returned to Alcatraz. There he had survived only by the force of will.

Two days ago, after the American bombing of Hanoi had begun in earnest, he'd been brought with other prisoners back to the Hoa Lo prison. While most of the others had apparently been quickly processed into the general POW community, Tom was still held incommunicado in some area of the block-square complex. Other prisoners told him via the tap code that he must be in what they called New Guy City, but in time it was apparent he was in some high-security cell they were not familiar with. It was hard to understand the lingering malevolence the North Vietnamese seemed to hold for him. Apparently conditions in the Hanoi Hilton had begun to improve a little after 1969, but Tom had never experienced any relaxation of the harsh treatment. Even now he was deprived of talking to men such as Alvarez and Risner, heroes whom he included in his daily prayers.

The bombing had begun on the eighteenth, and Hanoi, once off-limits, was being pounded by waves of Navy and Air Force aircraft. At the first sound of the air-raid sirens, Tom took the ten-foot-long mahogany plank that had been thrust into the cell with him. They told him with hand gestures to prop it against the wall, in case a vagrant bomb hit the jail itself. It fitted at about a forty-five-degree angle between the two walls, and when the bombs came, he huddled under it.

He had heard American raids in the past, but they had been individual sorties, with the aircraft, usually a fighter, dropping its weapons and then departing. As he had been warned by tap code, tonight was different. It was evident that the entire Hanoi area was saturated with fighters—no doubt taking out the SAM sites and the anti-aircraft batteries. Then there came the long rumble of bombs that could only have come from B-52s.

In his mind's eye Tom could see them flying in cells of three, dark, lethal looking, the crews inside intent on the mission, knowing that they would have to fly straight and level during the bomb drop, no matter if they saw the brightly burning rocket of a missile heading straight for them.

The key turned in the lock—Tom had not heard anyone coming, and his stomach flipped, it could only mean torture, they were going to punish him because of the Americans' bombing. A tall Vietnamese officer, the same one who had questioned Tom for the newsreel, came in, followed by one of the nameless guards. They both scuttled under the mahogany plank, pressing against Tom. The officer said, "The Americans will never bomb Hao Lo. They know you are here."

Somehow, they still considered him important. He looked with loathing at his tattered clothes, long nails, and dirty body and pulled himself up straight. He might be scruffy, but if they thought he was important, he was important.

Seven miles above Vietnam, Steve O'Malley realized that he had not made the wisest of career moves eighteen months before. General

Meyer, anxious to continue the "fighter-pilotization" of the Strategic Air Command, had persuaded him to shift from fighters to bombers, guaranteeing him an aircraft commander's slot and the command of a squadron within a year. "Persuade" was a euphemism. Meyer had told him what he wanted O'Malley to do, and O'Malley had done it. Now he was flying in Maroon 1, a jet-black Boeing B-52D, part of Wave Three.

In his mind's eye he visualized the flights of B-52s lumbering before and after him like multiple columns of Hannibal's elephants. They were moving exactly on track, on this, the third night of Operation Linebacker II, President Nixon's desperate effort to force the North Vietnamese back to the negotiating tables in Paris. So far, only two aircraft had been shot down out of more than three hundred sorties. If Linebacker II failed and the North Vietnamese continued their offensive into South Vietnam, as many as twenty-five thousand American servicemen would be taken prisoner. Worse, in the eyes of the State Department, the United States would have been dealt a naked military defeat, beaten by a tiny nation. And if they won, everyone knew there would be no release of prisoners of war; the North Vietnamese negotiations in Paris had made that quite clear.

O'Malley would have preferred to be flying his Phantom in another Operation Toro, mixing it up with North Vietnamese MiGs, but he knew how important this mission was. For a moment his mind drifted to Vance Shannon and his request for a relentless bombing of Hanoi and Haiphong. Well, Vance was getting his wish now, on a scale even he had not envisaged. O'Malley said a quick Hail Mary, praying that Tom Shannon, imprisoned somewhere below, would not be injured.

Shifting in his seat, he cinched his parachute harness and gestured to his copilot, Chet Schmidt, to do the same. O'Malley was acutely aware of how flawed the U.S. planning was. The bombers were replicating the courses they had flown on the two previous nights, and he knew from long experience that the savvy North Vietnamese gunners and missile men would have the B-52s' predicted track marked on their radar screens in crayon. All they would need would be the B-52s' altitude, and the MiGs flying formation with the B-52s could provide that. *It's a setup,* O'Malley thought—*and our own staff is the one setting us up.*

Linebacker II was a massive effort, one that Americans could be proud of in the midst of an unpopular war. Fifty B-52s stationed at U

Tapao RTAFB, Thailand, and another 150 stationed at Andersen Air Base on Guam were to carry the air war to the enemy without the foolish rules of engagement for the first time. President Nixon had recognized the emergency and finally lifted the barriers to the exercise of airpower in the Vietnam War.

The bombers were a mixture of the Big-Belly B-52Ds, capable of carrying up to 108 five-hundred-pound bombs, and the B-52Gs, which carried only 27 of the larger 750- or 1,000-pound bombs. To get the bombers to the target—a six-thousand-mile round-trip for the Andersen B-52s—required a massive effort involving multiple refuelings, a host of command and control aircraft, and the entire air-sea rescue force of the theater.

Planning Linebacker II had begun in August and was based on the firm belief that cells of B-52s, operating together, had enough electronic warfare equipment to jam the enemy air defenses, which were the strongest in the world, stronger than those surrounding Moscow. During the past seven years, Hanoi and Haiphong had built up a powerful integrated air defense system that combined surface-to-air missiles, tremendous anti-aircraft artillery, and numerous MiG fighters.

The MiGs were up tonight. O'Malley had done a double take when he looked out his window and saw a MiG flying formation on his left wing, no doubt reporting his course, airspeed, and altitude. The MiG peeled off but did not attack.

He had taken off from Andersen more than six hours before, call sign Maroon 2. Now he was turning over the initial point, ready to drive in on the target, the Gia Lam railroad yard, a huge facility that should have been destroyed long ago.

Even as he eased the B-52 precisely on course, he resented the fact that he was doing this in 1972, against heavy defenses, when it could have been done so easily in 1965. The same effort then would have spared the country seven years of war and more than fifty thousand deaths. Then things got busy.

Schmidt, his copilot, called, "Target is overcast."

His transmission was broken by a call they all heard. "SAM Threat, SAM Threat, vicinity Hanoi."

Gabe Rogers, the navigator, always acerbic, came on. "That's hardly news; what the fuck does he expect?"

O'Malley looked ahead. "There's some flak at our altitude, about ten miles away or so estimate, but it's hell breaking loose below. Looks like lots of 57mm."

The electronic warfare officer, Sam Greenberg, piped up, "They are really throwing the SAMs up. Looks intense."

O'Malley mashed his intercom button. "Let's cut the chatter; we're on the bomb run now."

John Rosene, the radar operator, said, "OK, pilot, I've got the target."

O'Malley saw a huge explosion on the right. Had to be a SAM hitting a B-52 square in the bomb bay. Schmidt started to speak, but O'Malley waved his arm. No sense in getting the crew shook up on the bomb run.

Greenberg, his voice rising a notch, said, "I've got an uplink."

He meant that his signals showed that a SAM had been fired, probably at them. O'Malley thought, *Pretty goddamn calm. Good man.*

Schmidt said, "Got a SAM, visual," then transmitted, "Maroon 1, got a visual SAM."

Greenberg followed with, "Another one, four o'clock, coming at us."

Rosene said, "Steady, skipper, one minute to go. Keep her steady."

Every fiber in O'Malley's body ached to pull the B-52 into a diving turn to outfox the SAM, but orders were orders—anyone who broke formation to avoid a SAM was going to be court-martialed, and this came straight from SAC headquarters.

Rosene called, "Bombs Away."

O'Malley wheeled the B-52 in a steep turning, shrinking into his seat as he did so, knowing that the turn moved all their jamming antennae away from the radar sites below. They were most vulnerable in the turn, and the North Vietnamese proved it to them by exploding a SAM into the right wing, just between engines six and seven. The force of the explosion knocked the control wheel out of O'Malley's hands for a moment.

"Schmidt, what does it look like out there?"

"Can't see anything but flames, boss; we'd better get out of here."

"Crew, stand by. I'm going to try to get a little closer to Laos before we bail out, but get ready to go when I call it."

There was a dead silence as each crew member strapped his parachute tighter and hunched down in his seat, hands hovering near the ejection seat handles.

O'Malley saw another B-52 burning to the left, spiraling down. He flew the plane carefully, watching the instruments, being posted on the fire. Suddenly the controls let go, and he knew it was time to go.

"Eject, eject, eject."

He fought the airplane, heard Greenberg's seat go, then saw Schmidt leave in a burst of flame, followed by a gout of debris—maps, lunches, thermos bottles—spewing out the open hatch. O'Malley called "Gunner? Nav? Radar?"

There was no answer and no more time. He pulled his ejection seat handles, the hatch left, and he shot out into the blackness of the Laotian sky.

CHAPTER SIXTY-FIVE

February 10, 1973
Palos Verdes, California

Jill was busy arranging the table, putting out not Korbel but Dom Perignon, for this was a real celebration that was the happiest in years. Word had come in two days before that Tom Shannon was in fact alive and well enough to be coming home in a few days. Steve O'Malley, back from his own adventures, was due there any moment, with a personal letter from General Meyer to Vance.

Everyone else—Nancy, Harry and Anna, Bob and Mae, the children, and inevitably nowadays, Warren Bowers—was already in the library, surrounding Vance and continuing to rejoice over the fact of Tom's delivery from imprisonment. The news had an astounding effect upon Vance, seeming to take twenty years off his age. He was jubilant, a totally different man than he had been only a few weeks before when the news of the peace treaty ending American involvement in the Vietnam War had been announced on television by President Nixon on January 27. Bitter about Tom's situation still being unknown, Vance had railed at the television set, denouncing Nixon for selling out the South Vietnamese but really hating him for selling out his son.

There followed almost two weeks of frustration and depression until Vance received word from Lieutenant Colonel Steve O'Malley that Tom was alive and, if not well, at least on the way to being well.

The doorbell rang and Harry sprinted to it, clasping O'Malley on the back and bringing him into the library to the cheers of the family. He walked right up to Vance, saluted, and said, "General Meyer wrote this out in his own hand. I don't know what it says, but when he gave it to me, he told me to congratulate you on your son's recovery, and that he felt that you deserved to know that the American air forces had performed brilliantly."

Vance opened the letter with his ancient Swiss Army knife, apologized to the group, and read it silently, tears forming in his eyes. He put it down for a moment to collect himself, then read it aloud:

"It says: 'Dear Mr. Shannon, my heartiest congratulations on the news that your son, Colonel Thomas Shannon, has been found in a North Vietnamese prison camp and will be repatriated as soon as possible. I understand that he has suffered much during his imprisonment, but is now in good spirits and looking forward, of course, to returning home to his family.

" 'I'm writing you today because I felt your many contributions to the strength of the air forces of the United States deserved special consideration, and because I well remember your visit to my office and your recommendation for the all-out use of airpower against the North Vietnamese.

" 'The Air Force, like all the services, is of course under direct civilian control, and as much as I was inclined to do so, I was unable to follow-up on your instructions. But as you know, the incursions of the North Vietnamese in the fall of 1972 forced the President to conduct Linebacker II, the bombing of Hanoi and Haiphong, and this effort forced the North Vietnamese back to the negotiating table.

" 'I thought you would be interested to know that we executed Operation Linebacker II exactly as you would have wished—and exactly as my predecessor as a SAC commander, General Curtis E. LeMay, would have wished. The USAF made fifteen hundred and ten sorties from December 18 through December 29. Of these, seven hundred and twenty-nine were B-52 attacks on Hanoi and Haiphong. Another two hundred and seventy-seven sorties were flown by Naval and Marine aircraft. The enemy defenses were totally suppressed. By December 29 when the last raid was made, there was virtually no opposition. Although I could not say so officially, it is my belief that if we had persisted in the attack, we would have forced the North Vietnamese to surrender on our terms.

" 'Sadly, we lost fifteen B-52s and six other aircraft in the attacks. The loss rate, however, was very low, only slightly over one percent.

We were prepared to accept a higher loss rate, if required, to achieve our objective, which was the total domination of the enemy airspace and breaking the enemy's will to resist.

"'I'm writing to you in gratitude for your son's service, for his valiant resistance during his imprisonment, and also in gratitude for the manifold contributions you have made to airpower personally.

"'With respect and admiration,

"'John C. Meyer, General, USAF.'"

Vance's voice shook slightly as he turned to O'Malley. "Steve, it was good of General Meyer to take time to write this, and good of you to bring it. I understand that you were shot down on the third day of the operation?"

"Yes, but we made it to Laos, and were picked up within a few hours. No one was badly injured—a couple of sprains, that's all."

Vance turned to Warren Bowers, saying, "Warren, here's the man you should write your next book about. Colonel O'Malley has been both a fighter pilot and a bomber pilot, and he sort of epitomizes the new age of flying."

Bowers, diffident as usual, said he would be pleased, but O'Malley laughed and said, "Warren, if you've only written one book about Vance Shannon, you have your work cut out for you. I've been studying the Shannon family for years, and between Vance, Harry, and Tom, they are the world of aviation in one family."

Vance jumped in. "And don't forget our partner, Bob Rodriquez, who did the initial work on the smart bombs."

Rodriquez had been hanging back, as usual, conscious that this was a family gathering but filled with emotion that Mae, young Bob, and he were so completely accepted. Diffident as usual, he said, very softly, "Warren, Colonel O'Malley is right; you've got another two or three books in the Shannon family alone. Think about what is coming along, the F-15 and the F-16, the B-1, lots more stuff, and maybe in another ten years or so a supersonic airliner. When they all are operational, the Shannons will already be working on the next generation, and I'll be proud to be helping."